Cleansing Evil

A Christian Rinaldi Thriller

By Derek Dorr

Derek Dorr

ISBN 13: 978-0692236567
ISBN: 0692236562

Published: Derek Dorr   July 7, 2014

Editing: **Heather Stocks Pixley**

Cover Design: Clarise Tan

Formatting by: Brenda Wright

This book is intended for a mature audience of eighteen and older.

<u>Acknowledgements</u>

First and foremost, I would like to thank my wife Janene for her support and all of the extra work she had to take on around our home to allow me the time to write. Three young children are a lot to handle alone and without her, this would never have gotten done. Thank you for believing in me when I didn't believe in myself.

Thank you to Brenda Wright for her guidance and her wonderful work in preparing the final copies of this manuscript for my readers.

Thank you to Chelle Bliss for helping me navigate through the ins and outs of this new world and steering me in the right direction.

Thank you to Heather Stocks Pixley for beta reading and your editing work.

Thank you to my fantastic Beta readers: Emily Bak, Jackie Day, Beth Drabik, Glenda Hibbard, Jaime Hume, Vanessa Morgan, Holly Strout- Fraser, and Lisa Roeber. Without your constant feedback and encouragement, I may never have finished.

Thank you to my friends and family who supported me and pushed me to make my dream come true.

Table of Contents

Chapter 1

Old onion skins and dirt. The musty scent of field dirt mixed with the skins of last year's onion crop filled Christian's nostrils and caused tears to start welling up in the corners of his eyes. The onions may have brought the tears to the surface but it was fear that was making them flow down the sides of his pudgy cheeks.

Even clear, dry eyes would have been useless to him. Darkness, so complete that he was unable to see his hands in front of his face—let alone the cellar walls—enveloped him. His other senses were only marginally better in the pitch black abyss of the root cellar. When he rested his back against the cool, flaking cement, small crumbles of dirt cascaded from above, first falling onto his neck before finding their way down the back of his shirt. At least he hoped it was dirt. He stretched his arms outward in an attempt to gauge the dimensions of his foreboding tomb, starting with reaching out in front of him and then to each of his sides. Each time his fingertips hit the barrier before his arms were at full length, his elbows remaining bent.

Christian tilted his chin upward to look where the sky should have been but in its place was only more darkness. When he squinted his eyes and strained to see, he thought he could make out the outline of the weathered, splintery, hand cut pine boards of the door inches above his head. He could crouch but not sit. No matter how he twisted and turned, his knees would painfully strike the sides before his butt met the ground. The slickness of the onion skins littering the floor made keeping his feet in one place almost impossible. More than once, an attempt at adjusting his position ended with his knees meeting one wall or another with significant force while the back of his skull cracked against another.

Christian tried in vain to clear away the offending onion skins but no matter how he turned, stretched or tilted, he couldn't extend his fingers to the floor. The only thing that worked at all was pressing his back firmly against one side of his cell, balancing on his left leg and using his right foot like a broom, to push the debris in one direction and then the other. He was usually able to maintain his balance for two or three sweeps, but inevitably he found himself falling with his right shoulder and ear slamming hard into the unforgiving cement.

Like everything else in the barn, the cement was at least 75 years old, and had been poured long before the local home improvement stores started selling mixes that used extra fine gravel to make it smooth. This was a homemade concoction of gravel, small rocks, crushed stone, powdered clay, and limestone. It was sturdy and would probably last forever, like the pyramids. Unlike the new mixes, which are meant to be smooth as well as beautiful, this old version was all about functionality, and certainly not about the aesthetics at all.

Stones, gravel, and other sharp things stuck out at odd angles, cutting and scraping any of Christian's exposed skin that had the unfortunate opportunity to make contact with the jagged edges. After each fall, he peeled himself off the wall, leaving some skin and blood behind. The right side of his face throbbed and he could feel a dampness forming in his hair, his own blood causing it to stick together before the same blood dripped down into his ear.

A dozen or so attempts later, Christian had managed to clear a spot large enough for both of his feet to get traction. Now that his base was as stable as it was likely going to get, he turned his attention to the door above him. Christian reached up through the oppressive darkness and felt around along the underside of the door. Splinters poked and prodded his tiny fingers as they searched. On the far right side, he found what he was looking for—the hinges.

Three rusty metal hinges attached the door to a shorter row of planks that extended about eight inches out over the hole. He gave each a slight tug and found a small amount of looseness with the one nearest to him. The other two were much more snug and would be of no use. He repeated this process on the left side of the door, but found the sliding lock to be as tight as a snare drum. Bracing his feet, Christian placed one hand on each side of the single weakened hinge, squatted as low as he could comfortably get, and called upon every last bit of strength that remained in his body. His thighs and shoulders burned as he drove his feet straight downward and pushed up as hard as possible against the weak spot above his head. The semi-rotted wood flexed and a grinding squeak emanated from the oxidized metal, but the door would not give. Mr. Melanson must have rolled a bale of hay or two over the door.

"I'm sorry. Please let me out! I won't say anything, I promise. PLEASE!" Christian's begging voice came out sounding like a mixture of screaming and sobbing. His first words since getting locked in the tiny 3 foot long by 3 foot wide by 5 foot deep root cellar were 100% full of fear, betraying his usually brave demeanor. He was more terrified than he could ever remember being in the entirety of his nine years on earth.

Christian's pleas went unanswered; his squeaky voice echoing in the barn above, causing him to feel even more alone. His, now confirmed, solitude only multiplied the horror he felt inside. In his mind, he might as well have been the last person left in the world. Waves of nausea overtook him and he had to choke back the acrid bile as it came rushing up into his throat. His head swam and spun, made worse by being unable to see anything at all in the darkness. His heart pounded, sounding like war drums in his ears, ready to burst through his small chest at any second. Adrenaline surged from the terror, and he summoned every ounce of strength that he could find for one final attempt at pushing his way through the door and into the freedom of the cool night air.

Unfortunately, much like the last attempt, nothing happened—no perceivable movement all. With the adrenaline fully dissipated, he could feel his head starting to throb, his face flushing to the point where he expected his cheeks to start glowing. Beads of cold sweat developed on his forehead and rolled into his eyes, the saltiness adding to the burning that was already there, compounding his discomfort. All of his muscles were sore and shaking. With all prospects for escape dashed and fading into memory, he tried the only option he had left.

"Please! Please, let me out! I didn't see anything, I promise."

That last part was not the truth, but Christian hoped that Mr. Melanson would believe him, if he was even listening. He had actually seen "something" but he was not sure what that "something" was. All that Christian knew for sure was that he had snuck into the barn's upper loft to see why the light was still on when Mr. Melanson had supposedly gone to hang out with his buddies for the night.

After hearing some noises, Christian had crept along the floor, staying as low to the ground as he could until he reached the edge of the loft overlooking the rest of the barn. In the center of the hay-strewn floor was a very dirty man with a scruffy beard, tattered clothes that looked to be at least two sizes too large, and a look of sheer, unadulterated terror in his eyes. This unknown man had looked as scared as Christian felt at this very moment. The stranger was sitting in a chair with ropes around each wrist, his ankles, his stomach, and another around his neck. He was just sitting there in the middle of the barn floor, but Christian didn't know why.

He heard a creaking behind him, followed by the darkness of a hand over his eyes. A second palm over his mouth and nose made it difficult to breathe. The hand blindfolding him moved to his chest, and he could see the loft disappearing behind him as he was dragged away from his perch. His feet banged against each step of the stairs. When they reached the ground level, he was tossed over Mr. Melanson's left shoulder: the familiar smell of cheap, hand rolled cigarettes, and even cheaper whiskey, made the new luxury of breathing again far less appealing. The last thing he saw was the open root cellar coming at him as he was tossed downward like a rag doll the door slamming shut above his head. Darkness closed in around him.

"I want to go to my room. I am sorry!", Christian yelled as loudly as he could while the small root cellar began to feel smaller and smaller.

Suddenly, out of nowhere, there was a loud scraping noise, the wooden door above his head creaked, and then light broke up the darkness. Not a lot of light, just a small amount seeping in through the spaces between the old pine boards of the door.

Peering through the tiny cracks, Christian could see a narrow section of the room above him. A small antique Coleman lantern sat on a picnic table about 15 or 20 feet away, and there were a couple more spread throughout the room. These were the lanterns that Mr. Melanson normally used to light up the barn when he was repairing his tractor or working on some other project. Christian couldn't make out a lot of what was happening; mainly he just saw shadows moving around. When a large shadow moved closer, he called out.

"Mr. Melanson, I have learned my lesson, can I please..." his words were cut off by any eerily calm but extremely angry voice.

"You need to be quiet now. You can come out when I am done. I would already be done if you hadn't interrupted me, and you know damn well that I hate to be interrupted."

Christian crouched in silence, surrounded by darkness. He was scared about what might happen – scared to move, but also afraid of staying where he was. He stuck his fingers out through one of the wider gaps on the left side of the door near the lock. The two fingers searched in frantic silence, hoping to find the small metal bar that slid into the metal loop on the other side. He found it!

The circular knob that normally sat on top of the slide bar was turned to the side and in the full lock position. Christian would need to push the knob back to the top position and then backward to be able to slide it out of the loop. He went through the motions in his mind and then tried to get his fingers to replicate those same motions. He wiggled the knob and managed to move it into position, but this minor victory came at a cost.

The old lock made a metallic grinding noise as it moved. Slowly, ever so slowly, he continued to move it towards the goal. Centimeter by centimeter, it crept along. The grinding noise seemed deafening in the silence, but he was almost there!

Suddenly, he saw a rapidly moving shadow rushing towards him. He simultaneously felt a searing pain and heard the crunch of bone against unforgiving metal and wood as Mr. Melanson's boot came crashing down onto his helplessly exposed fingers. Christian screamed in pain as he tried to pull his badly injured fingers back through the opening. The boot did not lift up; instead it twisted and crushed his fingers between the wood and the hard rubber sole.

Finally, the boot was gone and Christian had his hand back. He slumped down with his back against the cold cement once again, and his knees scraped against the opposing wall. Blood trickled down his shins but he barely noticed. He made himself as small as he could and clutched his possibly broken fingers with his only functioning hand. The sensation of a warm wetness filling his hand and something hard sticking out of the skin all but confirmed his diagnosis. It was possible that there was a huge splinter stuck into his finger but he doubted it. He was too scared to look, but he was pretty sure that it was one of his smashed finger bones.

"I told you I would let you out!" Mr. Melanson yelled down at him. "How am I supposed to trust you if you won't listen? You need to learn some respect, boy."

The hulking shadow standing over his makeshift tomb disappeared but Christian still didn't dare to move. He continued to sit in his crouching position and held his throbbing, likely broken, fingers in his good hand. He squatted there for what seemed like hours, but was probably only a few minutes, in complete silence.

The angry stomping of footsteps shattered the quietness, and the room became darker again. A chair was placed over the top of his door, blocking more than half of his available light. The ease with which the chair was moved indicated that it was empty, but it didn't stay that way for long.

The next sounds came from what appeared to be the tied-up stranger being forcibly dragged over to the chair. He was fighting as valiantly as he could, but being as restrained as he was, he didn't stand a chance. The door creaked from the weight of the man being slammed into a seated position on the chair. As Mr. Melanson tied the man down, Christian could hear the stranger crying and pleading through the tape that covered his mouth.

"Now I'm going to take the tape off but I do not want you to scream. Do you understand? No one can hear you out here and screaming will just make me upset. You DO NOT want to make me upset. Do you understand?" Melanson said in the same eerily calm voice.

A muffled sound of apparent agreement was followed by the tearing off of the tape. The man seemingly had agreed to stay quiet, but he didn't for long. Almost immediately, he began pleading his case.

"Mister, I have a family. Please let me go. I won't say nothing to no one. I swear. You won't ever see me again, I promise," the dirty, tied-up man sobbed.

"Did you hear that, Christian? He has a family. He says he won't tell anyone. Do you believe him?" Mr. Melanson asked, but Christian was still too scared to respond. "Sorry friend, this isn't your lucky day. It doesn't sound like Christian believes you either."

"Please, no, you can believe me. You have to," the man begged. Once again, his pleas became muffled; the tape was placed back over his mouth. He frantically started thrashing around in his chair and screaming, trying to get somebody's attention, anybody's. Sadly for him, there were only two other people in the room: one that couldn't help him, and the other was the source of his problems.

Christian heard Mr. Melanson walk away. It sounded as though he stopped at the far wall where he kept most of his farming tools. The man above Christian continued screaming and wiggling in a feeble attempt to escape, but he was not having any luck. Above the sound of screams, Christian could hear the scraping of metal tools against corkboard, and then footsteps as Mr. Melanson returned.

Something that the stranger saw must have frightened him because he became more frantic. His attempts to escape became so vigorous that as he rocked from side to side, his chair began to tip. He was successful in getting the chair to tip over, and he crashed with it to the floor, nearly falling through the wooden door. He wiggled and wiggled but he was now stuck on the cellar door above Christian. Christian covered his head and flinched, but the door held. A new smell filled the small space of the root cellar. This man had gone a long time without bathing—much longer than Mrs. Melanson would ever let Christian get away with.

Melanson's boots came to a stop just outside the edge of the door. The smelly man screamed and screamed. The boards separating him from Christian creaked mightily, and then came the creepiest sound that Christian had ever heard. It was laughter, but not the laughter of someone watching something funny; there was a demented sickness behind the laughter that made Christian's blood run cold. The more the man struggled, the louder Melanson laughed. After a moment or two, the laughter stopped, and Mr. Melanson spoke once again.

"I am sure that you would agree this has been fun, but I am expected elsewhere and Christian has already made me late."

The man struggled and screamed as Mr. Melanson struck him with whatever tool he had brought back from the corkboard. Each violent swing was accompanied by a sound similar to wet Styrofoam being stomped on. The blows continued to rain down. One became two, which became five, and then ten. Somewhere along the way the man stopped struggling, but the blows kept coming. Mr. Melanson repeatedly struck the man long after the gurgling sounds of his breathing stopped. Finally, mercifully, Christian heard Mr. Melanson walk away.

A new, sickeningly sweet smell took the place of the dirt, onions, and even the filthy man's body odor. Christian's face began to feel wet as something dripped on him from above. Feelings of nausea returned as he figured out where the wetness and smell were coming from.

Mr. Melanson returned and knelt over the presumably dead man. Through the small cracks in the door, Christian could see the outline of what Mr. Melanson was holding in his right hand, and a different kind of fear gripped him. In Mr. Melanson's hand was the antler-handled Damascus steel skinning knife that he took with him on deer hunts—some during the legal hunting season, some not. He normally used it to field dress and clean the deer, and the other animals that he slaughtered around the farm. Many pigs, chickens, turkeys, and even a few cows, had been skinned by that very knife.

He set the knife down on top of the door next to the unmoving man. He then reached over and grabbed the hook from his pulley that he used to hang up deer. He put the hook through the ropes that bound the man's feet, and then walked over to the far wall again. He pulled on the rope and the man slowly began to rise from the floor just as many deer, moose, and large game animals had in the past. He looped the rope around the hook on the wall and left the man hanging by his feet, the tips of his fingers lightly scraping against the door as he gently swung back and forth.

"Gotta get the blood out of him or the meat will turn bad," Mr. Melanson matter of a factly stated, as if what he was doing was no different than preparing a deer.

Christian watched in silent horror as Mr. Melanson knelt down, picked up his knife, and stepped toward the motionless man hanging by his feet from the rafters of the barn. He grabbed a tuft of the man's unruly, greasy hair and pulled his head back, exposing his neck. With a single, quick, seemingly practiced motion, the obsessively sharpened blade sliced deeply into the man's throat, nearly decapitating him. Only the bones of his spine kept his head from crashing to the floor.

For an instant, the man appeared to be alive, his eyes flew open, wild with fear. His return to consciousness was very brief and he soon went limp again. Blood poured out of his severed arteries and veins, showering down onto Christian like a thick, sticky, warm waterfall. The blood coated Christian's hair and descended down his body. His clothes stuck to him. Blood filled his shoes and his socks felt like warm sponges encapsulating his toes. When he tried to breathe, blood filled his mouth and nose with a metallic gelatin. The world began to spin, slowly at first and then faster and faster as everything became draped in a crimson hue, and then he fell into a black nothingness as the world faded away.

Chapter 2

Christian opened his eyes to his own reflection staring back at him from the window of seat 32A. The 5:20 AM DownEaster Amtrak commuter train barreled on its way from Portland to Boston. The lingering look of panic in his eyes, left over from his recurring nightmare, caused alarm bells to go off in his head. Nightmares were nothing new but he was far from used to them. 25 years had passed since that night, but it could easily have been last night. He could still smell the cellar. Onions always triggered memories, memories he wished were not his own. The nearby café car didn't help in this area as the kitchen staff prepared sandwiches for their cooler.

Looking to his left, he decided that he must have called out as he slept because the woman and young boy who had been sitting across from him at the beginning of his trip were no longer there. It was possible that they had gotten off at the Saco station, but he doubted it. Who would have paid 20 bucks to ride for 20 minutes at this time of day?

Christian focused on regaining his composure. He turned away from the center of the car, looked out the window, and tried to enjoy the view. Staring out the right-hand side of the southbound train, he was treated to flashes of pine trees and the occasional glimpse of a two-lane street. This told him that he was still in Maine and was less than an hour into the ride. Had they crossed into New Hampshire or Massachusetts, he would've seen the sun breaking through the darkened sky via the windows on the left side of the train because they would have been traveling in a more southerly direction. Instead, the gentle illumination was coming from behind. His current view was only of woods and sporadic evidence of a nearby town. The light dew that frosted the grass and gave it the hue of polished silver, told him that it was very brisk out, as April mornings tended to be. Christian was just happy that the snow was gone—well, mostly gone. It still hung on in places like the mountains and the deep dark sections of the forest.

Christian turned his head back to his left and glanced around the half-full train car. The 5:20 AM train arrived in Boston just before 8 AM and the station, North Station, was also a hub for the famous Boston T subway line, allowing people to get to almost anywhere in the city with minimal effort. This made it a favorite mode of travel for commuters arriving from the north. A monthly pass cost around three hundred dollars – another hundred would allow you to trade the gray cloth seats of coach for the slightly larger, red leather of business class – and was much less expensive than gas for even the most economical of cars. It was also a much calmer ride than the two and a half hours of chaos on I-95.

In Christian's opinion, I-95 in Maine was much more civilized and polite. In Maine, the pace was slower, there were less people on the road, and the highway was two lanes in each direction. The Massachusetts side was a different animal—3 to 4 lanes per side, filled to capacity with people who tended to be in the wrong lane. They usually figured it out at the last minute and then cut each other off while a cacophony of horns and expletives filled the air. It seemed that when people became mired in the constant gridlock, they forgot all manners—along with basic laws of physics. Simple laws, such as "two objects may not occupy the same space at the same time" were completely ignored. Drivers appeared to believe that the solution to this dilemma was a higher rate of speed. It was not. Christian had witnessed nature correcting that incorrect assumption (in a rather violent way) several times over the last few years.

No, the train was fine with Christian for when he needed to travel to "Beantown" for business, the Celtics, or the Bruins. If he was traveling down to see the Red Sox, he preferred to take the bus. Unlike the train it didn't make any stops, saving about 30 minutes each way, and it went to South Station, which was much closer to Fenway Park, their home since 1912. The train, on the other hand, went to North Station, which happened to be under the T. D. Bank Garden—home to both the Celtics and Bruins. It was also the train's final destination. If he wanted to go to other cities, like New York City, he would need to find his way over to South Station and catch the train from there.

A passionate fan of New England sports, Christian spent a lot of his free time watching a game, either in person or on the excessively large TV in his home theater room. The Patriots held the top spot in his heart, and the Red Sox and Bruins were in a dogfight for the number two position, with the Celtics in a very, very distant fourth place. In fact, all three local minor-league teams—the Portland Sea Dogs (baseball), the Red Claws (basketball), and the Pirates (hockey)—finished well ahead of the Celtics. These Celtics were not like the Celtics that he had loved as a child, with Bird, McHale, and Parrish at their core. No, this group was led by a selfish punk at point and his contagious sense of entitlement made the team almost impossible for Christian to watch.

As usual, most of the passengers were adults. Only a handful of children were ever on the early train during the week, especially at this time of year. On the weekends, during the summer, or even during the upcoming April break, they would fill the train as they went into Boston to visit one of the many museums, the Aquarium, the IMAX Theater, sporting events, or the beautiful Franklin Park Zoo. The majority of the train's current passengers were sleeping, catching up on work, reading the complimentary newspaper, or doing something on a smart phone, laptop, or tablet. The free Wi-Fi on the train was another nice selling point.

A minor sense of relief washed over Christian as he spotted the lady and her son who had been sitting next to him at the beginning of the train trip. She was seated eight seats ahead of him in one of the two quad seating sections and was facing in his direction.

The quad seating was intended for a group of four people to be able to sit facing each other so that they could talk and enjoy the ride more. Christian rarely sat in them, and if he did, he chose the side facing the front of the train. He hated facing in the opposite direction.

Something about moving away from where he was looking seemed to throw him off slightly, like being seasick.

This car had two sets of quad seats. The closest one was occupied by four men who seemed to be oblivious to each other's existence, and the second had just two people in it: the lady and her son. She was facing Christian but the only evidence of the boy was a pair of small Teenage Mutant Ninja Turtles shoes sticking out into the aisle. Christian had fond memories of the show from his childhood but he didn't like the updated version as much. Seeing the shoes made him feel better. She must have moved so her son could lie down and she would still be able to watch over him. Maybe Christian didn't bother them after all.

The pleasantness of this revelation was short-lived. The woman was reading from one of several pamphlets spread out on the seat next to her. Christian recognized them immediately and now had an unfortunate answer to the question of why they were on the train so early on a Wednesday morning.

The pamphlets showed happy smiling faces but the unmistakable Dana-Farber logo meant that things were not wonderful. The Dana-Farber Institute is the preeminent cancer center in the Northeast. Sadly, this meant that the 8 to 10-year-old boy accompanying her was in the early stages of one type of cancer or another.

Studying the woman for a minute, Christian quickly knew several pieces of information about her. He could tell that she was in her mid-30s, was very sleep deprived, hadn't yet told the boy a lot of details about his diagnosis, was headed for testing in hopes of a second opinion, the stress of the illness was causing issues in her marriage to either a high school or college sweetheart, and she didn't have a lot of close family or friends that were aware of her son's condition.

The age was easy to figure out; she looked like she was around Christian's age of 33. Bags under her eyes showed a lack of sleep and the darkness of the circles around the bags proved that it was more than a single night or two without restful sleep. The way the child had cheerfully bounced around as soon as they had gotten on the train, mixed with his generally healthy look, told Christian that he was either early in treatment or had yet to start treatment. That carefree happiness would soon go away as the effects of treatment took over.

The early hour of the trip pointed to an early appointment. Early appointments for a child generally meant that they were going in for tests. The first treatment appointments of the day were reserved for adults trying to get them in before work and the children had their treatments later in the day. Children going in early tended to be doing so to have a battery of tests before an afternoon appointment. Going to Boston for testing that could have been done in Portland pointed to this being a second set of the same tests already performed by his local doctor. Second set of tests equaled a second opinion.

The pamphlets showed Christian that the woman was early in the process as well. People usually only read them to learn something new. All five of the ones she had front of her related to diagnostics and not treatment, which also meant the treatment had yet to begin and that she was likely looking for something on those pamphlets that might show that the existing diagnosis was wrong.

She nervously twisted her wedding rings, an indication of tense thoughts towards her spouse. Stress over medical issues commonly causes marital problems and her spouse was not on the train with her, further confirming Christian's thoughts about a disagreement related to the cancer. It was possible that her spouse couldn't take time off from work, but appointments of this nature are scheduled weeks in advance, and most employers will understand a situation like having a child with cancer.

She wore three rings: an engagement ring with a very small stone, a second diamond ring with a much larger stone and a wedding band sandwiched in between. The smaller ring was at least 10 years old, making her in her early 20s when she got it –just out of high school or possibly in college. The small stone indicated a limited budget and the fact that she still wore it showed that it had a significant sentimental value to her. This information led Christian to assume that the small ring was given to her by a high school or college sweetheart. The larger ring was likely from a 10 year anniversary upgrade and looked to be only a year or two old.

The part about limited close family and friends in the know was pretty easy. If she had people that were close to her and she had shared this type of news with them then it would be safe to assume that at least one person would have been sitting with her. Christian's assumption was that no one knew because she refused to believe it herself, again pointing to this being a trip for a second opinion.

Lastly, knowing it was the child and not her that had cancer was also obvious. Had she been the one who was sick, the child would have been in school and not on the train with her. Children of that age were rarely brought along for moral support.

Christian hated that he was cold reading this woman that he didn't actually know, but it was second nature to him. He did it to almost everyone without even thinking. People try to hide things about themselves from everyone around them, but Christian could see what most people could not, either because they don't look hard enough or because they don't know how to "see" what is hiding there.

Mr. Rinaldi, the last in a long list of foster parents and the man who adopted Christian as his own, and had taught him how to read anyone. He said that he wasn't actually teaching Christian anything; what he did was more along the lines of nurturing a talent that was already there, something that needed to be focused and controlled—like a lot of Christian's other "talents".

This became Christian's "chicken-or-egg "question: did this skill make him a good psychiatrist or did his study of psychology make him good at reading everyone? Whichever it was, natural gift or trained talent, moments like this one made Christian wish that he couldn't do it at all. The other passengers would go about their day, blissfully unaware of this woman's struggle. Like Christian, they would never know what her days and nights of worry felt like. He hated the idea of any child suffering for any reason at all. Christian reminded himself that one of the noble truths of Buddhism was "life is suffering". He knew from experience that suffering at any age shaped your world as a person but he didn't have to like it.

No, these other passengers would probably not know her secret but then again they would never know Christian's secrets either. As long as he didn't make any mistakes, they would never know that on this morning they had shared a train with one of the world's most skilled and prolific serial killers.

It was at that moment that Christian realized that he had been staring at this woman for several minutes and he bashfully looked away. Thankfully, she had never looked up from her pamphlets or noticed him looking at her. As he looked away, he thought he saw something in the quad between him and where the woman and her son sat.

When he looked over at that quad, he saw four men: two were reading the newspaper, one was on the phone but the fourth man, seated by the window and facing Christian, was staring at him. As they locked eyes, the stranger averted his stare. Christian, trying to act as naturally as possible, turned toward his own window and in the reflection he could see that his new friend was looking at him again. Christian decided to watch the man via the reflection for a few minutes in case he was wrong about this man's intent. Over the next several minutes, the man only did two things. He rotated between looking at the tablet that he held in his hands and looking at Christian.

Christian did not recognize this man from any previous interactions. He was not someone that Christian knew as a former patient, coworker, or even a person that worked anywhere that he frequented. Based on the way he continued to look at his tablet and then at Christian, it appeared as though he was using one to confirm information about the other. Maybe he had seen Christian speak at an event or had read one of his books, but in any case, the length of time that he had spent observing Christian was now crossing over the line from curious to creepy.

The man looked to be in his late 20s and had dark hair, dark eyes, and a light complexion- possibly of English or Irish heritage. The Oxford shirt that he was wearing was of the "modern fit" style favored by men with a V-shaped torso—broad shoulders and a narrow waist—and the man filled it out well. His overall size was hard to estimate because he was sitting, but Christian guessed that he was around 5'10" to 6' tall based on how high his head extended over the seat back. Still unsure if this man was a potential threat, Christian decided to get a closer look.

Christian stood and stretched. Another benefit of riding the train was that it didn't have any overhead storage in this section, as buses and planes always did. This allowed him to stand without needing to stoop and shimmy his way into the aisle before standing up straight.

At 6'3" and 225 pounds, he was not huge, but he definitely took up more space than most people. As he bent down to grab his black leather messenger-style bag, he took one last look at the window and saw that his new friend was still looking at him. Christian needed a reason to walk by this man without alerting him to the fact that Christian had caught on to what he was doing.

Unfortunately, the café car was one car behind him, so that wouldn't work as a reason, but then he came up with an idea. He slipped his bag over his head so that the strap was on his left shoulder and the bag rested on his right hip, allowing him to keep both of his hands free. He then walked toward the man. As he passed, he could see the man, who he had begun calling his stalker, peeking over the top of his tablet at him. Christian watched him out of the corner of his eye as he continued to walk past him.

It is a natural human reaction to look at a person that is changing positions around you. If a standing person sits down or starts walking in your direction, your curious mind tends to instantly look at them. The only people who don't look are either too involved in what they were previously doing to react, or are already watching in the first place and are now trying to hide it. The more a person tries to hide it, the more suspicious they appear.

The man watching Christian was definitely in the latter category. As Christian walked by, he stared straight down while occasionally looking sideways at Christian— much like a dog that hopes you will not notice that he peed on your kitchen floor. The stalker clutched the tablet to his chest like his life depended on it. Christian looked over his shoulder as he walked by, hoping to catch a glimpse of the screen, but didn't have any luck. His stalker turned slightly as Christian passed, like he was getting ready to stand up to follow Christian, but he quickly relaxed back into his seat when Christian stopped at the next quad.

"Excuse me, Ma'am," Christian said as he came to a stop in front of the mom and her son. "I noticed that you were gone when I woke up. I wasn't snoring too loudly, was I?"

The woman glanced up from her fourth or fifth pamphlet and Christian got his first good look at her. He could see that she was someone who took great care of her appearance and had a natural beauty that was best exhibited without the aid of makeup. She had the petite form and long, defined muscles of someone who frequently ran or did yoga. She couldn't have been more than 5' 4" and maybe weighed 130 pounds, with chestnut colored hair and blue-green eyes that were similar to Christian's own. A weary smile spread across her face, and she looked like she was happy to have a distraction from her thoughts rather than being annoyed at the intrusion.

"Oh no, not at all. My son was getting tired and I wanted him to get a nap in before we got to Boston. We have a long day," she said as she instinctively leaned forward and covered over the pamphlets with her forearms.

Christian squatted down, like he did with his younger patients, knowing that seeing a large man with a crew cut and a shaggy, month-old beard staring down at you could be intimidating. He made his voice as soft and caring as he could, and spoke at just above a whisper. "It is a great facility. I have known a lot of people that have gone there and they all came back happy with the care they received. They also said that the first day is always the scariest but the staff there had made them feel right at home."

Even though they were speaking quietly, the young boy began to stir. The woman quickly glanced at him and then returned her eyes to Christian. The look on her face expressed the kind of relief that comes from not having to answer questions about diagnoses, types of cancer, stages of disease progression, or treatment plans.

The boy sat up, rubbed his eyes and gave his pants a quick feel, as young boys who were prone to bedwetting tended to do. Seeing Christian, who was still squatting and was at about eye level with him, he swiftly glanced over at his mother and asked, "Mom, who is this guy?"

"Honey, this is the man who was sitting next to us when we were back there," she said while pointing back to where Christian had been sitting. Turning to Christian she said, "I'm sorry, I never even asked your name."

"My name is Christian and it's nice to meet you both," Christian said while spending equal time looking at each person.

"Nice to meet you Christian. My name is Gina and this is my son, Charlie," the woman said, placing her left hand on her chest while acknowledging her son with a short sweeping motion of her right hand. The boy looked like a carbon copy of her, aside from his unruly hair that fell across his eyes.

"I won't keep you any longer. I just wanted to make sure that I hadn't started your trip off badly." Christian said.

"No bother at all. It was nice to meet you," she replied

"Have a great day in Boston. It is time for me to see if there's anything appetizing in the café car. Can I get you anything? Coffee?" Christian asked.

"No thank you, but thanks for asking," Gina said with a smile. Was she being flirty?

Christian stood and as he turned to walk toward the café car, he caught his stalker looking away quickly. *Not a very stealthy eavesdropper,* Christian thought to himself as he walked away. Whoever this man was, he was not great at hiding his nosiness.

On his walk past his stalker's quad, Christian attempted to see what the man had been looking at on his tablet. He didn't see the screen but he could see that the man had a hiking backpack between his feet, was wearing dark jeans that were tight but loose enough that he could move well, and had on hiking boots that looked more like the expensive L.L. Bean brand instead of army surplus or Walmart. A light jacket was folded on the left side of the seat. It was disguising a bulge on the man's left hip. It was a too small to be a gun holster but could easily have been for knife, or just a holder for a blackberry.

Christian gave Gina and Charlie a final wave and continued on his way to the café car. It was almost 20 feet away in the second to last car of the train. The final car on the train was business-class and the café car served the dual purpose of providing people with a place to eat slightly overpriced food while also separating the people who spent an extra $8 for business-class from the rest of the train. Christian opened the pocket door that led to the café car, stepped into the space between the cars where the restrooms were situated, and was about to close it when a hand shot in and stopped the door from closing.

The small hand slid the door open and Charlie came into view. The boy smiled at Christian and stood behind him waiting for Christian to go into the café car.

"Hey there, Charlie, did you change your mind?" Christian asked.

"Not really. I'm not too hungry, but I needed to get up. I had to get away from my Mom for a minute. She gets too sad when she reads those things. She said to stay with you and not wander off if that's cool," Charlie replied.

Christian wasn't thrilled about having another shadow but when he looked at Gina through the still open door, she had a look that seemed to be saying "Please" and "I'm sorry" at the same time. He gave her a smile, nod, and wave as if to say "sure, no problem". She mouthed "thank you" just as he turned away.

Christian and Charlie entered the café, and got in line behind four men in suits, none of whom looked away from their phones until they were asked what they wanted at least twice. Some looked up at the menu for the first time, while others held up a single finger signaling "one minute". They did it with the exaggerated flourish of someone who was being rudely interrupted instead of a person who was wasting everyone else's time.

Charlie stuck his head around the side of the man in front of them, looking at the cooler of prepared foods, fruit and drinks that sat in front of the counter. The self-important man in front of him turned and gave Charlie a look as if to say "do you mind?" but as Christian leaned in closer and looked down at him, his face softened with the realization that Christian was not a bear he wanted to poke. Fear will do that to someone with a big ego.

He stopped what he was doing and frantically scoured the menu for something to order so he could quickly get out of Christian and Charlie's way. He asked for an onion bagel with light cream cheese on the side, and he wanted it toasted a "golden brown". Upon hearing that onion bagels were not on the menu, he emitted a large sigh as if this was the worst news of his day.

"Figure out what you want?" Christian asked Charlie.

"O.J. and a glazed doughnut," he answered

Christian looked at him quizzically and said "Bro, those two things don't mix very well."

Charlie just shrugged his shoulders and Christian ordered for them both. "One chocolate glazed, an egg white omelet with peppers, mushrooms and mozzarella cheese, a large coffee, and this orange juice," he said as he placed the orange juice on the counter.

It was at that moment that Christian got an idea. He might have a way to find out what his new friend was doing without tipping him off. He turned and faced Charlie.

"Hey, can you help me with something?" he asked.

"Depends," came the suspicious reply from Charlie, who leaned away.

"No, it's nothing weird," Christian said with a chuckle. "I have a friend sitting near you and he and I have a bet going. You can help me win."

"What do I get if I help you win?" Charlie said, smirking.

Christian raised his eyebrow and said "You mean besides breakfast?"

"I mean, you must be getting something if you win so I want something."

"It isn't a big bet. We just get bored on these rides. He was going to pick up the tab when we hit the bars later tonight if I win and I have to pay if I lose," Christian lied "So how about five bucks?"

"Make it 10 and you have a deal."

"Fine. It is really simple. He's doing something on his tablet and I have to guess what it is. He also has something under his coat and he picks up dinner if I can guess what that is," Christian said, thinking to himself that the day had started out in a very strange way – being stalked by a stranger and getting shaken down by a little kid.

"How am I supposed to figure that out?" Charlie asked.

"Well, every time I walk by, he covers everything up and I never get a good look but he wouldn't do that if it was just you walking by. Just go back to your seat and ask your mom if you can eat breakfast with me and try to get a good look," Christian instructed.

Charlie just shrugged again and said "What the hell, why not?"

Christian didn't bother to correct the kid about his language. He knew that Charlie just wanted to act tough around another guy, and it wasn't Christian's place to say anything, so he just nodded to Charlie as he began his walk back to his mother.

Christian's stalker looked up when he heard the door open but when he saw that it was just a young boy he closed his eyes and rested his head back on his seat.

Charlie walked to his seat, looking back at Christian a couple of times along the way. Christian shook his head, partly at Charlie's lack of couth and partly because his brilliant plan hinged on a kid. Charlie glanced at the stalker on the trip to his seat but, thankfully, the man's eyes were still closed.

Christian could see Charlie talking to Gina and she seemed to be saying that she was fine with him eating with Christian, but then Charlie sat down. What was he doing?

Charlie's head popped up over the seat and quickly back down again. About 30 seconds went by with no perceivable movement from Charlie. All of a sudden there was a flurry of motion. Christian saw the stalker's coat go flying into the air. The man stood quickly and his tablet tumbled into the aisle. In a flash Charlie was picking it up and Gina appeared to be apologizing to the stalker. A look of shock spread across Charlie's face as he swiped his finger across the screen. The man stuck his hand out and Charlie handed him the tablet. Charlie looked at his feet.

Without further conversation, the man turned and sat back into his seat before Christian could get a good look at his left hip. After a few more words with his mother, Charlie headed back toward the café car. Christian gathered their food and found them a table to sit at. A few seconds later, Charlie joined him and gave him a confused look.

Christian spoke first. "That was a stealthy move there, Super Spy."

"Your game kind of sucks, man," Charlie said ignoring Christian's barb. "Is your buddy a security guard or something?"

"No, why?" Christian asked.

"He was wearing the same kind of Taser that my friend Eric's dad wears. He rides around on one of those armored cars for the bank."

"Huh, that is odd," Christian said acting surprised. Apparently, his stalker came prepared. "I saw you knock over the tablet, did you get to see what was on it?"

"Yeah," he said without elaborating. This conversation was like pulling teeth

"Well, Charlie? What was he looking at?" Christian asked, a little more impatiently than he wanted to.

"That is the weird part. It was just a bunch of pictures of you."

<u>Chapter 3</u>

Jeff Sullivan staggered over the cobblestone sidewalks of Portland's Old Port District, his feet barely skimming the top of the uneven, clay brown bricks. He listed to one side, and then the other, banging into trash cans, cars, railings, sides of buildings, and anything else that could hold him up for a moment before he moved on to the next.

Tripping over yet another loose brick—pushed up an inch or so higher than the rest by the spring frost—he fell forward, slamming shoulder-first into the curved lip of the circular black steel trashcan. He tried to catch his breath, but the pain only allowed him to take short, quick breaths. He placed both hands on the trashcan, one on each side of his chest, and pushed himself to his feet. He staggered on, in search of the next place to rest.

To anyone who happened by him at this early time of the predawn, he would appear to be another homeless drunk. Portland had become the Mecca for the homeless population of the Northeast, due in part to the beautiful location, friendly people, and of course the copious amount of programs that served the homeless residents of the area.

On most mornings, you would be justified in assuming that alcohol was affecting Jeff's gait, but not today. No, the half-bottle of wine, scavenged by his friend Alton and shared with a dozen others, had barely given him a buzz, and that weak buzz had worn off many hours ago. His affect was not caused by drugs—legal or otherwise. He hadn't even had a cigarette since he found that halfie stuck between some cobblestones the day prior. The reason that he bounced around like an aimless pinball was simple: pain. Lots of pain.

Jeff crossed Exchange Street, leaned against a beaten-up, rust orange, decade old Saab, and was thankful that it didn't have an alarm. The owner was likely sleeping in one of the apartments that filled the upper levels of the four-story brick buildings on each side of Exchange. The bottom floors were all retail shops, each one a mom-and-pop, never a chain or franchise store. Their brightly decorated window displays looked festive, even in the quiet darkness of the early morning.

The second floor was usually made up of offices or bars, but the top stories were apartments. These apartments usually housed college students, young professionals who were fresh out of college, recent divorcees, or the occasional building owner. The proximity to the bars and downtown made them very appealing to the young and unattached, but the lack of parking and late-night loudness was a turn off to most everyone else.

It had to be getting close to 5 AM; the "magic hours" would soon be over. The magic hours were the only safe time to walk around if you were homeless. The 100+ bars in the small area were open until 3 AM, and drunken young punk kids loved to screw with someone like him. It wasn't uncommon to be followed by a group of kids who would do everything from laugh at him and mock him to punch and kick him. The police would break it up quickly, and it didn't happen often, but it did happen enough to make traveling at that time of night not worth the risk.

The only people who were worse to deal with than the drunken twenty-somethings were members of the suit-and-tie crowd who migrated into the area starting around 6:30 or so. At that time of morning, everything changed. As soon as the first BMW, Mercedes, Lexus, or other overpriced foreign luxury car came rolling in from the surrounding affluent towns or better sections of Portland (the parts where you actually had a lawn), carrying its precious cargo of suit-wearing, self-important jerks, talking loudly into their Bluetooth while simultaneously checking their email and being completely oblivious to the "unimportant things" like red lights, stop signs, or human beings in crosswalks, it was time to be somewhere else. They frequently "nudged" people with their cars who were not walking fast enough, and berated the homeless for being "lazy moochers" with no provocation needed.

The kids might hit you but these guys made you feel completely worthless. The sticks and stones cliché was wrong. The physical wounds do heal and scar over, but deeply cutting insults will play over and over in your mind long after they were heard.

The plan was always the same for all of the homeless. If you slept anywhere other than the shelter, you crossed through the unfriendly zone after 3 AM but before 6:30 AM. Once you got to Monument Square, it was much friendlier. Monument Square was a more open area and the important things like the Preble Street soup kitchen and day labor agencies were right around the corner and would be opening at 7 AM. Warmth, decent food, a shower, and the potential to earn a day's wage were all available to you, if you were so inclined. There weren't always enough jobs to go around, but everything else was the same day after day. All you had to do was get in line and wait.

Jeff was running out of time, but making sure that he beat the crowd was the least of his worries. After resting against the cold metal of the car, he leaned forward, placed his hands on his knees, and rocked himself into a standing position before he started walking up the little hill toward the intersection with the next street. The pain was worsening and standing up straight was no longer an option. He stared down at his worn-out, duct tape covered army boots and shuffled along, inch by painful inch. The pain had moved from his lower back and was now in his groin.

When the pain started two days ago, he thought that he just had a sore back muscle. He assumed he had just strained his back on the construction site that he had worked on that day, or that he had slept on a rock. When it didn't go away yesterday, he went to the free clinic where he was told by a new nurse, who had all but pinched her nose closed while examining him, that he was dealing with a kidney stone. "Just drink lots of *water* and they will pass," she had said. She had emphasized the word "water" in a not-so-subtle way of telling him to avoid alcohol.

This morning, his pain was much worse and he was questioning her medical expertise. He had dealt with kidney stones before and while they had been extremely painful, they had never felt like this. This was a different level of pain that he had never experienced before. Additionally, he wondered what were the chances that he had kidney stones on both sides of his body at the same time.

The pain had gone from a dull throbbing to something akin to having been shanked in the back. Now the pain was on both sides of his back and moving down his front. An urgent need to urinate took over his thoughts and he quickly shuffled across the street, clutching both sides of his lower back. As soon as he made it across the street he turned left in the direction of Monument Square. He moved as quickly as the agony would let him. He staggered past movie posters in glass cases on the exterior of the Nickelodeon movie theater, posters that he had stopped looking at months ago. Even if he had the money to go enjoy a film, the stares and comments would make it an unpleasant experience.

He reached the corner but was unsure of where to go next. Directly in front of him was a statue of a man picking up a lobster. It was a nice statue and paid tribute to the top fishing industry of the state, but it just seemed weird to Jeff. It was big enough for him to hide behind, but he would still be seen from any other direction. For some unknown reason, as he stood there, the scent of saltwater intensified his need to find a bathroom.

The smell was coming from Casco Bay, a few blocks back in the other direction, and going there was definitely not an option. To his right was a parking garage, but the bathrooms were locked up, and the sight of the booth attendant squashed any idea he had of sneaking into the stairwell and letting it go in the corner.

Jeff looked across the street and spotted the solution to his problem. Dunkin' Donuts! There was an older lady with a thick Russian accent who worked the morning shifts, and she never had a problem with him using the bathroom or sitting at a table to get warm, as long as he bought something. He felt around in his front pocket and dug out what meager amount of change he had. Ninety-four cents was his grand total and would just barely be enough for a donut. Jeff doubted that he would be able to eat the donut because of the pain and he didn't want spend his last change on it, but what choice did he have?

Jeff tried to ignore the pain as he rushed to the first entrance. Just as he began to open the glass door, he noticed the red "occupied" sign on the bathroom door. He would have to wait. He hoped it wouldn't be a long wait. A motion on his left side caught his eye. He turned to see his Russian friend waving at him to get his attention. When their eyes met she began shaking her head while pointing to a woman who was standing next to the K-cup coffee display. The second woman didn't have on the standard brown visor and smock of an employee, so she had to be an owner. Ms. Russia mouthed "sorry" at him through the window and he knew that it was a lost cause. He was running desperately low on options, but he did know of one more place nearby. He just hoped he could get there in time.

Jeff's need to get to the bathroom was becoming overwhelming. The pressure building up his lower abdomen nearly pushed the pain from his mind but not quite. Jeff took a few staggering steps across the open courtyard before he had to lean against the brick exterior of the One City Center office building. His legs felt weak, like they would give out at any time. He continued on, staying within a foot of the building in case he needed to fall over and be held up. More often than not, his right shoulder scraped against the jagged brick as his jacket caught on the rough surface every few feet. Finally, he saw the dark corner that would be his salvation.

Just to the right of the stairwell leading up to the building was an alcove where the building's transformer and a couple garbage dumpsters sat. He chose a spot between two overflowing rusty dumpsters and pressed his right shoulder and upper body against one while he fought with his belt buckle. Once the metal tongue was free, he let his ill-fitting army surplus cargo pants fall to the ground. Jeff's ass was peeking out beneath his old green army issued BDU jacket, but he could not have cared less. *Enjoy the show* he thought with a touch of amusement.

To his surprise, the urine barely trickled out. The constant pressure continued to build like water pressing against a dam but there seemed to be something blocking it off. Jeff groaned from pain and pushed like a woman in labor. He took a deep breath and pushed down as hard as he could until the blockage moved. A small pinging sound of something hard hitting the rusty iron dumpster made Jeff think that maybe the nurse was actually right about the kidney stones, but he couldn't be sure if that was what he actually had heard. At last, the pee flowed freely. It was a deep orange and had an odd smell that Jeff couldn't place at that moment. He was just happy that he wasn't pissing himself.

Jeff finished peeing, gave his battle buddy a shake and then reached down to grab his pants. Even after pulling them up and buckling his belt, he didn't feel much better. The pressure was gone but the pain remained. Instead of the physical relief that he was expecting, he actually felt worse. The agony in his lower back and abdomen spread into a stabbing pain running from the bottom of his rib cage to the top of his hips. He needed to rest, preferably somewhere warm and nearby.

Jeff emerged from the shadows of the utility alcove and grabbed the cold hollow tube railings of the stairway. Pain shot through his body as he lifted his left leg and then his right up each of the 8 inch tall gray concrete steps. He slid his hand up the railing incrementally, stripping off layers of chipped paint as he did. He lifted his left foot onto the next step, followed by his right, landing unsteadily on the same step as its counterpart. Slowly, methodically, he repeated this effort a dozen more times before reaching the top step where a new decision awaited him.

The decision wasn't a difficult one. There were only four possible locations that he could get to right away where he could sit and be warm. The closest option, One City Center, and the furthest one away, 2 Monument Square wouldn't work. They were open to the public, but each had a security guard stationed near the entrance. That left just two choices. Dunkin' Donuts, which was back down the stairs, and probably still had the same issue that it did 10 minutes ago, was out. The final option was the Bank of America ATM kiosk. It was directly in front of him and was only 50 feet away, but it did have two challenges—getting there, and getting in. Challenges or not, it was his best option. His decision was made.

Jeff started inching forward. His feet moved but did not lift above the ground as he crossed the 25 foot expanse with nothing to hold on to. The brick surface was flat, but the lack of support made it difficult. His arms shot out straight to each side, and he wobbled like a tightrope walker with no pole to steady him. Each shuffling step barely covered one of the 4 inch long bricks. His pain became worse and worse, and each step required Jeff to rely on his force of will just to get his feet moving.

A full two minutes passed before he reached the base of the last remaining set of steps. The ATM kiosk at the top of the final seven steps loomed like an oasis in the desert. He grabbed the railing with his left hand. His journey across the 25 feet had been more of a diagonal stumble than a straight shot, causing him to end up on the far side of the stairs. A new determination filled Jeff as he pressed his hip against the middle rung of the railing and tried to swing his right foot up onto the first step. His hip bone crunched against metal and his body hung halfway over the railing as he attempted the first of the final seven steps. His right boot landed with an uncoordinated stomp. His left barely made it onto the top, the steel toe of his boot dragged over the lip. Stomp and drag, stomp and drag, he continued, one pain-filled motion after another.

Jeff made it to the final step and fell forward onto the glass door. His right cheek and shoulder pressed against the glass, and he put his hands on each side of the frame as he willed his left foot forward. Leather boot collided with the metal doorframe. The bang was loud enough that he worried that he would draw the security guard away from his comfy desk.

He couldn't feel his right foot anymore. All control over it was gone. He stood as tall as he could and dragged his useless right foot until it was almost even with his left. It moved sideways rather than forward, and when he stepped down on it, his ankle bone touched the ground. This was definitely not kidney stones. That stupid bitch was going to hear about it when he got back to the clinic.

Jeff grabbed the grooved metal handle on the outside of the glass door and pulled back as hard as he could. Instead of swinging open, there was a metal clanging sound and no movement at all. Frantically searching for an answer, he noticed a sticker on the doorframe. It showed a credit/debit card and pointed to a small slot like a vertical version of the key card locks on hotel doors. Apparently, he needed a bank card to open the door, but did it have to be a card from this bank or would any one work?

Jeff reached into the cargo pocket on the outside of his right knee. He felt around, searching through the gently used tissues and various other items he had scavenged on his travels and believed might be useful, until he found what he was looking for—his old debit card. It didn't have any money on it, his paltry military pension had been used up days ago, but it might be useful in this situation. He lined up the strip on the back with the arrows on the door and slid it in. He kept his eyes closed and said a silent prayer. He opened them to see a red light. He pulled battered plastic card back out and looked it over again. There were deep scratches on the back and a fair amount of dirt. He blew on it and when that didn't work, he spit on it. He fished out one of the tissues from his pocket and wiped off the spit and dirt. The tissue came away with deep red and brown splotches. Blood? He slid the card in again and hoped that the cleaning had worked. Green!

Jeff yanked on the doors hard as he could and nearly fell backwards down the stairs when it popped open. He swung his left hand up and grabbed the door to catch his balance. He staggered through the doorway and warm air wooshed around him. The clicking of the closing door echoed in the small glass room. He stumbled over to the corner on the other side of the ATM and slid his back down the wall. His left shoulder and face pressed against the glass window that separated the kiosk from the actual bank. The red neon lights of the clock on the wall in front of him read 6:45 AM. Jeff closed his eyes hoping for a few minutes of uninterrupted rest before someone came in who actually had business with the bank itself or the ATM on his right.

His whole body screamed with pain. Bright white flashes streaked across the darkness created by his closed eyes. A warm fluid spread over his groin. Rather than opening his eyes, he felt around with his right hand, first his pants and then the floor. Both were damp. *Great, I pissed myself* he thought. His hand flopped lifelessly to the cool tile floor and landed with a wet splat. Too tired to care, he just sat there in the expanding puddle as the world around him seemed to fade. The white streaks became further away and he found himself dozing off.

The sound of the metal door scraping against the aluminum threshold stirred him back to consciousness. He tried to open his eyes but only managed to create a small opening that allowed in a tiny slither of light. All he could see were the shoulders of two people and the blurry head of a woman who he heard ask "Is he okay?"

"Hey buddy, are you alright?" asked a second voice, this one male.

Jeff felt two large hands, presumably the man's, shake his shoulders. Suddenly, the woman screamed and Jeff fell back against the wall as the man released him.

"Holy shit!" exclaimed the man as Jeff heard them running to the door. "Call 911!" the man screamed to the woman.

Seconds later, Jeff heard her say "Hello, we need some help. We found a man sitting in a puddle of blood inside the Bank of America kiosk at One City."

The world started to fade away again. The man's voice sounded very distant as he said, "Hang on man, they are on their way."

Those were the last words that former staff Sgt. Jeffrey Sullivan ever heard.

Chapter 4

"Got my 10 bucks?" Charlie asked, sticking out his right hand.

"Yeah, sure," Christian replied as he reached for his wallet that was sitting next to his phone on the Formica-topped café table he shared with Charlie. Handing a pair of five dollar bills to Charlie, Christian asked, "Are you sure he was looking at a picture of me?"

"Yep, definitely. I saw a couple of them before I had to give it back to him. There was one of you that looked like one of my class photos and another of you walking up the stairs of a big brick building," Charlie said, nodding as he spoke.

A picture of his office building flashed in Christian's mind as he thought back through the recent weeks, trying to think of any time where he might have seen the man. Drawing a blank, he felt a combination of anger, confusion, and adrenaline surging through his body in anticipation of a potential confrontation.

Inner Circle's song "Bad Boys" brought him back to focus. Immediately recognizing the ring tone, he wondered why he was getting called this early in the morning.

"Sorry Charlie, I need to take this," he said before picking up the phone. Charlie was too involved in his breakfast to do more than grunt in acknowledgement. "Agent Brooks, what can I do for you? More importantly, what could have gotten you out of bed this early in the morning?"

"Hey, Dr. Rinaldi. You there? Can you hear me?" came the loud voice on the other end of the line.

Christian pulled his phone away from his ear. Agent Brooks must have been using his Bluetooth. For some reason, he always yelled when he was using the hands-free device on his phone, no matter how many times he was told not to.

"I can hear you just fine, Agent. You will need to speak more quietly. I am not alone on the train," Christian said, hoping that Brooks would take the hint.

"Okay," Brooks said in a marginally quieter voice. "I am heading to a crime scene over by your office and was thinking that maybe you and I could grab a coffee."

"Sorry, but I'll have to take a rain check on that. I'm on my way to Boston for a day or two. We can catch up when I get back. What is the FBI doing at a crime scene in Portland?" Christian asked.

"Double whammy. The vic had a military ID on him and he dropped in a bank."

"Foul play?" Christian asked.

"I'm not sure. All I know is that a couple of hippies found him in the ATM kiosk, covered in blood and barely conscious. He was DOA by time the medics arrived on the scene."

"Well, you have my number if you need another set of eyes."

"Okay, I will call if I need anything. I'm driving up now, so I gotta go. Enjoy Boston." With that, agent Brooks was gone.

When Christian put his phone back on the table he was startled by Charlie's voice. He had almost forgotten about the kid.

"Wow, that guy is really loud. What's his deal?" Charlie asked.

"He still can't figure out that sound travels," Christian laughed.

"Did he call you Doctor? What kind doctor are you? What is an FBI agent calling you for?" Charlie asked in rapid succession.

"Whoa, slow down, Charlie. One question at a time," Christian said holding up his hands and leaning back.

"Okay, what kind of doctor are you?"

"A psychiatrist."

"You mean for like crazy people?"

"No, different stuff. Mostly, I'm a therapist. I try to help people who are going through a tough time. Besides, everyone's a little crazy," Christian's attempt at a joke fell a little flat.

"Why is the FBI calling you if you're just a therapist?" Charlie asked, crossing his arms and raising an eyebrow like he had caught Christian.

"You ask a lot of questions for a kid. What are you? 10?"

"Eleven. You never answered the question," Charlie said impatiently.

"You would make a good lawyer, Charlie," Christian said before continuing. "Ever heard of profiling?"

"Yeah, like that show where they use Jedi mind tricks to find psychos, right?" Charlie answered.

Christian cringed at the term "psycho" and at the idea of the show Charlie was referring to. He was talking about *Chasing Killers*, a show about a team of good-looking profilers who always caught the bad guy red-handed as he was attempting to kill his final victim. He hated how neat and tidy they wrapped up all of their cases, and how easy they made it appear. The real job was rarely that easy or exciting. It almost always consisted of Christian looking over reports, crime scene photos, or watching suspect interviews by himself, or occasionally with his semi-friend, Agent Randy Brooks.

"Sort of, that show isn't totally accurate..." he began before wondering why he was sharing all of this information with an 11-year-old who he barely knew. "What are you doing watching that show?" he asked Charlie.

"I like to watch it after my parents go to sleep. Besides, Jessica is really hot," Charlie said with no signs of embarrassment.

"They never look like that, Charlie. Most of the ones I work with are fat 45-year-old guys with bad mustaches and comb-overs," Christian joked, striking out again. This kid must not have a sense of humor.

"That sucks, dude," was the only response.

"It's not all bad. I get to help them figure out the reasons why some people do the things that they do. It has its fun moments"

Thankfully, Charlie appeared to be getting bored with this topic or was daydreaming about Agent Jessi.

Christian peered over Charlie's head and through the windows of the door to their car. Gina was looking at them, craning her neck to get a view of her son. Christian waived and she relaxed back into her seat.

"I think breakfast time is up. Your mom is getting a little antsy back there," Christian said to Charlie.

"Thanks for the food and the money," Charlie said as he got up and walked back to his seat. His tray remained on the table.

Rather than calling the kid back, Christian just picked up the garbage and threw it away himself. It gave him a chance to create a little distance between him and Charlie so they didn't walk back together, hopefully keeping Christian's stalker from getting suspicious about Charlie's "accident" earlier.

Christian grabbed his bag, phone, and wallet before starting his walk back to his seat in the passenger car. He walked to the door, paying careful attention not to make eye contact with the man who was already staring at him as soon as the door opened. When he reached his seat, he took a look at the man in the window as he pulled his bag off his shoulders and set it down in the seat nearest the aisle.

He sat back down into his seat and opened up the bag to take out his e-reader. For the next few minutes he pretended to read while he came up with a plan on how best to handle his new friend. He had to confirm that he was being stalked, and if he was, he would need to find a quiet place to lure the man into so they could have a little "talk".

Christian's original plan for the day was to take the T from North Station to Copley Square, and then walk to his meeting from there. He couldn't deviate from that route too much, or the man would know that something was up. That, of course, is if the man knew where Christian was going. Christian decided that he would have to assume that the man knew everything about his schedule. It was safest that way. He would need to make sure that the man was able to keep up with him but also keep a buffer zone between them. To make his plan work, he had to treat his friend as if he were both an idiot and a genius at the same time.

To find the best place to get his friend alone, Christian started with his final destination, Boylston Street, and worked backwards, trying to think of a location that was both quiet and that he knew well enough to have home field advantage. He settled on a spot near the off-campus dorms for Emerson College, but left himself open to any spontaneous choices that might present themselves along the way. He would have to get off the subway earlier than usual, but he could also use that to his advantage.

The train left the final station on its way into Boston, and a few new people who had just gotten on from the Woburn, MA station filled some of the empty seats in Christian's car. There wouldn't be any stops until North Station in about 20 minutes. Twenty minutes was plenty of time for the first phase of Christian's plan.

Christian stood and took his bag with him toward the café car. He could feel the stalker's stare on his back the whole way. Instead of going into the café car, he opened the door to the restroom and went inside.

The restroom was very tight. Christian hated being in a room that small, and the window was so tiny that it only provided a marginal amount of solace. The room was positioned in the area between the cars, over the gap where there are no axles and wheels. This caused the room to pitch back and forth frequently.

Evidently, many men still chose to stand in the tiny, unstable room while relieving themselves. The evidence of that was on most of the flat surfaces, including the walls. Christian pulled off a handful of paper towels and used them to cover sections of the countertop that were relatively urine free. He placed his bag on top of them and dug around inside the flaps that hid several special compartments.

He pulled out several items, each one was compact, and in his hands, very deadly. First was an item that looked like a credit card. It was actually an origami knife. It was made of Kevlar and had a ceramic blade that folded flat. By pressing the sides together, it opened up. The sides came together to form a handle as the blade unfolded outward and locked in position. It was small, but also sharp enough to push through a person's ribs or into their liver. He put it into his back right pocket. Next he took out a collapsible blackjack. With a downward flick of the wrist, a 4 inch long metal tube became a 2 foot long baton strong enough to break a clavicle or kneecap. This item found its way into the sleeve of his shirt and secured against his forearm.

The final item was a pair of 3 inch long plastic handles. If you pulled them apart you would find that they were held together by a single gray string. The string looked innocuous, but was actually a 500 pound parachute cord. It was about half as thick as a pinky but was constructed to hold up to 500 pounds before breaking. This perfectly compact garrote found its home in the small pocket inside the right front pocket of Christian's jeans.

Christian reached for the door just as the train jostled, slamming him into the wall one final time. Christian grabbed his bag and walked back to his seat while pretending not to notice that his friend was still staring at him.

Christian sat down, choosing the aisle seat this time over his usual window seat. His watch read 7:46. He took it off and placed it inside his bag. It could also be used as a weapon, if needed. Coiled underneath the stainless steel and glass face, just above the precision Swiss timing gears, was a full foot of thin, sharp piano wire. A pull on the small knob on the side released it. Without leather gloves it could slice through a finger and not just the throat of the person that it was used on. He didn't want to kill this man, nor did he want to take a chance on breaking the watch, so into his bag it went.

The train yard came into view and the slumbering masses began to stir in anticipation. The final few minutes always had the feel of a beehive to Christian. Everyone was in a hurry to get off. Christian was not. He planned to wait until Gina and Charlie were as far away from him as possible and then he would set his plan into motion.

The train plunged into shadows as it entered North Station. It stopped at its platform under the protection of the cement and steel outdoor covering. As expected, everyone started to stand. Everyone that is, besides Christian and his friend. Christian grabbed his possessions and after seeing Gina and Charlie exit, he stood with his bag over his shoulder. This time he positioned it so that the bag was on his left hip, allowing access to the surprises hidden on his right side.

Christian's friend stood. Christian made sure his shadow had a chance to keep up as he exited the train. He kept two people between them as they walked down the aisle and off the train. One person would be too close, you can reach around a single person to strike or stab someone. Three people would make it easier to lose track of another person, but two people was the perfect distance.

Christian used the reflection in the glass entryway of the TD Garden to keep track of his friend as they entered. He noticed that the man was falling behind, so he slowed and held the door for a pair of elderly women. It was just enough time for his friend to close the gap.

Christian entered the lobby and slowed again, this time to look at the Celtics and Bruins displays that advertised the ticket office and team stores that were elsewhere in the facility. When his friend got within 10 feet, Christian turned and headed toward the stairway that led down to the subway.

A dozen or so MBTA agents and police officers scanned the crowd. They looked more like electronic mannequins than protectors of the people: ready for action.

The sea of people bunched together in various areas at the bottom of the stairs. To the left were rows of Charlie ticket stations where people waited to buy tickets for the subway. Another handful of MBTA agents, dressed in robin's egg blue uniforms, assisted various people in figuring out how to use the machines. Several more agents were in the middle of the room near the newly added gates. They stood watching the people who were trying to get through the doors that opened from the middle and then slid into the sides of the ticket taker. A couple of lines were stalled by people unable to get their freshly purchased tickets to register, causing a bottleneck of impatient people.

To the right of the gates was a row of lockers that could be rented by the hour, or by the day. Beyond them was Christian's next stop, the men's room. It would be the site of the first test for his new friend.

Before Christian could open it, the pale blonde wooden door swung open in front of him, nearly hitting him in the face. The short stocky man who opened it looked at Christian as though he shouldn't have been standing there at all. His shoulder brushed roughly against Christian's ribs as he pushed by. Christian caught the door with his forearm and entered the restroom. It was better than touching the germ-infested handle.

A couple of men were standing at the urinals and all six stalls had their doors closed. Occupied or not, the smell in the small bathroom made the idea of using them unappealing. Thankfully, that wasn't why he was in there.

The wall nearest to the door had air dryers on one side and paper towel dispensers on the other. Christian walked to a bank of sinks, depressed the button on the soap dispenser and rubbed the fluffy pink foam over his hands. The faucet sprang to life when he waved his hand in front of the sensor. Thirty seconds passed and there was no sign of his friend.

Christian chose to use the towel dispensers to dry his hands because they were on the side of the door that was obstructed when it opened. While he meticulously dried his fingers, the door swung open, nearly hitting him again. As it closed, he placed one freshly-dried hand on his hip pocket. The door closed and he could see that it was not the man that he was waiting for. He decided that his friend was not going to be coming in, so when the door opened a second time he used his left elbow to hold it and walked out.

Christian scanned the area for his friend but did not see him. He walked over to the gate lines and continued scanning the room. When it was his turn, he placed his plastic Charlie ticket near the sensor, listened for the beep that signaled the gates were about to open, and walked sideways through the opening just before it slammed shut again.

The mass of people surrounding Christian made it difficult to pick out the man he was looking for. They continued to move, even when he wasn't. Several people firmly bumped into his back as though he was somehow invisible. After 2 or 3 passes, he found his target.

The man was standing in the middle of the platform by one of the support beams and was trying hard to blend in, without luck. Every time someone walked in front of him, he leaned around them to keep a constant lock on Christian's position. He was anything but inconspicuous, but he had chosen a good spot to wait. No matter what train Christian chose to take, his friend would have a great vantage point.

Christian walked over to the giant floor to ceiling map that showed where each line went and what stops it made along the way. His usual route involved taking the Green Line over to Copley Square because it was closest to his office, but today he wanted to go a different way. His friend seemed to know his schedule and Christian hoped that a slight deviation would throw him off. After careful review, he settled on taking the Orange Line to

Chinatown and then he could walk to Emerson College for the final step of his plan, if the man didn't make a move first.

A rumbling echo let him know that the Green Line was on its way to the platform, and Christian took a few short steps in its direction with the rest of the impatient masses. Out of the corner of his left eye, he saw his friend waiting about 15 feet away.

The doors opened just a few seconds after the cars came to a stop. People getting off the train pushed against those trying to get on in the urban version of salmon struggling to swim upstream against the current. Shouts between temporarily separated companions added to the usual calls of "excuse me", angry grunts, and swearing. Christian had several, "What is wrong with you? Get out of the way" comments tossed his way when he did not move forward, but he was unfazed. He had no intentions of getting on this train, but his friend had yet to notice that.

The man had just stepped over the gap between the platform and the train car when he looked over his shoulder and saw Christian standing exactly where he had left him. Christian noticed a brief moment of panic in the man's eyes just before Christian turned to walk toward the back of the line.

The man frantically pushed against the forward flow of people in a last ditch attempt to get back off the train. This effort was met by even more resistance and comments. Most of the hits were unintentional but at least one fist landed squarely in his stomach. He made it back onto the platform just before the doors closed on his bag. He attempted to look calm and collected, but it was clear that this small change had thrown him for a loop. Definitely an amateur.

The man rushed over to the map to try and figure out what was going on while keeping Christian in his eye line. He traced his finger along one of the lines on the map, his brow furrowed with confusion. Seemingly satisfied with his answer, he walked back toward the edge of the platform nearest to Christian. He was still a car length away, but this time he stood back further, unwilling to be fooled again.

The Orange Line train pulled into view and without hesitation, Christian joined the throng of people who were headed onward. He stepped over the threshold onto the car and walked up the three steps to the seating area. Most of the seats were full so he chose to stand with one hand on the pole nearest the door. One door down, his friend mirrored his stance. They both stood in the same position, each pretending that they had no interest in the other, until the stop for the Theater District (Chinatown) neared.

By the time the car came to a complete stop, Christian was one of several people already crammed onto the stairs. The doors opened and he pushed his way out into the open with only slightly less effort than a newborn baby making its way out of the birth canal. He didn't bother looking for his companion as he walked up the stairs that provided his escape from the dank subterranean commuter hell and into the open sunlight.

The early morning hustle and bustle was well underway as Christian stretched in the spring sunshine.

He loved the morning time and always tried to appreciate each new day with the verve of a man who was feeling fresh air on his skin for the first time after a year in solitary. In this personally ritualistic moment, he was nearly oblivious to anything around him.

Remembering that he was not alone on this beautiful day, he brought his focus back to where it needed to be. Turning on his heels, he walked in the direction of Boylston Street and used the windows of the stores along the way to look for his unwelcome shadow. He was beginning to think that he had lost him before catching a glimpse of the man as he reached the crosswalk.

Christian stood in the middle of a herd of people waiting for the walk-don't walk sign to change in his favor. Nearly everyone in the cluster of humanity was preoccupied by their phone. He was far from a technophobe, but he just didn't get that mentality. Why couldn't they just enjoy the day? What could be so pressing that they needed to be looking down the whole time? Even when the light changed, they continued to look at the handheld devices as they all moved forward in unison. How they didn't constantly run into someone else or a car was beyond Christian.

Once the group finished crossing the busy intersection, they split off into smaller groups and went in several different directions. Christian found himself in a small group of younger people, most around 20 years old and likely headed to an early class at Emerson. They had a different appearance than he remembered from his college days. Overstuffed, back injury inducing backpacks had been replaced by messenger bags with their textbooks now on tablets. These differences made the age gap seem larger than it truly was. One of the few exceptions was his shadow, who was now hanging back about 20 feet. He kept the same leisurely pace as Christian for the next few minutes, seemingly content with the proximity.

The St. Francis House, a local homeless shelter, came into view in the distance and this marked the beginning of the next phase of Christian's plan. He sped up his pace slightly to increase the distance between him and his friend without alerting him. The store window reflections showed that he had doubled the space over the last half block. As he got close to the corner of Tremont and Boylston, he prepared to make his move.

Christian moved to the left side of the crowd, where he had a little more space to work with. He could see that the walk sign was counting down for the crossing ahead. It was at six seconds and the crowd was beginning to slow. He, on the other hand, did not. The sign flashed three seconds as he got within fifteen feet. He inched his way to the front of the line while his friend came to a stop in the middle of the pack. Christian paused at the edge with one second left. He knew that there would be a standard three second delay from the time that the sign changed to "Don't Walk" and the traffic light turned green. He moved his right hand to his bag and lifted it up just enough so it was half way between his arm pit and his hip. The sign changed, Christian waited a half second and then moved into action.

Horns honked as Christian sprinted out into the crosswalk. Glancing over his shoulder, he saw his friend look up at the sound of the horn and tried to push to the front of the line. Others pushed back and glared at him, not wanting to be pushed off the sidewalk. He wasn't going anywhere until the light changed. Just as Christian's foot hit the curb on the other side, cars started moving and his friend's hopes of catching up were dashed.

Christian paused on the opposing sidewalk until his friend was looking at him again. Christian met his stare, his message was simple, *I know you are following me*. Christian could have chosen to continue running toward his final destination but he still had no idea why this man was following him. He wouldn't feel safe having the man follow him to the office, so he made sure that the man saw him walking down Tremont.

Ten seconds later the man was out of sight, but Christian knew he would be along soon enough. This section of Tremont was much quieter. Christian was behind one of the off campus dorms for Emerson, and he doubted that many of the students would be wandering around the area at this time of day. Only the off-campus kids got up early. An alley between two of the buildings provided him with what he was looking for: a place to set his trap.

He walked to the center of the entrance to the alley and took inventory of the space. The quick look showed several places to hide, including a couple dumpsters, one illegally parked SUV, and several sections of building that jutted out into the open. He wanted to get into position, but he had to wait until he knew that his prey had seen him go in. He looked back toward the corner and saw that the group was now crossing. That was good enough for him.

Christian bolted into the alley, running toward the dumpsters on the left-hand side. When he got to the second one, he walked around the side and placed his bag down on the cement. He pushed it to the front edge where it would be partially visible but give the appearance that it was meant to be hidden. He then backtracked about 15 feet and cut across to the other side of the alley.

The large, black, American-made SUV was parked at a lazy angle, causing its front end to stick out into the alley more than the back end. Christian took up his position behind the car, using the unnecessarily monstrous tires to block the view of his feet. The deep darkness of the tinted windows should be enough to obscure his stalker's view. Unfortunately, that camouflage worked both ways. Christian would have to rely on sound, instinct, and a touch of luck.

Just as Christian settled into position, he heard a pair of feet running toward the alley and coming to a stop. Those same feet now shuffled slowly into the alley. Anxiety filled his chest as he could only listen without having a visual of the man. He slowed his breathing and listened intently to the slow shuffle of boots on cement. The light scraping got closer and closer, and then stopped. Christian hoped that the man had just noticed the bag. From his crouch, he could see just over the top of the hood of the car. Glancing past the windshield, he could see the black plastic cover of the dumpster where his bag was "hidden". The shadow of his friend darkened the dumpster as he moved closer.

Christian crouched a little deeper and inched his way to the front of the car. Peeking around the edge, he could barely see the dumpster, but it was enough. The man was now at the dumpster and was preparing to turn the corner, likely thinking that he had the drop on Christian. He unclasped his Taser, pulling it out into his right hand. He flipped the safety switch off just before he made his move. He might be an inept stalker, but he apparently meant business.

Christian thought over his choices for weapons and settled on the blackjack. Unhooking the loop in his sleeve, the cool metal tube slid easily down his forearm and into his hand. Using his thumb and forefinger, he gave the ball bearing style knob at the end a push to loosen it in preparation for rapid deployment. He moved into position behind the front quarter panel of the SUV and waited for the man to make his move.

In a flurry of motion, the man spun around the edge of the dumpster and Christian sprang to his feet. Christian snapped his wrist downward, the blackjack sliding open with a loud click. Christian was 3 steps away, blackjack raised to shoulder level, when the man realized his mistake. He turned toward Christian with the Taser out in front of him. Christian swung viciously downward and the blackjack crashed onto the man's wrist. The bone cracked loudly and his hand released the Taser, but it did not fall to the ground. Christian had failed to see the wrist strap holding it on.

Christian stopped about 3 feet away from the man who had managed to step backward and get the Taser back into his badly injured hand. He found himself walking in a semi-circle around the man with the blackjack still in his hand. He positioned himself so that his right foot was back, his left forward, pointing toward his adversary, as they took a few steps to the left and then back to the right, sizing each other up. He pressed the button on the side of the blackjack, collapsing it. He put it in his back pocket to give him freedom with both hands. Should he blitz the man and hope that he surprised him or should he wait for his opponent to make a move? He chose the latter.

Christian didn't have to wait long. The man lunged forward, jabbing the Taser toward Christian. Christian moved his weight to his back foot and stepped to the side. As the man's hand came closer he reached out and grabbed his wrist. He squeezed the injured wrist and pulled the man forward, using his own momentum against him. The Taser dropped and dangled at the end of the wrist strap. Christian stepped behind the man as he stumbled forward. Christian instinctively wrapped his left arm around the man's neck. The man tried to get his chin down but it was too late, his Adam's apple was now resting in the crook of Christian's elbow.

Christian tugged at the loop on the man's arm and the Taser fell to the ground. With that danger gone, he turned so that his left hip was against the man's back and his right arm moved upward. He used his right forearm to protect his own face from an attempt at a head butt. With each second that passed, his grip tightened on the man's neck. He grabbed his right bicep with his left hand and used his right wrist to push his enemy's head downward, increasing the pressure. Between his airway being choked and the pressure of Christian's arms on the arteries in his neck, the man only had a few moments of consciousness left. Christian used that time to ask a question.

"Why are you following me?" he asked without reply.

The man's attempts to escape, although valiant, were proving to be futile, and he began to slump. A few seconds later, he fell to his knees. Christian tried one last time to get his answers.

"Tell me why you are following me or I am not going to let go until you stop breathing," Christian growled in the man's right ear.

He only heard a gurgled attempt at breathing. He heard no response, nor did he hear the slow patter of footsteps behind him. Instead, the first thing he heard was a metallic click at the very moment that he felt something cold and hard on the back of his neck. The person behind him spoke and simply said, "I wouldn't do that that if I were you."

Chapter 5

The aluminum handle of Labor Ready's glass door slammed loudly against the building's light brown brick exterior. Ricky Hayes stepped through the open doorway, cigarette in hand, angrily searching his pockets for his lighter. Every motion exhibited a fury that was more childish tantrum than it was powerful or intimidating.

"What the fuck, Ricky? It isn't my damn fault. Come back in an hour and we might have something," the recruiter yelled out the door. "If you are going to be an asshole, I'm going to stop trying to help you."

Without turning around, Ricky simply raised his right hand and stuck up a single crooked finger; it was not his thumb. "Go fuck yourself," he mumbled, his lips tightly pressed around the freshly lit Marlboro.

The limp that he normally tried to hide was extremely obvious when he was angry, which was about half of the time. An accident on a lobster boat two decades earlier had left him walking like one leg was 4 inches shorter than the other. Sure, it hurt most of the time, but it didn't stop him from being able to work. Fishermen don't usually have disability insurance and a couple hundred bucks a month from social security was barely worth filling out the paperwork, so every morning he played the same game.

At 5 o'clock in the morning, without the aid of an alarm clock, Ricky would wake up on whatever shelter cot, park bench, or friend's couch he had slept on the night before, and then take the bus to Labor Ready. He waited in line with everyone else for the first round of jobs. He usually didn't get picked, so he went to Trader Joe's for a coffee and came back for the second round. They weren't as picky, but they didn't pay that well either. Half the time, he would get chosen for some sort of crap job and the rest of the time he walked back to the bus stop and went to the big hardware stores to see if any contractors needed help for the day. He hated the daily hustle, but he didn't really have many other options.

The walk to and from Trader Joe's always screwed with his leg. It was four blocks of hills and the badly healed muscles burned with every step. Ten minutes into the walk, he reached the small grassy area behind Trader Joe's and decided to sit on the bench to rest. He sat on the end with one leg on each side; the rounded sides were oddly comfortable. After rubbing his sore thighs for a minute, he leaned back so that he was lying flat on the length of the bench and closed his eyes.

He ignored the sounds of cars as they drove by and the occasional shout from some jerk calling him a "lazy bum", but he did look over when he heard a truck idling near him. The man behind the wheel honked and he sat up.

"Yeah?" Ricky yelled to the driver.

"You looking for a hard day's work?" the man asked.

Hearing those magic words, Ricky pushed himself off the bench and walked to the passenger side of the truck, putting all the effort he could muster into not limping or wincing. When he got to the door, the electric window rolled down.

"Sure, I could use the work. Whatcha got?" he asked the stranger.

"Boss needs some help getting the fields ready to plant. You any good with a tractor?" the man asked.

"If it starts, I can drive it. If it won't start, I can fix it," Ricky said confidently, leaning in the open window. He flashed his best smile—not great by most standards, but it was genuine. Years of smoking, poor eating, and fistfights had cracked or knocked out a handful of his teeth and discolored the rest. Ricky was capable of many things, but do-it-yourself dentistry was not one of them.

"We need someone for the next couple of weeks to start with, but if you're good, you might get to stay through harvest and plow under time. We have a bunk house if you ain't got a car," the man said, his downeast accent softening some letters and making a lot of the "R's" disappear. Car sounded a lot like "cah", and that was comforting to Ricky. He preferred to work for a local over some transplant from Massachusetts.

"Sounds good. When do I start?" Ricky asked.

"Grab your stuff and hop in," the man replied.

"Nothin' to grab. All I need is these two hands," Ricky said as he opened the door and sat down.

The two men rode in silence until they were outside the city. When the truck passed through the toll booth for 95 North, Ricky broke the quiet.

"Where is this place?" he asked with more curiosity than suspicion.

"Oh, up the road a stretch. Right on the edge of Poland," the man answered. He was in his late 30's or early 40's, around 10 years younger than Ricky and had the weathered skin of a lifelong farmer. Knuckles twice the size as they should have been poked up from the top of the steering wheel. Years of abuse and arthritis tended to do that to a man's joints. Ricky had his fair share of things that creaked and cracked when he moved but this guy looked way more torn up than he should for his age.

"What do you grow?" Ricky asked.

"Bit of everything. A lot of nothing," the man replied.

"What's the boss man like?"

"Good guy, likes hard workers, but doesn't put up with the mouthy or lazy."

"You been with him long?"

"Hey man, you have a lot of questions that you don't need to be asking. Why don't you practice being quiet?" the man said curtly.

Ricky was both surprised and angry at that response. Who was this little shit to be mouthing off to someone he didn't know?

"I kinda like to know where I am going and what I am doing. If it's going to be like this, just pull over and let me out," Ricky said with irritation in his voice.

"You got some spunk for an old guy. Hope you got more of it. You're going to need it," the man said, turning to face Ricky. He smiled but not in a "just kidding" kind of way. This smile had some bad intentions behind it.

"Just pull over and let me out. I ain't interested in no weird stuff," Ricky said, unnerved by the change in the driver's demeanor. The driver didn't speak.

"Listen asshole. I don't want the job. Just pull into the next parking lot and let me out," Ricky said with a little panic in his voice.

"You wanted the job. Now, you are going to do it."

"And now I don't want it. It doesn't feel right and I don't want to go. I am not asking you again. Pull over or I am jumping out," Ricky yelled.

"Not gonna happen," the man said.

Before Ricky could respond he heard the door lock click. He looked at the door and saw that the lock was missing. He pushed the window button but it didn't open. Scared and furious, Ricky turned back to face the driver. "I am tired of the games. Pull this truck over or I am going to knock you the fuck out."

"Buddy, our game is just getting started. Now sit back and shut up. We will be there soon," the man said in a frighteningly quiet voice.

Ricky turned almost completely around in his seat so that he was facing the man. Just as he was about to protest one more time, he saw the man reaching down beside his seat with his left hand. When it came back into view, it was no longer empty. It was now holding a black 9 mm pistol.

Staring straight ahead, the man said "Boy, are we gonna have some fun with you."

Chapter 6

Christian let go of the now unconscious stalker and slowly stood, raising his arms in the air, but keeping them tight to his body. They were only an inch or so from his ears when the man in front of him collapsed into a heap on the ground. As he moved, the gun pressed into the back of his neck, just below his skull, moved with him.

"Your buddy here made the mistake of following me, and now you have too," Christian said through bared teeth.

"I wouldn't be so cocky if I were you Dr. Rinaldi. You are the one with a gun to his head, not me," said the faceless voice behind him.

This new man had certainly gotten the drop on him, but that didn't mean that Christian was ready to give in. He moved his head slightly to see how twitchy the man was. There was no reaction, so Christian knew that he had some leeway to work with. Even with some room, he was only going to have one shot to make it work.

He ran through his options in his head. He could kick straight back and hope he hit a kneecap, but that was too risky. He could dive toward the SUV and hope that he made it out of the gunman's range in time but, again, that was too risky. He settled on a third option. He would still need to be fast, and it was definitely dangerous, but if it worked the gunman would be on the ground next to his buddy.

Christian took two slow, deep breaths to calm his body and steady his nerves. If he made a mistake, he could end up with a bullet in the back of his head. He opened up the fingers on both hands and silently counted down from three. When he reached zero, Christian spun swiftly to his right, making an extremely tight turn. His right hand clamped around the gunman's wrist from the side and simultaneously squeezed, and pushed the hand away from him. A rapid twisting motion locked the man's arm from wrist to shoulder.

The gunman was startled and off balance, his body turned toward the wall as Christian wrenched his assailant's arm downward. Christian placed his left hand on the man's right shoulder and pushed down, completely immobilizing the arm that held the gun. For good measure, Christian drove the heel of his foot into the back of the man's right knee, buckling it. The man fell to his knees and the gun clanged impotently against the cement.

"Buddha, it's me for Christ's sakes, calm down!" the man screamed.

Only a couple of people called Christian by that nickname, and he thought he recognized the voice. He used his left hand to spin the man by the shoulder and the terrified face staring back at him filled him with a sense of relief. Relief and rage.

"Darren? What the hell were you thinking? Who is that guy?" Christian asked the man sitting at his feet.

"I heard you were coming down today, and I thought I would have a little fun," Darren said with a smirk

"Pulling a gun on me is fun? That is a good way to end up eating through a tube," Christian said humorlessly.

"Okay, that was a mistake but I thought you were going to kill him. Safety was on the whole time, I swear," Darren said, raising his hands up innocently. "Now can you help me up so I can see if I need a new Regulator?"

Christian clasped Darren's open hand in his own and yanked him to his feet. He pulled more sharply than he should have, just to emphasize his irritation. When Darren was standing and Christian got a good look at his friend, he thought that 'Buddha' was a better nickname for him. His shaved head barely came up to Christian's chin, but he easily outweighed Christian by 20 pounds. With his shaved head and prominent beer gut, Darren would have been a dead ringer for a 'fat Buddha' statue—if he could even get into the lotus pose, that is.

The nickname was an obvious one. Christian is a practicing Buddhist and Darren just loved the fact that a Buddhist was named Christian. Darren was a devout atheist, who after a few drinks would tell anyone and everyone that they were "ignorant sheep" for having an "invisible friend to talk to".

"That is your new reg?" Christian asked, nodding at the first man who was now stirring into consciousness.

"What happened to what's-his-face? The kid from Jersey."

"He couldn't take all the fresh air and nothing to do at night, so he transferred somewhere more exciting," Darren said with a shake of his head.

"To each his own, I guess," Christian said, shrugging his shoulders. "How long have you had this one?"

"Fresh out of the box, man. I got him in the last cycle. He was completely green, so I thought I would break him in a little," Darren said as he gave the downed man a light slap on the face.

"Breaking him in by having the poor bastard stalk me on the way down here? You must really hate this one," Christian chuckled. "If you had waited another 30 seconds, a cleaner would have been taking him out of that dumpster and putting him in a bag. You are going to want to take him to a hospital. I broke his wrist for sure."

"You break it, you buy it," Darren laughed.

The man seemed to be almost fully awake but still wobbly as Darren helped him to his feet. He rubbed his neck, looking back and forth between the two men. He stuck his good hand out toward Christian, nearly losing his balance as he did.

"I am sorry about that, Mr. Rinaldi. It is nice to meet you. I'm Greg," the young man said, waiting for Christian to acknowledge him.

"Dr. Rinaldi, kid. It is Doctor not Mister. He spent too much money and time in some third world shrink school for you to call him anything else," Darren said sarcastically.

Christian shook the kid's hand and said, "Christian is fine. If he ever asks you to follow me again, refuse. It never ends well."

"Yeah, I was thinking that same thing just before I blacked out," Greg said, still rolling his head in circles and rubbing his neck.

Christian reached over to pat Greg on the back, but the kid flinched and Darren broke down laughing. Christian placed his hand on the embarrassed young man's shoulder and they all started to walk back down the alley. When they reached Tremont St, Greg dropped back a step, as though he wasn't supposed to be with them. Christian looked over his shoulder at him to see if he was okay but the kid seemed fine, aside from a bruised ego and broken wrist.

"How long are you here for?" Darren asked Christian as they made the turn onto Boylston.

"Just for the night. I am here to meet with Grayson and pick up my new reg. Wait, you are seriously 'Greg the reg'?" Christian asked over his shoulder.

"Umm, yeah, I guess so," said the embarrassed young man.

"Not really all that funny, Doc," Darren said. "Do you have any idea who you are getting?"

"Not a clue, but Alex said she has been here all week and she has her eye on one. She is going to work her charms on Grayson to get him assigned. I can't handle one like that kid you just had. I want a reg that is going to stay out of my way and not be all over me all the time. They are regulators, not babysitters," Christian responded.

"Those are some great charms she is working with, so she will get what she wants. Hell, I'd buy her a house. Seriously though, good luck with that. I don't know where they dig some of them up lately. No offense, Greg," Darren said but his "no offense" came out more like "yes, I mean you."

The three men stopped in front of their final destination, a non-descript, twelve story brick building that looked exactly like the five buildings on either side of it. They walked toward the glass doors, which automatically opened, and the cold air of an overpowering air conditioning unit enveloped them, sending goose bumps up Christian's arms.

"AC is on already?" Darren complained as they stepped inside the building.

Ahead of them were two lines of people waiting to go through the metal detectors. Luckily for them, the security guard knew them and always let them go around the side.

Darren led them toward the side entrance, but stopped dead in his tracks. The man in front of them was not their usual security guard. Christian would be fine if he had to go through the metal detectors, but what was Darren going to do? Christian had the blackjack and a small knife that would be looked over and handed back to him, but Darren had at least one gun on him. Knowing him, it was likely three or four.

Christian passed through the scanner and waited patiently on the other side for his bag to come off the conveyor belt when he heard the guard speak to Darren.

"Sir, you can't go over there. That area is off limits to visitors," the man said firmly.

"It's cool, man. Frank lets us through here all the time. We are going up to nine and we are in a hurry," Darren responded, trying to act calmly.

"I am not Frank. Everyone goes through the scanner. No exceptions."

Darren walked closer to the man, leaned inward by the slightly smaller man's ear and softly said "Look, I know you are new but this is how we have been doing it for years, and I am running really late. How about I show you my ID, you let us through, and when my meeting is over, I can come back down and walk through your scanner?"

The guard was not interested in listening to Darren. "Sir, step away from me and get back in line. I am not going to tell you again."

"Just call Frank. He will tell you that it is fine."

"I am not calling anyone. You are going to get in line like everyone else," the guard said sharply, his limited patience gone.

"Okay, okay. Calm down, sweetheart. I am just going to go outside and wait for Frank. Come on, Greg, let's go," Darren said, turning away and raising his hands up in mock surrender. As his arms lifted higher, his thin jacket pressed tightly against his back, showing the outline of what was hiding underneath.

The security guard jumped out of his seat and reached for his sidearm. Before Darren had taken five more steps, the guard was though the detector. His youthful exuberance was reacting before his brain. The blaring alarm caused Darren to turn.

"Everyone down, this man has a gun!" the guard foolishly yelled.

Screams of panic filled the air as everyone fell to the ground. On the other side of the barrier, Christian stood silently, not sure of his next course of action. Greg dropped to the floor with everyone else besides Christian, Darren, and the guard who had his gun pointed directly at Darren's chest.

Chapter 7

Ricky had been staring out the window for the past twenty minutes, trying and failing to not think about the gun or the man holding it. Why hadn't he just gone and gotten his coffee? None of this would have happened if he had just kept walking. The sound of gravel crunching under the truck's tires broke his train of thought.

They pulled off of the main road and onto a long unpaved driveway that cut a single line through a forebodingly dense forest. Ricky looked at the clock, 8:25, and the speedometer, 25 miles an hour, so he could try to figure out how long this driveway was when they got wherever they were going.

Two minutes and about a mile later, the roadside opened into a large clearing. A white two story farm house was ahead to his left, and several enormous barns were to the right. Horses, cows, and chickens ran loose in various fences on each side of the driveway. The driver pushed a switch on his visor that looked like a garage door opener and the long gate blocking the road ahead slowly began to open.

Ricky's captor pulled the truck to a stop behind a huge barn and honked the horn three times in succession. A shaggy haired man around Ricky's age came out of a smaller building at the end of the field and started walking toward the truck. The impatient driver pressed the horn and held it down for one sustained "HOOOOOONK", and the older man picked up his pace a step or two.

"You do everything that Old Jim tells you. He is going to get you settled and show you around. If you try anything, I will shoot you myself," the driver said as he opened his own door and left Ricky alone in the truck. He walked over to Jim, towering over the old man's bent frame, spoke a few words to him, and slapped him hard enough on the back to make the old man wince before walking away.

Jim opened Ricky's door and said "My name is Jim. I am not here to hurt you but I need you to stick out a leg." When Ricky hesitated, Jim followed up with, "Don't make this harder than it has to be. If I don't get you squared away, he is going to kick my ass and shoot you. That big bastard has got a helluva temper on him. Mean streak like an old junkyard dog."

Reluctantly, Ricky turned in his seat so that his legs stuck out through the open door. Jim wrapped something around Ricky's ankle and hooked it together in the back. It looked like a cross between a house arrest monitor and a scuba diving weight belt with a metal clasp and a few red and white wires.

"Don't go past that gate you just drove through and whatever you do, do not screw with this thing. Those little pouches are full of C-4," Jim said, pointing to the three bulges on the outside of Ricky's new ankle accessory. "If you try to take it off or go across that line, it will beep three times for a warning. You hear those beeps, you better haul ass. You have ten seconds to get back over the line before it blows. I have seen it happen twice, and it is not pretty."

"What the hell is going on here? This guy just picked me up and asked me if I wanted a job. Halfway here he got all weird and pulled a gun on me," Ricky asked.

"You'll see soon enough. Just thinking about it makes me sick. I sure don't want talk about it. Just keep your head down and your mouth shut, and you should be okay. Just do whatever they ask you to do and don't complain," Jim explained solemnly.

Without another word, Jim turned and walked back toward the same building he'd just come out of. Ricky hurried to catch up, his new ankle bracelet rubbing up and down on his lower leg with the softness of sandpaper. The idea of having something that could explode connected to his body still hadn't sunk in yet. Everything seemed surreal. How could this day get any worse?

Jim pushed on the screen door that led into the small building and waved for Ricky to follow him in. Ricky stepped up the four concrete steps and into the dingy structure. This must have been the bunkhouse that the driver had mentioned. It was about 30 feet long and 20 feet wide with metal bunk beds lining both sides of the room. It reminded him of all the old war movies he saw as a kid, where the men slept in barracks like these while in basic training. There were six sets of bunks on each side, but there was no one else in the room. There didn't seem to be any electricity, running water, or any other basic comforts. The walls didn't have sheetrock or insulation. They were just framed-in walls with rotting, untreated planks on the outside. Most were weathered a muted gray, but some were still fading from a pale off white color and had to be recent editions. Daylight seeped in through hundreds of gaps in the floor, roof, and all of the walls. The floor and roof were not in any better shape. It had to be 50 years old and only one spot was repaired during that time.

"This here is going to be your bunk," Jim said, pointing to the second one from the end on the left-hand side. "Don't have anybody sleeping on the top or bottom, so I guess you have your pick. It doesn't look like you brought any stuff with you, so I don't have to tell you where put it. Change out of the clothes you have on and put on those coveralls. Take good care of 'em because they are gonna be the only things you have for a while. Get changed, and I'll take you out to where everyone else is."

Ricky walked over to his new bunk and just stared. The mattress was blue-and-white striped and could not have been more than 3 inches thick. It didn't give much cushion from the bare support bars underneath, but it couldn't be any less comfortable than those cots at the shelter. It came with a similarly flat pillow, a fitted sheet, and a dark green wool blanket. He quickly changed into the new mud brown coveralls, which were a couple sizes too big. He rolled up the pant legs and put on the brown military surplus style tee shirt that sat with it. He changed his clothes like he was in a hurry to get somewhere but didn't know why. He couldn't tell if he was more curious or fearful.

"You ready yet?" Jim yelled in a hoarse, lifelong smoker's voice from the other end of the building. "Better hurry up. We don't want to keep them waiting."

"I'm not sure I can work in these pants. They are way too big," Ricky said as he shuffled quickly to meet Jim. He felt like a little boy trying on his older brother's clothes.

"Don't worry, we can tape 'em up later. Don't think you'll be working today anyway. We've got something way worse going on," Jim said in the voice of a broken man.

"What could be worse than being dragged here at gunpoint and having a bomb strapped to my leg?" Ricky asked.

"You'll see," Old Jim averted his eyes as he said those two words. His shoulders drooped like he had just had fifty pounds dropped on him.

Ricky walked beside the old man, slowing his natural pace down so that he wouldn't get ahead of Jim. He didn't think he was going to get any answers out of the old fellow, but he didn't want to be alone just yet. They walked down another dirt path, about as wide as a one-ton truck, which led them through another small patch of woods and into a large, partially plowed field. Three tractors sat in various places on the overturned soil, unmoving and riderless like sentries standing guard.

"Where is everybody?" Ricky asked.

"They are in another field on the other side of those trees," Jim responded, nodding to the trees on the right hand side of the opening.

They skirted around the edge of the fields, along the tree line, until they came to a small footpath that was so narrow that Ricky had to walk behind Jim. He found it awkward to walk with one foot on each side of a small grassy mound that ran down the middle of the path. He waddled like a duck more than he walked like a man. His bad leg was begging for a break.

Five hundred feet later, they entered another clearing where he saw around fifteen to eighteen men sitting on logs and facing a clearing in the woods. The logs were makeshift seating with room enough for three or four men to sit on each one. There were nine logs on each side, with an aisle down the middle. Each log was angled so that it helped form a semi-circle around what looked like a central staging area. The forest surrounded the clearing on all sides and Ricky couldn't see any other paths in or out.

All of the men wore the same brown coveralls that Ricky was now sporting. Some were too tight, some were too big but very few fit. Each man was dirty and the closer he got to them the stronger they smelled of mud and sweat. They were all in various stages of ragged dishevelment, and Ricky wondered if that was how he could tell how long they'd been here. He felt like he was in a movie about POWs in some foreign land. Everyone had the same defeated look. What insignificant amount of hope remained in Ricky was rapidly going away.

"Go take that open spot, there in the middle. Don't ever sit in the front and never be the furthest guy back. You want to blend in and not stick out," Jim said pointing to an opening between two other men on the left side.

Ricky walked down the small aisle that divided the rows of logs. He gave the men a slight nod as he shuffled in front of them, trying not to bang into them or the person in front them, and sat down. Neither man returned the nod nor did anyone else even look at him. They all stared straight ahead at the empty clearing.

Well, the clearing was not completely empty. There was a hole in the center and a post-hole digger leaning against one of the trees along the edge. Ricky wondered what the hole was for. The answer to that question came a couple of minutes later.

Ricky heard groaning and scraping coming from the path he had just walked down. If anyone else heard the same sounds, they didn't show it. He turned to look but he was the only one who did. He could see three shapes coming down the path, but at first he couldn't make them out. There appeared to be three men walking single file. The first man was wore a hood and was carrying some small items in his hands. The second man was carrying something large on his back, and the third was mostly hidden by the first two, aside from a hood like the first man. Half a minute later, Ricky wished that he hadn't looked at all.

As they emerged from the shadows, their clothing and what they had with them came into clear view. The first man was carrying a round-headed, short handled wooden mallet and a handful of thick, long metal nails. Ricky had used those same spikes when he was building his kids' treehouse back in the day.

The third man carried a large spear-like rod with a sharp metal point on the end of a stiff wood shaft, and something else that Ricky couldn't make out. As frightening as those two men were, it was the sight of the middle man that sent a cold chill through Ricky.

He was dressed in a white linen toga, with long hair and a shaggy beard. He had a wooden beam across his back with ropes securing it to his wrists and arms. A second wooden 4 x 4 ran down his back, dragging on the ground behind him. He was dressed like Jesus and was dragging a cross on his back! What the hell was this place?

The men continued to walk, without speaking to anyone else or to each other, into the clearing in front of the seated men. Once they reached the center, they stopped and turned to face the crowd. They stood there in silence with heads bowed, and stared at the ground. After what felt like an eternity, the man with the hammer and spikes flipped back his brown hood and spoke.

"Brothers, I am pleased that you could all join us today. We have had a thief in our midst. But alas, he has been caught, tried for his crimes, and now is his moment of reckoning," the man's voice boomed in the clearing. He spoke clearly and slowly with the same pitch and tenor as a Southern preacher. Something about his voice was off, and the speech seemed more mocking than genuine.

The man was an inch or two taller than the one who had driven Ricky to this place, but he was narrower across the shoulders. He looked strong and agile, even under the brown robe that he wore. His outfit was reminiscent of a Franciscan monk or a Druid; Ricky didn't know for sure. There were no markings on the robe. It was a deep brown with large sleeves that stopped in the middle of his hands. It was a simple design with a hood and twisted gold colored rope for belt. It reached all the way to the ground and covered the man's feet. It seemed almost costume-ish.

Ricky recognized the third man as the one who had picked him up this morning. He was wearing the same outfit as the first man but his hood was still covering most of his face. In one hand, he carried the spear, and in the other he held a dagger about a foot and a half long—a full foot of it was a double-edged blade.

"Brother Gene lied to you all, stole from you, lived off of your hard work, while shirking his own. My brothers, it is time to remove the snake that has been living among you. We do not pass judgment here. We only carry out the execution," the first man continued on. "We need some volunteers who are willing to do what they know is right. Raise your hand and be counted."

No hands were raised and the man spoke again, his voice harsher this time. "I cannot see your hands, brothers. Who will help us carry out Brother Gene's sentence?"

This time, a few hands tentatively lifted from laps and into the air. Once three hands were visible, everyone else followed suit. Monk #1 pointed out into the crowd at three different men who each stood and walked to the front of the log benches. They continued to look at the ground, hands clasped in front of them until he spoke again.

"Brother Robert and Brother Mike, please grab a side of the cross. Brother Stephen, please lift up the back end and guide it into the hole."

The men did as they were instructed and walked the man called Brother Gene, along with his wooden burden, backwards until the base of the cross was at the edge of the hole. Gene stumbled and fell but they continued to carry him. None of the men looked Gene in the face.

"Raise him up!" the first monk yelled. Robert and Mike lifted their sides of the cross and Stephen grabbed the shaft of the vertical pole and pulled it backwards until it started to slide deeper into the opening. He then ran to the front and helped tilt it up until it was straight. The men grunted from the effort of lifting a cross and motionless man. The base of the cross hit the bottom of the hole, jerking Gene from side to side, his legs swaying lifelessly. His arms were tied to the horizontal beam, but that was all that held him in place, causing him to sag lower.

Gene appeared to be only semiconscious and possibly drugged. His eyes fluttered open briefly and then rolled back in their sockets. Ricky was surprised that he had been able to carry the cross that far. The cross probably only weighed fifty or sixty pounds, but it was at least a quarter mile walk from the barn to the clearing and all of it was field and woods. That is a long way to carry something on your back, even if you weren't only half conscious.

The first monk stepped directly in front of Gene and turned to face the hanging man. "Brother Robert, please hold Brother Gene's arm. "

Robert stepped forward and placed one hand in the middle of Gene's forearm and the other between his elbow and shoulder. He pressed it firmly against the wooden cross member, shifting his body so that his right leg was behind him to brace himself. The first monk placed all but one of the 6 inch long galvanized steel spikes into his robe's pocket.

"All the stories you've been told about crucifixions are wrong. You cannot drive a spike through a man's palm and have it hold him in place. It would tear through his hand and he would fall to the ground. We do not want Brother Gene to suffer, so we will carry out his sentence in the way that the Romans truly did," the man said as he turned toward the still unmoving man.

Gene slumped flaccidly forward, his head bowed, shoulders drooped and legs hung impotently. If he knew what was going on, he certainly didn't act like it.

The first monk placed the point of the first silver spike just below Gene's wrist bones. He held it in place with his thumb and two fingers, his right hand held the wooden mallet. He pulled his arm back over dramatically and held it high in the air. Robert, Mike, and Stephen all looked away as the mallet moved forward. Its flat wooden face struck the head of the nail and drove it a couple of inches forward, more than enough to pass through the soft skin, sinew and bones in its way. Gene's head jerked straight up, his eyes wild and he let out a guttural scream. It was the most horrifying noise that Ricky had ever heard.

The mallet struck the nail over and over. The monk repeated this motion until the head of the nail was no longer visible on Gene's blood soaked wrist. Blood flowed from the wound and dripped to the ground. The green-brown grass below was now a deep crimson. The monk moved across Gene's body to his right arm. Without being told, Mike ran over and secured Gene's remaining undamaged arm. The first monk placed the spike in the same location as the first one and repeated the process. This time he did it more quickly and unceremoniously.

Gene thrashed furiously, his legs swinging from side to side in a feeble attempt to break free. He moved the fingers on both hands, reaching for the nail. Each movement caused blood to flow faster.

"Stephen, grab his legs," the monk yelled.

Stephen attempted to catch Gene's legs just above his ankles and struggled to hold them in place. He pressed his own shoulder against the back of the cross, and wrapped both arms around Gene's lower legs. He appeared to be sobbing but only lightly.

The monk pulled out an even larger spike from his robe and pointed at Gene's feet. Mike seemed to understand the wordless instructions and grabbed Gene by his ankles. The monk positioned Gene's feet, and bent his legs at the knees so that he could stack one foot on top of the other. He nodded to Mike who held the feet in that position. The monk placed the final spike over the middle of the exposed foot and swung the mallet with a flourish of speed and force. A morbidly loud crunch filled the air and blood squirted profusely from the freshly impaled feet. A man in the front row watched as blood splattered onto the toes of his boots. He pulled them back against the log but didn't wipe them off.

The monk stood and spun in a circle, his arms extended to the sides and head tilted upward. He seemed to find pleasure in what he had just done. When he stopped spinning, he looked out into the crowd and spoke again.

"Everyone thank our helpers. They did a wonderful job, didn't they?" he said in the same manner that a magician thanks his volunteers at a cheesy Vegas show. Unfortunately, this was not an illusion. "Now it is time for the second half of the sentence to be carried out."

Hearing his cue, the second monk flipped his hood back onto his shoulders and upper back. He slid the dagger into his rope belt and walked to the middle of the clearing. He continued down the aisle separating the two rows of logs, and stood about twenty feet away from the freshly crucified Gene. He lifted the spear to his right shoulder, cupping his hand around it securely but loosely, like a javelin. He took three steps backwards, pulling the spear behind him as he went, until the back tip of it almost touched the ground. He shuffled forward while swinging his arm in a rapid arc. The spear left his hand so quickly that he stumbled forward as he let it go. He held that position, standing on his left leg, torso twisted and bent over with his right arm still pointing at his prey.

Everything seemed like it was in slow motion to Ricky. The spear left the man's hand and wobbled as it flew towards its target. It struck Gene between his right shoulder and the middle of his chest.

The first monk yelped with glee, ran over, and viciously pulled it out, leaving a gaping hole. Blood flowed from the gaping wound and soaked the front of Gene's robe. The red stain spread, and air sucked in and out of the hole from an apparent puncture to Gene's lung.

The first monk handed the spear back to his compadre, who then got back into his throwing position. He let the weapon fly one more time. The projectile landed in Gene's upper thigh with a dull thud. The monk left it there and walked toward Gene. He nodded to the first monk who responded with a smile and nod of his own.

The second monk pulled out the dagger from his robe's belt and the first monk removed the spear from Gene's thigh. Monk number one stood to Gene's left while monk number two took up a position behind the cross. Number two reached across Gene with his right arm, holding the dagger in his hand. Gene's head drooped lifelessly and the man used his left hand to pull Gene's head upward by his hair. He pressed the blade against Gene's throat. A bead of blood appeared at the blade's razor sharp tip. Monk number one held the spear in both hands and nodded to his cohort. He stepped forward and plunged the spear into the side of Gene's exposed rib cage while monk number two slid the blade across Gene's neck. Both men smiled with an unearthly giddiness.

Number one yanked the spear out violently and number two wiped the bloodied blade on the side of his robe as they walked to the middle of the clearing and stood side by side, triumphantly preening before the captive audience.

"Robert, Mike, and Stephen—you stay behind, and when he's done bleeding, pull down the cross and fill the hole in. Tonight before it gets dark, you need to drag him out and put him in the back of the green truck. DO NOT take him off the cross. If it doesn't fit in the truck bed, trim off some of the wood. I don't want any sticking up. Cover him over with tarps and put some tires on top of that. I want you to come to our bunkhouse and let us know when you're done. That is your only job for the day. Everyone else, go to the bunks and get some rest. We have fields to plow after lunch," the first monk said. The pomp and circumstance was gone from his voice, as was the southern drawl. His new voice sounded like any other Mainer.

The men walked one by one down the dirt path toward the bunkhouse. Ricky tapped Jim on the shoulder and asked "What the hell was that? Is this some kind of religious cult?"

"No, it ain't no cult. I don't think either of 'em has ever found religion. Just be glad you were in the audience. It's usually one of the volunteers that goes next. That's why those three boys are shittin' their britches now," Jim said with no emotion in his voice.

"You mean they just do this for fun?"

"You don't want to know what these guys do for fun. This was nothing; they really liked Gene. You should see what happens when they are pissed."

The men walked in silence all the way back to the bunk house. Each and every man stretched out on top of their blankets, without a word. Ricky stared at the bunk above him, unable to sleep. He was tired, but he didn't dare to close his eyes. Even when the line from the lobster trap had wrapped around his leg, pulled him off the boat and into the ocean, he hadn't felt fear like he was feeling now. At that moment, Ricky knew he was never going to leave this farm alive.

Chapter 8

Christian stared in disbelief at the scene in front of him. The new security guard had just panicked at the outline of Darren's gun. The young man could not have been any older than 25. He had the look of a man with aspirations of becoming a full-fledged police officer someday. His company-issued blue and black uniform was crisp and pressed like it had come from the dry cleaners. It was too perfect to have been done on an ironing board at home. Most of the guys who had been on the job for a while looked like they picked what pieces they could find of their uniform off the floor, gave them a shake, and put them on. His was still shiny; all the buttons were polished, as were his shoes. The holster he drew his glossy black Beretta out of barely had a crease. The leather on the clasp was tight, as was the holster itself. So tight that it almost squeaked when he drew down on Darren. Christian was sure that this was the only time the weapon had been drawn, outside of while the guard was home in front of his bedroom mirror.

Christian thought the man's silver plated nametag had said Johnson but he wasn't 100% certain. Regardless of his actual name, "Johnson" had created a chaotic atmosphere. A dozen men and women were scattered around the room, face down on the beige Travertine tile floor. Some had hands over their heads, others were crying. All were shocked. As for Johnson, adrenaline and youthful bravado were getting the best of him. His overreaction had created a situation that his mind and body were not prepared for. His outstretched arm was tiring. The Beretta was shaking; so was his voice.

"Sir, I need you to do exactly as I tell you. Do you understand?" he said, his voice cracking like a teenager asking a pretty girl to dance. "Put your hands on top of your head and get down on your knees."

Darren started to speak in protest but Christian shook him off, motioning downward with his hands to tell Darren to relax and comply. As twitchy and inexperienced as this kid was, someone could get hurt. Darren dropped to his knees and put his hands on his head. Same position as requested but wrong order.

"Lay flat on your stomach and keep your hands where I can see them. I mean, put them out in front of you," Johnson said, his confidence growing.

A hollow grinding noise filled the air. It was familiar, but in the midst of this drama, Christian couldn't place it. A second later, a high-pitched ding caused everyone to look at the elevator. The startled guard turned on his heels and pointed his gun at the bank of elevators behind Christian. Instinctively, Christian moved to the side, out of the fire line. The center elevator stopped on the ground floor, and everyone waited for the doors to open.

The mahogany-covered doors parted from the middle, and standing dead-center in the opening, framed like a museum quality photograph, was a stunning woman. Her Amazonian frame- 5'11 in bare feet—eye level with Christian in the spike heeled patent leather boots she had on—filled the doorway like it was made just for her to walk through. Her meadow green eyes registered a hint of fear, but that was quickly replaced by a fire that Christian had seen many times before. Alex loved the thrill of anything dangerous. A man pointing a gun at her turned her on more than it scared her.

Alex strode toward Johnson with the confidence of a jungle cat stalking its cornered prey. The heels of her stripper boots clacked against the tile, pin points of sound echoing in the cavernesque silence of the building's foyer. Ever the exhibitionist, today's ensemble was equal parts dominatrix and Catholic school girl. She managed to evoke lustful stirrings in most men and women whose paths she crossed. Either one was fine with her.

The leather boots ended just above her knee, her green and red Irish plaid skirt fell to the middle of her thigh, allowing 2 inches of toned, muscular leg to peek out. A tight white oxford shirt, barely containing her ample milky white figure, left little to the imagination, and a lot to be desired. She only wore shirts that were tight enough to be corsets. Christian couldn't think of a time when she had less than 4 buttons open. A Wiccan pentagram necklace found a happy home in her exposed cleavage. A single black stripe outlined her pouty lips, emphasizing her blood red lipstick. Shadowy eyeliner and a touch of rouge accenting her high regal cheekbones finished the almost Vampiric Goth look. All that was missing in this juxtaposition between innocence and seduction was a pair of pigtails.

If Johnson had caught his breath, it wasn't noticeable. He seemed to be caught in her gaze like Perseus meeting Medusa. Unlike Perseus, Johnson didn't stand a chance. Alex had almost closed the gap between the elevator and Johnson before he had even spoken.

Alex stepped through the still beeping metal detector and closed to within four feet of Johnson before she made a sound. His eyes followed her hand as she reached out, placing her hand on the top of his gun. She gently pushed it away from her and the barrel pointed to the ground as she stepped closer. Johnson's eyes reached her chin but they peered straight down the front of Alex's shirt.

"What seems to be going on here? Is there a problem with my friend there?" she said, her voice floating through the air like a smoky whisper. She placed a single fingertip under the soft skin of Johnson's chin, tilting his face upward until his eyes met hers.

"Well, umm he has a gun and this is a gun free zo..." Johnson said, turning his face towards Darren, his confidence substantially lower than it was only a minute ago.

"Shhhhh," Alex stopped Johnson mid word. She turned him back to her. "Of course that man has a gun, silly. He is my bodyguard. You wouldn't want something happening to my body, would you?"

"No, of course not, he didn't... He should have told me."

"False alarm. Everyone go about your day," Alex yelled to the stunned crowd, startling most. A woman slapped the man next to her, who was caught in Alex's trance.

Alex waved to Darren, who came loping over like a new puppy. Greg started to follow him but Darren stopped him. "Go get your wrist X-rayed and come back."

Greg walked toward the street to hail a cab while Alex put an arm around Darren to guide him past Johnson. Neither of them spoke again until they reached the elevator where Christian was waiting, smirking. Alex pushed the up arrow and the center elevator reopened. As soon as all three were inside, Darren started jabbing at the "close door" button even though they don't actually close the door any earlier. Once it closed, Alex pressed 9 and her 4 digit code on the security box above the floor buttons to start the elevator moving. Anyone could press floor 9-12 but the doors would not open without the individualized pin.

The car jerked into motion, slowly rising upward. Christian leaned against the back right corner, arms crossed and eyes closed. His heart pounded, a cold sweat broke out on his forehead. He took a couple slow, deep breaths to hinder his growing anxiety. The small metal box was now close to 100 feet up the shaft, and slowed to a stop. The 4 seconds from the end of the ascent until the doors opened crept by, feeling like minutes. Christian moved up to the front, close enough to hug either companion if he wished, and herded them through the open door as swiftly as he could. He could now breathe again.

Neither Darren nor Alex dared to say anything about their hulk of a friend's claustrophobia or the odd irony that a well-known psychiatrist couldn't correct that peccadillo for himself. Both knew a little about why he was afflicted by this fear, but neither wanted to open *that* door. The darkness behind it was not a place that anyone ever wanted to be.

Alex was the first to break the uncomfortable silence. "What the hell happened to Greg that you had to send him off to the ER?"

"I, kinda, sorta had him do a field training today and it didn't go well," Darren said sheepishly.

"What sort of field training?" Alex asked, stretching the final words out suspiciously.

"I might have sent him down on the train with a picture of Christian and told him to follow him and maybe subdue him a little?" Darren said, holding his hand up and pinching two fingers close together when he said "a little".

"Did you give Christian a heads up?" Alex asked.

"Negative," Darren answered, looking at the floor and smirking.

"You idiot, are you trying to get him killed?" Alex asked. She punched him in the shoulder playfully. She then laughed and pushed a strand of her fire red hair out of her eyes, moving it behind her left ear. Multiple piercings held the strand in place. She claimed to have many more in other areas, and frequently offered to let Christian "hunt for them".

They found the room they were looking for at the end of the hallway. Darren opened the ornate door and they all walked into the observation room. They each grabbed a seat in one of the plush theater style seats that faced the "magic window". It wasn't magic in any way; it was just a run of the mill mirror like any of the ones you would find in a police station line up or interrogation room. The new class of regulators on the other side would never know who was watching them at any one time.

The clock read 9:20, and most of the participants had arrived on both sides of the glass. Christian recognized a few of the men on his side of the glass, but none on the other. Most of the people involved were men. Alex was something of a unicorn. Female serial killers are very rare, even more so at her level of skill and viciousness.

Christian had just settled in when he heard a muffled yet familiar sound. "Bad boys, bad boys, whatcha gonna do..." was playing in his bag. He opened it up, grabbed his phone, and answered the call while holding up an apologetic hand to the rest of the room.

"Agent Brooks, I am about to go into a meeting, can this wait an hour?" he asked while crossing to the other side of the room.

"Sorry about that, Doc. I just have a real head scratcher from that DOA this morning and thought you might want a puzzle to think about," Agent Brooks yelled into the phone, using the magic words that he knew would grab Christian's curiosity.

"Ok, give it to me," Christian said with a sigh, hating himself for being so predictable.

"Ok, so this guy bleeds out all over the damn bank floor. Blood comin' out of every hole below his belt, but he doesn't have any obvious injuries. Liver, kidneys, all the other usual suspects are all intact. Any ideas there, smarty-pants?" Brooks said with a laugh. The laugh was in fun, but Christian knew that he would not be calling if it weren't important.

Christian stood silently in the corner of the observation room and closed his eyes. He liked to get a picture of everything in his mind and work through it.

"Agent, can you tell me what he had on him?"

"Sure, nothing much to tell, really. Basic bum pack stuff, tissues, a fork, a couple knives, a plastic container with water, old military ID, salt, pepper, crackers, sugar packets, some loose change. That is about it, maybe a few other odds and ends."

Christian pictured each of these items on a table in front of him. The fork and knives would have left puncture marks on him, so they were out, but nothing else seemed to fit, until...

"Agent, the salt, is it in a packet or a shaker?"

"Uh, let me look. It is in a basic white diner shaker, why?"

"There is your murder weapon. If you shake some out on your finger and rub it you will find the answer."

"Oww," Brooks said in obvious pain. "That was rough, kind of sharp, too. What the hell is it?"

"Glass. It is an old mob trick. People would grind up glass and put it with salt or sugar and over time it perforates the intestinal track and other organs, causing major but slow blood loss. The holes are so small you wouldn't see them without a microscope. Have the M.E. verify, but that is going to be your cause of death."

"How would that have happened?" Brooks asked, still not getting the whole picture.

"Look at the shaker. It might have the name of where it came from. Someone intentionally put that glass in there."

"Yeah but this had to take a while. How would they have known that he was going to take it?"

"They didn't but they probably did know that, like most homeless people, he is territorial and would have claimed the same seat at the same table day after day. Same table, same shaker. They might have just gotten lucky when he took it. No way to tell if he was the target, or if the killer was just hoping to get anyone who used it."

"Ok, Doc, I will look into all that and let you know if it checks out. Talk to you later," Brooks said before hanging up abruptly.

Christian walked back to his seat where his buxom friend sat waiting for him. When he sat down, she pointed through the mirror and said, "That one right there, second row, third over? That is your guy. His name is Mick something. We called him McDraper at eval because he always had his hair parted to the side like that dude from *Mad Men*. I think you will like him, though."

Christian stared through the window at the man Alex had pointed at. He carried himself like a military man, par for the course when it came to regulators, but he seemed to be unsure about something while he sat in that room.

He wasn't a huge guy. Maybe Darren's height, but he was barrel-chested and built powerfully like a bulldog. His reddish blonde hair stuck out in the group of a half dozen men that were milling around in the training room. He couldn't have been over 30, but it was hard to tell with the red hair and freckles. Didn't most people grow out of those?

Christian leaned over and jokingly said, "You picked out a leprechaun?"

Alex moved even closer, and ignoring Christian's question, whispered into his ear, "I want us to go to lunch alone. I need to talk to you about something."

Christian turned his face to hers. She was close enough to smell her jasmine scented body lotion. "What is it?"

Alex leaned in closer, so close that her breath tickled his ear and neck, "I need you to kill someone for me."

Chapter 9

Mick Healy tapped his foot against the tile floor, impatiently waiting for the day's meeting to begin. He still had no idea why he was here or what he was doing. The classroom felt like one of his evaluation training rooms back in Army AIT School. It was clean, almost clinical. The walls were bare aside from a few of the obligatory corporate signs with the cheery sayings about "Leadership", "Perseverance", and other crap like that. All that was missing from this menagerie of clichés was the poster of a cat dangling by its paws from a clothes line, with the words "Hang in there" written on it.

Not knowing what was going on was wearing on him. He needed something to occupy his mind, but no one had been allowed to bring in any electronic devices, phones, or even a notebook. The last two weeks had been very hush-hush, and he was ready for some answers. Hopefully today was the day for that.

Two weeks ago, Mick had been sitting in the base admin office, waiting to fill out his paperwork to re-up for another 4 year tour when his Commanding Officer called him in to his office. When he got there, a man in a very expensive Italian suit was waiting. His C.O. said that the man was from a government contractor and left the two alone to talk.

The suited man said he was interested in evaluating Mick for a private sector position working with his company's "Assets" in the field. He had been selected from a huge pool of candidates and they thought he had what it took to succeed with them. There would be some danger involved from time to time, but it was limited. When Mick asked if the company was a government company, the man said, "Let's say that we are government *adjacent*." That was the only answer Mick received about anything other than salary. That number was substantially more than he was ever going to make while enlisted.

After about 10 minutes, the man left, saying that he needed an answer the following day, and that Mick was not to speak to anyone about it other than his C.O. His C.O. reentered the office and the officer said that he had heard of the company, but knew very little about it. He said that there were rumors about who they were and what they did, but they were more secretive than the CIA *and* were better funded.

Mick had heard rumors about these types of backdoor offers, but didn't know anyone who had been approached. Black ops companies, recruiting people like him who were smart, skilled, and had no family or any other real connections to get in the way, was supposedly commonplace, but he didn't have any true examples come to mind. He knew that he didn't want to disappear off the grid, but he was intrigued by both the mystery and the money.

At 6:00 the next morning, Mick's phone rang and the voice on the other end instructed him that a car would be there to pick him up in five minutes. It would only wait for sixty seconds. He didn't need to pack, and he was not allowed to bring his phone. He had two choices: walk out and get into the back of the waiting car, or do nothing. Once the car left, that was it.

Mick sat on the end of his bed and looked around his room. It looked like every other single guy's room on base. He had a few personal possessions, DVDs, a laptop, books, clothes, an oversized flat screen TV, and a bunch of video games, but that was it. There wasn't anything in the room that would tell you that it was *his* room. He didn't have any pictures or mementos from his childhood, or even from the last 12 years in the Army. There was nothing.

He thought he heard a car idling outside but he had no idea how long it had been there. What was his decision? Mick still wasn't sure, so he chose to run down the stairs and if the car was waiting, he would go, if he missed it then that was his answer. As he made it to the heavy metal doors, he looked through the thin slotted window and thought he saw a man walking from the back door to the driver's seat. Crap he was going to miss it!

"Wait! I am coming!" he yelled as he pushed down hard on the metal lever to open the heavy door. He ran down the walkway toward the car. Thankfully the man, dressed in a black suit, white shirt and thin black tie, stepped over to the rear door of the jet black town car. He had his hand on the door's handle and only said one word to Mick.

"Name?" the driver asked.

"Mick Healy," Mick responded, panting with his hands on his sides.

The man did not check a list or even respond. He simply opened the door and waited for Mick to climb in. As soon as Mick's butt touched the seat, the door closed. The back of the car had two sets of seats facing each other, a small mini fridge between two seats in front of him, and nothing else. The partition window separating Mick from the driver was tinted and up. He settled into his seat and tried to lower the divider to ask where he was going, but it did not work. The car drove away, and Mick was left in silence for about 15 minutes—just him and water from the fridge.

When the door opened again, Mick found that he was still on base. He was at the airstrip on the south side where they regularly took off for jump training. This time though, the plane on the strip was not a little puddle jumper for skydiving. This avionic masterpiece was stunning. A sleek jet, the color of a platinum watch, sat quietly humming on the runway in front of his car. The driver closed Mick's door, and without a single word, sat back down in the driver's seat and took off, leaving Mick standing almost alone.

The only other person on the tarmac was a man standing at the base of the jet's stairway. He was dressed exactly the same as the driver, and when Mick approached, he also only asked Mick for his name. Mick answered again and the man stepped aside for Mick to walk up the stairs. Once at the top, Mick cautiously peeked inside and saw seven other people sitting in individual, leather captain's chairs.

The chairs were in groups of four with a table between each pair. There were three sets on each side of the cabin and the people were spread out. Only two had chosen to sit together. Mick saw another man wearing a grey Army PT shirt, matching the one he had on, so he decided to sit near him.

Mick walked over to the man and asked if he could sit. He only received a nod for an answer, but that was good enough. He took a seat on the aisle side, across from the man, facing the rear of the plane, and tried to relax. The brown leather chair was more comfortable than any bed Mick had ever slept on. If this was the deal, he could get used to it.

"Do you have any idea what is going on?" Mick asked the man in front of him.

The man said he had no idea what was happening, either. He described a scene similar to what Mick had experienced. A man showed up at his base yesterday and gave him the option of going to this meeting, or not going. He told Mick that none of the other men had a clue either. They continued to talk as the door closed on the jet and it barreled down the runway. The takeoff was so smooth that if Mick hadn't looked out the window and saw the base getting smaller below him, he could have been convinced that he was still in that luxury town car.

When the plane leveled off at altitude, a door opened at the rear of the plane and the same man from the C.O.'s office walked into the cabin and sat down. Everyone swiveled their chairs to look at him.

"Good morning, Gentlemen. You can call me Lincoln. Now that we have our last guest, I can give you some information about why you are here. This information will be all that I am permitted to share. You may ask me anything that you wish when I am done, but it is unlikely that I will be able to answer you to the extent that you are looking for," the man began. He was dressed in another beautiful suit, this one with a paisley pocket square, but otherwise almost a carbon copy of yesterday's.

"As I told you yesterday, you have been chosen to apply for a very important position with my employer. Unfortunately, I cannot share any details about that position with you until you finish your preliminary testing. You are all here because you are exceptional in one or more areas and appear to meet our needs. You have been evaluated by our operatives over the past several years and have met all of our requirements to date. This does not guarantee you a position with us. That is what the next two weeks will be about," Lincoln continued without pausing, his gaze moved from person to person.

"Everything you need for your time with us will be supplied. You did not bring anything with you because there is nothing that you will need that is not already with you or provided by us at our facility. For the next two weeks, you will be living on grounds. You will not be leaving for any reason, unless we determine that you are not the right fit for us.

"You will be tested physically and mentally. If at any point we determine that we were wrong and that you are not an ideal candidate, you will be returned to your home. If you do successfully complete the evaluation, you will be relocated to your new assignment. Any personal belongings currently at your prior residence will be delivered to you. Do you have any questions?"

Several hands shot up. Lincoln pointed to a man in front of him in a Navy sweatshirt who asked, "What is the name of your company?"

"I'm sorry, I can't answer that," Lincoln said before pointing to a Marine on the other side of the plane.

"Are you guys like CIA, FBI, or something like that?"

"Yes and no. We are like them and work with them, but are neither of those, and I promise that you have never heard of us."

There were more questions about where they were going and about the job, but Lincoln was never able to answer anything. After the fourth question, Mick just wanted everyone to shut up. This guy was obviously not going to provide any meaningful responses. After another ten minutes, everyone gave up. They sat quietly until they landed. Some made guesses about where they were, but no one knew for certain.

The jet landed at another airfield, and they were driven to a warehouse where they did various tests for the next 2 weeks. They never knew when they would be called down to an evaluation or what it would be. They all wore the same grey sweats. The group that Mick arrived with was one of three, and they brought the total number of applicants up to 24. They only ever saw each other at meal time and the numbers started to dwindle soon after arrival. At first, they weren't sure if people were leaving or if they were just too tired to come down to eat.

The testing was rigorous and included everything from psychological testing, combat skills, quizzes on basic knowledge, and meetings with psychiatrists. Mick thought he was doing well, but the instructors didn't give any feedback. Most of the instructors were men, and all were called by the names of former Presidents. He only saw one woman over the whole time, a tall redhead, but she never spoke to any of the recruits.

At the end of the two weeks, the remaining men were told that they would have a letter on their pillow with a single word on it. That word would tell them which jet to get on the next morning. Mick's said "left" so when his name was called, he went outside and got on the jet on the left side of the tarmac. In total, five other men got on the same plane that he did, and the rest got on the other. Once the plane was in the air, Lincoln emerged from the back again.

"Good morning. You may be wondering why there are two planes. One is for the group who is going home and the other is headed to our corporate headquarters for the last phase of your training. You are on the latter. Tonight you will head to a hotel near our office and are free to enjoy the night off.

"You may do anything that you wish, other than talk to anyone about what you are doing there. You may speak to the men on this plane with you about that topic, but only in the privacy of this plane or your hotel room— not on the phone or in public. At 9 tomorrow morning, you will meet in the lobby and will be driven to our office where you will receive answers to all of your questions, and your assignments. Congratulations, men and welcome to Sicari."

That conversation took place yesterday, and now Mick sat, impatiently waiting for someone to come in and tell him something, anything. At exactly 9:30, the door to the room opened and a grey haired man in his late 50's walked in. He looked like the average corporate CEO. Everything about him screamed "average". He was average height, maybe 5 foot 9 or so, just like Mick. He had an average build, and nothing about him stood out. The only thing that made anyone take notice of him was that he exuded power. The man carried himself like he owned the world and anything in it. He walked to the front of the room and just stood there, looking at the six men in front of him.

"Good morning, men, my name is Grayson. I am the President of Sicari Associates, and I want to take a second to welcome you to the team. You have worked hard to get here and I, for one, am happy that you made it. Eighteen other men tried and failed where you succeeded. A position with us is yours if you want it, but you have to decide now. There is no going back. There is no shame in not wanting to give up your home and life for a company that you know nothing about. I cannot give you any more information until I know who is staying. I will start my presentation to you in one minute.

Between now and then, you may leave if you feel that this is not for you."

A minute later he spoke again to the six men. None had chosen to leave. "As long as people have existed, they have lived together, built communities, fell in love, had families, hunted, grew crops, fought each other, started wars, and killed others who had what they wanted or that they disagreed with. They felt compelled by nature to do these things. Some things have always been considered polite, acceptable behavior and others have been condemned as wrong or evil. Good people have always committed bad acts and no "evil" person has ever lived a life fully absent of good.

"We have killed each other over land, women, food, property, money, and most often in the name of religion. Some have been forced into a soldier's life, and others, like you, have chosen it.

"Some men and women have found pleasure in taking the lives of others, and have done so out of an enjoyment that neither you nor I could hope to understand. Society has demanded that these people be hunted down, captured, jailed, or even killed as penance for their transgressions. That is the world that we all know. However, there is an entirely different part to that world.

"There has always been another group of men and women who feel the need to kill. They are compelled to take life. Unlike the others, they do not do it for fun. It is a desire that builds in them until they cannot control it. They *must* kill to make that nagging itch in the back of their brains go away, even for just a brief moment of relief.

"An even smaller group of those same people have devoted their lives to feeding that insatiable need by killing those among us who bring our society down. They kill the undesirables among us, the rapists, the people who kill for money or greed, the people who hurt children, and so on. I ask you, are these *killers* wrong for removing those horrible people from our society?

"I don't think so. I believe that they provide a service to the world. That service is one that is needed to keep civilizations from falling apart. The justice system makes mistakes, people fall through the cracks, and truly evil people, who commit the most heinous of acts, walk free.

"Who does it fall upon to clean up that mess? Who rights those wrongs? These men and women do. Yes, they should be controlled, they should be watched and they should always make sure that they are only killing the most evil creatures among us. They also need to be protected from themselves, and from the prying eyes of those who would jail them and stop them from providing that necessary service. That protection is where we come in."

The men looked around at each other, not sure of what to make of this strange little man and the craziness of his speech. Could this be a joke or the final test?

"Our company has been around for hundreds of years in many forms. Some call us a secret society, and at one point we were just that. We were a group of likeminded men and women who felt the compulsion to kill and to kill the truly evil people in the world. We started by helping each other in various ways like providing shelter, alibis, money, or whatever was needed. We understood each other, and we did our best to keep ourselves hidden from the normal world. We lived in everyday society as teachers, doctors, lawyers, farmers, tradesmen—every profession you could imagine. We had no real organization or rules, just loose guidelines that everyone agreed to follow.

"That was the case until 1456 when Vlad Dracul went crazy in Bucharest. He had a true bloodlust and was a horribly demented man. He killed everyone that he could get his hands on. He and his army killed over 80,000 men, women and children over a six year period. He slaughtered them in horrifying ways, and he did so in public view for his own amusement. Finally, we were able to sneak one of our men into his castle to stab him in the heart while he slept. I am sure you have heard about him before, as he was the inspiration for Bram Stoker's *Dracula*.

"After that very public incident, we decided that we needed a code, some very basic rules to live by. They started out very simply and grew in scope and number over time. Many of those early rules are the same ones we use today.

"We agreed that children were never to be killed, period. Even now, we only rarely allow for the death of a woman, but that is seldom necessary. We primarily have approved the death of women who have hurt children. No innocent people or collateral damage is permitted.

The person you are killing needs to be verified as beyond reparation. We call that process "being vetted", and require an independent internal assessment. Your target can never be someone you know personally. You cannot kill for emotional reasons, such as revenge. By the way, we hate the word "killing". We prefer "cleansing", because we are ridding the world of something toxic."

A brave hand shot up and interrupted Grayson, who seemed unfazed and just pointed at the man, who asked, "What if the person is really evil and you have a personal relationship with them? Do they just get to live because of a technicality?"

"That is a good question. The answer to that is simple. You ask us for what we call a "proxy kill". You can suggest someone for the job, or we will find one. The approved cleanser must have no relationship with the person, and it must be approved by us, but then we will allow it. You will learn more about the specifics of the day to day process later this afternoon. My presentation is about the history of us as a group," Grayson answered. He took a drink of water and then continued on with his talk. He never moved once while he spoke, other than to look around the room.

"Other rules that are meant to keep us out of the limelight are things like no pictures, videos, or souvenirs. If you are questioned by the police, you are not permitted to talk at all. If one of your bodies is found, you do not go to the crime scene. The cleansing should never take place in public, unless previously approved. Never allow a body to be found. There are many more, but you will learn them when you are in the field. One of our trainers will tell you more about it today. You will not be told what role your trainer plays within the company, so please do not ask them. Does anyone have any questions?"

The same guy raised his hand and was called on. "Are there any famous killers that were part of your group who didn't follow the rules? If so, what rule did they break? How was it dealt with?"

"Yes, there have been an unfortunate few who decided that they were above our laws. We always try to be creative about cleaning up the messes, and sometimes the public helps us without knowing it. One example of that was in 1764: one of our members brought a long-haired hyena home to the French countryside from a trip to Africa. He trained it to hunt people, and over the next 3 years, it attacked 210 people and killed 113. We found the man and his pet, and they were both cleansed. By that time, survivors and other people had seen him go into the forest before they saw the large hyena. They assumed that he had changed into the beast, and that is where the story for the modern day werewolf originated. We just let that story run wild, and it solved the problem for us.

"Another famous story, which was a little different, was Jack the Ripper. He was the son of a Duke who had forced his son's membership through. He was not of sound mind due to syphilis he had contracted from a prostitute. He decided that all "women of the night" needed to be cleansed, and before he could be stopped, he killed seven women. Only five were actually confirmed by the constables as his murders, but there were a total of seven in his initial spree.

"When our council finally made it to Whitechapel, they convinced his father to lock him in the family home. The killings stopped, and people assumed that he was gone. He escaped six weeks later and the syphilis, combined with being locked in a room alone, made him devolve even more.

"On December 29, 1888, he killed the first person that he had seen since he was found next to Mary Kelly's mutilated body. Unfortunately, that person was a 7 year old boy named John Gill. His death was never attributed to "Jack", and before we could catch him, he climbed onto a ship headed for America. He killed an unknown number of women in New York before we caught up to him in 1891. We could not afford to let him be apprehended, so he was cleansed on the spot.

"The Ripper Mishap, as it is known around here, led us to two changes, and that is the last thing I will tell you about before you leave for lunch. The council knew that one of the reasons that Jack escaped was that he knew that we were coming for him. He knew the council members and knew why they were there. That familiarity contributed to his escape.

"To avoid a recurrence, it was decided that we needed an internal cleanser. This would be someone who we could count on to eliminate these problems if they came up. Our Assets now know that if they break our rules, someone will come for them. The Assets fear this man and you will hear stories of the "Reaper" and guesses about who it could be. However, there are only ever four people who know who he or she is. The Reaper knows, his regulator may possibly know, I know, and the person that the reaper cleanses will find out—for a brief period of time, anyway.

"You are probably wondering what it actually is that you do. Your training this afternoon will get into more details, but here are a few basics. When the Ripper Mishap occurred, we also decided that we couldn't trust our Assets completely, and we needed eyes and ears on the ground. That was the second change, and that is your role. If we were the FBI, you would be called a "handler". Here you are a "Regulator", or "reg" for short. You will live with and assist your assigned asset in their day to day life. The two terms for discussing them with us or with other employees are "Asset" or "Cleanser".

"To the outside world, you are their personal assistant, employee, intern, or some other applicable role. The reality is that you work for us. You do not work for them. You send in their requests to us for approval, you perform initial, in-field vetting of targets in the local arena, you report anything that is out of the ordinary to us, and you pull the plug when there is a problem with a cleansing. You may like the Asset you are assigned to, but you are not there to be buddies. You can have a pleasant relationship, but do not let it cloud your judgment."

With that, Grayson gave instructions to not talk with anyone about what they had just learned. They could talk to each other about it, but not in public. They were dismissed for lunch and were told to be back at 1 o'clock for more training. It was a lot to digest, and Mick just wanted to be alone, so he left the building and went for a walk. What the hell had he gotten himself into? Was he really going to live with a serial killer?

Chapter 10

Christian studied the faces of the six men on the other side of the glass, while Grayson gave his never-ending history lesson. Some looked confused, others appeared to be shocked, and one even seemed to think that Grayson was going to stop and let them know that everything he had said was an elaborate joke. It wasn't.

The person that Christian was most interested in was Mick, the 30-ish, ginger-haired kid who Alex had picked for him. His facial expression barely changed throughout the long soliloquy. He never registered as being anything other than interested in what Grayson said. There was no hint of fear, disgust, or confusion. He was taking mental notes much the same way anyone would at any new job. He might actually have the right temperament for his new position. For his sake, he had better.

As the class ended and everyone, on both sides of the glass, prepared to leave for lunch, Alex grabbed Christian's arm, sliding hers through his and locking elbows.

"Where do you want to get lunch?" she asked as though she was about to go have a nice chat about her next art exhibit, not plan the death of another person.

"Dealer's choice. I am good with wherever. Maybe somewhere close. I would rather walk," Christian responded, uncomfortable with her closeness.

"Okay, I have just the place then. Ray's Back Bay Bistro. It is kind of new, but I have heard it is good," Alex said as they walked down the hall toward the elevator.

They were just about to leave, when a shout behind them asked for the elevator doors to be held. The six newly hired men squeezed into the space that was already too cramped for Christian's liking. Each of the young men took a few glances at Alex, who gave her best angry stare but actually loved the attention.

"So, do you actually think there is a 'Reaper', or is it some BS that they tell each other to keep the strays in line?" one of the men asked, the same one who had interrupted Grayson to ask about rule breaking. No one answered. The lack of a response seemed to keep him from asking any more questions, and a minute later the doors opened.

Frank was back at his post, and there was no sign of Johnson as the eight people from the 9th floor walked past the metal detectors and out onto Boylston St. Christian and Alex turned left, and thankfully the others turned right. Five of the men walked together, but Mick hung back. A couple blocks later, Christian and Alex found themselves at the hot new bistro in the midst of the lunch rush.

A tall, thin, brunette (who Christian was pretty sure should have been in a high school classroom somewhere) showed them to a small table on the upper patio, overlooking the busy street below. As she handed them their menus and told them that their server would be over shortly, she peered over the edge of the patio at the growing line forming at her hostess station. The sight of the crowd left her frazzled, and she abruptly walked toward the stairs, tugging at her tightly fitting black skirt as she went.

Christian flipped through the four-page vinyl menu and immediately knew what he was going to have. He closed his up, placed it on the table, and stared at Alex while she looked at page after page, from front to back and then to the beginning again. He wasn't exactly comfortable with her choice of venue for the topic that she'd wanted to discuss. Alex had a loud voice that tended to carry, but Christian held out hope that she may try to rein it in a bit, given the nature of the subject.

"Do you want to split an appetizer?" Alex asked as though they were just two coworkers out for lunch, without a care in the world.

"Not really. I'm not very hungry and besides, I don't think we have that much time before we have to be back to teach class."

"I think we have enough time. I'm going to go with the steak," Alex responded to a question that was not actually asked.

"Isn't there something you wanted to talk to me about?" Christian said impatiently. He wasn't comfortable with having this conversation in a public place and he just wanted to get it over with.

"Okay, I see *somebody* is all business today. Hopefully you won't be later," Alex said with a hint of a wink. "So, do you know my friend Gary?"

"It's possible. Is he the guy who drives the Porsche and has the snotty looking wife with the tortoiseshell sunglasses that she wears everywhere, even inside?" Christian asked trying to place Gary in his memory.

"Sort of. He used to drive a BMW, and that does sound like his wife. That isn't the important part. Anyway, he's been a sales rep for a big software company for a few years. He was doing really well..." Alex started to say but she stopped when their waitress appeared table-side.

"Hi, there. How is everyone doing today?" the bouncy waitress said without waiting for an answer. "My name's Courtney, and I will be taking care of you today. Can I start you off with some drinks? Our margaritas are amazing. "

"I'll just have water with lemon, thank you," Christian said to the young blonde. He cringed at the use of the word "amazing" to describe the margaritas. He hated its constant overuse to describe everything that anyone ever found remotely pleasing. Sadly, Alex's regulator used it so often, you would swear she was getting paid to.

"Same for me," Alex said in an abrupt and dismissive way. She wanted the girl to leave so they could finish the conversation.

"Did you want to hear about our specials, or will you be ordering off the menu?" the persistent server asked. She was young, maybe 23 or so with her blonde hair back in a ponytail. It was simply done, but looked like it would work whether she was doing yoga or here at her job. She stood with her weight mainly on her left leg, closer to Christian than Alex.

"We'll be ordering off the menu, but I think we're ready now," Alex said. "I'll have the New York strip, medium, with the fries and coleslaw."

"And I will have the Cobb salad, hold the avocado. Thank you," Christian said to Courtney when she turned her blue eyes towards him. Unlike Alex, he found it best to treat anyone who would be touching his food with an extra helping of politeness and respect.

"Okay, so where were we?" Alex said, dropping a not-so-subtle hint that the waitress should be on her way. The girl complied and stomped off, obviously irritated by Alex's treatment.

"Gary worked for a software company," Christian reminded her.

Alex leaned forward, her chest barely staying in her shirt, and began her story again. "So, Gary has been working for the software company for a bunch of years, and he's one of their top reps. Well, like a year ago, he ended up having to have some emergency surgery. At first the company stood behind him and said that there was no problem, and that they would wait for him to heal up. Then all of a sudden, while he was home recovering, he got a phone call from their HR department saying that they would be terminating his contract at the end of the month."

"Isn't he protected by a law like FLMA?" Christian asked.

"Nope. He wasn't an employee; he was a contractor, so they could legally fire him anytime they wanted to. The surgery was pretty nasty and took him three months to recover. He didn't have any income coming in, and his wife was basically allergic to working, so she was useless. Their bills started to pile up, and then his wife filed for divorce and custody of their son. She got a big alimony award, even though he couldn't pay it, and custody of the kid. Then the bitch moved out of state with her new boyfriend."

Courtney was back with their drinks, and she placed Christian's glass of water, ice, and a lemon wedge gingerly on the table in front of him, along with a straw. She wasn't so gentle with Alex's. The glass of plain water and a couple lonely ice cubes was placed on the table in such a quick motion that the top quarter inch of tepid water splashed out onto the table and Alex. Before Alex had a chance to say that she must have forgotten her lemon wedge, Courtney turned and disappeared back down the stairs.

"It's nice to see you making friends," Christian said, amused.

"*Anyway...*" Alex said, sarcastically, trying to change the subject back to what she had been talking about. "Gary couldn't afford to pay the alimony or anything else for that matter. His unemployment check went straight to his ex, so he couldn't afford his house or his car or anything while he looked for work. After six months, he still hadn't found work, lost his house and car, and had to move back into his parents' place. He couldn't afford to drive to Pennsylvania to see his son, and his ex-wife was making his life miserable. He got so depressed that he never left his parents' house. Then, a couple months ago, he jumped off the Casco Bay Bridge."

"Wow, I am really sorry to hear that. I wish I'd known sooner and maybe I could have talked to him," Christian said with a touch of sadness.

"He didn't talk to anybody about it. None of us knew," Alex said, stopping again as Courtney and another server brought their food out.

Courtney placed Christian's Cobb salad in front of him and asked him if he wanted any more napkins. When he shook his head no, she reached over to the platter that the other server held, grabbed Alex's plate and began to set it on the table in front of her.

When the plate was about 4 inches above the white tablecloth, Courtney let go. The oval shaped white ceramic plate clattered against the table, rocking in a ragged circle. The steak sloshed around in its own juices, splattering Alex's Oxford shirt and the table. Overcooked French fries flew off the plate and onto the floor. The coleslaw was nowhere to be seen. Even from where Christian sat, he could tell that Alex's steak had barely touched the hot grill. When she cut in to it, blood flowed onto the plate, soaking into the French fries. It was about as raw as steak could get.

Alex was not about to let some young girl get the best of her, so she just cut into her steak and ate it. It couldn't have been pleasant. Christian could see that the fat was still hard and had not even begun to melt. It had to be cold in the middle, but Alex kept eating it.

"Okay, I understand his story, but what are you looking for from me? If this has anything to do with the wife, I can tell you right now that I'm not interested. Grayson would never allow that," Christian said trying to distract Alex from a lunch that looked like it could have been walking around on hooves just a few minutes prior.

"No, the mark isn't the wife. It's Gary's old boss. I know he's visiting the area for the next few days. I have Asher tailing him right now."

"This is something that I'm going to need to think about and talk to Grayson," Christian started to say, but was interrupted by Alex.

"I already talked to Grayson. He said he was fine with it. He even said that I could watch," Alex said with a sadistic gleam in her eye. "He also told me some other interesting stuff."

"Oh yeah? And what would that be?" Christian asked as he took another bite of chicken, tomato, and bacon.

"Well, he said that you still have all of your tags left. He also said that you haven't even sent in a request in months and that he wants *you* to plan this, just to keep from getting rusty," Alex said, arching one eyebrow. "Is it true? Are you still all tagged up?"

"Yeah, I just haven't found the right situation. I also haven't really felt the need. You know that I go into hibernation in the winter," Christian said, using enough truth mixed with lies in hopes that she would believe him.

The reality was that Christian had very little interest in finding someone to kill. He still felt the urge growing, but he was fighting to keep it at bay. Unlike a lot of the others, he found absolutely no pleasure in taking someone's life. It wasn't something that he looked forward to, or took lightly. No matter how evil the person was, Christian always felt a level of sadness about the life lost. At some point, the target had been a child with hopes and dreams for a future before they committed the acts that put them on his radar. However, he was also realistic: he knew that he wouldn't be able to stop permanently, even if he really wanted to. The company would always send names his way, and the need would always be there.

"I have already used like half of mine. I am hoping that I can stretch the rest out," Alex said as though they were talking about something frivolous, like makeup or leftover candy from Halloween. "I *really* hope you can do this for me."

"Let me think about it. When do you need to know?" Christian asked as he scraped up the last pieces of lettuce and Roquefort cheese and dipped it into the light red wine vinaigrette dressing.

"I was thinking that we could do it tomorrow night."

"Wow. That's pretty sudden. Why so fast?" Christian asked, nearly choking.

"This asshole leaves to go back to Pennsylvania on Friday. Who knows when he'll be back in this area again?" Alex said. Her eyes grew wider, like Bambi from the children's movie. It was an old trick that Christian knew well. She might use her other charms on almost everyone else, but this was the look she used on Christian. She used it because it worked every time.

"Okay, I will think about it tonight and I'll see if I can come up with anything. I'll let you know in the morning," Christian said, placing his napkin on his plate and pushing his chair back.

Christian walked over to where Courtney was standing and asked if he could have the bill. She asked if everything was okay, and Christian said that it was. He paid, leaving a generous tip, and then Alex and Christian began their walk back to the office.

Christian had been trying to avoid killing for months and had been successful for nearly five straight, but now his hand was being forced. He was going to have to take Alex's word that this man, who he did not know and had never met, needed to die a painful, unnatural death.

Chapter 11

Christian patiently waited outside of the observation room for Alex to finish changing into a new shirt. Her previous one was likely ruined from lunch. She emerged wearing a new oxford that was nearly identical the old one and they walked into the adjoining classroom.

The six new recruits finished their conversations and took a seat as the pair entered. As usual, twelve eyes followed Alex as she walked in. Christian could have been invisible, and that was perfectly fine with him. True to her nature, Alex took the lead.

"Good afternoon, I hope you all had a good lunch. My name is Alex and this is Christian. We are here to go over some of the basics about what your day will be like in the field, what your responsibilities will be, and answer some of your questions. We are not allowed to answer specifics about what our roles are here in the company, other than to tell you that I am an artist and I teach at an art school. Christian is a psychiatrist and author. He will be able to answer questions that you might have regarding the inner workings of the minds of the Assets that you will be working with.

"I have a few topics that I am required to cover, but otherwise, I would like to keep it informal. Usually, I let your questions guide the conversation. The goal is for this to be an informational primer session, but, as with most jobs, you will learn a lot more by doing the job than hearing about it. Who has the first question?"

A dark haired man with a Marine haircut raised his hand. "If we are all in the company now, why is everything still so secretive? I mean, we are going to be working together, right? What does it matter if you tell us that you are a secretary or an Asset?"

Christian could see that the use of the word "secretary" got under Alex's skin, so he decided to jump in and answer this one. "The easy answer is that it comes down to plausible deniability, but the bigger answer is more complicated than that. You each have been watched and evaluated for several years, and based on those evaluations, we *think* that we understand you as well as we possibly can, but you are about to enter a strange new world and there is no way for anyone to accurately predict how that environment will change you.

"Keeping you all in the dark about certain things that are not necessary for you to know yet will protect you and everyone else. The more you know about each person that you meet here, the more familiar you will naturally want to be with them.

"The goal is for all of us to be nearly independent in the "real world". I know Alex outside of these walls, but our relationship must always appear to be different than it actually is. We cannot be perceived to be close friends. I can be someone who buys her art and attends her shows as an acquaintance, or she could be my patient, but we are not having each other over for BBQs.

If something happened to go awry in the field, you will need as much distance from each other as possible. Does that make sense?"

The man nodded. "Is that why you have not asked any of us for our names?"

"That is part of it. We will have no idea who you are or where you will be assigned. We can assume that you are here to be Regulators, but there is also the possibility that you could end up as internal analysts or in another role. If you are an analyst, we need you to be unbiased when you review requests. As a hypothetical, let's say that you were an analyst and were assigned to review a request from Alex, and that you knew from previous experience that she had always thought her plans through and had never made a mistake. Your familiarity could make you complacent or sloppy by allowing you to assume that she did everything perfectly this time as well. That is when things can go wrong.

"There could be an obvious hole in her plan that you would have caught had you been putting in your best effort. For that reason, each file that comes in is assigned a number and does not include any Asset-related names. Only the analyst who vets a target will know their name. They could guess based on the location, but each state has several Assets. A separate analyst will review the plans which will only include words like "Asset" and "target" instead of names. We do not list city or landmark names like "Casco Bay Bridge" or "Maine". Instead we say "location" and "bridge" to keep it generic.

"A second analyst in each department will independently assess each part of the file, and they never know if they are conducting a first look or second review so that they must complete the work independently and send their report to the Board of Directors, who makes the final decisions. The more layers there are, the better we are all protected." Christian explained.

Another hand raised in the back corner. "So how many Assets are there?"

It was Alex's turn to answer. "Only the Board of Directors knows for sure. They are basically the new school version of the original council. I know that the total number of Assets that we carry at any one time is based on a few things such as: the population density of the specified area, the anticipated crime rate, the number of and frequency of available potential targets, and a few other things. If there were too many Assets cleansing too many targets, there would be no way to hide all of that activity. By the same token, if a particular area has a justice system that does a good job of solving crimes and putting away the perpetrators, then our services are not needed as much. On the other hand, if you have incompetent people at any level in a particular jurisdiction, then more criminals will walk free who should have been incarcerated. We are more than happy to supply enough Assets to correct that issue."

The questions started to come in rapid succession. Most came from the Marine, a man wearing a Delta tee shirt, and a blonde guy who wore a suit for some unknown reason. He must have bought it while visiting Newbury Street, because most recruits showed up in sweats or casual clothing. They weren't allowed to bring anything with them to the evaluation, so there wasn't a real dress code at the introductory meetings.

"How much does the local law enforcement know about us and what we do?"

Christian answered "Most of the people in law enforcement who are aware of our arrangement are high level officials. Only the board knows for sure. The police and field agents are almost never aware of what is happening, but they are handled if they get too close or too suspicious."

"Does anyone in the community know who isn't a part of the company?"

Christian took this question as well. Both he and Alex have classes at local colleges that they teach, so they intuitively tend to take control of the classroom. The tricky part was not stepping on each other's toes while answering. After five years of doing these trainings, they had gotten pretty good at this instructional ballet. "There are some aspects of our jobs that require assistance from outside vendors. Some of these things are accomplished internally by Assets who have careers in a particular field such as an undertaker or medical examiner. Other aspects are handled by hired contractors who are aware of what we do and have a vested interest in helping us. We rarely have any issues with our vendors."

"If we, as Regulators, are sending in all of the Asset's requests, wouldn't there be a paper trail?"

"That is a very good question. Everything we do here is done electronically. You will all have access to a protected room, sort of like an SCIF. For those that have never heard of one, an SCIF is a Sensitive Compartmented Information Facility. Some people call them "Red Rooms". They contain secure, self-deleting computer systems that purge all information from your local systems as soon as it is sent. Everything is stored in a secure cloud database that can only be accessed based on your level of clearance.

"You can only see what you are approved to see. You only have access to your particular files. Any needs that you might have for historical documents or files related to other Assets are only made available if you get high-level approval. Assets do not have access to the SCIF or the Cloud. You should not share your access with them for any reason.

"All messages are all encoded, and the red rooms have a special infrared lighting system that kills all trace DNA after you leave it. The surfaces are made from specially-made nonporous polymers that do not allow fingerprints to adhere. If someone, somehow, managed to get into an SCIF who was not supposed to be there, they could not access anything, and the room would lock itself down and do a fire purge. The flames burn so intensely that all that is left behind is ash. That ash is then contained and destroyed. There are contingencies for the contingencies," Alex answered.

The Marine continued to press about positions within the ranks. "Well, we know that women serial killers are extremely rare, so why couldn't we just guess that you are an analyst or secretary, and since Christian is a shrink, couldn't we also guess that he is part of the

Board or is another analyst? Neither of you seem like you would be killers."

Christian thought to himself that this guy was pushing it, and hoped that Alex could control her temper. If he only knew the truth, this guy would not be tempting her. She looked like she was just your average Goth hipster, but underneath she was a stone cold killer. Even Christian didn't know how many men she had taken. She has always been one of the most creative body disposal people that he had ever heard of. Most remains went into one of her high temperature kilns and were reduced to ash. She used that ash to mix into her pottery clay, or with pigments for colors. The remains of an unknown number of men sat on the shelves of hundreds of her art buyers around the world.

Christian knew the story about one man who was a corrupt city official and rapist who managed to slip through the hands of the justice system. He didn't get by her. She sealed him up in a metal sculpture that she then donated to the city. It was perfectly enclosed by her masterful welding skills. No fluids or smells would ever escape.

He was permanently entombed within sight of his former office. His former coworkers and constituents walked by him on a daily basis without ever knowing. Others have been added to the cement bases of other displays. She loved knowing that they were right under the nose of the general public.

While Christian had drifted off in thought, Alex answered the question at hand. "That is kind of the idea behind why this works. Assets should blend in and not be suspicious. Would it make more sense to be unassuming and blend in, or to look like the prototypical Hollywood depiction of a serial-killing monster?"

"Yeah, I guess you are right."

Rather than take a follow up question, Alex went into monologue mode. "Okay, so I don't get sidetracked, here are some of the important things that you need to know about the role that a Regulator plays."

"Each asset is allowed a certain number of what we call "tags" each year. Think of them like deer hunting tags. Assets can use them all up, or only a few—that is up to them. The number of tags assigned varies from Asset to Asset and is based on their skill level, frequency of compulsion, and local demographics that I mentioned earlier. When they are gone, they are gone. There are very few exceptions.

"The only time an Asset can use more tags than originally allotted is if they are assigned one specifically by the Board. That usually happens when they have someone that law enforcement has asked them to handle, or if a proxy request comes in from another Asset.

"Your role is to send in the requests and plans for approval. Your Asset may ask your opinion, or have you review their plans for any obvious flaws before you send them in. It is a good idea to review them even if you aren't asked. That saves the analysts a lot of time, and you will have first-hand knowledge that the analysts don't.

"Once the Cleansing is complete, you will submit the final report to the Board. You will explain any deviations from the approved plan and what the resulting alteration was. You will also explain any possible exposure that may have occurred.

"If you feel that your Asset is having any sort of issues, it is your job to report it. Things can go downhill very quickly and you need to be able to recognize when something is not quite right and inform the Board. Outside of these duties, you will play your public role that is assigned to you, and will never discuss your real position with anyone else. Is that clear?"

The classroom door opened and a man walked in. He didn't look at anyone or speak. He just walked up to Christian and handed him a slip of paper. Christian opened it, read the contents and handed it back to the man, who then left the room. Christian walked up the Alex and leaned in close to her ear.

"I have to go see Grayson," he whispered before turning to the group. "You all will have to excuse me for a minute. I may not be back before the end of the class, so if not, I wish you luck. Welcome aboard."

Christian left the room as Alex continued on, explaining about the ins and outs of the day-to-day role, and he hoped that she kept her composure in his absence. He went to the elevator, entered his code, and hit the button for the 12th floor. He leaned against the back corner, even though he was alone, and took several deep breaths. Once he emerged, he stuck to the inner portion of the hallway. This section of the top floor had huge windows overlooking the city. The 120 or so feet of open air between him and the concrete jungle below was more than a little unnerving to Christian. Walking as far away from the glass as he could get kept him from feeling the panic.

As Christian approached the final corner office Grayson's personal assistant stood. Christian could never remember his name, but after this many years of working for the same company, he would feel foolish to ask, so he didn't. At this rate, they could both retire with Christian not knowing his name.

"Mr. Grayson said you could just go on in, Dr. Rinaldi," the nameless man said.

Christian just nodded a quick "thank you", opened the huge mahogany double doors, and entered Grayson's expansive office. Fifteen-foot-tall bookshelves lined two of the huge walls, and artifacts from around the world were scattered around the room like Grayson's own personal museum.

Christian's personal favorite was a 400 year old Japanese Katana that hung directly behind Grayson's oversized desk. It was hand-forged and the steel was said to have been folded 300 times. The blade was "live" and gave new meaning to "razor sharp". Only a handful of the ancient master forger's creations still existed, and their value was immeasurable.

Grayson was already sitting behind the oak monstrosity that he called a work desk and motioned for Christian to take a seat across from him. Grayson never stood when he didn't have to if he was in the presence of an Asset. He was a half-foot shorter than Christian, and the size difference became apparent when they shook hands. He wanted to appear as powerful as possible, and looking like a child standing next to Christian's large, muscular frame would diminish that.

His ornately carved desk held many more ostentatious artifacts from places that Grayson had never been, but he had the money to own them, so that was close enough for a man like him. The appearance of experience was more important than the memories of actually experiencing something dangerous. He reminded Christian of the stereotypical high school sports coach who never played on any major level but filled his office with his team's trophies and other memorabilia that could be purchased on an online auction site.

The only modern implement in the room was a computer. It looked oddly out of place in the midst of the other items. Grayson leaned back into his throne-like seat and interlocked his fingers, resting them on his stomach as a king would, while waiting for the court jester to entertain him.

"Good to see you, Christian. How are things?" Grayson asked without actually being interested in the actual answer. "I wanted to talk to you about a few important items."

"Sure, sounds good," Christian responded. He had an idea of what three of the topics would be, but the rest were a mystery.

"First thing's first. The recruits are going out tonight. They are taking in a baseball game, and I am sure they will want to hit the town afterwards. They have been cooped up for a couple of weeks. They deserve the break, but they also need a chaperone. I am sending you, Alex, Darren, and Greg. The other Assets had them last night. You will be sitting a few rows back, so you don't actually need to talk to them all that much. Just keep an eye on them."

Christian nodded. "Sounds easy enough."

"Let's hope so. They are past the point of no return, so they had better make it. As I am sure you can guess, one of those guys is going to be assigned to you. We tried to give you time to get past the last incident and didn't assign you anyone from the last group, but we think it is time to move on. Alex has given me her opinion as to who she thinks you should be assigned, several times actually, and I am inclined to go with it unless you have any objections," Grayson said. When Christian didn't say anything, he continued, "Did she mention anything to you about a proxy?'

"Yeah, we went over the background about it today. She says that you already approved it. I don't know anything else, other than it has to be tomorrow night. That is a little tight, if you ask me," Christian said. He didn't expect agreement from Grayson, nor did he get it.

"It is short notice, but that is the window we have. I am sure you can come up with something. I need you to give me the details in the morning, but I think you will be fine. That brings up the last subject. I know you haven't had a Regulator for a while, but I am still surprised that you haven't used a single tag this year.

"We don't have anything on the horizon for you, so I really need you to step up your planning. I know you have a good grasp on your needs, but you know as well as I do that they can sneak up on you. I can't have you getting overwhelmed and then end up being sloppy because the urges clouded your thinking. You are too good for that. How are things with Agent Brooks going?"

"Everything is fine there. He has been calling me more and more, but it is all case-related stuff. He has settled in to his new post nicely, so I don't think he is going anywhere. Before you ask, he doesn't have any curiosities about me, or about what happened to Agent Reston. He thinks everything that I am doing is related to my practice or my writing. I am the last thing on his mind."

"Good, I am glad that he is working out. Try not to beat yourself up. What happened to Agent Reston was not your fault. You couldn't have seen that coming. Franklin was not on anybody's radar."

Christian looked at his feet. It had been six months since Reston was killed, and he had just started to forget about it. That wasn't true. He still thought about it when he went to Brook's office or drove by the river near his home, but it was not constantly on his mind anymore. No matter what anyone said, he still felt responsible. He should have noticed something was wrong before it was too late, but in the end he had handled it. He hadn't cleansed anyone since.

"That is all I have, so unless you have anything for me, we are good here. Do me a favor, try and trust the new guy and have a little fun," Grayson said. He looked back down at something on his desk and Christian stood, knowing that this meant the session was over. *Good talk, boss.* He thought as he walked away.

Christian walked through the huge doors and past the nameless assistant who was engrossed in whatever he was doing. He didn't notice Christian. Alex had apparently finished the class and was waiting for him outside of the doors to the executive wing.

"Everything good?" Alex asked before he had even reached her.

"Yeah, everything is fine," Christian answered, but everything was not fine. To an outsider, the conversation would have appeared innocuous enough, but Christian knew the deeper meaning behind the questions. Grayson was not happy about Christian's lack of "production" and was hinting at retiring him. This could become a serious problem. Retirement for an Asset was not about getting a gold watch at a going away party and then sitting on the beach during your golden years. No, retirement was more like being buried in a shallow grave under that beach.

Chapter 12

At 6 o'clock, Christian left his new hotel room and walked down the hall to Alex's. Several of the recruits were milling around in the hallway, waiting for their chaperones so they could head off to the Red Sox game against the Tampa Bay Rays. Christian had a lot on his mind and some serious planning to do, which had him wishing that he could stay in, but when the boss says "jump", you suck it up and do it. Grayson did run a company of serial killers, after all.

Christian knocked on Alex's door and it swung open before his knuckles touched it a third time. Alex had traded her psycho school girl look for tight jeans with rips in several strategic places, running shoes and a bright pink Red Sox Jersey. It was unbuttoned at the top, and she wore a white men's V-neck tee shirt underneath. She had her hair pulled back into a short ponytail that stuck out through the back of an equally pink Red Sox hat.

"Going for the full pink hatter look, I see," Christian said, with one eyebrow cocked suspiciously. Alex was not a pink hatter, but she was sure as hell dressed like one.

The term pink hatter came about after the 2004 World Series. The Red Sox had just finished a playoff run that was nothing short of miraculous. They had been down three games to none in the American League Championship Series against the hated New York Yankees before rattling off one thrilling win after another, becoming the only team in MLB history to come back from being down 0-3 to win a series.

They then swept the Cardinals in four straight games to win their first World Series in 86 years, breaking the "Curse of the Bambino". The people of Boston, New England, and anywhere else that long-suffering Red Sox fans called home, went crazy. Red Sox Nation was born, and merchandise started flying off of the shelves.

Wearing Sox gear became trendy, and many non-sports fans jumped on the bandwagon. In particular, wives and girlfriends of sports fans started buying up the cute pink jerseys and hats. True blue fans wouldn't touch those if you paid them, and the pink attire became the unofficial uniform of the uninformed fan. The "fake fans" started being called pinks hats, and the name stuck.

"Nope, just going undercover tonight, right? Besides, I look hot and you know it," Alex replied with a giggle. The giggle was also fake. She was going all out on the ditsy front tonight.

"Okay, let's get moving then. They guys are waiting for us. Darren is already in the lobby."

"What is the hurry? The game is in an hour, and our seats will be waiting no matter when we show up. It is only going to take like 20 minutes to walk there," Alex stated. She hated to be rushed. For her, "on time" meant being fifteen minutes late. "They can go on ahead and we can catch up," she continued with a flirty tilt of her head.

"You know we have to keep them in sight all night long," Christian said, ignoring her advance. The flirting happened all the time, so he was good at ignoring it.

"Fine," Alex said with a childish pout as she closed her door. They joined some of the others and took the elevator down two floors to the lobby where Darren was waiting impatiently.

For the next 15 minutes or so, they all walked in two groups through the streets of Boston as they headed for Fenway Park. When they turned the final corner onto Yawkey Way, the oldest functioning MLB park in America loomed before them. It always felt like walking back in time when Christian approached the century old structure. There had been improvements made since it opened in 1912, but the old bones were still the same.

The group had seats in the right field bleacher section so they looked for gate C on Landsdowne Street. The last stretch of street was full of vendors, bars, restaurants, and souvenir shops. Half of the people were wearing jerseys; some wore team tee shirts, and a few others wore suits but the overall feel was that this was a blue-collar team in a blue-collar town for everyone to enjoy. The ticket prices on the other hand, told a different story.

The smell of grilled sausages and French fries filled the air. The buzz of over 38,000 people, all walking toward Fenway, made the atmosphere feel electrified. It was a beautiful thing, and Christian loved every second of it. He even loved the cheap seats that they were going to be sitting in. It was his favorite section of the park. You could see the whole field and were as far away from the suit-and-tie crowd as you could possibly be while still attending the same event. The outfield bleachers did get more spirited than he liked at times, but otherwise it was great.

They walked through the turnstiles and gave their tickets to men who scanned the bar code and screened any bags that people brought with them. A couple of steps later, and they were in the concourse under the seats where they would soon be sitting.

Because they were facing home plate, everything was backwards from what the name would have indicated. Right field was to their left, and left field was on their right. To the right were the stairs that led up to the left-field Green Monster section. This was an area where you could sit on top of the most famous wall in baseball, a 37 foot tall green steel wall, full of dents from hundreds of balls slamming into it year after year. The seats had a great view, but came at a hefty price.

All of the support beams that held up the stadium were green, aside from white letters and numbers that let you know what section you're under. More food vendors and souvenir kiosks filled both sides and center areas of the concourse.

Christian dodged someone trying to sign people up for a Red Sox credit card and got in line for one of his two favorite foods at the park—the Fenway Frank. He always got one of the iconic foot-long hot dogs and a bag of kettle corn. It was a tradition that bordered on ritual.

Alex got an order of fries and a $6 beer before they headed up the cement walkway and into the open air majesty of Fenway Park, "America's Most Beloved Ballpark", according to all of the advertisements. Christian paused to look at the field before proceeding to his seat.

Christian folded the hard blue plastic seat down and stared out at the immaculate grass-covered playing surface as he sat. On one side of the field, men in red and white warmed up, as did their blue clad counterparts on the other side. Just in front of their section was the home bullpen where tonight's starting pitcher was going through his pregame routine.

Christian and Alex settled into their seats and she leaned in closer until they were shoulder to shoulder. She was always very touchy-feely when they were in public. It used to bother Christian, but it was just another thing that he had gotten used to. He didn't have anyone that he was dating and the attention was kind of nice. Most people in their profession found it tough to balance a home life with this very private life. Very few actually tried. He zoned out and tried to avoid thinking about the plan that he needed to present to Grayson in the morning, but it was not going to be easy.

Over the next three hours, Christian and Alex talked, cheered, booed, and kept an eye on their charges. Darren and Greg were a few seats away and never let on that they knew each other. Finally, the right fielder caught the 3rd out of the 9th inning and put an end to the Rays' misery. The Red Sox had crushed them 8-1, but it wasn't even that close. The Standells' song "Dirty Water" played as everyone squeezed their way through the crowd. Once the whole group met up across the street from the exit, the new guys said they wanted to grab a drink or two. This was not what Christian wanted to hear, but he went along with it.

Three streets away, they settled on one of the hundreds of packed sports-themed bars, and everyone went in. Christian, Alex, Darren, and Greg found an open table and the others spread out between the bar and pool tables. Darren grabbed a pitcher of beer, to presumably share, and a scotch for Christian. Everyone looked exhausted and ready to leave, but orders were orders, and they had to stay until the recruits wanted to leave. Greg pushed a straw under his new cast, digging at an itch somewhere under the plaster.

"I am really sorry about that, Greg. I wish I had known. Sorry, bro," Christian said to Greg, truly feeling badly about the situation.

"No worries. You were just defending yourself. I don't blame you," Greg responded, shooting a nasty look in Darren's direction.

Darren shrugged it off and simply said, "It'll heal."

The four of them made small talk about how things were going in their "real lives". It was always awkward to find topics to discuss in public when the one thing that tied them all together was too taboo to mention.

Greg was settling into the quiet of Maine. Darren was getting him used to working at his family's gun shop. They didn't dig into the politics of that field, something that Christian and Darren passionately disagreed about. Christian was a hunter and only used what few guns he owned for that purpose. Darren was significantly more fast and loose with his arsenal. His distrust of all authority figures was so extreme that he had a "bug out shelter" that he could move into if the world came to an end.

Alex talked about her latest shows and that she was hoping to "interview" some of the potential models for the school's nude form drawing class. Darren made a crude offer to come sit on her "casting couch" and she pretended to throw up.

Christian didn't have much to share and blamed the "boring life of a writer". His publisher was pushing for a new book soon, but that was about all he had going on. They all took turns making jokes at Greg's expense until Mick and another recruit came over to the table.

"Excuse me, sorry to interrupt you all," Mick said. This was the first time that Christian had heard him speak. "The other guys want to stay for a while, but Joe and I were hoping to just go back to the hotel. Is that cool?"

"Technically, one of us is supposed to be with you at all times," Christian said, looking around the table for a volunteer. He didn't want to stay but alcohol, Alex, and Darren made for a potentially combustible situation.

"It's cool. I am getting tired, so I am ready to go too," Greg said, getting out of his chair. "Good night, all."

The four remaining recruits were playing pool and the alcohol was starting to make two of them more loose with their words than Christian liked. He thought he heard "Regulator" a couple of times and decided to go check in. Alex stood as well, saying she was going to go get the next round. She rarely paid for anything, so she never said that she would buy the next round.

"Hey Christian, how are you doin', man," the Marine yelled when he spotted Christian coming his way.

"Guys, I am glad you are having fun. I know the last couple of weeks haven't been easy, but you have to chill. We want as little attention as possible," he said, addressing the group. The two quieter ones looked away like puppies that had just gotten caught on the furniture. They caught what he meant, but the Marine was not as quick on his feet.

"It's okay, man. We are just having fun. We aren't gonna see each other again, so we are making some memories," the Marine reassured Christian.

Before Christian had a chance to respond, he felt a hand on his shoulder. It was Darren. "Hey Buddha, we might have a problem. There is a guy at the bar that is getting too friendly with Alex. He isn't taking 'no' very well."

Christian scanned the bar and finally caught sight of Alex and a couple of men who were talking to her. She was shaking her head with a smile on her face but Christian could tell she was not happy. Their eyes met and the look she gave set his feet in motion. He walked past the first guy and leaned up against the bar, between Alex and the other pursuer.

"Hey Babe, I was starting to think that you got lost," Christian said to Alex. He called her "Babe" because he had yet to size up the situation at hand.

"Sorry Hun, it is just taking longer than I thought," she responded. Her response told him that the situation had the potential to get ugly. It was why she didn't use his name either. No names made it tougher to find them later. "Your timing is perfect. I could use a hand with all these drinks."

Christian grabbed a couple of glasses and Alex picked up a new frothy pitcher of beer, and they started toward the pool area. They had only made it halfway when Christian heard a couple of loud voices behind him.

"Where are you going? We weren't done talking," the man from the bar yelled at Alex.

Alex ignored him and kept walking. Christian stopped so that she could walk ahead of him and then followed behind, weaving through the high-top tables until he reached the pool table. He set the drinks down on the small table nearest the pool table that the remaining recruits and Darren were using. He had a feeling that the man was still behind them. He was right.

"What the fuck? Are you some kind of tease or what?" the man yelled again.

"Screw you," Alex replied, flipping the man off.

Christian turned around and the man was only a foot or so behind him. He was a couple inches shorter than Christian and walked with the "tough guy swagger" that alcohol only seemed to make more pronounced.

"I think you need to go back to the bar," Christian said to the man in a low voice.

"No, I think me and my boys are going play some pool. You got a problem with that?" the man responded, obviously looking for trouble.

"No problem. I see an open table over there," Christian said calmly, pointing to a table on the other side of the bar.

"Nah, we like this one. We'll just wait until it is free," the man said as four other men joined him at his side.

"Time to pack up and go home," Christian said to the recruits, hoping to stop the situation from escalating. Darren started handing the recruits their various coats and other gear. Christian didn't move. He was planning on being the last one to leave.

"I was starting to think that maybe you were her boyfriend," the drunken man said, stepping towards Christian. "No wonder I didn't get anywhere. Guess she only likes pussies."

"That's funny," Christian responded. "You can have your table and your little jokes, but we are leaving. You and your boys have fun holding each other's *sticks*."

Christian turned to follow the rest of his group when the man yelled one last insult at them: "I guess bitches stick together."

Christian stopped, as did Darren. Unlike Christian, Darren didn't stop out of anger. He stopped because the man had disrespected a woman around Christian, and he knew that wouldn't lead anywhere good. Christian spun and walked briskly back to the man who puffed out his chest as Christian approached. The cartoonish bravado was almost laughable, but it was the smirk that pissed Christian off.

"Apologize to the lady," was all that Christian said as he got closer.

The man continued to smirk. "I ain't apologizing, but I will give you the first shot if you want it."

"Look buddy, you don't want any part of this. I am sure you are used to making mistakes, like your choice in clothes tonight, but this is one that you would regret for a long, long time," Darren said. He had come up behind Christian and had his hand on Christian's chest pushing him towards the door. Thinking better of the situation, Christian complied. Alex gave him a nod and they walked out of the bar.

The group of four new recruits, Alex, Darren, and Christian had just turned down a quiet side street when they heard footsteps running toward them from behind.

"Get back here, we ain't done yet!" yelled the drunken fool from the bar. The situation was never going to end.

Christian stopped and faced the group of men as they got closer. The side street that they were walking on consisted of businesses that were closed for the day, so they were the only people on it. The man caught up to Christian's group and he and his four buddies spread out in a line in front of Christian.

"You are making a huge mistake," Christian said. "It is time for you and your boys to be on your way before you say something that I don't like."

"We aren't going anywhere, asshole. We thought maybe your girl would want to go hang out with some real men. Don't worry, we'll be gentle, slut," the man said, blowing a kiss in Alex's direction.

The recruits and Alex stepped forward but Christian held a hand behind him telling them to stop. Months of bottled up rage boiled inside him. It may have just found a reason to come out.

"You are a little outnumbered here. I think you should leave," Christian growled.

"You only got six and there are five of us. That is close enough. The bitch ain't gonna fight us too, is she?" the cocky man shot back.

"You aren't going to be fighting with them. You only get me. They are leaving, and you should too," Christian said, his eyes locked on the man in front of him. "Either leave on your own, or in an ambulance. You choose."

"This is going to be fun," the man said as he pulled his hand back to swing at Christian.

Christian stepped back and stood with one foot forward and one foot back. The man swung a big looping right hook at his head. Christian stepped into the man's swing, turning his back as he caught the fist in his hands. As he turned, he bent forward and the man's momentum flipped him over Christian's back. He landed hard on the sidewalk, and the wind rushed out of him. He just stayed there, gasping for air.

His buddies charged at Christian. The first swung and Christian ducked, swinging his right foot in a sweeping arc across the ground, tripping the man. A quick punch to the sternum left him struggling to breathe as well. The next man took a spinning back kick to his abdomen and crumpled to the ground. The three of them flopped around, trying to take in some much needed oxygen like fish on a riverbank.

That left two more men squaring off with Christian. They looked at each other, and the one on the left rushed in. He dove for Christian's midsection like a Greco-Roman wrestler. Christian stepped back, letting his legs spread out behind him. As the assailant grabbed at his legs, Christian slid his right forearm under the man's neck. He pulled the head into his armpit and cranked upward. The man couldn't breathe, but he still tried to finish tackling Christian. Christian swung his legs forward and wrapped them around the man. They both dropped to the ground, and within seconds, the man was unconscious. Christian rolled the dead weight off of him and scrambled to his feet.

The final man stalked towards Christian and finally swung with his left hand. Christian wasn't prepared for an attack from that side, but he improvised. In a similar motion to what he used on the first man, he stepped forward and grabbed the man's wrist as he swung. This time, however, Christian spun toward the man and crashed his elbow into the bridge of the unfortunate man's nose. He fell to the ground, grasping his bleeding face.

Christian turned his attention to the ring leader, who was wobbling to his feet. Christian stepped over and grabbed the back of the man's neck with both hands. He interlocked his fingers and began slamming knee after knee into the attacker's stomach, kidneys, and liver. The formerly macho man tried to fall to the ground to stop the beating, but before he could, Christian gave him a final knee to the jaw and let him go. None of the other men had decided to get up.

Christian rejoined his group, and they walked back to the hotel. No one spoke for the rest of the way. There was little doubt left in the recruits' minds as to what Christian's role was in their new company. The four battle-tested soldiers had just seen their own version of Dr. Bruce Banner turning into the Incredible Hulk. The way he dispatched the five attackers was both beautiful and terrifying. They were just glad that he was on their team. He was on their team, right?

Alex walked with her arm around Christian and offered to let him "cool off" in her room, but he declined. He had a lot of planning to do. In 24 hours, he had to kill a man that he had never laid eyes on.

Chapter 13

Just down the hall from Christian, Mick struggled to sleep. There were too many questions in his head. Is this job something he really wanted? He didn't feel like he had a choice. He had no idea where he would end up or who he was going to be assigned to. He hadn't gotten the impression that he had a lot of say in anything that happened from here on out, and he wasn't completely comfortable with that arrangement.

He was striking out with what few channels his hotel TV carried and decided to go for a walk to the vending machine. He only had a little cash left from what he had been given before their night out, but he was willing to settle for whatever the machine had to offer. He grabbed his room key and headed down the hall.

When he reached the small alcove that housed the vending and ice machines, he found that he was not alone. Greg, the man who had walked back from the bar with him, was rubbing his cast on the edge of the soda machine.

"Hey Greg, I don't think a genie is going to pop out of that thing, no matter how much you rub it," he said, trying to make a joke.

"Oh, hey.....I'm sorry, I didn't catch your name," Greg responded, looking embarrassed that he had been caught.

"It's Mick. Don't worry, I don't think I actually told you. Having trouble sleeping, too?" Mick asked.

"Yeah, damn cast is driving me nuts. I can't really get comfortable."

"Well, I am going to be up watching TV or something if you are bored. I don't think I will be sleeping much over the next couple of days," Mick said.

"You must be getting assigned tomorrow, right? Yeah, it takes some time to transition," Greg said before realizing that technically they were in public and shouldn't be having this conversation. Then again, he hadn't had anyone to talk to about the job since he took it and it might be nice to vent. "I think I will take you up on the offer. The Bruins are playing in L.A. tonight, so I was just going to watch the end of the game anyway."

"Sounds good to me," Mick said as they walked in the direction of his room. Once they were safely inside, each grabbed one of the queen beds and stretched out with their vending machine treasures.

"Your head must be spinning right now. I know mine was. One day, I was just chilling on base, trying to decide between reenlisting and becoming a civie, and the next minute I was on a plane to who knows where. Then after all the exams, you find out that you are going to be living with a serial killer? That is not easy to get used to," Greg said, unloading some of the thoughts that had been lingering in his mind for months.

"How long have you been here? I am assuming that you work with one of the people from tonight?" Mick asked, not expecting an answer.

"I started last fall. I work with the short bald guy from tonight, named Darren. We are only a few hours away from here up in Maine. Same with the other two, they work out of the southern part of the state, and we are kind of up in the middle," Greg said, the pain killers making him open up more than he should.

"Is Alex Christian's regulator?" Mick asked.

"Oh no, as far as I know, they are both Assets. I just met them both today. Christian is the one that gave me the cast."

"I thought he was a psychiatrist, not an ortho doc?" Mick asked, not understanding Greg's meaning.

"No, he didn't put the cast on me. He is the one that broke my arm. It wasn't his fault, though. Darren wanted me to practice my surveillance skills on him. I was supposed to follow him down here, get him alone, and Darren was going to pop out to tell him about the joke. Christian caught onto me and everything went off course. He switched up his route on me, and it threw me off. He ended up leading me down an alley and surprising me. Darren was like a minute and a half too late.

"Christian is one tough bastard and fast, too. Dude has some crazy skills. I'm no slouch when it comes to hand-to-hand, but he is a different level. He took me out fast and when I woke up, he had taken Darren's gun from him and put him down too. He is like a ninja or something. Crazy," Greg said, shaking his head.

"I heard some of the guys talking when they got back. They said something about some guys following them and trying to start a fight," Mick said, hoping that his new chatty friend would keep on talking.

"I wasn't there, 'cause I was here with you and that other guy, but Darren said that some guys were messing around with Alex and followed them out of the bar when they left. Christian doesn't like men messing with women or kids. That is like his nuclear button.

"Basically, these five guys tried to start some crap with them and Christian beat the hell out of them all. No one else even had a chance to step in and help. He just went through them all one by one," Greg paused to let that part sink in. "Darren is a crazy sonofabitch, but even he won't mess with Christian. Darren hasn't told me much about him, but from what I can tell, he has some serious Jekyll and Hyde shit happening. He can go from the nicest guy in the world to making you wish you were dead real quick. Darren loves the guy though. He says he is the closest thing he has to a brother. These guys are like most of us, they don't have any family or friends."

"Do you regret getting in their car and coming here?" Mick asked, afraid of the answer.

"No. I mean, it can get boring as hell up where I live sometimes, but I am starting to like all of the outdoorsy stuff. Darren is pretty cool and the money is good. Most of the time it is like just hanging out with a buddy."

"Yeah but you are hanging with a buddy that kills strangers," Mick quipped.

"No, it's not like that. I know every assignment is different, but Darren only has five tags a year. I have only been around for two of the Cleansings, and they deserved it. Part of your job is to check these people out to make sure that they really are as bad as the Asset thinks they are. Most of the Assets seem to have a "type", if you want to call it that. That is what Darren says, anyway. He hates pedophiles. That is his big target group. I read hours of court docs on these guys. They were raping kids, man. That is fucking sick. They got away with it because the kids were too scared to testify. By the time we got the approval, I wanted to kill them myself."

Mick nodded. He was beginning to see the other side of the coin. Maybe it wouldn't be so bad. Maybe he would get assigned to someone that he would get along with well. Hopefully his Asset would be someone that was cool to hang with and was into some of the same stuff that he was, but just so happened to kill some seriously bad people every couple of months. He was pretty sure his conscience could deal with a half-dozen dead pedophiles a year.

They caught the last period of the Bruins game and chatted about where they were from and where they grew up. It turned out that Greg was former Army, too, and had grown up in Indiana, not far from Mick's home in Chicago.

Who knows, maybe they will end up working close enough together to catch a beer every once in a while. They both got tired and Greg left at around 2:30, which left Mick 3 hours until his wake-up call. Things were looking up. Mick just hoped that they stayed that way after he got his assignment.

Chapter 14

"Take the goddamned knife, Christian!" Melanson screamed. "Stop the damn crying and grab the knife!"

Christian stared at the weapon in his foster father's outstretched hand. His tears made everything blurry, but he reached for the knife anyway, hoping that he wouldn't grab the blade again. His back still ached from the beating he received after grabbing the blade and cutting himself last time.

Now that Christian was holding the knife in his tiny hands, Melanson's whole demeanor changed. He knelt down in front of Christian and placed his hands on Christian's shoulders. "I need you to be my good brave helper. I am not always going to be able to do this. You know how twitchy my hands can get. I might not be able to do it, but it still needs doing. I need a big, strong helper who can step in for me when I can't. Can you do that for me?"

"Yes sir, I can do that," Christian said, fighting back more tears. He didn't want to help Mr. Melanson. It didn't feel right. He hated doing it, but he feared the punishment he would get for not doing it even more. If he didn't do as he was told, Mr. Melanson would use one of the other kids, and they were too small to know any better. Christian would need to do it to protect them and himself.

Melanson stood and turned Christian so that he faced the task that he wished that he didn't have to complete. They walked together to the center of the barn where a table was set up. A burlap sheet covered over the table's wiggling contents. When they reached the edge, Melanson grabbed the top of the burlap and pulled it off. Christian looked into the terrified eyes of the farm's handyman, Dave. This was going to be tougher than he thought. He really liked Dave.

"I'm gonna leave you to it, boy," Melanson said before he turned and walked away.

Christian stood, staring at Dave for several minutes. He knew that if he did what he wanted to do and cut Dave loose that Melanson would catch him. He would bring Dave back, make Christian do his job, and then beat him for disobeying.

"If you promise to be quiet, I will take the gag out," Christian said to the man tied to the table. Dave nodded over and over and Christian reached over and pulled the soiled rag out of his mouth.

"Christian, let me go. We're friends, you know that. Haven't I always been good to you? I will go get help and bring them back to get you, I promise," Dave pleaded.

Christian wished that he could, but he knew it wouldn't work. It would take Dave hours to get back to town and find someone to help them, and Melanson would find him long before then. There was only one way that this could end. Christian didn't like it and he knew that Dave sure wouldn't.

"I want to, Dave. I really want to, but I can't. I have tried it before and it never works. This way is the best. I will make it quick. I am pretty good at it now," Christian said. He was not proud of those facts, but that is exactly what they were—facts. He had gotten good at knowing where to cut to get the most blood, or to make it hurt more than other spots. He also knew how to end it quickly. His first couple of times had been messy and the people had screamed for a long time. He hated that part. He wanted it to be over as fast as possible with the least amount of mess. He always had to clean up any mess he made.

"Hurry up, boy! We got shit to do!" Melanson yelled from behind Christian. How long had he been there?

Christian turned his head and looked at his foster father who was limping toward him in a hurry. His cane creaked from the excess weight. It was meant for a much smaller man. Christian briefly thought about taking the cane, beating Melanson with it, and running away but he didn't want to end up some place worse. Melanson was now only a couple of feet away. The closer he came, the more nervous Christian became.

"What the fuck are you waiting for?" Melanson demanded. He only used that word when he was very angry, and it sent a streak of fear through Christian.

"Please, I will do better. I don't even know what I did wrong. Can't we talk about this? You've proven your point. I just want to go back to work," Dave begged.

"Too late for apologies, Dave. Christian, get this over with. NOW!" Melanson bellowed. He yelled so loudly that his jowls jiggled under where his first chin should have been. Well, the actual chin was in there somewhere. It was just really well hidden.

Christian turned back to Dave, knowing that there couldn't be any more stalling. This one was going to hurt more than the others. Dave was really nice. He played catch with Christian and taught him to throw a football. There wouldn't be anyone to do that with now. His sadness quickly turned to anger. He raised the knife above his head, grasping it with both hands.

"No, please, NO!" Dave screamed.

"Do it. NOW!" Melanson ordered.

A single tear ran down Christian's cheek as he slammed his hands downward. The six inch double sided blade sliced through Dave's chest. The knife was so sharp that it barely slowed as it passed through the ribs on its way to Dave's heart. The hilt was the only thing that kept the knife from going all the way through to the table.

Christian's fear and anger were replaced by something else, something electric. He both hated what he had done and loved this new tingling rush. He pulled the knife out of Dave's chest and blood oozed from the wound. If his heart had still been beating, it would have squirted. Dave was dead. Even knowing that the job was done, Christian raised the knife up and plunged it down again and again until he felt a hand on his shoulder.

"I think he's dead now, Christian," Melanson said. His maniacal laugh filling the air. "You did good, boy. Real good."

* * * * *

Christian woke up in a full sweat and jumped out of bed. He shook his whole body as if the memories would just fall away. It was 4 AM, and he was definitely not going back to sleep. He preferred to sleep naked, so he needed to find something to put on before he decided what to do next. He grabbed a pair of shorts and an Italian soccer jersey and headed down to the gym. It wasn't open yet, so he changed his plans and just went for a run.

The crisp morning air felt great on his skin. Even at this early hour there were a few cars out and about, but not many. He jogged past a bakery and the smell of freshly-baked bread and donuts made his stomach rumble. *Not today stomach, not today.*

An hour later, he finished his run and was back at the hotel. The gym would be open in an hour, but he wasn't sure if his legs could take any more today. Just as he slid his key into the slot, he heard his cell ringing inside his room. The reggae ringtone sounded like a jet taking off in the darkened stillness. He made it just in time to avoid losing the call to voicemail.

"Agent, these calls are getting to be a little early don't you think?" Christian said into the phone fighting to catch his breath.

"Oh shit, I didn't interrupt you banging some broad, did I?" Brooks asked when he heard Christian's voice.

"Get your mind out of the gutter. I was out for a run. What can I help you with?"

"I need to get you back here. Portland is falling apart since you left."

"What are you talking about, Brooks?" Christian asked.

"Two bodies in two days—that is what I am talking about. I am at Deering Oaks Park right now at another damn crime scene," Brooks responded.

"What happened?" Christian asked. Even being the largest city in the state, Portland rarely had two homicides in a month, let alone in back-to-back days. "I am jumping in the shower. I have a couple of early meetings, but I should be able to get back to Portland around lunch. Send me anything you have this morning and I will review it on the way back. I will call you before I get to your office."

"Okay, I will see you this afternoon. I will send everything over as soon as the techs have it ready," Brooks said.

"Agent, is it safe to assume that you have ruled out everything other than foul play?" Christian asked.

Brooks' response was half sarcasm and half due to confusion. "I sure as hell don't think this guy crucified himself."

Chapter 15

Mick's nerves were making it difficult for him to sit in the plush high-backed parlor chair outside of Mr. Grayson's office. In just a few moments, he would know where he was going and who he was assigned to. He had no idea how many options there were, and that prospect was frightening. He had always been told where he was going to be stationed while in the Army, but he usually had some lead-time to prepare before being shipped out. He would be in his new home in a matter of hours, but where that home happened to be was anyone's guess.

An hour ago, he had been sitting in the classroom with the five other recruits when Jenson, Mr. Grayson's assistant, came to get them. Jenson's immaculate appearance and flamboyant mannerisms reminded Mick of the character Jack from the show *Will and Grace*. He looked like a mannequin who just came to life one night. His purple and grey diamond plaid sweater, matching argyle socks, pressed khakis, and oxblood patent leather slip-on shoes looked like they were hand-delivered by a personal shopper this morning. His alabaster skin was baby soft and shaved so closely that Mick wondered if he even had hair follicles. His hair was tightly cropped on the sides and spiked on top, with each blonde highlighted/chocolate lowlighted strand crisp and in its proper place. He walked into the room and asked the waiting men to follow him before turning to leave with the flourish of a prima ballerina.

The six men followed Jenson as he—the only word Mick could use to describe it was "sauntered"—to the elevator. Once he entered his code for the 12th floor, he turned into a tour guide. He told them that floor 10 was where the analysts reviewed files and took emergency calls. The 11th belonged to security, the internal internet servers, and the recruitment team. Lastly, the 12th floor was where the local members of the Board of Directors had their suites. Only a few members actually used their offices, and of those few, only two were in residence daily. They were about to see one of those men, Mr. Grayson, the head of the U.S. division.

They entered the waiting area near Jenson's desk and waited for their turn to see the man who held their fate. Three of the other five men had already gone in to see Mr. Grayson and had come out 15 minutes later, like clockwork. Each one had looked straight ahead and walked out of the room without saying a word. The fourth recruit had gone through the huge, ornately carved double doors thirteen minutes ago. Mick and Leon, the only other recruit left, silently stared at the door, waiting as the final 120 seconds counted down in their heads.

The doors opened inward from the middle, and number four rushed out, eyes locked on the exit. The sound of Mr. Grayson's voice caused Mick to jump in his seat. "Mr. Healy, would you please join me."

Mick rose from his seat and walked toward the open doors. He paused as he reached the entrance, and

Mr. Grayson stepped aside, sweeping his arm forward to usher him in. The office was barely lit, but its enormity was still evident. Over three-quarters of the expansive room was taken up by displays of various sorts. Most of the wall space was occupied by bookshelves, exotic animal heads, artwork, and framed pictures. Several of the pictures showed Mr. Grayson with celebrities and former Presidents. One was of him shaking hands with a former President, signed with the message: "Keep up the 'killer' work." Mick thought that it reflected an interesting sense of humor for the leader of the free world.

Feeling a new level of intimidation, Mick waited for Mr. Grayson to position himself behind his desk before sitting. Mick had been in tanks that were smaller than this desk. Mr. Grayson pulled out a folder that had Mick's name on it and opened it in front of him.

"How are you finding our little company, Mr. Healy?" Mr. Grayson asked without looking up from the papers in front of him.

"It has been very, um, interesting to say the least, Mr. Grayson," Mick replied, hoping that his nerves didn't show.

"Just Grayson, don't worry about the formalities. I would agree that we are definitely an interesting place to work. Are you still satisfied with your decision to join us, or would you rather be back on base?"

"Yes sir, I am happy that I am here. Not knowing where I am going is a little disorienting, but nothing that I can't handle. I would be lying if I said that I had slept well last night."

"Well, by the time you leave this room, you will know where you are headed and what we will be expecting of you. Do you like a challenge, Mr. Healy?" Grayson asked.

"Yes, I do. I prefer a challenge to boredom any day of the week, so I am ready for whatever you are about to tell me," Mick said. He hoped that his enthusiasm would leave a good impression. It couldn't hurt.

"I am glad you said that. Your assignment is rarely going to be boring. Unlike the others in your role, you will be assigned to a man who is extremely busy, travels often, and works directly with law enforcement all over the country. It takes a steady hand and a discerningly discreet tongue to fill this role. Are you up for that?"

"I would say that I am. It sounds like an intense situation, and I am very proficient in those."

"Good. Your Asset is going to be Dr. Christian Rinaldi." Grayson said while smiling, as though Mick had just won a prize.

Mick's heart pounded, but he didn't know why. "I met him yesterday, Sir. He seemed like a good guy."

"He definitely is a good guy, as you said. He is special in a lot of ways. His story is unusual and I normally don't get into the personal histories of our Assets, but you should be aware of a few things. They will give you some important insights that I doubt he will be willing to share with you on his own."

"Ok, whatever you think I should know."

"Christian was found by one of our former Assets. The Asset was assigned to Cleanse a man named Melanson who had been on our radar for quite some time. He was a sadistic son of a bitch who got off on torturing and killing migrant workers and vagrants. He and his wife, who we believed was unaware of her husband's perverse hobby, also took in foster kids. Christian was one of those kids."

"The Asset had been given the green light to Cleanse Melanson, but when he arrived he encountered something that he hadn't planned on. Melanson was suffering from some sort of physical issue and was limping around with the help of a cane. One of his hands was barely functional, but he had found a way to keep on killing.

"He had started using Christian as a surrogate. He forced the child to kill dozens of men, and he was only 12 at the time. When our Asset reached the location, he found Christian committing the act, and not Melanson. He knew he couldn't leave a witness alive, but our rules prohibit killing children. That left him in an awkward position.

"He made a judgment call. He took Christian away from Melanson and told the man that if he killed again or had anyone else kill for him, that he would be back to finish the job."

"Rinaldi, our Asset, took Christian in and raised him like his own son until Christian was an adult. Rinaldi was an FBI agent by trade and worked hard to focus

Christian's newly acquired need to kill. He sharpened the kid's skills and turned him into the perfect combination of intellect and physical prowess.

"Christian went to medical school and became a psychiatrist, but the need was still there. He started writing books in an attempt to live vicariously through his characters rather than commit the acts himself, but it didn't eliminate the urges completely.

"When Rinaldi died 8 years ago, we needed a replacement, and Christian was the perfect fit. We recruited him and saw how special he truly was. He became our "Sicari venator" which translates to "Assassin hunter". Others call him the Reaper. They just don't know who he is."

Grayson paused to let that sink in and sinking is exactly how Mick felt. He was going to be working with the man who hunted and killed other serial killers? Could there be a more dangerous job?

"He has tags of his own, but he is always available for our needs. He has six private tags, but if he wanted more, we wouldn't question it. That brings me to your first challenge. He isn't using his tags. For some reason, he has stopped cleansing, and we need you to get him started again," Grayson said as though he was asking Mick to motivate a lazy student.

"Wait, you basically want me to convince a guy, who sounds like the most dangerous man on the planet, that he needs to kill more?" Mick asked, shocked.

"*Cleanse more,* but yes, it is the same idea. There is a reason that he has gone dormant, and we don't know why. If you can't turn him around, he is of no use to us. You can follow the subsequent chain of events for yourself on what would happen then," Grayson matter of a factly said.

"Do you have any ideas as to why he has stopped? I mean, these guys don't usually quit cold turkey, right?" Mick asked. It was barely setting in that his life was contingent on getting another man to kill.

"All I can say for sure is that it started around the time that he lost his last regulator. He has not been active since then. That was six months ago. Other than that, we have no clue, and he isn't sharing anything with us."

Fear washed over Mick. He wished that he had Dorothy's ruby slippers that could take him back to base. As soon as he could breathe again, he asked the obvious question that he was afraid to have answered. "If that was the event that caused this to happen, I need to ask you—what happened to his last Regulator?"

Mick winced like he was about to get hit. Grayson looked him directly in the eye for the first time and said the three most terrifying words that had ever entered Mick's ears.

"Christian killed him."

Chapter 16

A cacophony of animal calls filled the morning air as Ricky followed Jim around the edge of the pasture's fence. His disproportionally weighted wheelbarrow titled sharply to the right with each and every bump. At least if it tilted to the left, it would hit the wooden slats of the corral and he wouldn't have to fight so hard to keep it from tipping over.

Pigs, cows, horses, goats, and sheep all raced along on the opposite side of the barrier. They had separate food and eating areas, but were all living together in one open field. Geese ran loose everywhere, turning the dirt an odd green color from their never-ending supply of droppings. Several of the incessantly honking crap-machines chose to stalk him and took turns nipping at the feed bags that hung over the sides of the rickety wheelbarrow. Even after taking several bags off, Ricky didn't notice a difference.

"I can tell you one thing, Jim. Before I do this damn job again, I am finding a pump for the tire on this thing. Is there even any air in it at all?" Ricky grumbled as he rocked the wheelbarrow back and forth in an attempt to get it over a rock or a clump of dirt.

"Probably got one 'round here somewhere. Couldn't tell you where, though," Jim said. He lifted a forty-pound sack of dried corn off of the wheelbarrow, and hoisted it onto the top of the fence. The bag was lying across the roughhewn top rung of the fence with more than half of it leaning into the pen. He dug out a well-used folding knife that looked like the one that Ricky's father had brought back from WWII, and cut the threads sealing the top of the bag. The dried corn poured out, bouncing like small pebbles off of the hard packed ground below.

Sheep and goats rushed in and didn't seem to mind the corn waterfall crashing against their heads as they ate. When the front half of the bag was nearly empty, Jim lifted the back end to pour out the remaining contents. He swung it from side to side to spread the corn out for some of the less brazen animals. The empty bag was stuffed into another empty sack so that it could be repurposed later.

"Next stop is four posts down," Jim instructed as he walked onward.

Ricky struggled to get the wheelbarrow moving again, and the older man had to come back to him. Jim grasped the forward lip of the 'barrow and rocked it to help. A couple of tugs later, and they were back to making sloth-like progress. At their current pace, they would barely be done feeding the livestock before it was time for lunch.

"How long have you been here, Jim?" Ricky asked.

"Oh, must be five or six years, now. The time has been blending together."

"Wait a second; you have been living in that shitty bunk, working for these guys with a bomb on your ankle, and watching people get killed for FIVE FUCKING YEARS?" Ricky screamed in a whisper.

"No, it wasn't always like that. At first, a guy would go missing here or there, but we just thought that he got fired or something. Maybe a year or two ago, it started getting to be more often, and then they gave us our new jewelry. These crazy bastards didn't start killing people in front of us until a couple months back."

"What changed?"

"Dunno for sure. We all got some ideas, but the best guess is that the old man that owned the place must have left, kicked off, or got too sick to control these sick bastards anymore. Hell, they've been here longer than I have, but they weren't always this bad." Jim explained.

The conversation was interrupted by a shout from behind them. They both turned and saw the man who picked up Ricky, waving to them. Ricky still hadn't caught his name. Everyone just referred to the two men as "Sir" or "The Big One" and "The Small One". A couple of the younger men had shortened it to "Biggie" and "Smalls".

"Better go see what he wants. You are a damn sight faster than me. Just be happy that it is him and not the other one. He is a mouthy little prick, but he is much better alone. No one to show off for, I guess," Jim said to Ricky.

Ricky ran down the hill to see what Smalls wanted. He tried his best to disguise his limp, but 2 hours of pushing that damn wheelbarrow and smashing his knee into it hadn't done him any favors.

"New guy, what's your name again?" Smalls asked as Ricky got close enough that they could speak to each other without yelling.

"It's Ricky, Sir. What can I do for you?" Rick replied.

"Ricky, you can come with me, is what you can do. We need to go get another guy to help you, and I don't like repeating myself. Is that understood, Dickey-boy?" Smalls responded, purposely calling Ricky by the wrong name to get a reaction. Ricky didn't give him the satisfaction.

"Yes, Sir, that makes sense. No point in saying somethin' more times than you need to," Ricky replied, hoping to earn some points.

Smalls didn't respond. He simply turned and started walking toward the open area between the barn and the bunk house, where some of the other men were sanding and painting doors that were spread out on the picnic tables they used for all their meals. As they stopped in front of the working men, the men all stopped and looked at Smalls. Ricky recognized 3 of the men as the volunteers from yesterday. In total, 7 sets of eyes looked at Smalls with fearful anticipation, waiting for him to speak.

"Stevie, you come with me and Dickey. Y'all got a job to do," Smalls said before turning and walking off again.

Relief washed over the six remaining men but Stephen looked like he had just been told that he had contracted an incurable illness. He fell in line behind Ricky and followed along, his eyes looking at his boots and his shoulders slumped.

The three men followed the narrow path all the way back to the site of yesterday's execution, stopping a single time at a storage shed to grab two shovels. The only reminder of the prior day's events was the sitting logs. The post hole had been filled in and even the blood had been washed away by the overnight rain showers.

"You boys got your listenin' ears on?" Smalls asked the men as they approached the open area where Gene had met his maker less than 24 hours prior. Neither man spoke, but both nodded. Smalls continued with his instructions.

"I need you to dig a hole right here," he said, dragging the toe of his boot through the grass in front of him. "It needs to be at least six feet long, three feet wide and three feet deep. I want this done before lunch, got it?"

Ricky nodded and Stephen stepped forward to start digging. Smalls left the clearing without another word. Ricky backed up about six feet away from Stephen and started digging as well. Time and time again, the shovels plunged into the top soil, removing a chunk that was then tossed aside. Stephen was throwing his clumps toward the tree line and Ricky followed suit. They dug in silence for several minutes before Ricky made an attempt at conversation.

"I am sorry that you had to go through that yesterday. It had to be rough," Ricky said, not knowing how to break the ice.

"It wasn't easy, but at least it wasn't me on the cross. Then again, sometimes I wonder if Gene and the others are better off than we are," Stephen said without taking his eyes off his shovel.

"Did he really steal from you guys?" Ricky asked.

"What could he steal? We ain't got anything that anyone can take away. Gene just started slackin' off some and Biggie didn't like it. It was just dumb luck more than anything else. He never should have come here. None of us should have," Stephen said. He spoke in a rhythm that could have lost a foot race with cold molasses, and a sadness that was almost as thick.

Ricky couldn't think of anything else to say so he just kept digging. In less than an hour, they were standing waist deep in the fresh hole. Regardless of the circumstances, Ricky was proud of himself for keeping up with the younger man, bad leg and all.

"I think Smalls is going to be happy with this hole. We did a great job, if I do say so myself," Ricky said, smiling for the first time since he had flashed the fake one at Smalls on the side of the road yesterday.

Ricky climbed out of the hole and stood facing Stephen, who was sitting on the edge with his feet dangling over the side. Ricky walked over and offered the tired man a hand to help him up. Stephen just looked at the outstretched offer of assistance and did not move. After a minute or so, Ricky grew impatient. He didn't want Smalls to think that he was slow or lazy. He wanted to get back to Jim.

"What's the hold up? You aren't worried that he is gonna catch us sitting around or think we took too long?" Ricky asked the listless man.

"It doesn't matter. You go on ahead if you want to, but I am going to enjoy sitting here for a bit."

"You sure don't look like you are enjoying yourself. What's your deal?" Ricky asked, growing more impatient by the second.

"You don't get it do you? Gene was the one that dug the hole for the cross. I was a volunteer yesterday and now I am digging today. You just got here but it's obvious to everyone that you have a bum leg. You think they want to keep some cripple around here?" Stephen said, his voice getting louder with each angry word.

"I work hard even with a sore leg. If I keep my head down and do what they say, I will be alright. They keep Jim around here, and he ain't much of a worker," Ricky said, trying to convince himself as much as he was Stephen.

"Wow, you really are an idiot, aren't you? Stephen said, his anger replaced by an odd amusement, or perhaps pity. "They always make the person they are going to kill do the prep work. That means that this hole is for you, me, or both of us. At least one of us is dying in this pit tonight."

Chapter 17

The muffins and oatmeal from Mick's hotel breakfast fought valiantly to stay in his stomach. It wasn't just that he was in an automobile with the single craziest driver he had ever ridden with, or even the nerves about heading somewhere he had never been before that was making his stomach do flips. Yes, moving in with a man who he had spent less than an hour with was not something he did very often, but the military had prepared him for frequent changes. It was also true that Alex's style of driving—a terrifying combination of aggression, excessive speed, and a complete lack of awareness for her surroundings—was causing his life to flash before his eyes, but he had spent months driving through active war zones where explosives and insurgents dotted the landscape. No, these things simply compounded the uneasy feeling he had developed in his meeting with Grayson.

After the revelation that Christian had killed the man who had formerly held Mick's new position, Grayson spent the remaining few minutes asking him to spy on Christian. The Board was very concerned that Christian was teetering precariously between continuing to provide the services that they needed him to, and shutting down completely. He emphasized that the Board needed to trust Mick and that he had to be their eyes and ears in the field.

Mick wasn't totally comfortable in his new role to start with, and now they wanted him to basically lead a potentially volatile killer to believe that he could open up to Mick while feeding that personal information back to the people Christian didn't want to have it. Mick struggled with the integrity involved, or the lack thereof. He had been on the job for only a few hours and he already had lost respect for his boss. Not a good start.

Mick had emerged from the meeting in a daze similar to the one everyone else had walked out in. He didn't even remember walking by the final recruit or Jensen. If either had spoken to him, he didn't hear it. When he made his way through the glass door and into the hallway, he didn't find Christian waiting for him as he was expecting. Instead, Alex was leaning against a wall outside of the office suites. He was still too shocked to speak but managed a confused look before she spoke.

Alex informed Mick that Christian had gotten an early morning call from the FBI agent that he consulted for, and was needed back in Maine. He had met with Grayson to quickly go over a plan of some sort and boarded the train back to Maine at about 9 or so. She was going to give Mick a ride back to Portland and then take him shopping for some clothes. Christian was going to meet them at the Maine Mall in a few hours. He followed her to a two-year-old grey crossover style SUV and climbed into the front seat. Mick thought that she might have said something about needing a huge car so that she could transport art, but he wasn't listening.

The last 45 minutes had felt more like a movie about two convicts trying to escape a city before the police caught them rather than a leisurely commute from Boston to Portland. Mick had been fairly quiet the whole time, but he doubted that Alex had noticed. She hadn't stopped talking, and most of the conversation seemed to require her to turn and look at him while talking, as though her words wouldn't reach him if she wasn't aiming her mouth at his ear. The road and other drivers were barely a consideration to her. He decided that if he had to spend another couple of hours in the car, that maybe he could distract himself by trying to get some information from her. She definitely seemed willing to talk.

"So, have you always lived in Maine or did you get relocated here like me?" Mick asked.

"I've pretty much always been here. Well, that's not totally true, I was born in Florida but I moved to Maine when I was like 3 years old, so I don't remember much about living down south. My mom kinda had some addiction issues and I didn't have a dad who was around, so my mom's aunt and uncle took me in when she went to jail. I lived with them until I turned 18, moved to Portland, and have been there ever since. How about you? Where are you from?"

Mick didn't want to tell her about his childhood, but it was his own fault that she had asked. Besides, if he wanted her to give him the real lowdown information on his new roommate, then he needed to build some trust. "I was born in Chicago and lived my whole life in the same apartment on the South Side. My parents were in their 40's when they had me, so I was their "miracle baby". They died when I was a senior in High School."

"Oh, I am sorry. What happened?" Alex asked.

"Car accident. They were stopped at a light late one night and some guy behind them fell asleep at the wheel. He rear-ended them going like 45 and their car got pushed out into the intersection and got t-boned by a city bus," Mick said. It had been almost 13 years, but the wound was still fresh. He felt odd opening up to a stranger about it, but at the same time, it was nice to say the words out loud.

"Holy shit, that sucks. I don't have anyone left either. My mom died in prison and my aunt and uncle just got old and died a few years back. We are pretty much a company of orphans, so you aren't alone," she said with more than a touch of sadness.

A horn honked somewhere behind them as Alex cut over into the next lane without looking or using a blinker. They were about to connect back with Interstate 95 and would be in Maine in an hour or so. Mick hoped he made it that far. Feeling a little more secure, he began asking the questions that he really wanted to know.

"How long have you known Christian? Is there anything you can tell me about him that I need to know? I want to make this as smooth as I can," he asked.

"Well, that is kind of a wide open question. He is a really sweet guy when you get to know him, but that can take some work. He is kinda closed off. He's been screwed over by a lot of people, so be honest with him all the time. He likes that. You'd think he would be some alpha male type by looking at him, but he isn't. He doesn't like to hang with the overly-macho guys, either, so keep that in mind. He's kind of a homebody. He spends like almost all of his time either at home or in his office. Hmm, what else is there...." Alex rambled.

"Ok, what does he do for fun? Does he even have fun?" Mick prodded.

"Oh yeah, he is a lot of fun. He is hilarious, too, but in a dry, sarcastic way. Sometimes I don't know if he is serious or kidding. He is crazy deadpan when he is joking around. That is a good way to know that he is getting comfortable with you. If he starts busting your balls, you are getting closer.

"What does he do for fun? Hmmm, okay, he loves sports—football on Sunday is like holy time for him. You don't want to try to get him to do anything when football is on. He is big into hockey, baseball, MMA, and stuff like that. If you like NASCAR, you are gonna be watching that by yourself.

"He lives on a river and there are a lot of lakes near his place, so he does a lot of swimming, hiking, and fishing. He works out like every day. I don't work out, but sometimes I go over there just to watch him get sweaty. I think that is about it."

"So you guys seemed kinda close the other night. Are you like a couple or something?" Mick asked, testing the waters on personal questions.

Alex laughed. "A couple? Umm, no. I've thought about it before and like to flirt with him, but there is nothing going on. Christian doesn't date, and I am not good at sticking with one person. Don't get me wrong, I think we could have some majorly dirty fun, but he isn't interested. He doesn't trust people enough to let them get that close. It's still fun to try, though. I haven't ever seen him on a date with anyone, so who knows? Maybe you have a better shot with him than I do."

"How did you end up working for Sicari? You don't really seem like a killer to me," Mick said, ignoring Alex's attempt at humor.

"That is a long story. I don't really want to get into all the details right now, cool?" Alex responded.

"Yeah, sorry, I know that is way personal. Let's forget I asked," Mick said sheepishly.

"No, don't worry about it. I don't have a problem telling you about some of it, there are just some things that I don't like to think about. I wasn't some freak that liked torturing bunnies or anything.

"I am not even sure when I started feeling the urges. I know that when I was in high school, I used to get in a lot of fights with some Barbie doll-looking bitches. They made fun of me because I came to school with paint all over my clothes from my work and stuff. They gave me shit about everything, man. I used to cut my hair when I was upset, so they made fun of how that looked. I didn't like to do sports in gym class, and they would try to push me around and stuff.

"They used to push me in the pool all the time. So one day, they tried and I pulled one of them in with me. We were in the deep end and I had her under me. She got all freaked out and it was awesome. I just remember that I didn't let go of her and someone had to pull us out. I felt really powerful, like I was the one who decided whether she lived or died. I loved that feeling. They didn't screw with me again."

"But you didn't kill her, right? When did you start?" Mick asked, not sure if he wanted to know. Alex seemed like she was getting a little too excited by this story. Her cheeks turned a red and she was breathing differently. He didn't know what was going on, but she was acting really weird.

"No, she lived. I didn't kill anyone then, but I think that it is when I started thinking about it. I dreamt about holding her under water until she stopped breathing. I really wanted to kill them all. Wow, that must sound crazy," Alex said, seeming a little self-conscious about the topic.

Mick didn't want her to close up so he tried to reassure her that she was ok. "No, I get it. I was in the Army, remember. When did you do it for the first time?"

"Not until I was in college. There was this professor that I kind of had a thing for, and one night he came into my studio and started hitting on me…" Alex started.

"Oh no, umm, I didn't mean sex. I meant the first time that you killed," Mick corrected himself, his cheeks glowing from embarrassment.

"I know what you meant," Alex responded. She started rambling in one long thought. Each sentence came right after the previous one as though she only had the length of one breath to tell the whole story. "You see, I was in art school and we each had our own working studios in the school. Mine was on the floor with ceramics and painting classrooms. He came in and started hitting on me and I was into it at first. He kissed me and I liked it but then he started trying to go too far. He grabbed at my shirt and tried to push me onto my back. I pushed him away, and he started saying stuff like 'You know you want it', and I stood up and walked out.

"I went into the ceramics room where there were some other people and he just stopped in the doorway. Later, when everyone else left, I stayed to load the pottery into the walk-in kiln. He came up behind me and put his arms around me. He started squeezing my breasts and I told him to let go. He didn't, and I slammed my head back into his face. He slapped me, hard.

"I pushed him back, and then when he stepped towards me, I pushed him again. I was crying and so mad that I kept pushing him, and then he slipped and fell on the floor of the kiln. I kicked him in the face. I kept kicking him, and he was just lying there on the floor. I thought I killed him.

"I got scared and I ran out of the kiln and closed the door. I thought I was going to get kicked out of school. I didn't know what to do, and then I saw the start button on the wall. I turned on the heat and started throwing wood in the fire pit. The door has a brick that you can pull out to look in the kiln to see if it is firing right. I looked in and he was moving on the floor but he didn't make any sounds. I just left him in there."

"What happened when you opened the kiln? I mean, wouldn't they find his body in there at some point?" Mick asked a little confused.

"There wasn't much of anything left. Those kilns get really hot. They can get up to between 1500 and 4000 degrees, depending on what you are firing in there. I didn't know it then, but the human body turns to ash at 1292 degrees. After a couple of hours in there, he was just ash, a couple of ends of bone, and a greasy spot."

"What did you do with the bone?" Mick asked

"We have a pneumatic press that we dump the messed up pieces of ceramics that were broken or just came out wrong and it crushes them to dust. The bones were almost falling apart anyway, so I just tossed them in there and that was it," Alex said.

"So, then what happened? How did you get here?"

"I majorly freaked out, thinking that I was going to get caught, but then nothing happened. I started thinking about what I had done and it reminded me of how I felt when I almost drowned that bitch. I liked it a lot," she said as a satisfied grin crept across her face.

Alex continued. "A couple of months later, I heard another girl talking about how her boyfriend was cheating on her and had hit her when she called him out about it. I had seen him around before and knew where he worked, so I followed him when he walked home from there one night.

"I pretended to run into him and he started hitting on me, too. He asked me if I wanted to go somewhere to be alone and I said that I wanted to. We went to a beach and walked up to a lighthouse. He asked me if I wanted to sleep with him and I told him that I wanted to go up to the top of the lighthouse so we wouldn't get caught. When he was getting undressed, I pushed him off the platform. He fell onto the rocks and that was it."

"Ok, but how did you find out about Sicari?"

"Damn, you're impatient. I am getting to it. I started liking the rush of killing these cheating bastards, and I kept doing it. I did it for like 2 years without getting caught or even questioned. Then about 6 years ago, I had just graduated and I was thinking about going to do post grad work at an art school in Savannah, when a guy came to my apartment. He told me that he knew what I had been doing, and that he was going to turn me in.

"I thought about killing him on the spot, but then he told me that he had a way to help me keep doing it and never get caught. He worked for a company that hired people like me. I told him that I was interested, and I went for evaluations. It was sort of like yours, but not completely. Afterwards, I met with Grayson and he told me all about Sicari. He said that he could get me a job teaching at my art school, I could do my art on the side, and they would pay me.

"They would leave me alone as long as I followed their rules and let one of their employees live with me. It was perfect, so I signed right up. They let me have 8 tags a year, and my reg is awesome. Her name is Asher and she hates the same kinds of guys that I do. It is pretty damn perfect."

"How do you pick your targets?' Mick asked, curious about how the process worked.

"Asher helps me a lot. She is quite artistic and has a day job as a courtroom artist. She does those sketches that you see on TV from trials, or of suspects that the police are looking for. She is in courtrooms or at the police precinct a lot, so she knows when people get away with shit that shouldn't, and she gives the names to Grayson. He lets everyone know about some of them that fit their type. Some of us hate pedophiles, or wife beaters, or whatever. I go for the rapists or domestic abusers. Unfortunately, there are way more of them than the number of tags that I get."

The conversation had done such a good job of distracting Mick that he didn't even notice that they had passed through New Hampshire and were already 25 miles into Maine. The large green sign on the side of the highway said that Portland was only 20 miles away. The traffic was much lighter, and Alex's aggression had also diminished. He only had about 15 minutes or so before they got to the mall, and he still had one important question that he needed to have answered.

"Alex, I am so glad you stuck around to give me a ride. I was kind of freaking when I left Grayson's office, and you have helped a lot. I am pretty sure that I will be good now. It's just that a lot of what he said had me worried about living with Christian, you know? I mean, there is still the one thing that is bugging me, but otherwise you have made me feel better," Mick said, leading the conversation down a potentially dark path.

"Well, I don't want you to be nervous about being there. He is a super great guy. What is the one thing?" Alex asked.

"What happened to the guy who had this job before me?" Mick asked, turning to face Alex.

"What did Grayson tell you?"

"All he said was that Christian killed him. Is that true?" Mick pressed.

Alex didn't speak for what felt like forever. For the first time on this drive, she stared straight ahead with both hands on the steering wheel. Mick could tell that this question was not one that she was prepared for. He wasn't going to apologize this time. He waited in silence, intent on not being the next one to speak.

"Yes, it is true, but it isn't what you think. You have to understand that our testing doesn't catch everything, and deep down Franklin was a sick guy. He started off fine. He asked a lot of questions and he even trained with Christian. They lived together for over 7 years and became close, like family. Christian trusted him and he started to let his guard down.

"Franklin started spending more time away from Christian, and we all just thought that he had met a girl and didn't want to bring her into our world. The truth was that he had developed a taste for killing. He grew tired of watching from the sidelines and knew that he was not sanctioned to do it himself. He needed an outlet to feed his desires and chose to hide it from everyone.

"He started getting moody and no one knew why. He would go into New Hampshire or other parts of Maine for a weekend away and come back like a different guy. He was happy again for weeks, and then back to moody. Christian thought that he possibly had a mood disorder, but never thought that he might have homicidal tendencies. The truth about his trips was that he was killing people while they were hiking or camping in the woods.

"Agent Reston, the guy who worked out of the FBI office before Brooks, started putting it together. He noticed that every time that Franklin went away someone went missing or had a freak accident in the area that he had been in. He told Christian about his suspicions and Christian didn't believe him. I guess Reston confronted Franklin about it and Franklin killed him. Christian caught him trying to move Reston's body and..." Alex stopped mid-sentence, visibly upset.

"...and he did what needed to be done," Mick finished her thought for her.

"Yeah, it crushed him to do it. He thought he should have seen signs or something, but he didn't. He trusted Franklin too much. He thinks that if he had confronted Franklin himself, then Reston would still be alive," Alex finished.

Neither spoke again until they reached the entrance to the Maine Mall. Alex's sadness filled the car like a black cloud. He wished that he hadn't asked because of how it had affected her, but he needed to know the truth. Mick had started this ride fearing the man who he was supposed to live with and spy on, but he ended it feeling sorry for him. He wanted to explain that he was nothing like the last guy and that Christian could trust him, but he could now see why that would take a lot of time and effort. Hopefully, it would be worth it.

Chapter 18

"It's gotta be some religious whackadoodle, right Doc?" Agent Brooks asked as he paced around his small office, "I mean someone's gotta be way, way out there to nail someone to a cross, right?"

Christian stared at the crime scene photos that covered the top of Agent Brooks' desk. They tilted at a variety of angles due to the copious amount of paperwork, soda bottles, and other garbage that littered the desk underneath. He could tell that Brooks was extra nervous because of the speed that he paced and because of his new tendency to end every sentence with "right?", as though he needed the constant confirmation that his cop's intuition was on point.

"Agent, I would say that you could be looking for a group of men, possibly as few as two, but I would hazard to guess that between four and six strong men were involved in this killing. At least one was extremely well organized and the others were either organized as well, or very willing to take direction from the first man.

"Yes, the crucifixion aspect would lend itself to a religious element, but whether the killing was meant as a 'righteous killing' or was meant as a defiant counter-religious statement, I cannot tell at this point. I would say that the man or men who chose this particular ritual were versed in history more than religious zealotry," Christian said in a slow calming voice in hopes of settling Agent Brooks' nervous energy.

"What do you mean? Like a cult or something? Why do you say it had to be that many men, and why history?" Brooks asked in rapid succession.

"It could be a cult, or it could just be a group with a strong leader. I say it was four to six at minimum because of the way he was killed. First, unless someone is completely subdued, it would be virtually impossible to get them attached to a cross. Secondly, the mud on the bottom two feet for the base means that it was standing. One man would have an extremely difficult time lifting over two hundred pounds of man and wood up and into a hole. The distribution of the weight across the crossbar would be awkward at any height or weight."

"Couldn't he have used pulleys? I can take a three hundred fifty pound motor out of my car with a pulley, and I am only a buck seventy on a good day," Brooks interrupted.

"He could have, but didn't. There are no holes on the cross other than the ones from the nails, so there wasn't anything attached to this for a pulley to lift it by. To answer your question about why I think the man with the plan on this one was historically versed is simply the placement of the nails. If this was meant as religious tribute, most people would have put the nails through the palms, as the Bible references. All pictures of Christ show the stigmata on his palms, and this was done through the wrists. That is where the Bible cannot be historically accurate. All civilizations that performed this punishment used the wrists for stability reasons," Christian explained.

"Yeah, but the spear was like the Bible, Right?" Brooks pointed out.

"Yes and no. That depends on the interpretation that you read. Christ had either a lance or spear driven through his side. That was done here as well, but this man also had a wound to his upper chest and thigh, which are different than the Bible, as was the slitting of his throat. Also, if this was meant to be similar to the death of Christ, he would have had lash marks on his back and a crown of thorns on his head. Neither of those were present in this slaying."

"Okay Doc, I think I got it. I will have the boys start looking around," Brooks said before being interrupted by his ringing phone. "This is Brooks. Okay, perfect, that makes the day a little brighter. Thanks, Sergeant."

Christian waited for Brooks to speak before he asked about the call. Brooks finally stopped pacing and dropped into his chair with a thud, causing it to swivel almost a full half turn. The apple-sized spot of thinning hair on the back of his head now faced Christian. He repositioned himself behind the desk and started gathering up the pictures. His mood had certainly improved.

"I don't know how you do it sometimes, Doc, but you always do. You must have a crystal ball or something," he said with a hint of a smile peeking through. "That was Sergeant Penn over at Portland PD.

One of the overnight staff at the shelter admitted to putting glass in some of the salt shakers. The guy said that he was tired of watching them get stolen and wanted to teach somebody a lesson. He didn't care who it was, he just wanted to send them all a message. You were right, again."

"I guess congratulations are in order. Good job, Agent Brooks. I am sure you have some work to do, and I have to go pick up my new intern. I don't mean to cut this short, but I have to get going. It is going to be a busy night with trying to get him settled in and all, but you can swing by my office tomorrow if you need me," Christian said as he stood.

Brooks stood as well, extending his hand to Christian. "I couldn't have done it without you, so thanks. Maybe we can grab lunch tomorrow and I can meet this new kid. What's his name again?"

"Mick, Mick Healy is his name. He seems like a good kid, but I don't know him all that well yet. I am sure we could do that tomorrow. I will let him know. Have a good night, Agent," Christian said as he headed for the door. If he didn't get out now, Brooks might end up tagging along. With the plans Christian had for this evening, that would not be a good thing.

Christian left the FBI satellite office and walked down the single flight of stairs that led to the side of the building. The office was on the second floor of a strip mall, above a Chinese restaurant. The strip mall housed a handful of eclectic shops, and a couple of other buildings in the parking lot contained a bank, a fast food restaurant, and a large sporting goods store. Mick and

Alex were waiting for him across the street at the much larger Maine Mall.

While he waited for the light to turn green, Christian sent a voice text to Alex and told her where to meet him. He was hoping that they would be waiting for him when he got there so I could avoid hunting for them in the crowded mall setting. Alex responded with a smiley face, and he took that as a positive sign.

Christian caught a glimpse of Alex as she walked out through one of the clothing stores, and pulled into a parking spot. Alex and Mick walked through the parking lot, each carrying about a dozen shopping bags. Mick looked like a man who had spent too much time following a wife or girlfriend through the mall as they tried on everything ever made in their size.

As they neared the car, Christian popped the trunk, and Mick placed several of the bags that he was carrying in the large empty space. One of the bags, presumably dropped in error, had the telltale pink and white stripes of the world's most famous women's underwear and lingerie store. Alex had two more in her possession and Christian couldn't resist the chance to give the new guy a hard time.

"Ummm, Mick, I know we just met, and I don't know what you were told about your role with me but..." he lifted the bag out of his trunk and pulled up the strap on one of frilly bras inside "we are *just* roommates. You do have your own room. We aren't sharing one. I appreciate the effort, though."

Mick turned three shades of pink when he saw the bag. He was embarrassed, but tried to hide it by playing along. He reached out for the bag and said "Damn, way to ruin the surprise. I was just trying to make our first night special."

Alex laughed as she took the bag away from Mick. "I tried to get him to model it for me but he wouldn't. I couldn't even get him anywhere near the dressing rooms. Somebody's shy, isn't he?" she squeezed both sides of his face as she said the last line.

"Ok, I think the poor guy has been tortured enough. Thanks for bringing him with you. We have got to get home if he is going to get settled in, and I am going to need time to get everything ready for tonight. When will you have the package delivered?" Christian asked Alex.

"I will be there around 8 or so to help you, and then Asher should be there between 10 and 11 with the package. She is going to call first."

"Ok. See you then," Christian said as he opened his door. Mick followed suit and climbed into the front seat.

"It is pretty nice up here. I wasn't expecting it to be so busy," Mick said trying to kill the potential for uncomfortable silence off the bat.

"Yeah, this area is more built up. Portland and the small towns around it are about as congested as you will find in Maine. I hate to disappoint you, but where I live is much smaller."

"How small are we talking? Ghost town small or no cell reception small?" Mick asked

"Cells can get spotty, but they still aren't that bad. My closest neighbor is about a mile away, so it is nice and quiet. Dublin only has about a thousand people total. It's one of those, 'everyone knows everyone and all their business' type of places," Christian responded.

"Well, they can't know all of your business, right?"

"They are like everyone else. They know what I want them to know. They knew my father, and his father, and way back down the family tree. It is a town that was settled by the Irish a couple hundred years ago and he was the only *Italian* in town," Christian said, emphasizing a hard "I" sound in the word "Italian". "You have the right kind of name and look like you could be the poster child for the Emerald Isle, so you should fit in fine."

"I am used to base living, and they are basically the same way, with everyone knowing everything about their neighbors, except they have more people. How far away is your place?"

"It takes like 25 minutes to get home from the office on most days. It is about the same from here. The 15 miles from the house to the outskirts of Portland takes basically the same amount of time as the last 5 miles of driving through town. I know you have had a busy few days, but are you cool with talking some business for a minute?" Christian asked.

"Sure, no problem. I want to make sure that I don't screw anything up. Just tell me what you need me to do, and I'll do it. You're the boss," Mick said, before remembering that he doesn't work for Christian. "Well, you know what I mean."

"No worries, I get it. This is a weird kind of situation to be dropped into. As long as you remember the basics, you should be fine. As far as everyone knows, you are here because you are working on your Doctoral thesis and are interning under me. You are kind of like a research assistant."

"I don't know much about psychology," Mick interrupted.

"Don't worry about it. Most people don't know as much as they think they do. So as long as you are confident about what you are saying, you should be fine. If all else fails, say something like, 'That is an interesting point of view, let me think about it some more,' or 'There are several differing views on that topic, I think that most have their own merits,' and you should be fine," Christian said.

"So, fake it until you make it," Mick said with a snicker.

"Pretty much, but since you will be here for a while, you might want to do some research of your own, or sit in on some of the classes that I teach," Christian said.

"Okay, that makes sense. I will do whatever you think I should do. I don't want to blow our cover," Mick said, taking mental notes.

"As far as settling in up here goes, your stuff has all been delivered from your base housing. I have a couple of vehicles that you can use when you are not with me, or you can go get your own. Grayson will pay for a car if you want to go that route. The only guideline is that it shouldn't be flashy. We try to blend in as much as we can.

"My cars are all a couple of years old, dark colored, and are one of the more popular styles. A guy in a new BMW convertible will be memorable if they are in the area of a crime scene. The same guy driving this car— a 3 year old black Honda Accord—won't even be noticed. See what I mean?" Christian explained.

"Yeah, I am good with that. I am not sure if I will get one or not. I didn't even have one on base. If you are cool with me using yours, I will probably just do that until I find something. So does anyone else know the real reason that I am here?" Mick asked.

"Only the other Assets, their Regulators, and a few people that deal with Grayson know about you. Everyone else, including my personal assistant, and the people I work with at the FBI, have been told your cover story. Aside from the people that you contact at Sicari, you will only occasionally see people that are informed about the truth. Even if you see one of them in a public setting, you are to act as though you only know them via the job that they do."

"You mentioned other Assets and people that work with Grayson, so it isn't just Alex and Darren?" Mick asked.

"No, there are around a dozen Assets in various parts of the state, and more in each of the surrounding states. We occasionally need the help of people that can assist us with certain parts of our job, like disposing of evidence, and they are in the loop as much as they need to be. Those relationships are all set up by Sicari. You will meet two of them tonight. When I say 'meet' that isn't to say that you will actually see them. They will show up, do their job, and leave," Christian continued.

They were now well outside of the suburbs of Portland, in an area that consisted mostly of woods and farms. A few houses were sprinkled in here and there, but it was much quieter than anywhere Mick had been lately. It was like another planet.

"Here we are. Home sweet home," Christian said as they turned off the main road and onto one named O'Connor's Glen. Mick would have missed if it if he had been behind the wheel. The only indications that it was there at all were a small green sign with the name and a bright yellow dead end sign.

Two miles and a grand total of four houses later, the road came to an abrupt end in a driveway. Christian's house sat at the end of the road/driveway on about two and a half acres of beautifully manicured lawn. Dense woods surrounded the property on all four sides, except for one spot on the left where there seemed to be a fairly large boathouse on a river. Mick doubted that there was another person within a mile of where he was standing.

Christian's home struck Mick as palatial as it sat in the middle of the golf course quality lawn. A three story grey colonial with a farmer's porch that covered the entire front and swept around the side loomed over them as they pulled up to the garage. Christian pressed a button on the roof of his car, and the second of three garage bays started to open. Tools lined the organized walls and a pressure washer sat in the far right corner. Aside from the Accord, the garage was home to a grey Toyota Venza, an either original or fully restored '69 Mustang, and three motorcycles. As they got out of the car, Mick couldn't help but stare.

"I might as well start the tour in here. That door in the back leads to the basement. There is one on the other side that goes out into the back yard, and this one leads into the house," Christian said, pointing to three doors on the left side of the garage.

Mick followed Christian as he walked through the open garage door and into the late afternoon sunshine. The door lowered and closed as soon as they were both through it. Christian turned right, walked over a short stone walkway, and then onto the porch. Mick joined him as he began pointing out various parts of the property.

"Over there is the boathouse. You can fish right off the dock there or take the boat out. The river is fairly narrow around here, so there aren't a lot of people on it. It is great for kayaking or canoeing if you are into that. There are a couple of each in the boathouse," he said, pointing to the far side of the lawn. He walked around to the end of the house, and the giant porch continued on. Mick could have stood there on the grey composite decking with his hands on the stark white railings and just gotten lost in the stillness. He had never been anywhere that was so peaceful and quiet. It was as though they were completely alone.

"Back here..." Christian started, his voice breaking Mick's daydream. "Back here is just the back yard, where I like to have barbecues and just chill."

Mick reached the back side of the house and fell in love. The yard was huge. He stepped down off the back porch and onto a stone patio area. There was a fire pit, cooking station with outdoor sink, fridge, large stainless steel grill, and a smoker. Beyond the patio was a fenced-in area that held an in-ground pool covered by a large winter cover. Nestled in the back corner of the porch, up against the side of the garage, was a six-person hot tub. *What better place could there be to relax after a hard day of killing criminals,* Mick joked in his head.

"You can go hiking back here, if you want. The property extends for just over 40 acres, and beyond that is a nature preserve, so there isn't anyone back there for miles. There are some trails cut and I have a couple ATVs and side by side vehicles in the shed in the far end. The shed over by the pool is where the yard tools are. Ready to go in and settle into your room?" Christian asked.

"I could just sleep here," Mick said pointing to a free standing hammock under a tree that was just outside the pool area. "It is absolutely beautiful back here. I am jealous."

"Thanks, but it is your place now, too. There are only a couple things that are off limits—the mustang, my Harley, and my seat in the theater room," Christian said, only half-kidding.

If Mick was impressed with the yard, he was completely awestruck when they got back to the front porch and entered the house. The deep maroon entry door opened to a huge open space with hardwood floors as far as the eye could see. As they walked in, Christian continued his tour. There was a short wall in the middle of the otherwise open room that had hooks for coats and keys to various cars and other toys. Each hook was labeled.

Directly ahead was the kitchen. Stainless steel appliances filled the space, a huge gas cooktop sat in the middle of a granite island, a double convection oven was on the left side, and dark oak cabinets lined the walls. The fridge was a double wide that had two doors on top and a slide out freezer on the bottom. A dishwasher sat in the middle, next to the double sink.

"The laundry room is over there and the door to the garage is in there, as well as a half bath. I use it as a mud room to take off clothes if I have been out in the woods," Christian said, pointing to a door on the right side, just before the kitchen.

They next turned left at the end of the wall, just before the kitchen, and the rest of the room was completely open. The section closest to the kitchen, along the back side of the house, only had a 6-person table with dark wooden legs and a granite top that matched the kitchen island. Glass sliding doors on the back wall opened to the porch. The front half of the room had a large brown sectional and two recliners that faced a 60 inch flat screen. Aside from the coffee table and an area rug, the rest of the room was bare. The walls were sporadically covered with framed black and white photographs of nature and sporting scenes.

The wall on the far right was not the end of the house like Mick initially thought. It had an eight foot wide stone fireplace in the center, with French doors on both sides. Christian walked to the doors on the left and opened them wide. Mick stepped into the room and saw that the fireplace was visible on both sides. There was a large desk on the front wall that looked like it could have been from the 18th century. The rest of the room was covered with shelves of books. Two windows let light in from the side porch, or would have, if the curtains had not been drawn. A deep brown leather couch sat under the windows.

"This is my home office. I use this space to write, and to work on files that Agent Brooks, my FBI liaison, brings by. You are welcome to come in here and relax or read if you want. I just ask that you are quiet if I am in here writing," Christian said.

Mick noticed that both sets of doors led into this room. It seemed like a waste of space to him, but maybe the guy liked the symmetrical look that they created. With the amount of money that this place must have cost, he could do whatever he wanted.

They left the office and headed back to the wall in the middle of the room. Christian pointed toward the front of the house and said that the stairs to go up were over there, and the basement stairs were on the back side, which is where they were going.

At the bottom of the stairs was the entrance to a completely finished basement. It was split into a couple different parts. The side closest to the stairs had sporting tables, a pool table that was so old that it had handmade leather nets for pockets, a foosball table, a ping-pong table, dart boards on the wall, and a vintage Pac Man game. On the same wall was the door that led back up to the garage. Christian led Mick to the far wall, which had two doors as well. He opened the first and turned on the lights. Mick nearly fell over. The room was a huge home theater. The entire front wall was a movie theater style screen. There were four rows of leather stadium seats, and the walls were covered with signed sports and movie memorabilia.

"I like to come down here and just relax and watch a game or a movie. It is all yours unless there is a game on. You are always welcome to join me, but don't talk crap about the Pats and absolutely no NASCAR. I don't want to watch three hours of people turning left. Open wheel racing is a different story," Christian said.

Mick didn't want to leave the room, but he had to follow Christian, who was still talking. "This door over here leads to your SCIF. I am not supposed to go in there and I don't even know the code. When you get it sent to you by home office, just memorize it and destroy it."

Mick stared at the door for a second. The only thing that seemed different about it from any of the other doors was the key pad until he knocked on it. The hollow thud told him that it was a reinforced steel door like the ones used in safe rooms. At least he had somewhere to hide if Christian snapped.

The men left Mick's dream room and headed back up the stairs. They moved on to the second floor where Christian pointed out a couple of guest rooms, a guest bathroom, an open room that was likely intended to be a children's play room, and then they came to his room. It was on the far end of the house on the side closest to the river. The room itself was pretty large, about fifteen feet square, with additional rooms on each end. Four windows provided him a view of the river.

On the wall closest to the rear of the house was a walk-in closet and full bathroom. The bathroom had a walk-in shower and separate whirlpool tub. Travertine tile and Italian marble covered most of the surfaces. The side closest to the front of the house also had a door on it. He walked through the door and found that he had his own private den. One wall of the den had a door that walked out onto the top of the porch and created a balcony. The den had a desk about 5 feet wide and a recliner, along with boxes that hopefully held the contents of his old home.

"My room is on the other end, above the garage. I don't think you will have much of a reason to come in there, but if you do, I just want to warn you that I sleep in the nude," Christian said. Mick tried to get that image out of his mind as Christian continued. "That is basically the whole house. There is another floor, but it is just an open room with studded walls and plumbing and electrical run for lights and a bathroom. I hope I can get that finished, eventually. I hope your room is ok. If not we can figure something else out."

"Are you crazy? This place is friggin' awesome. Did you rob a bank or something?" Mick said before catching himself. "I mean, it's none of my business, but this is a lot of house for a guy so young."

"Don't worry about it. I know it is a little over the top, but it is everything that I could ever want. When my Dad was dying, he told me about how he owned this land but hadn't done anything with it, and that I should build my own personal Shangri-La. I think he figured that if I had everything here that I could possibly want, I would interact with people less in the real world. He was worried about, well you can guess," Christian said with a touch of sadness. "Before he died, we had the land cleared and we started having the house built. When he passed, he left me everything, including a sizable life insurance pay out. He also had squirreled away a lot of money over the years from Sicari. He lived off his FBI salary and saved everything else. This is what he wanted me to do, so I built it to honor him. I don't need all this stuff, and honestly, sometimes it makes me feel like a fake. Buddha taught us that material wealth is not the path to happiness, and this is an excess of material possessions."

"I don't think I would ever want to leave if this was my place," Mick joked.

"Seriously, think of this as your place. I want you to use anything here that will make you be able to feel at home and relax. My world has a lot of beauty in it, but it also has a lot of stresses. You are going to be with me for all of it.

"I spend my days working with children and adults who are going through some pretty horrible stuff and it can wear on you. When I am not doing that, I am helping the FBI on unsolved homicides. There is very little joy there, aside from catching the bad guy. I spend my free time writing about serial killers and some pretty nasty stuff. This place and all of the toys are how I get the images out of my head that I see day after day."

"I am sure that can't be easy," Mick interjected.

"You know the final piece of my life that the others don't, and it is the hardest part for me to live with. I have no idea what you must think of us, but I want you to know that I would give anything to not be this way. I fight the thoughts and needs every day. The only solace that I have is in knowing that the person that I am killing really deserved it. If I can stop them from hurting someone else, I can live with that. It isn't easy, but I am very good at it, and for now I need to do it," Christian said, opening up more than even he was expecting to.

"I would be lying if I told you that I knew what I thought yet. I have a lot of thoughts in my head. You seem like a great guy, and I believe that what you are doing is necessary, but I know how I felt when I had to pull the trigger in war. I still have nightmares and question myself about whether what I had to do was actually the right thing. I don't know exactly how you feel, but I understand the regret."

Both men stood in silence, the air seemingly heavier from the words they had just spoken. Seconds passed, but they felt like minutes. Mick didn't know what to say, and neither did Christian. Christian looked out the window, and the sight of the boathouse brought him back into the present moment.

"Feel free to unpack, or rest, or whatever you want. I need to set a few things up before Alex gets here. I will be running back and forth between the boathouse and the sheds if you need me. I plan to grill some steaks around 6 if you are hungry," Christian said, breaking the silence.

"I can help you if you want. I know my way around a grill pretty well. If not, I will probably unpack some and catch a cat nap. I am guessing that we are going to be up pretty late tonight."

"High tide is just before midnight, so we will be up until at least one o'clock. I am sorry but you will have to be there to document the whole night for Grayson. I know that you didn't have a lot of training on what to do, but Asher will be here and she can help you with the stuff that I don't know," Christian said.

"What do the tides have to do with tonight?" Mick asked.

"Don't worry about it yet. It is better that you don't know until tonight. You have plenty of time to deal with this stuff going forward. Get some rest," Christian said before leaving Mick alone in his new bedroom.

Mick quickly poked around the boxes to get an idea of where everything was before he stretched out on his new bed. He set his phone to go off at 5:30 and tried to sleep. One thought played over and over in his mind. *What is happening at high tide?*

Chapter 19

Ricky grabbed a steak from the plastic serving tray and put it on his plate with the potatoes and beans. These guys might be crazy, homicidal assholes but they sure did feed him well. He looked around for Old Jim and found him sitting alone at the picnic table at the far end of the clearing.

"Mind if I sit here?" he asked the old man as he approached.

"I don't mind at all," Jim responded before adding, "I was starting to wonder where you went off to earlier."

"Smalls took me and that Stephen guy back to the little clearing and had us dig a hole. It was only three feet deep but Stephen didn't want to leave when were done. He just sat there bitchin' about dying and us bein' next to go," Ricky explained.

"So you were gone that whole time to dig a hole?" Jim asked.

"Yeah, Smalls wanted it to be 6 feet by 3 feet and 3 feet deep. We did it right where they killed that Gene fella. What have you been up to?"

"Well they had me take some guys out to the back fields to show them where there were some good sized stones that were in the way. After that, Biggie had me put down some of them humane traps to catch some big rats that have been around here. Same weird shit, new day," Jim said.

"You don't think that Stephen was right about them killing one of us tonight, do you? You said that it doesn't happen that often and they just killed Gene last night," Ricky asked, hoping that Jim would agree with him.

"I don't know what to think any more. It doesn't make much sense to dig a hole out there unless they were gonna use it, but they don't normally kill people that close together. Hell, it could be for a damn pig roast for all I know," Jim said. He went back to stabbing his fork at a few random beans scattered around his plate.

The rest of the men ate in relative quiet. Each table held a conversation of its own, but there was no laughter or fun going on anywhere. The low hum of a dozen or so voices stopped when Smalls walked into view. Biggie stood next to him, and they whispered to each other, pointing in Ricky's direction.

The two men walked in unison around each of the picnic tables. They stopped in front of Ricky and Jim. Ricky's heart pounded in his chest as he waited for one of them to speak.

"Thanks for putting out those traps, Jim. They did a great job. We caught 3 huge rats. Mean bastards, too," Biggie said to Jim before turning to Ricky. "New guy, I heard about the hole you dug. Everyone is real happy with the job you did, but we need you to do it faster the next time."

The men turned and walked away from the tables, toward the nicer bunkhouse. They stopped at the final table and looked at Stephen. "I need you to come with me, Stephen. It's time," Biggie said to the seated man.

Stephen started crying, his sobs growing louder as the seconds went by. At first it appeared that he was not going to get up, but he eventually did. He walked next to Biggie and Smalls, his legs wobbling. They walked up the small hill and into the nicer bunkhouse. Stephen's cries grew louder and louder. He begged them not to choose him next. If he was being answered, no one could hear it. The rest of the men did nothing to help. None of them looked sad or even remotely upset. They all just turned and went back to eating. As long as they weren't chosen, they couldn't care less who else lived or died.

Ricky was appalled that no one else cared about Stephen's impending death, but he also felt immense relief that it wasn't him. He couldn't decide what was worse: dying or becoming like these other men who didn't care about anything other than their own survival.

Chapter 20

Christian and Mick sat in two patio chairs next to a fire in the huge stone pit at the far left side of the patio. It was shortly after 8, and they were waiting for Alex to show up. Christian had set everything up for the night's festivities, and now they just needed their guest of honor to arrive.

"Wasn't she supposed to be here a while ago? Do you think something went wrong?" Mick asked.

Christian laughed. "It is so cute that you think that Alex works with the same sense of time that the rest of the world does. She is on Alex time, and Alex time is at least 15 minutes behind the rest of us. She will be speeding down the road any minute and then she will get out of the car in a hurry like we are the ones that are slowing her down."

"So this is normal then?"

"It is as normal as anything gets with her," Christian said, taking a swig of his root beer. Normally, he preferred to sip scotch by the fire, but on the day of a Cleansing, he didn't drink alcohol. He wanted his senses to be as sharp as possible. "Seriously, if I ever need her to be here at a specific time for something, I give her a time that is at least an hour before I need her. That usually works out well. Usually."

As if on cue, the silence was broken by the roar of an overworked car engine. Within seconds, it sounded like it was right on top of them, as though the only thing stopping them from being run down was the enormous house behind them. Brakes squelched as the roaring beast came to a stop. A door was slammed shut with such force that it must have done something to piss Alex off. Footsteps pounded up the steps and onto the porch.

"Hey, Princess, we're out back," Christian yelled into the darkened night.

The footsteps got closer and closer. "Yeah, I noticed, asshole. I could see the smoke from like three shitty towns away. Are you trying to burn the forest down, or lure Smokey the Bear over for a chat?"

"Oh, just sit down and relax," Christian said to Alex before turning to Mick. "Isn't she sweet?"

"Like a church mouse," Mick laughed.

Alex grabbed one of the empty chairs and brought it over to where the men were sitting. "So are we good or is there something that we still need to do?"

"Everything is ready. All we are waiting for is your girl and her new friend to show up. Chill for a minute. It is going to get intense enough later," Christian reassured her. He tilted his head back onto the top of the chair's cushion and stared at the starlit sky. Orange sparks from the fire's embers popped and floated into the air, contrasting against the simple black and white of the perfectly clear night sky. It was almost hypnotic.

* * * * *

A lone bell rang in the distance, and Ricky followed the other men outside. Ten wheelbarrows were lined up next to the path leading to the fields. Half contained chunks of wood and the others held rocks, each at least the size of a basketball.

"Everyone grab a wheelbarrow and follow me," Smalls instructed.

The men rushed to get one of the first five. They held the wood and looked to be lighter. Everyone else settled for the rock carriers until they were all gone. Four men were left without anything to do, including Jim, who ran up to Ricky and offered to help with the stone filled wheelbarrow that he had been stuck with.

The first few men were able to stay close enough to Smalls to be guided by his flashlight, while the others had to rely on the full moon. The moonlight worked well until they reached the last path through the thick forest. It was almost pitch black. The only light came from the clearing in the distance. Several times during the short walk, the men bumped their wheelbarrows into the legs of the man in front of them, resulting in swearing and insults.

"Take the wood over to the pit and the stones to the back tree line," Smalls said to each person as they entered the clearing. He stood at the edge of the trail and used his flashlight to point as he spoke. The clearing practically glowed in the moonlight, so the flashlight was unnecessary.

"Everyone, toss the wood into the pit and make sure it's all in one pile. We'll spread it out after it is roaring," Smalls called out.

The men did as they were told. They took turns pulling wood from the wheelbarrows and tossing it into the darkened pit. When each wheelbarrow was empty, it was moved to the back tree line with the others. Smalls told everyone to take a seat on the log benches and then poured kerosene into the pit from a five gallon jug that he had carried with him. He lit a cigar with a book of matches and then tossed the flaming matches into the fire.

The lit matchbook met the combustible fumes long before it touched the woodpile, sending a ball of fire into the air. The heat from the bonfire was so intense that the men in the front row of logs had to turn away. Blue and orange flames danced around the pit. Smalls walked to the tree line and came back with what looked like banana leaves sticking out of a metal wash tub.

Ricky turned to Jim, feeling a sense of excitement and relief. "Hey, you might be right. Maybe we are having a pig roast or a clambake. This is how we used to do it back home. Or maybe we are making bean-hole beans."

"I don't think so," the old man replied.

"Why not? We have everything that we need. I have a bonfire to burn down to coals, wet banana leaves to put over the coals to make steam, and rocks to put on top of...." Ricky stopped when he noticed the missing item.

"The pig, we have everything but the pig."

* * * * *

"Okay, that was Asher. She is on her way and will be here in like fifteen minutes. Are you sure we are all set?" Alex asked Christian as she hung up her phone.

"Everything is good. We are ready. Do you want to take a walk around so I can show you everything?" Christian asked.

"Sure, we might as well get the plan together," Alex replied.

Alex and Mick followed Christian around to the front of the house. He pointed to a metal storage container that looked like it belonged on a ship, but was about a third of the usual size. "Asher and Mick will clean the car out and throw everything in the fire pit. Then we will put the car in there and RJ will be back for it around 6 tomorrow morning."

"What happens to it after that?" Mick asked.

"RJ is one of our vendors. He will take the car to his auto yard, strip any parts that he can resell, give them a new clean VIN number, and then crush the rest for scrap. He will melt it down after that. It is clean and there is nothing left," Christian explained.

Christian pointed to a dark object, just outside of the boat house. "After we are done, we will put the body in the pine box and then bring it up here," he tapped the ground and it sounded hollow. "There is a shallow hole under here that we can use for storage. You just cover it back over with dirt and it blends right in. Alfred will come by before dawn and pull the box out. He owns a funeral home and will cremate the remains before most people are even out of bed tomorrow."

"Another vendor?" Mick asked, getting the hang of the way things worked.

"No, he is an Asset. He helps us out and we help him out if he needs it," Alex answered before Christian could.

"Where is the actual Cleansing going to take place?" Mick asked.

"Inside the boat house," Christian answered.

"Won't we have evidence in there to dispose of, too?"

"It is going to be very clean. There shouldn't be a drop of blood spilled. Once he is down there, we won't even have to touch him again until it is all over. We will just wipe down a few things and we will be good," Christian responded.

"How are we going to manage that?" Mick asked.

Before Christian could answer him, a pair of halogen headlights lit up the road in front of them. The car slowly made its way down the driveway and came to a stop in front of them. As they each held up an arm to block the vibrant white light, Alex said, "Get ready boys, its game time."

* * * * *

The fire in the pit had died down, leaving behind a six foot expanse of glowing coals and embers. The acrid smell from the burning kerosene lingered, filling the noses of the silent men. Smalls stood at the edge, staring like a mesmerized zombie waiting for something to happen. A walkie talkie on his hip crackled to life.

"Hey, you on here?" came a distorted version of Biggie's voice.

"Yeah, I got ya coming through. What's up?" Smalls responded.

"I need you to come down to the field and meet me. My damn flashlight died and I can't see shit in the woods."

"No problem. I'm heading your way now," Smalls said as he started to walk toward the path. He turned to the men. "Don't you go getting any stupid ideas. The boundary isn't too far in the woods and if you make a run for it, BOOM! You are getting splattered all over a squirrel's house."

After leaving everyone with that adorable image, Smalls ran down the path toward the waiting Biggie.

Jim turned to Ricky and said, "I have been looking around but I haven't seen Stephen anywhere, have you?"

Ricky scanned the remaining faces and Stephen's was not one of them. He didn't respond to Jim. He just looked the old man in the eye and shook his head.

The feeble beam from Smalls' flashlight lit the path like a train coming out of a tunnel. When he came into view, he was accompanied by Biggie and another staggering man who looked like Stephen.

"New guy and Mike, get up by the pit," Biggie yelled.

Ricky and Mike tentatively walked up to the edge of the pit and waited for further instructions.

"Cover the middle of the coals over with the banana leaves but don't put the fire out," Smalls ordered.

Ricky and Mike reached into the wash basin and pulled out several dripping banana leaves each. They tried to gently drop them from above the pit and into the middle of the embers. A strip of orange disappeared as each leaf hit the bottom. The coals sizzled and a light steam wafted up. The fire was burning low but it was still hot. When the last one was placed in the pit, the center was completely dark but the edges continued to shine with a grey and orange hue.

"All set, Boss," Rickey called to Biggie and Smalls.

The men began walking towards them, half dragging the third man who was presumably Stephen. As they got closer, his identity was confirmed.

His head slumped backward and Stephen's face became clearly visible in the moonlight. He appeared to be in a similar state as Gene was when Ricky first saw him. His eyes were vacant and his muscles lax. *They must be giving them some sort of sedative before bringing them out,* Ricky thought.

"Don't just stand there with your thumbs up your asses. Come grab a goddamn leg," Biggie yelled at Ricky and Mike.

They quickly joined the three men at the far edge of the pit. Mike grabbed Stephen's right leg and Ricky the left. Biggie and Smalls each had an arm. As Stephen's legs

235

were lifted and his body became parallel to the ground, his head dropped back as though he was completely unconscious.

"Lower him in but be gentle. We want him on the leaves as much as possible," Biggie instructed.

All four men walked in unison, straddling the edge of the pit as they walked with two on each side. They then slowly lowered Stephen toward the center of the pit. Most of his body landed safely on the leaves, causing a rush of steam to shoot upward. His right hand flopped lifelessly to the side and landed on the coals. He didn't immediately react. Flesh sizzled as it rested on the hot wood embers. A new smell of burning hair filled the air. Stephen did not scream, he just aimlessly pulled his hand off the coals and to his side.

Ricky couldn't believe what was happening. He had dug that very hole less than fourteen hours earlier with the same man that he had just lowered into a pit to be cooked alive. How could anyone be that cruel?

Biggie yelled to the men and made the heinousness of the event even worse with one sentence. "Mike, go get one of those other wheelbarrows and bring the rocks up here."

* * * * *

A short, slender woman climbed out of the driver's seat and hugged Alex. She removed the blonde wig from her head revealing a short brown pixie cut.

"Hi Christian, how are you doing? You must be Mick? I'm Asher," the new arrival said, introducing herself.

"Nice to meet you," Mick responded.

"Is he good to go, or do I need to be prepared for a fight?" Christian asked.

"I slipped him a muscle relaxer. He should stay out until you want to wake him up." Asher replied.

Christian walked to the passenger side door and pulled the well-dressed middle aged man out of the car. He must have weighed over 180 pounds, but Christian lifted him onto his shoulder like he was a bag of potting soil. Christian carried the unconscious man across his back, fire fighter style, and headed for the boat house.

"Mick, you and Asher handle the car, and we will get set up down here," Christian yelled over his shoulder with no sign of strain apparent in his voice.

Mick and Asher rushed to remove all the contents from the man's car. Anything that had a name on it went into a cardboard box. The car was a rental, so there wasn't much in it to remove. Asher told Mick to throw the box in the fire, and she would put the car into the container. A minute later, they met on the lawn and started walking toward the boat house.

As they reached the door, Mick hesitated. He wasn't sure that he wanted to see what was on the other side. It was like Schrodinger's cat: as long as he didn't open the door, all possibilities were still on the table. When that door was opened, the truth would become his reality.

Asher stepped ahead of Mick and pushed the door open. They both stepped into the house and looked around. It looked like what the average person would expect a boat house to be. The walls were covered with fishing poles, kayaks, canoes, and marine tools. The floor was wood and had a few other related tools on it, but was mostly clear of clutter. The center of the floor was open to the water below and a boat sat in the slip. A garage style door took up most of the river side wall and was lowered to water level. Aside from Christian, Alex, and Asher, the only thing that Mick saw was a large diver's cage like you would see people use when they were swimming with sharks on TV.

Inside the cage sat the semiconscious man. Alex scooped water into a bucket from the exposed river behind the cage. The cage itself was on a pulley and hovered just above the open water. Alex threw the water onto the slouching man who popped back to alertness.

"What they hell is going on. Where am I?" the man yelled as he looked around the boathouse. He looked down, saw the water below him, and backed into the corner of the cage as though that position was somehow safer.

"It is possible that this is a big misunderstanding, Sir. Maybe you can help us clear that up," Christian said, trying to focus the man's attention on him.

"You! You drugged me you fucking bitch! Let me out of here!" the man yelled when he caught sight of Asher. He recognized her immediately, even without the blonde wig. She needed to work on her disguises.

"Sir, I am going to ask you again. What is your name?" Christian repeated.

"My name?" the man responded as though he was perplexed by the question. "My name is Dean. Dean Costa. Can I get out now?"

"I am sorry. I wish I could let you out but you are, in fact, the right man," Christian said. "I appreciate your honesty and your continued truthfulness will be necessary for the rest of our time together."

"I am in a cage that you say I can't get out of. What good will playing along do?" Costa asked.

"It will get you a merciful death," Christian said.

Mick noticed a change in Christian and Alex. She seemed to be more amped up and ready to bounce off the walls. She paced back and forth like a wild tiger in a zoo, angry and predatory. Christian, on the other hand, was even calmer than usual. It was creepy how reserved he was.

"You are going to kill me? What the hell did I do to you? I don't even know you!" Costa begged.

"You are right. You don't know me. Let's talk about someone that you do know," Christian said. "Remember, honesty is your only friend here tonight. Tell me about an employee that you had around here named Greg."

"Greg? Is that what this is about? Hey, I am sorry about having to let him go but business is business. I have to make the bottom dollar work, or my bosses are going to chew me out. Greg knew that when he signed up. Is he still bitching about getting canned? That was like a fucking year ago."

"Greg isn't bitching. He is dead you fucking prick!" Alex yelled, grabbing the bars of the cage.

"Alex!" Christian yelled. "You either get your shit together or you are going to have to wait outside."

"Mr. Costa, you said it yourself. You believe that you should put profits ahead of people. I disagree with your priorities, but that is not the point here..." Christian said.

"What is the fucking point? Is the point that you are all nuts? I saw all your faces and you are all going to jail. All of you," Costa yelled as he grabbed the bars of the cages and pulled. The cage began to swing back and forth on its metal wire. It nearly hit the bow of Christian's boat. He dug around in his suit jacket's pockets and then moved to his pants. His wallet and cell were both gone. He wouldn't be calling the police after all.

"As I was saying before you so rudely interrupted me," Christian continued in his eerily calm tone, "The point of this all is that you chose to put your own personal business gains ahead of the health and welfare of a loyal and valuable employee. Your actions put a hard working family man out of a job. The loss of that job led directly to him losing his family, his home, and eventually pushed him into taking his own life. What do you have to say about that?"

"I say it isn't my fault that his marriage sucked and that he was too much of a loser to find another job. Life is a bitch. Deal with it and move on," Costa yelled. "Now, let me out of here!"

"I wish that you were at least bothered by the death of one of your own employees, but since you seem to see no problem with your behavior, it is time to move on to the next phase of our evening," Christian said as he walked over to the far wall.

Christian pushed a button on a switch that was hooked to the wall. The pulley's winch screeched into action, slowly lowering the cage toward the water. Alex stepped forward and guided it over the water until the bottom had safely dropped below the floor. Christian stopped the winch and walked to the edge of the opening where he knelt down to face Costa.

"Even though there is nothing that you can do to prevent this situation, I am going to explain to you what is about to happen. I am going to lower this cage into the water until you touch the bottom. You will be standing in about 3 feet of cold water. The tide is coming in and the water level will rise over the next hour.

"Much like Greg could see his troubles piling up and knew that he was powerless to stop them, you are going to feel the water rising around you. It will continue to come in, wave after wave, inch after inch, until the tide is at its fullest point. The water level will stop, but by then it will be about 4 inches over the top of the cage when it does.

"You will struggle to draw in every breath possible as you watch the water get higher and higher. There will, however, come a point when you will know that nothing you do will stop the inevitable. You will give in to death, and you will feel genuine regret for what you have done. Unfortunately for you, it will be too late, just like time ran out for Greg."

Costa's eyes filled with terror as Christian's words sank in. Christian pressed the button and the cage lowered little by little. Costa's expensive leather shoes filled with water. The cool liquid moved up his leg, submerging his ankles, then his knees, and finally his waist. The cage jerked to a stop as it sank into the muddy river bottom.

"Now, we wait," Christian said, sitting on a bucket by the edge of the water.

* * * * *

"All of you get up and form a line over here," Biggie yelled to the men who were still sitting on the logs.

The men walked around the edge of the pit without looking in. They may have been happy that they were not in the hole, but that didn't mean they wanted to see the man who was. They dutifully formed a line next to the first wheelbarrow.

"Each of you will now pick up a stone," Biggie commanded and they all complied. "One by one, you will walk to the edge and place the stones on top of Stephen. Do not put it on his head and try not to drop it on him, please."

Each and every man walked up, one after the other, and placed the heavy stones into the pit. Ricky put his on Stephen's leg so that he wouldn't cause him too much pain. Other men attempted a similar tactic but it didn't go unnoticed. The first wheelbarrow quickly emptied.

"Go grab the next wheelbarrow," Biggie yelled. "All of these go on his chest. If I see any of you put one somewhere else, I will beat you to death with the damned thing."

The men did as they were told. The stones soon covered Stephen's chest. He was still in a medicated stupor but as Ricky lowered his stone on to the pile he could hear Stephen straining to breathe against all the pressure and weight.

"I'm sorry," Ricky whispered before getting back in line.

"We don't want to kill him yet. Spread the rest of the stones out on the other parts of his body," Biggie instructed.

One by one, the stones were removed from the wheelbarrows, and eventually they all sat empty. The collective sadness was darker than the now cloud-filled night. The men solemnly stood as they waited for their friend to be slowly crushed to death under the immense weight that they had each helped to create. Each time he exhaled, the rocks compressed his chest more, making less room for the next breath. It wouldn't be long now.

"Are you boys gonna cry? Don't worry, we aren't done yet," Biggie mockingly said to the group. "Go grab the shovels."

* * * * *

The water continued to rise. It was now nine inches from the top bar of the cage. Costa could no longer stand without being under the surface, so he treaded water and held on to the top of his watery prison. Even as his imminent death drew nearer, he stood defiant in the face of his accusers.

"You are all just like Greg. He wasn't man enough to face up to his responsibilities, and you had to drug me and put me in a cage. You didn't have the balls to face me in a fair fight," he hissed at the quartet of onlookers.

No one took the bait, and the water continued to rise. Soon, it was almost level with the top bars. Costa began to break down. "OK, I give in. I am so sorry. I would fix it if I could, but I can't. Greg's dead, and there is nothing we can do about it," he sobbed.

The water level incrementally rose, and Costa had no choice but to stick his mouth and nose through the top bars to try and breathe. The gentle waves lapped at the outside of the boathouse. Inside the room, they sloshed over Costa's face, thwarting his attempts at breathing. Sensing the end was near; Alex walked over to him and stood on the top of the cage. Water rolled over the tops of her sneakers.

She knelt down and said "This is for Greg. I hope you like hell, asshole," she placed the top of her right foot on Costa's face and pushed it below the surface. The water churned as he grasped at her leg, trying to push it away. Fifteen seconds passed, and then thirty. A few more and the thrashing stopped. Costa's hands dropped into the water and fell out of sight.

Christian walked over and gently pulled her onto the floor. He held her in his arms and whispered, "It is all over now." Alex sobbed loudly into his shoulder. Asher stood and waved at Mick. He followed her out of the room and left Christian and Alex alone for a private moment between friends.

* * * * *

"Fill in the pit," Biggie commanded.

"But he is still alive in there," said a voice that Ricky did not recognize.

"Not for long, he isn't," Biggie said with a laugh.

There were only two shovels so the men took turns walking over to the area where Ricky and Stephen had thrown the clumps of sod. They each walked over, got a shovelful, and dumped it into the pit before handing the shovel off to the next man in line.

"I need someone to come dig him up tomorrow before breakfast. I'll come knocking bright and early and tell you who I want to do it. Same drill as before, wrap him in a tarp and put him in the back of the truck," Smalls said.

The men continued to fill in the hole. They left his head for last, but it didn't seem to matter. His breathing got weaker, and dirt began to fall from the mound on his chest and onto his face. He appeared to try to spit some out of his mouth. It was the first sign of life that Ricky had seen. He prayed to a God that he didn't believe in that Stephen would stay unconscious until the end. He grabbed a shovelful of dirt and slowly walked to the edge of the pit. Partly out of pity but mostly out of mercy, he lowered the shovel into the pit and let the dirt and rocks slide off the metal spade, covering Stephen's face. That small amount of dirt brought an end to the suffering of the man who Ricky had only shared a day long friendship with. Two days at the farm, and two men were dead. Ricky almost hoped that he would be next.

Chapter 21

Mick's alarm started playing but it didn't wake him. He had been staring at the ceiling in his new bedroom for hours. After wiping down the boathouse and helping Christian, Alex and Asher carried the pine box containing Dean Costa to the "spider hole" hiding spot near the driveway. He had gotten to bed just before 1 AM.

He had fallen asleep relatively quickly but didn't stay there for long. Right away, dreams of being locked in the diving cage as it slowly filled with water began. He awoke in a dark room that he didn't recognize with a light scent of something burning in the air. He was initially alarmed by the smell before realizing that it was just from the contents of the cardboard box he had tossed in the fireplace.

The few hours since his dream had been spent lying on his new bed and listening to the sounds of nature in the nearby woods. He had never been somewhere so quiet before. He was at least 500 feet from the closest tree line, but he could hear the nocturnal animals scurrying about. Owls hooted in the distance and a scattered band of various insects serenaded him. None of these things helped him to get his thoughts to move on from what he had witnessed just hours before.

The oddest part of his thoughts was that he wasn't really sure how he felt about what had happened. He had known for several hours that Costa was going to die, but seeing it happen was a whole other ball of wax. He had expected something vicious, like all of the violence he had encountered during deployment, but this was almost...poetic.

The ravages of war had shown him more battered, bloody, and dismembered corpses than he had ever wanted to be near. Maybe that is why the stillness of Costa's body had been so unnerving. He looked like he could awaken from a deep slumber at any point.

He had prepared himself for a near monstrous transformation to occur in Christian, but it never came. He had remained cool and calm the whole time. After the vile man had succumbed to the cold embrace of his watery demise, Christian did not seem happy or satisfied. Mick even thought that he saw a twinge of sadness. This left Mick wondering what he had actually just experienced.

As Mick got out of bed and into the shower, another thought entered his mind: Had Christian actually killed the man? Christian *had* prepared the boathouse. He *had* carried Costa to the room but did he put him in the cage? Mick assumed so, but he did not see it happen. He did push the button that lowered the cage into the water, but it was Alex who had forced the man's life to leave his body. Sure, he would have drowned soon enough anyway, but she made it happen on her terms. Christian was supposed to perform the Cleansing; but did he? Is this the kind of thing he was supposed to report back to Grayson?

Mick finished his shower, dressed in his brand new clothes, and went downstairs to the kitchen. After spending the last 12 years in Army issue clothing, it felt odd to be dressed like a civilian. It almost felt like he was playing "dress up".

Christian was standing behind the island, cooking on the flattop. His bare chest was still damp from his shower. Mick couldn't help but stare. How was a psychiatrist that ripped? The guy looked like one of those anatomical drawings that showed all the muscles. When did he even have time to work out? Mick remembered something that Christian had said the afternoon before that made him turn away. *I like to sleep naked.*

"Hey Christian, you are dressed, right?" he asked.

"Yeah, I have shorts on. I just didn't want to get anything splattered on my shirt while I made breakfast. I am making omelets. Want one?" Christian asked.

"Sure, I will have whatever you are having."

Five minutes later, Mick sat on the other side of the table from his still shirtless roommate. The egg white omelet, whole wheat toast, grapefruit, and some sort of smoothie that Christian had made him had nearly been devoured. A man could get used to living like this. It sure beat the hell out of the mess hall.

"I am going to go throw on some clothes and be ready to go in five. Does that work for you?" Christian asked as he cleared his dishes and some of Mick's off the table.

"Yeah, I am ready whenever you are," Mick replied. He finished clearing his plates and then walked out onto the porch. It was just before 7:30, and the morning was beautiful. The air was noticeably chillier than he was used to, but he could easily adapt to it. This place felt like paradise.

Mick looked for the container that held Costa's rental car, but it was gone. How had he missed that being picked up? A tow truck dragging a heavy metal container onto its flatbed must have made a hell of a racket. A quick look in the spider hole revealed that it was empty as well. It was as though last night was just a dream. Nothing about this picturesque location said a man was murdered here last night.

A garage door loudly opened behind him, causing Mick to turn his head. The Venza was backing out into the early morning sun and when it stopped, Mick climbed in.

"It is so beautiful here. I have never seen anything like it. I am glad I came," Mick said. It was an awkward thing to say but it felt right.

"I am sincerely glad you like it here, Mick. It is really important to enjoy yourself. I think you will find that this area has a lot to offer," Christian replied.

Neither spoke much for the majority of the ride into the city. Mick stared out the window at the people who were just getting into the flow of their day. Children stood at the end of driveways while waiting for a school bus to pick them up. Cars and trucks turned into the parking lots of several different coffee shops and roadside diners. This place was like a throwback to the "good ol' days". He half expected to see Sheriff Andy and Deputy Barney Fife around the next turn.

"Even though it is against my nature, I am not going to ask you about your feelings regarding last night. You can always talk to me if you want to but I am not going to push," Christian said as they entered the relative hustle and bustle of Portland. "I do, however, need to ask you a favor. You don't need to do it. That is your call, but I do need to ask."

"Sure, what is it?" Mick asked.

"Alex was concerned about what you saw last night. We technically broke the rules by letting her be there. Grayson had permitted her to be here last night, but allowing her to finish him off violated about forty different regulations by itself. It is up to you about how you want to file your report, but I know what she is hoping for. Normally, I wouldn't have let her be there, but this was very emotional for her. She needed the closure to move past her friend's death," Christian explained. "I know that the analysts don't see that concept as important, but as a therapist and her friend, I knew that she wouldn't have been as able to move on if she hadn't been there. It was my call and I will deal with the consequences if you decide to report the violations. I just wanted to let you know why I made that decision."

"I understand. I don't see why it needs to be brought up. The plan was flawlessly executed and there is nothing left that could track it back to anyone who was there last night. As far as I am concerned, it was a clean cleansing," Mick said. He surprised himself that he felt so secure about lying to Grayson about it. It seemed like the right thing to do, but who knows how he would feel when it came time to do the actual paperwork later.

The car pulled into a quiet parking garage under Christian's office building. They got out of the car and took the stairs to the third floor. Once there, they walked around the corner and Christian opened a glass door that simply said "300" on the outside. There was nothing that indicated what the office was for or to whom it belonged.

"Good morning, Anita. Did you miss me?" Christian asked a short blonde woman of around fifty who sat at the desk nearest the door.

"Immensely. I could barely stand it," Anita responded. "How was the trip? Is this the new intern?"

"The trip was basically uneventful. Thankfully, I shouldn't have to do it again for a while. Yes, this is Mick Healy. Mick this is Anita. She is the only reason that we stay open," Christian said with a smile.

"If I didn't schedule the appointments and bill the insurances, no one would have a job here. Dr. Nice Guy over there would just do this for free if I let him. Nice to meet you, Mick," Anita said before diving into the day's schedule. "You are open until 9, but then you have back to backs and then nothing from 11 to 1. Do you have anything you need me to add?"

"Yes, Agent Brooks will be coming by around noon to go to lunch with Mick and I. I don't know how much time he will need. You know how he is. Do I have anything else scheduled for the afternoon?"

"I have one of those pharmaceutical company guys coming in to pitch you some new ADHD drug at 1, but that is it."

"Okay then, I will be in my office with Mick until 9. Just buzz me if the patient arrives early. I am sure he will want a break from me by then," Christian said before walking down the hall.

Christian's office was not what Mick had expected. After seeing "Castle Rinaldi", he had expected something more ornate. This was pedestrian by anyone's definition. The room barely consisted of anything other than a desk, computer, comfortable chairs, and books. Maybe he didn't want anything to distract his patients or something. If that was his goal, he succeeded.

Christian and Mick had barely settled in to their seats when the phone rang. Christian hit the speaker button. "Yes, Anita?"

"Dr. Rinaldi, there is a young man here who is asking to see you. He says he is your brother?" Anita said as more of a question than a statement.

"Go ahead and send him on back, thank you, Anita," Christian said, puzzled.

"Brother? I thought you were an only child and adopted?" Mick asked.

"You are right on both counts. Believe me, I am as confused as you are," Christian said as he waited for the door to open.

The mystery brother knocked on the door and Mick opened it. The man's face was familiar to Christian, but he didn't readily recognize him.

"Christian?" the man asked as though he was not sure who he was talking to.

"Yes. I don't mean to be rude, but you told Anita that you were my brother?" Christian said quizzically.

"Yeah, sorry about that," the man said, rubbing the back of his neck nervously. "I didn't know how to explain that we were in the same foster home around 20 years ago and that you might not remember me. Brother seemed easier."

Christian stared at the man. He seemed very familiar, but 20 years ago would have made Christian 13 and at that time he had been with Vinnie for a year. It was just him and Vinnie, no other children or even a pet at that age. The man in front of him would have been around 10 years old back then. There is a huge difference between what someone would have looked like at 10 and the man Christian saw in front of him.

This brother was almost Christian's height and was lean and muscular like a swimmer. Christian tried to think of any 10 year olds he knew with sandy blonde hair and blue eyes from when he lived with his adoptive father. He couldn't think of any. The man must have meant the placement before moving in with Vinnie which would mean...

"Andy?" Christian guessed. The only boy at the Melanson house that was around that age was a quiet little guy named Andy. It had to be him, right?

A smile crept across the young man's face. "Yes, holy crap, I didn't think you would remember me!"

"Mick, this is Andy. He and I shared a bedroom at my second to last foster home. Andy, this is Mick. He is my new intern. Today is his first day, actually," Christian said, oddly relieved.

"Nice to meet you, Andy. I'm Mick Healy. Well I guess he already said that," Mick said laughing at himself.

"Andrew Melanson. I haven't been called Andy in like 15 years, but that is cool," Andy said.

"Melanson? Did you get adopted? That is so great!" Christian said, trying to hide his disdain for the name that filled his nightmares.

"Yeah, I guess it wasn't long after you moved. Mom decided to adopt those of us who were in the house. That was it. They didn't take in any more kids. Well, with Dad's issues, they really couldn't," Andy explained. He got more somber as he talked about an apparent illness.

Issues? Did he know what Mr. Melanson had been doing? Is that what he means? Christian thought to himself.

"How are they? I haven't seen them since I was moved," Christian asked. He had been quite fond of Birdie Melanson. She was extremely nice; the polar opposite of her husband.

"They are both gone. Mom passed away a few years back and the Muscular Dystrophy finally took Dad last fall," Andy explained.

"I am really sorry to hear that. What have you been up to for all of these years?" Christian asked.

"I went in the Navy after high school, but then Dad got worse and I started coming back here more often. After my 8 years were up, I left the Navy and just moved back here to help him out. He left me the farm and now I am trying to make that work," Andy continued.

"Wow, so you are running that big old place by yourself? That can't be easy," Christian said before turning to Mick. "The farm we are talking about is pretty huge. They used to grow like 15 different vegetables and raised around a dozen types of animals."

"That is crazy. You do that all by yourself?" asked Mick.

"Oh no, I couldn't do that. We've scaled back the operation quite a bit and I mainly handle the logistical stuff. Dad had a couple of guys, brothers actually, who started helping him back when I enlisted. I convinced them to stay on and they basically have full run of the farm and oversee the guys that work there. They only come to me if there is something they need from me."

"Well that is good to hear. I don't want to cut you short, but I have a patient coming in a few minutes. Maybe we could catch up sometime outside of here," Christian offered.

"I am free for lunch if you are," Andy suggested.

"Oh, I can't today. I have a meeting," Christian said. When he saw the look of disappointment on Andy's face he added, "I am free for dinner. Would that work?"

Andy's face lit up once again. The shy boy that Christian remembered was still hiding in the body of a fully grown man. "Yeah, that would be great. Do you mind if I bring a couple of my farmhands with me? They rarely leave the farm and I think they could use some time away."

"No, that sounds fine. Here is my address," Christian said, writing his address on a scrap piece of paper. "We will walk you out."

"Awesome, thank you. I am really looking forward to it," Andy said as they walked down the hall toward the doors.

An unexpected surprise met the men at the front door. Two men in Portland Police Department uniforms were waiting in the lobby.

"Good morning, officers. Is there something we can assist you with?" Christian asked as Andy slipped out the door.

"Yes," the first officer said as he held up a picture. "We would like to talk to you about this man."

Mick recognized the face before the officer finished his statement.

The officer handed the picture to Christian and said, "His name is Dean Costa."

Chapter 22

Christian stared at the photo for several seconds before showing it to Mick. Mick struggled to appear calm on the outside while his heart pounded. He was going to jail. He didn't do anything other than help move a body, but that would still be enough to put him away for a long time. He was unable to speak, so he just shook his head.

Christian was much more balanced under pressure than his new protégé. "I am sorry officers, he doesn't look familiar. Should I know him?"

"He isn't a local. He is visiting from out of state and we got a missing person's call when he didn't show up for his meeting," the first officer explained.

"I didn't realize that you investigated people who missed meetings," Christian said.

"Normally we don't. Apparently, he is very punctual and his local coworkers went to his hotel room and his stuff was there but he wasn't. They got worried and called us," the second officer added.

"And you have reason to think that we would have seen him?" Christian asked.

"No, he had a meeting in this building yesterday and that was the last time that he was seen. We are just checking to see who might have crossed paths with him during the course of yesterday," Officer one continued.

"Oh, that makes sense, but we were not here yesterday. I was in Boston until the afternoon. I was with FBI Agent Randy Brooks after that. Today is Mick's first day in Portland," Christian explained. "The only person in the office yesterday was my office manager, Anita. It is possible that she saw him."

"Okay, Sir. Sorry to have interrupted your day. Enjoy the weekend," Officer two said before walking to Anita's desk.

"Not a problem. If you will excuse me, I am expecting a patient to arrive any second," Christian said.

"She didn't see him either," the returning second officer said. "Thank you for your time."

The two officers left and Mick could finally breathe again. He stared at Christian, who just shrugged his shoulders and walked toward Anita.

"Well that was exciting," Anita said as he stood in front of her. "I don't think your new guy could handle much more. PTSD?"

"No, I just think that being a civilian takes time to get used to," Christian said, glancing at Mick, who still hadn't moved.

Mick snapped back into consciousness and said, "Oh, sorry, I just didn't sleep well last night. I am not used to the quiet."

Thankfully for Mick, the excitement calmed down for the next hour. Christian had seen his first patient and was on to his second when there was a knock on the door of Mick's new office. He was trying to get it set up, but he didn't really have anything to put in it. He looked up and saw a man standing in his doorway.

The man was around his height and was about his weight, but it was distributed differently. This man had a less developed physique and a little bit of midlife flab around his waist. Not a lot of fat, but just enough to push the top of his belt down. His brown suit was ill-fitting and likely off the rack at a retail clothing store. The holstered gun on his hip gave Mick an idea as to who he was.

"Hi there, you must be Mick," the man said, extending his hand. "Randy Brooks."

"Nice to meet you, Agent Brooks," Mick said as he shook the man's hand. "I am sorry, but Christian, I mean Dr. Rinaldi, is with a patient."

"That is ok, I just got here a little early and thought I would pop in to meet you," Brooks said.

"Of course, have a seat. I really don't have anything in here to offer you, but I think that chair is supposed to be comfortable," Mick said, pointing to the only other piece of furniture in the room.

After several minutes of awkward silence and questions about how they each liked living in Maine, the conversation naturally fell to their only common connection.

"How did you meet Dr. Rinaldi?" Mick asked.

"Now, that is actually an interesting story," Agent Brooks started as he leaned back in his seat. This was going to take a while. "I had been here for a few weeks and I was going stir crazy. Homicides that required our assistance or other federal crimes were very rare around here. Finally, one Saturday night we got a call about a death at the home of a very wealthy family a couple of towns over. The local PD called us in."

"Because of the death or who it was?" Mick asked.

"It was the money piece that brought us into the picture. Well, it was also because it happened at a party with dozens of other wealthy people in attendance." Brooks continued. "It was around mid-November, and the party was a late Halloween costume thing. It was very over the top. They had a band, two stages set up, fog machines, laser light shows, caterers in tuxes, and the whole deal. This thing must have cost half of my annual salary.

"Once we found our way through the partygoers and into the most expensive house that I have ever seen—yes, it was even bigger than Doc's place—we found the wife and her lawyer waiting in the dining room."

"Wait, her lawyer beat you guys to the scene?" Mick asked.

"He was already at the party," Brooks answered. "Anyway, I was talking to the wife and she said that her husband had gone down to the basement to have a cigar in this giant, walk-in humidor. She went in to check on him two hours later when he hadn't returned, and she found him dead in the closed room. She didn't even open it, she called a friend down to look and they called the police. The coroner said that he appeared to have had a heart attack. He did a liver temp check and estimated the time of death at an hour earlier. The guy had some heart and lung issues but still had a cigar every night. Seemed like an easy report."

"But...?" Mick asked.

"But, a tall man dressed in a super hero costume walked up and said, 'Agent, this was a homicide and I know who did it'. I didn't know who he was, so I told him to go give one of the officers his statement and we would look into it," Brooks shook his head as he spoke. "It looked like an open and shut case. Home security cameras showed that the last person to enter or leave the property was the wife, just after the husband went into the basement. She left again 45 minutes before T.O.D. so we didn't see any way that she could have done it.

"The guy came back again and told me that the wife did it, and that he could prove it. I told him that there was no reason to believe that there was any foul play. He gave me his card and told me to give him a call when the autopsy showed that, aside from a possible heart attack, we would find abnormally high levels of carbon dioxide in the man's blood, and a blue tinge to his lips and fingers. He also said that the man would have an unfinished cigar in his hand, and it would not have burned down to a stub or have been stamped out by him."

"I am guessing that all of those things came back as true," Mick said.

"Yes, but I only found out because I looked into the reports myself. I had a nagging voice in the back of my head about what he said. I actually thought he might be a suspect until I mentioned his name around the office. They told me that he had consulted with the previous Agent in Charge and that he had some sort of gift for seeing what people missed. They jokingly called him 'The Witch Doctor'" Brooks laughed. "I figured that I should go check this guy out. I came here to this same office and showed him the test results. He restated his belief that the wife had done it."

"Was he right?" Mick asked.

"Do you have somewhere you need to be or do you want to hear the story?"

"I'm sorry, go ahead," Mick apologized.

"Okay, so where was I? Well, I put the file in front of him and told him to tell me why he thought it was a homicide and why the wife was his suspect. He asked if he was right about everything and I told him that he was. I also pointed out that no one had been in the house since the wife left, and multiple witnesses placed her on the stage, butchering several really good songs with the band, at the time of his death. I said that the guy was all-alone in the humidor, and that there was no sign of poison or anything other than the few abnormalities that Doc had already guessed.

"He asked me if the door to the humidor had hissed when it was opened. I didn't know what the hell he was talking about, and it wasn't mentioned in the notes. He asked me to call the officer that opened the door, so I did. The officer thought about the question and confirmed that there was a weird hissing or sucking sound when he opened the door. I asked Doc how the wife could have done it, and he pointed to the security camera photo of the wife walking into the house with a couple cardboard boxes.

"She had made two trips into the house just after the husband went in, and she carried two of the same boxes in with her each time. She didn't bring anything out of the house with her when she left. Doc dug out the photos of the humidor and pointed to the same boxes in that picture."

"What was in the boxes?" Mick asked, growing impatient.

"That was the weird thing. They were empty. They were just plain cardboard boxes with the party planner's logo on the outside and a clear trash bag inside each one. The kicker was that they were *sealed* with tape and unopened. The only open spot on the boxes at all were the holes where you put your hands in to carry them," Brooks said. "Do you have any ideas?"

"I have no idea," Mick answered.

"I didn't either. I asked him what was in them and he said that the boxes had contained..." Brooks started.

"Dry ice," Christian interrupted. Neither man had noticed him walk up to the door. "The boxes had dry ice in them for the fog machines. The wife brought them in the house and asked her husband to put them in the humidor to keep them out of the way. The dry ice melted in the humidity-controlled room. The thing about a humidor is that in order for it to serve its purpose, it needs to tightly seal when the door closes so that nothing gets into the room, not even air.

"The air that we breathe is about 21% oxygen, 78 % nitrogen, just under 1% argon, and less than a percent is other gases, including carbon dioxide. Most carbon dioxide in the air is from us exhaling. The humidor has lower levels of oxygen so that the tobacco leaves in the cigars don't mold. The carbon levels are also slightly lower.

"When dry ice melts, it doesn't turn into a liquid because it is pure carbon dioxide. The carbon dioxide level in the room skyrocketed when the ice melted, and when you mixed that with the already low oxygen levels in the room and the man's preexisting medical issues, he suffocated. He would have just gotten sleepy and passed out. His heart would go into cardiac arrest because of the low oxygen, and he would die right there."

"Okay, but how did you know about the blue lips, fingers, and the half smoked cigar?" Mick asked, stunned and confused.

"Oxygen is what turns blood red. Carbon dioxide turns it blue. That is why you see the two different colored arteries and veins if you look at your arms right now. One is leaving the heart and lungs with fresh oxygen and the other is full of old blood coming back so the lungs can get rid of the carbon dioxide. People with low oxygen levels will have bluer blood in their lips and extremities because the body sends the limited "good blood" where it is needed most," Christian answered.

Mick looked at his arms and studied the veins and arteries for a second. "Ok, and the cigar?"

"The cigar? It was just the same basic principle. The smoldering ash at the end of the cigar needs oxygen to keep burning. When the oxygen became so low, it burned slower and slower until it went out," Christian explained.

"And that is how we met," Brooks said, finishing the story.

"What happened to the wife?" Mick asked.

"At first she was adamant that she was innocent and that he had died from a heart attack. Then we brought Doc in to talk to her. They knew each other socially, and he thought she might talk to him. Her lawyer told her not to say anything, and then the Doc here, he just explained why he knew that she did it. An hour later, she took a plea deal," Agent Brooks said with a satisfied smile.

"So, enough about ancient history. Where do you want to eat lunch today, Agent?" Christian asked.

"Well, I was hoping that we could eat somewhere over by my office," Brooks replied with a sheepish smirk. "We picked up a guy who met most of the religious nut criteria that we talked about yesterday, and I was hoping you could give us an opinion. He seems to be a little out of it and that is kinda your specialty, right?"

"So, you basically picked someone up who fits one part of the profile, the part that I said I didn't think was accurate, and you want me to interview him?" Christian asked.

"Yeah, that's about right. I just have a hunch. If I am wrong, I will buy the steaks tonight."

"Oh crap, I forgot that we were having dinner tonight," Christian said, embarrassed. "I invited my old foster brother over for dinner, so I hope that is cool."

"Not a problem, it would be fun to meet someone who knew you as a kid. Maybe they can tell me why you are so damn weird," Brooks said laughing.

If you only knew, Christian thought to himself. *You don't want to know about me as a kid.*

Chapter 23

Rolleston "Rollie" Ambrose spastically twitched in the interrogation chair. Unfortunately for him, he was on the wrong side of the table. The good side had two chairs that actually moved. His was bolted to the floor. The good side of the table was flat and smooth. His had a metal loop that secured his handcuffs. The other side was the much better one to be on.

Agent Brooks, Mick, and Christian stood in the room adjacent to Interrogation, watching the extremely confused man from the "good side" of the two way mirror.

"This isn't our guy," Christian said, shaking his head and looking at Rollie's file.

"You haven't even talked to him yet," Brooks responded. He hated when Doc made snap decisions. Okay, he only hated them when those decisions disagreed with him. The rest of the time, he was happy that they saved so much time. Christian was always able to see the whole movie from beginning to end while everyone else was still waiting for the previews to be over.

"I will interview him and I *will* keep an open mind, but I can tell you right now that he is not capable of committing these crimes," Christian explained.

268

"Maybe he is, and maybe he isn't, but he might know who did it," Brooks said, grasping at straws.

Christian took the file and left the room. Fifteen seconds later, he reappeared on the other side of the glass and took a seat. He took the first minute to just look over the file, which he had already memorized. One of the great benefits of having an eidetic memory is never having to read the same thing more than once. This review was just for show.

"Ok, I have a question," Mick said as he watched his new mentor prepare to question Rollie. "Why do you keep calling it an interview? I thought the term was interrogation. It is even on the door."

"It is a stupid thing, semantics really," Brooks explained. "When I do it, it is an interrogation. Doc isn't officially a member of law enforcement, so he isn't allowed to "interrogate" a suspect. However, he is allowed to "interview" anyone he wishes. If the information gathered during his interview just so happened to be observed by a member of law enforcement, then they would be obligated to use that information. That is, of course, as long as the suspect had been read his rights at some point prior to the *interview* occurring."

"Okay, I get it, but why aren't you in there with him?" Mick asked.

"People are more open with him when he is alone. As soon as they even sniff a badge, they clam up and ask for a lawyer. Sure, he is a big son of a bitch, but after five minutes, everyone tells him what he wants to know. Hell, half of the time I don't think they even realize that they are doing it."

On the other side of the glass, Christian stared at Rollie. Rollie was rocking erratically from side to side and swatting at the air around his head as though there were mosquitos buzzing. Rollie still had brown leaves in his knotted and gnarled hair from yet another night of sleeping in the park. Homemade tattoos—crosses of varying sizes—dotted his exposed skin. He had circular scars on the palms and backs of both hands. His files said that he carved them with a broken plastic spoon during his last stay at Summer Bay Psychiatric Hospital. Christian knew it was a waste of time, but he attempted to ask the man some questions anyway.

"Rollie, my name is Christian. How are you doing today?" he said as he leaned in and rounded his shoulders to make himself appear smaller. He normally introduced himself as Dr. Rinaldi to separate himself from the police and FBI agents in the minds of the suspects, but in this instance, his profession would have made it worse. Rollie had spent more time than you would have liked around doctors and psychiatrists.

Rollie mumbled several nonsensical words, but not in response to the questions posed. He was speaking in the general direction of whatever he was swatting at. Christian repeated the simple question two more times, and after receiving the same responses, he thanked Rollie for his time and walked out.

"I told you that he isn't our guy," Christian said as he walked through the door to the observation room.

"Yeah, I know he is a little whacky, but if we get his meds into him, he will be much clearer. We can try again later," Brooks said.

"He is a diagnosed delusional schizophrenic. He has been off his meds for more than the 2 days since the homicide was committed. He would not have been capable of committing the act, or organized enough for the planning and execution of it," Christian argued.

"He could have had help. It took several people. You said so yourself. He could have been the ring leader," Brooks protested.

"Would you take orders from that guy?" Christian asked. "Besides, even if he was organized enough and had been on his meds, he wouldn't have done it the way that it was done. Look at his hands. He carved the biblical stigmata in them. He would have done the same thing at the crucifixion, and you know that didn't happen."

Before Brooks could attempt to continue the debate, his phone rang. He listened to the person on the other end and a look of disappointment crossed his face.

"Fine, you are right. He isn't our guy."

"I am glad you came around," Christian said.

"Don't pat yourself on the back too hard there, Doc. There is still a killer out there, and he has been a busy boy," Brooks responded. "That was Portland PD, and they have another body. Different park than the last one, but if it the two are related, it couldn't have been Rollie. The M.E. says the time of death was last night, and Rollie was in holding all night."

The same nervousness from earlier in the morning hit Mick like a ton of bricks. The undertaker, Alfred, couldn't have screwed up or double crossed them, could he? Hoping to get the right answer, he asked "Do you have an ID on the victim?"

"Not yet, but that might be because of the injuries," Brooks answered.

"Injuries? What kind of injuries?" Mick asked. Costa hadn't had any injuries, so this had to be good news.

"I might have heard him wrong, but the officer said the guy looked like he had been crushed and cooked." Brooks said, shaking his shoulders. "The creepy shit gives me the willies."

Chapter 24

Ricky and Jim sat in silence. Jim sat in his usual spot at the end picnic table and kept his back to everyone else. Ricky picked over his ham steak and just couldn't bring himself to eat it. After watching and participating in what happened to Stephen, he didn't see meat being easy to eat for a while.

"Jim, I have to ask, why do you always wait for this seat to open up?" Ricky asked.

"If I sit right here and look straight ahead at the woods, I can pretend that I am somewhere else. I get to be happy for a few minutes and just forget about everything," Jim said.

"Does it remind you of home?"

"I haven't had one of those in over 30 years, but I don't like to think about that," Jim said, taking his eyes off of the forest for the first time all meal.

"Why not?"

"It isn't something that I like to talk about either. I am sure you don't like questions about your leg," Jim replied. He knew that his statement would sting, but he wanted to make his point.

Ricky was surprised by Jim's reaction, but that only made him more curious. "You are right. I don't like to talk about my leg, but I will tell you all about it if you tell me about you."

Jim mulled over the idea of finally sharing his pain with someone else. It had been years since he had said anything about it to another person. "Okay, you go first."

Ricky took a deep breath and started his story. "Twenty years or so ago, I was working on a lobster boat out of Winter Harbor during the summers, and in the sardine cannery all winter. I had been on the same boat for almost 12 years. My captain was great. His wife and my wife were best friends, and our kids played together every free moment that they had.

"Chris, the captain, decided to buy a new boat, and this one was different than the old one that we had been using. Instead of tossing one trap over at a time with a line and a buoy on each one, this boat had an open back deck and the traps were dropped over in groups of ten. Each string of traps had a beginning line with a buoy, and a line that connected each trap to the next, with the last one ending with a final line buoy. All that you had to do was send the first one over the end, and as it sank, it pulled the rest of the string with it. We had eight strings of ten traps each, and then we would go back the next day and pull them in.

"I didn't like the new boat, but Chris said it was because I was just too set in my ways. Anyway, I was doing the best I could with it, but it was too much action for just one guy to watch. Chris brought his kid brother on board and he was supposed to help keep an eye on the traps as they went over. With all the rope going into the water, everyone on deck needed to keep their focus at all times and communicate well."

"This is a sweet story but we only have a half hour. Is there an end coming?" Jim said, half joking. In truth he was hoping that Ricky would talk so long that he would forget about Jim's story.

"Sometime in the third week of working with Benji, Chris's brother, I had my accident. Benji was only like 23 or so and had just proposed to the mother of his 11 month old baby. So, there we were one morning, out several miles off into the Atlantic, and he was dragging ass. I asked him what the deal was and he said that the baby was crying all night and he had barely slept in days. He wasn't paying enough attention to what he was doing, but he was going be able to take a nap as soon as we got the traps checked and then back off the boat.

"We made it to the fifth string and I had been paying more attention to where his feet were than he was. It had been dicey a few times, but I always managed to get him to wake up enough to stay safe. We finished baiting the string and just as the first trap went over the edge, I saw that his foot was in the bite."

"The what? I don't speak boat talk," Jim asked.

"The bite is when a rope gets looped up in a circle while it is sitting on deck and your foot gets stuck in it. If there is something in the loops, the rope will tighten up and it feels like getting bitten." Ricky explained.

"Okay, I get you," Jim said.

"Ok, so I saw his foot in the bite and I yelled to him like I had a dozen times that morning, but he didn't hear me. I saw the traps going over and the only thing I could do was to grab him. I ran down to where he was and pulled him to the edge. I was too busy yelling at him to notice that I had hooked my foot in the rope when I was running.

"A couple more traps went over and there were only a couple left when I felt a warning tug. I looked down just in time to see the rope get tight around my ankle. It pulled me over and I slammed onto the deck face first. Benji yelled to Chris and he came running. They grabbed the end of the buoy line and tried to stop me from going over. They were able hook the buoy on something that I couldn't see so that it stopped me from going over, but I was still hanging with my leg part way over the back of the boat.

"The eight traps that had already gone over were pulling me toward the water and Chris and Benji were holding me on board. My leg got crushed. The rope had moved up my leg when I was dragging and was looped around both my ankle and knee. I was finally able to get my diving knife free and I tried to cut the rope below my leg, but I couldn't reach it. I had to cut the rope above me and the next thing I knew, I was in the freezing water. I fought with the cut end of the rope and barely managed to get it off of my leg. I made it to the surface and passed out. I woke up a day later in the hospital. My leg had been shattered and my muscles were torn up.

"I was out of work for a long time, and with all of that free time, my wife and I started fighting more, and eventually she left me and took the girls. I haven't seen them in 18 years."

"I am really sorry, Ricky. If you get out of here, you should really try to make peace with them," Jim said.

"They don't want to see me. She turned them against me years ago. I am not sure that it is even worth the hassle now. They moved on, and so did I," Ricky explained.

"Trust me, you don't know how long you have with the important people. Don't leave things in a bad way," Jim said. "I was kind of hoping you wouldn't remember to ask about my story, but it is clear that you need to hear it. It isn't as long as yours though."

"I am all ears," Ricky said.

"I was in my early 20's when my wife and I settled into our first home. It wasn't much, but it was ours. It was a rundown dump with more rotten wood than good. The electrical was bad, and I didn't know how to fix it, but I bought some manuals and taught myself. I did the drywall and electrical, room by room and we lived in what was done while I worked on the rest. I finished the kitchen and the bathroom, and then one bedroom that we shared with our daughter," Jim started.

"That sounds nice, Jim," Ricky complimented.

"Most of it was. My wife was wonderful. She was everything that I ever hoped for, and more than I deserved. Our little girl was an angel. I was the problem. I worked in a wood mill on the night shift, and I was too exhausted to do a lot of work around the house some days. The crying baby and windows with no curtains to block the sun made it hard for me to sleep. I took my wife asking me about when I was going to finish the room as nagging. I started hitting the bottle. I never hurt them, but I was a real asshole about it. I didn't want to hold my daughter or talk to my wife.

"I started going to the bars when we got off shift at 4AM and came home still drunk a lot of the time. Then I started doing the work on the house. I went on a bender for a week straight and didn't do anything but go to work, go to the bar, come home to work on the house, and then pass out for a while. I didn't even go into the finished part of the house unless I had to.

"One night while I was at the bar after shift, I heard a fire truck speed by with sirens blasting. A few minutes later, a buddy of mine came in and told me that it was my house that was on fire. They tried to put it out, but it was too late," Jim paused and looked at the table.

"Was your family okay?" Ricky didn't want to ask but he had to.

"No, they found my wife and daughter cuddled together on the mattress in our bedroom. The doctor said that they never woke up. The smoke just got to them before the fire spread. They never knew what happened. That is the only peace that I have: knowing that they didn't suffer. The electrical work that I did when I was drunk caused the fire. It was all my fault. If I had done it right, then it wouldn't have happened. If I had gone home instead of going to the bar, then I would have been able to save them," Jim started to tear up.

"I am so sorry, Jim. That is horrible," Ricky said, putting his hand on Jim's shoulder.

Jim shrugged him off and said, "I just wandered the streets for the next thirty years. One day, I happened by this place and saw the help wanted sign at the end of the long ass drive way. I came in, and have been here ever since. I got along well with the old guy that used to run the place. I think that is the only reason that I haven't been killed yet."

Jim stood and started to walk away. He looked back at Ricky and said, "I am going to go take a nap for a bit. Come get me if they need me for anything."

Ricky sat in silence after Jim walked away. He thought about his girls, all of the fun times that they had spent together, birthdays, holidays, and the ones that he had missed since. They probably had families of their own, but he was now determined to see them again.

A shadow appeared on the table. He looked up and saw Smalls standing there. "Ricky, I need you to come with me."

"Sure, what's up?" Ricky asked as they walked. Smalls didn't respond until they were near the nice bunkhouse.

"It's time, Ricky. You are tonight's chosen one," Smalls said.

Before Ricky could protest, the door to the bunkhouse opened and Biggie jabbed him in the arm with a needle. The world grew fuzzy, and Ricky stumbled into the house. He felt himself being guided to something soft, and then everything went black.

Chapter 25

Christian squatted in front of the stark naked body at the center of the crime scene. He had to call the person he was looking at "the body", or he ran the risk of feeling some sort of human attachment to it. Once he left the crime scene and started interviewing suspects, he went back to the personal pronouns and names to feel a personal connection that would fuel his need to know why this had happened.

Mick leaned in closer to Agent Brooks and said, "He has been kneeling for like 10 minutes without speaking. Should we be doing something? I mean, the techs are all just standing around waiting on him."

"They know the drill by now. It drove me nuts the first couple of times, but when he stands up, their jobs will get a hell of a lot easier," Brooks responded.

Christian scanned the dirt around the body, looked at each path taken by everyone who had walked around it, and at the grass beyond the edges of the tape. Satisfied with his assessment, he stood.

"Agent, are you sure that only the Medical Examiner has been near the body and no one else?" he asked.

"The man who called it in said that he didn't get within ten feet, so it was just the M.E. And now you," Brooks responded.

Christian walked over to where Mick and Brooks stood. "We are looking for two men between 5' 10" and 6'2'. They are well-built but not overweight, and are driving a large pick up. The man was killed late last night and disposed of early this morning. He appears to have been laying on something, possibly coals and then buried alive with rocks or cinder blocks, and then dirt. You will probably find sedatives in his system like our crucified friend. He was dug up and brought here before 5 AM."

"Okay, I will pass it on," Brooks said before starting to walk away.

"Whoa, wait up. Let's hold on for a second here," Mick said, stopping Brooks in his tracks. "I get that you have some crazy power or something, but I need to know why you are going to just put that information out to the police without even asking how he knows this."

"I trust what he says. Until he is wrong, I will continue trusting him. It works for me. Does it work for you?" Brooks asked.

"Do you want to know why?" Christian asked before Mick could answer.

"Yes. I am not questioning you, but I would like to see what you see," Mick responded.

"That is fine. Here is the basic run down. The wide tire tracks that end about ten feet from the body do not belong to the police vehicles, nor do they belong to a truck from the parks department. They only use small ATV maintenance vehicles on the grass.

"I know that there were two men because there are three sets of tracks. The M.E. is wearing plastic slip-ons over his shoes, so the two sets with tread patterns are not his. The size and depth of the depressions gave me the height estimates. They were roughly the same as mine. I know that he was killed last night because of the limited amount of rigor that had set in when I tried to lift him.

"When I lifted him, I noticed that the ground under him was dry, but he was damp, and the two sets of prints all had water in them. The only time that it rained in the last two days was around 5 o'clock this morning. The visible burns on his back were red but not deeply burnt or charred, so I knew that he wasn't in contact with direct flame. The bruises on his torso are of varied patterns and are fresh, so I could tell that they were made by heavy objects that are not uniform in size. He was alive at the time, because they would not have bruised in that pattern. Dirt on his face and hair but not on the rest of his body would indicate that he was buried after the heavy items were placed on his chest and legs. Does that about cover it?"

"You left out the sedatives," Mick laughed.

"Would you just let this happen to you? There are no marks that would indicate that he was restrained, so he had to be drugged."

Brooks joined them again. "The M.E. seems to agree with you so far. The techs are taking tire and footprint impressions, and we will run them through. You can take off if you want."

"I really think these last two are linked. Can you bring over any unsolved homicide files with you when you come to dinner? I have some hunches, and if I am right, there are more out there," Christian asked Brooks.

"Sure thing, Doc. I will grab what I can. I doubt there are too many of them out there. How far back do you want to go?"

"I am thinking we should go at least two years."

"Sounds good, I will pick up the steaks and some beer and head on up in a few hours."

Mick and Christian walked to their waiting car. Mick was both impressed, and oddly scared, by Christian's intellect. How was he supposed to stay ahead of a man who saw everything that no one else did? How long would it take for him to catch on to Mick? Did he already know that Mick was there to spy on him?

Chapter 26

"There are more here than I thought," Brooks said, pointing to 3 boxes of files in the trunk of his FBI-issued black sedan. Christian pulled out two of the 30-inch-long cardboard file boxes and left one for Mick. Brooks was already half-way to the porch, towing a blue and white cooler behind him. He always brought his own beer. He liked to joke that Christian was an "uptown doctor" for drinking scotch and whisky, and that he was the "blue collar cop" and the beer backed him up.

"You know where the fridge is. We will take the files into the study," Christian called up to him.

"The butcher gave me a great deal on some New York Strip, so I hope that is good enough for you boys," Brooks yelled back.

"Works for me," Mick replied as he headed into Christian's study with his files. He found the box to be heavier than he expected, but just ahead of him, Christian had one under each arm.

Brooks walked into the study and took a seat next to Mick on the leather sofa. "Ok, you said you had an idea?"

"Yes, I noticed something on the last two bodies that could be something, or it could be just a coincidence. I didn't mention it at the scene because I didn't know for sure," Christian explained.

"Ok. What is it?" Mick asked.

Christian dug out the files for Gene and Stephen and walked over to the seated men. He handed them each an autopsy photo of the men. "Do you see anything odd about their legs?"

Brooks and Mick stared at the photos of the men's corpses. These file photos had become old hat for Brooks, but this was a first for Mick. He had seen plenty of crime procedural shows and recognized the V-shaped incision used to open the chest cavity, and then the Y that it is sometimes turned into so that the coroner could have access to the abdominal organs, but this was somehow too real. He had never met the men, but he had seen the second man earlier in the day at the crime scene. He was glad that the directive was to look at the legs; looking at faces made this even harder.

"I think I have an idea of what you are talking about," Mick said pointing to Stephen's leg, just below his knee. "He has a lot of hair on his left leg but nothing on the right except for a rash or something."

"Yeah, now that you mention it, this guy has one calf that looks like my ex-wife in winter and the other is the summertime version," Brooks joked.

"What would have caused it?" Mick asked.

"I am thinking that these men had something on their legs that was somewhat heavy and snug. It was on for a while because there is no hair left on the lower parts of their legs. They must have lost some weight

285

recently, because only the top part of their bald spots show any rash. I am guessing that the weight loss allowed whatever it was to move higher than it had been, and the redness was from newly ripped-out hair follicles. It almost looks like they had house arrest bracelets on," Christian explained.

"Neither man had any recent arrests or criminal history that would have had them on house arrest," Brooks said.

"I am thinking that these are homemade devices. They were probably used to monitor them, or possibly were used to secure them to something, like a flexible shackle. It could be a coincidence, but I don't think so," Christian continued.

"So I am guessing that you want us to look through these files and look for similar marks?" Mick asked.

"Yes. Grab a box and go through it. Look at the pictures as well as the coroner's report. They may not have mentioned a bald spot on a leg. I want to have one pile for people with similar abrasions, and a second pile for any odd method of killing. There may be a second link with 'out of the ordinary' methods."

Over the next hour, the three men worked in near silence. Each concentrated intensely on the files in their box. None wanted to miss anything, and would occasionally ask the others if they thought a particular murder fit the criteria for being odd. Once the final file was reviewed, there were seven new additions to the abrasion pile and four in the odd death stack. Two of the odd deaths seemed to fit the pattern better than the others, but the file didn't have pictures of the victims' legs, and the coroner didn't mention anything about bald spots or rashes.

Christian wiped a large white dry erase board clean and wrote the date, location of body dump, and cause of death on one side of the board for the nine from the abrasion pile, and did the same for the four others on the opposite side. All in all, the dates ranged from about two and a half years prior to that morning. The dates were fairly far apart in the beginning, but had picked up significantly in the last two weeks. This was common with serial killings. Many of the first killings were for practice, and as the killer's skills improved or something set them off (commonly called an escalating event) the frequency increased.

Just as the men started to discuss potential connections between the murders, the doorbell rang. Christian left to answer it, and Brooks followed a few steps behind. Mick stayed and looked at the board. Something seemed familiar about this pattern, but he couldn't put his finger on it.

Mick gave up and left the study, careful to close the doors behind him. When he rejoined the other men, he found two more had joined them. He recognized the first man as Andy from earlier in the morning, but had no idea who the other man was. Luckily, he had arrived just in time for introductions.

"Andy, you have met Mick. This is Randy Brooks. He is a friend and colleague," Christian said, leading off the exchange of names.

"Three psychiatrists in one room? I am not going to be crying about my rough high school years by the end of the night, am I?" Andy joked.

"Oh, I am not a shrink. I work for the FBI," Brooks corrected.

"And I am just an intern right now, so Christian is the only real doctor here," Mick added.

"FBI? I thought you said that you worked together?" Andy asked.

"We do, but that is a long story that we can get into later. Who is your friend?" Christian asked, pointing to the large man standing behind Andy. He was about an inch taller than Christian and squarely built, like he spent his days wrestling hay, or possibly black bears.

"This here is Clint. He is one of the men that I told you about that basically run the farm for me. He and his brother are life savers. I couldn't get anything done without them," Andy said, stepping aside so that Clint could shake hands.

"Nice to meet everybody," Clint said, dipping his head a little as he spoke.

Clint shook each man's hand, and Christian was both surprised and impressed by the power of his grip. The strength of his squeeze was as natural as it was painful. It was obvious that he wasn't applying the vice-like grip out of a macho display as a lot of self-important alpha males did. His rough, calloused hands were just stronger than most men's from the years of continuous strain and use. He fit the cliché of a man who "doesn't know his own strength". Mr. Melanson used to refer to it as being "farm boy strong".

"What's in the bag?" Christian asked, pointing to the brown paper bag Andy was holding.

"I hope you don't mind, I brought some fresh steaks and some chicken from the farm. It is all natural, grass and grain fed stuff. We dry age the steaks for a couple weeks to make them really tender," Andy said.

"Sounds fantastic. We were just about to go fire up the grill. Let's grab some drinks and head out back," Christian suggested.

Brooks took out the steaks and a six-pack, and the five men walked toward the patio. Mick hung back and helped Brooks get some more drinks for everyone. He studied Clint, the big farm hand, for a minute. The man seemed nice enough, but there was something about him that felt off. He didn't know what it was, but there was something hiding in the huge, quiet man.

* * * * *

"Jim, you gotta wake up. It's time to go," Mike said loudly.

Jim sat up and narrowly missed hitting his head on the bunk above him. The bunkhouse was darker than when he had started his nap. It had to be close to dinner time. "I'm not hungry. Go ahead without me."

"No, Jim—it isn't time to eat. Smalls wants us all to get out to the clearing."

"What? When did this happen? This is getting nuts," Jim said.

"The whole thing is nuts, but everyone else left already, and we need to get moving," Mike said as though his words were also in a hurry.

Jim stood and followed him out the door. His sixty year old bones and muscles were not built for this life. Every step and the pain that came with it reminded him of all the poor choices he had made. Only one decision was worse than coming here.

He should be enjoying retirement with his wife and spending his days watching his grandkids instead of being here. One series of bad choices had taken that option away from him forever. The priests and councilors who frequented the various homeless shelters he had been to over the last 30+ years had all told him that everything happened for a reason, and he needed to forgive himself. Forgiveness was not in the cards for Jim. He had hated himself for the selfish bastard that he once was, and no amount of penance would fix that.

Jim looked for Ricky as he joined the back of the line. The hazy darkness and matching attire made it difficult to pick anyone out of the crowd. They all looked like slightly different-sized copies of each other. The only people that stood out were the person pushing the wheelbarrow a few steps behind Smalls, and Smalls himself. Another man staggered along next to Smalls, but Jim couldn't tell who it was from this distance.

Jim finally made his way to the clearing and took an open seat in the back row, breaking his own rule. He looked for Ricky, but still didn't see him. He scanned the crowd without any luck, and then looked at the man with Smalls. He could be Ricky, but Jim couldn't tell because the man had his head down. *"Please don't be Ricky, he is one of the only good people here,"* Jim thought to himself.

"It is punishment time again, my friends," Smalls said loudly. He didn't have the same power in his presence as Biggie did, but he was still intimidating enough. For that matter, where was Biggie? He never missed a "punishment".

Jim frantically searched the clearing for any sign of Ricky. He didn't see him with the other men. All that Jim could see was the men on the logs, Smalls, the drugged man next to him, a rope hanging from one of the large limbs that reached into the clearing from the nearby trees, and the lone wheelbarrow. The contents of the wheelbarrow were not visible from Jim's seat. All that he could make out was a burlap sack and something square underneath.

"It has been determined that our newest member is not pulling his own weight around here," Smalls continued. "I blame myself for this unfortunate hiring. I was the one who picked Ricky up on the side of the road."

A cold sweat broke out across Jim's forehead at the mention of his new friend's name. He had only been here for a couple of days, but he was the only man who actually cared about Jim enough to ask about his life and how he felt each day since the old man who had run this farm when he first got here. Jim had refused to make a meaningful connection with another person since his wife and daughter, then the old farmer had passed, and now Ricky was being taken as well.

Something inside Jim snapped. He had stood by while other men had been taken away and then murdered in front of him, and he had done nothing to stop it. Not this time. He could not sit in the crowd and watch Ricky have a slow agonizing death.

"This isn't fair. He has only been here for a few days. He is still learning. Give him a chance," Jim yelled at Smalls.

"Who is that back there? Jim, is that you?" Smalls asked, startled that someone had questioned him. Without Biggie by his side, he wasn't being shown the same respect, and he couldn't allow that. "Jim, just sit back down. The decision has been made. This is going to happen."

Before he knew what he was doing, Jim stood and walked to the front of the clearing. Along the way, he tried to stir the other men. "We are tired of this. We don't need to put up with this anymore. We all came here to work, didn't we? We didn't come here to be shackled to bombs and to watch each other die. I am not letting this happen anymore. Who is going to help me?"

No one responded or even moved. Jim walked up to Smalls and looked upward at the much taller man. "This is not okay, and you know it. What happened to you? You used to be such a good man."

Smalls leaned forward and spoke to Jim in a quiet voice. "Jim, I have always liked you and respected you. The old man was very fond of you, and that is the only reason you weren't up here a long time ago. Don't say something that you will regret. Go back to your seat and cool off."

"Or what? What are you going to do if I stay right here? I am not going anywhere. Let him go, now!" Jim said, his voice getting louder with each word.

"Jim, I am not going to tell you again. You need to go back to your seat, or I am taking you back there myself," Smalls growled. He had to give the old man a chance to make the right decision, but he also couldn't lose face in front of the others.

"I said I am not going anywhere. You do what you have to, but I am not moving," Jim defiantly said.

Smalls had reached his limit. He stepped in front of the wobbling Ricky and put his hand on Jim's shoulder. Jim pulled his hand back and punched Smalls square in the nose. Smalls' eyes began to water and he felt a trickle of blood escaping his left nostril. Purely out of reflex, he struck the elderly man on the side of his wrinkled cheek. Jim fell to the ground and nearly blacked out.

Jim struck the ground hard, unable to break his fall. Smalls stood over him and, just before he punched Jim again, Jim heard him say, "Congratulation old man, you are getting your wish. Ricky gets to live another day. You are taking his place."

* * * * *

"The food is great. Thanks, everyone," Christian said as he cut into his second chicken thigh.

The five men sat around the teak patio table and enjoyed their dinners by the fireplace. They were all stuffed to the gills with the steaks, chicken, salad, and roasted vegetables that Christian and Brooks had prepared together. Each had washed the food down with several drinks apiece, and the mood was jovial.

"It is hard to believe that you two haven't seen each other in over 20 years," Brooks said. "I've gotta ask, what was Doc like as a kid?"

"I don't really know. I mean, we lived in the same house for about a year, but we rarely saw each other. He was either always reading, or with Dad. We were all pretty sure that he was Dad's favorite until he just up and left," Andy answered.

Christian hated to think of Mr. Melanson as anyone's Dad, and he definitely didn't spend time with the man by choice. "I am sorry that I left in such a rush. It was a surprise to me, too. I didn't know anything was even in the works until I was picked up. Everyone was already asleep when Mr. Rinaldi came for me, and that was that."

"So, Clint, how long have you been working with Andy?" Mick asked, sensing that a change of topic was in order.

"Well, I came here with my younger brother the summer after Andy left for the Navy. We came to Maine to go rake blueberries for a month, but when we got there, the man said he gave away our spots. We didn't have anywhere to go or any money, so we couldn't go far. We saw an ad in the paper for farm hands and went to check it out. Mr. Melanson was starting to get pretty sick and needed lots of help. He asked if we could work the fall harvest, and so we did. When everyone started to head south, he asked us if we wanted to stay. We didn't have anything better planned, so we stayed on," said the quiet giant.

"Now, we couldn't live without them. After Dad passed, I had no idea how to run things. Most of the crew took off and left, and I thought we were going to have to sell the place. Then Clint and Marty stepped up and said that they would take care of finding new employees, and that they would handle all the labor issues. I just had to make sure that everyone had what they needed and everyone got paid. Hell, outside of these two, I am not sure I could tell you the names of any of the employees. Clint runs a tight ship," Andy said with a smile. He reached over and slapped the big man on his shoulder. "So, how about you? How did you end up working with the FBI?"

"Just dumb luck, really. My adoptive father worked for the FBI," Christian began. "He worked out of the Portland office, and it was pretty quiet. He retired about 15 years ago and passed away around 7 years later. Well, one day a new field agent came to my house to look for him, and I had to tell him that he had died a couple of months earlier. I asked him if there was something I could help him with and he told me that he just had some questions about a cold case that he was working that Dad had worked on. I offered to take a look to see if I could remember him talking about it at all. I didn't recognize the case but I gave him some tips on what type of person I would look for. I guess he ended up solving the case, and he came back to ask me if I was willing to offer my assistance from time to time. We developed a good relationship until he left last year, and that's when I met Agent Brooks."

"What happened to the last guy?" Andy asked.

"I am not exactly positive. All I know is that he just retired one day out of the blue," Christian repeated the same lie he had given everyone else who had asked.

Clint looked at the sky, and then at Andy. He pointed to the spot on his massive wrist where a watch would normally be, if he wore one. Andy looked at his own watch and nodded back to his helper. "I am sorry guys. I know it isn't polite to eat and run, but Clint is right. We should get going. I am still not used to this farm time. If we are going to get up before the sun, we need to get to bed soon. Thank you for dinner."

"It's too bad that you have to run so soon, but we have a case to get back to anyway. Give me a call sometime and we can do this again. Maybe your brother can come as well," Christian said.

Clint whispered to Andy who then turned to Christian. "I appreciate that. I do have a question for you. Would it be possible for Clint and Marty to come by and put a boat in on the river sometime? They love to fish."

"I don't see why not. How about you send over some of Birdie's pickled beets and strawberry-rhubarb jam, and they can take my boat," Christian offered.

"You have a deal," Andy said as he walked around the side of the house and to his waiting truck.

* * * * *

Ricky stared through blurry eyes at the scene in front of him. His mind was foggy, but clearing. His vision and hearing were returning, but his body still refused to move. He remembered standing a while ago and walking somewhere, but now he thought he was sitting against a tree. He could see the outline of a small man on the ground, and he could hear Smalls talking to someone on a phone as he paced in the clearing.

"I fucked up, man. I really need you to get out here. Yeah, I am in the clearing. Are you almost here?" he said into the phone. "Okay, good. Is he still with you? Well, make up some excuse and ditch him. I need your help more than he does."

Ricky faded back out of consciousness again. For how long, he didn't know. Biggie's low angry voice woke him. When did he get here?

"What the fuck did you do? Is that Jim, for Christsakes? You know he was the old man's favorite. How are we going to explain this one, huh? We aren't going to be able to say that he just took off, or that we fired him like the others," Biggie angrily yelled.

"Well it is too damn late now, isn't it? I can't go back on this now. We'd have a damn coup on our hands. Are you going to help me or not?"

"What do you need me to do?" Biggie asked.

"Put the rope around his feet and go pull him up."

Jim started to stir, and he thought he felt something being wrapped around his feet. The next thing he knew, he was being dragged along the grass. His legs lifted off the ground, and then the rest of his body.

297

"Wrap a rope around his waist and tie his hands, too," Smalls ordered, and the bigger man complied. Smalls turned to the crowd. "Jim made the biggest mistake of all tonight. He chose to challenge us, and then he physically attacked me. We loved him like a brother, and now he has spit in our face. This offense cannot go unpunished."

Ricky watched as the wheelbarrow was brought closer to Jim. He didn't know what was in it, but he knew it couldn't be good.

Jim hung upside down with his face dangling at about the same height as Smalls's belt. Unfortunately for him, he recognized what was in the wheelbarrow even though the burlap sack still covered it. He had set those traps in the barn just two days ago. The agitated squeaking told him that they were full.

Smalls pulled the sack from the wheelbarrow and handed it to Biggie, exposing the three humane animal traps underneath. Each one held a huge black rat. The rats banged around inside the cages, baring their sharp front teeth. Smalls removed one of the large rodents from the cage. It thrashed as he held it by the scruff of its neck. Bright red eyes scanned the crowd as Smalls began to speak.

"Most people think that rats are dirty scavengers that like to steal food or eat the remains of dead animals. Those people are partly right—Owwww!" Smalls yelped in pain as the rodent swung his head around and bit him in the web between his thumb and his fingers. He tossed it into the sack, and Biggie closed it up. The rat fought to free itself from the heavy cloth bag. "That perfectly illustrates what I was about to say. Rats will eat anything, but they love to eat fresh meat."

Smalls reached into the cages and pulled the other two rats in the sack as he continued to speak. "They are also very attracted to salt. Do you know where you can find a lot of salt?"

Jim stared at the sack in absolute horror. He knew where the rats could find salt. He struggled to free himself as the opening of the bag enveloped his head. He would not give them the satisfaction of screaming. He felt the sack being tied to his body, his neck and face completely inside the bag. Over the squealing of the angry, hungry rats that he had trapped, he heard Smalls answer his own question.

"Tears, sweat and even your own saliva have salt in them. Your face has more sweat glands than even your armpits. Rats can see well in the dark, and the smell of salt and blood will soon drive these hungry beasts into a feeding frenzy. The worst part for our friend Jim isn't going to be that they are eating him alive, it will be how many little bites it takes," Smalls laughed.

Ricky willed himself to his feet and staggered forward. He struggled to get to his friend's side to save him. He made it to within a few feet of Jim before his body gave out. He fell forward and landed on his face. Smalls rolled him over and dragged him across the grass. When he stopped, Ricky opened his eyes, and directly above him was the brown sack around Jim's head.

Jim felt several little paws reaching out and touching his face. Another rat climbed up and onto his chin. Their whiskers tickled as they sniffed his nose, ears, mouth, and eyes. He squeezed his eyes and mouth shut as tightly as he could. He knew that these were prized areas in the animal kingdom, the first to be eaten. Sometimes the tongue was all an animal ate from the face of its prey.

A vision swept through his mind. He saw his wife and baby, sitting in a white room calling for him. They looked so peaceful. His wife was practically glowing she was so beautiful. He missed them so much. A tear formed at the corner of his eye and rolled down his eye lids. He felt the little clawed paws touching on each side of his left eye, the one that had betrayed him with the tear. A small pinching pain came from his eye lid. The thin flap of skin was a poor protection against the sharp incisors of the rat.

The sight of his wife and daughter returned as the rat bit into his eyeball. He didn't feel the ocular fluid squirt out; their presence filled him with a contented peace. He was ready to go. He wanted this tortured life to be over. He didn't know if there was another life after this one or not, but he knew he was leaving this life as a good man who had made one terrible mistake. A last thought entered his mind and he needed to share it.

Ricky saw Jim stop fighting and he thought that his friend's life was now gone, but then he heard his friend yell. It was muffled but he knew what he meant.

Jim yelled. He wasn't sure if he was heard or not. As soon as his mouth opened he felt the rat move from his chin and the furry bastard jammed his head in Jim's mouth. Jim tried to spit him out but it was too late. The rodent bit into his tongue. Blood filled his mouth and spilled out.

Ricky heard his friend's last message and saw him start to thrash wildly. A long minute later, the only motion left was from the rats moving in the bag. Blood pooled in the bottom of the sack and began to drip through. The drops landed on Ricky's face, but he chose to think of his friend's final words. He had chosen to use his last breath to give him this one final piece of advice. *Ricky make up with your girls.*

Chapter 27

Christian rubbed his hands up and down the sides of his cheeks. He, Brooks, and Mick had been staring at the two lists of unsolved homicides for over five straight hours and still weren't any closer to a connection between them. They had fallen into a pattern of long silences that were occasionally interrupted by what felt like breakthrough after breakthrough, only to be disappointed once again.

"Maybe they are all religious rituals?" had been one suggestion that seemed promising until an electrocution from several months ago didn't fit the pattern.

Everything from victim type to occupation to location to time of day or night was tossed around as prospective links but each was eventually shot down. Mick had long since passed the point of mental exhaustion and he began to hope that he would not have many of these nights in his future. The TV shows all made solving cases seem so easy.

The late hour had even the veterans of night-owl file reviews wearing thin. Brooks hadn't spoken in almost an hour, and Christian had begun to think that he was sleeping with his eyes open. They were in desperate need of a break.

"Why don't we take a few minutes and just step away from this?" Christian suggested. "Maybe we can come back to it in an hour or so with fresh eyes."

"Good idea, I am getting a beer and then I am going to toss one of those farm fresh steaks on the grill," Brooks said.

"Make it two," Christian replied. "How about you Mick? Do you want to join us out by the fire?"

"Nah, the couch is calling my name. Wake me up when you come in," Mick said as he headed for the brown micro-suede sectional in the living room. He kicked off his new sneakers, and his feet immediately felt lighter. Reclining on the chaise end of the sectional, he turned on the enormous flat screen in front of him. The screen itself was five full feet from one corner diagonally to the next. The actors were nearly life size, and Mick loved it.

Even though he was ready to slip off into a deep slumber at any second, Mick still wanted to find something good to watch. He hit the guide button on the satellite remote and began scanning through the 250 or more available options. Christian had recorded the Red Sox game so Mick didn't dare to put on any sportscasts. Infomercial after infomercial clicked by until he finally found an acceptable show. Thank you, BBC America!

Mick clicked the enter button and the British drama *Serials* filled the screen. It was a rerun from the first season, but Mick was happy to watch it. The irony about watching a TV show about serial killers in the home of a serial killer and his unwitting FBI friend was not lost on Mick.

Mick remembered watching the first 3 seasons of *Serials* on a weekend long marathon when he was stuck in his room with the flu a few years back. By the time he came out of the tight studio apartment-style room, he had gained three pounds and the place smelled of old pizza, chips, and beer.

He put his head back and began to doze when he thought he heard something interesting. Mick sat up and hit the playback button on the remote that skipped the show backwards 15 seconds. Yes, he was right. They had said something about the victim being electrocuted while standing in a tub of water. One of the unsolved cases was an electrocution in the same manner.

Mick checked the TV's guide again and there were several more episodes on in a row. He stood and walked to a spot where he could see the TV but could also turn and see the white board. He clicked on the next episode. The description read "Liam and the team race against the clock to catch the Hangman before he strikes again." Death by hanging was on the list too.

Mick walked into the study and dug out his phone. He brought up the episode list for Serials on his movie app. He looked at Season 1, or Series 1"as it was called in the UK. He looked from his list to the board and back to the list. He found matches for nearly every one.

Mick ran out to the porch, nearly crashing through the closed glass doors. "I've got it!" he yelled. His voice boomed in the still night air.

"Got what? If it is an STD, I don't want to know," Brooks joked, the lack of sleep had made him oddly loopy.

"What do you have?" Christian asked, ignoring his buddy.

"The connection. I have figured out how the murders are related," Mick said excitedly.

Christian was up the steps and next to him in five long strides. Brooks struggled to his feet and joined them 30 seconds later in the study.

"These murders match the style of killings in the first season of *Serials*. It looks like they are correcting the final scene where the Ass...I mean *killers* get caught in the act. They are completing those cleans—those *killings*," Mick said, catching himself as he started to use the Sicari terms.

Over the next several minutes they put the unsolved cases in chronological order. In the end, they excluded two from the second list and were left with a total of 11 matching murders. They lined up perfectly with episodes 6-16 of season 1.

"That should mean that there are five murders from back before these ones," Brooks said.

"Mick, what is the next episode about? It would stand to reason that if we have the pattern worked out correctly, then the next murder will match episode 17," Christian said.

"Let's see here, episode 17 was the final episode of that season," Mick started.

"That is odd. Aren't most seasons either like 13 or 24 to 26 episodes long?" Brooks asked.

"I think so, but remember, this is a British show. They do things a little differently there," Mick answered. "Okay, so 17 was about an arsonist who used fires to cover up his murders."

"That will be tough to figure out. Where the hell would they do that? They have been just dumping the bodies in local parks," Christian said.

Brooks grabbed his coat. "I am going to have the park's department check out every building in every park. Maybe we can catch these guys in the act."

"I would also look to see if there are any online communities devoted to this show. We are probably looking for a deranged fan, and those types of obsessive personalities flock to the internet discussion boards," Christian said to his departing friend.

"I'll make some calls and get the web nerds on it. They are probably up playing video games in their moms' basement anyway," Brooks sarcastically said as he left.

As the door slammed behind Brooks, Mick looked at Christian and asked, "Do you think he'll catch them?"

"I am not sure. They have killed on consecutive nights. If that pattern holds, we may already be too late."

* * * * *

Ricky rubbed his eyes, pushing away the crumbling remnants of Jim's dried blood and his own tears. The clearing was deafeningly silent. The only sounds came from the rats' bristly fur rubbing against the rough interior of the burlap sack and their increasingly infrequent squeaks.

Ricky's muscles fought against his requests for them to move but in the end, they lethargically complied. He looked at the lifeless body of the man who had stepped in and saved him when no one else would. A man who he had only known for days had sacrificed his own life for Ricky's, and that brave soul now hung upside down in front of him, swaying in the gentle nighttime breeze. He deserved better.

Ricky had never been good at dealing with his emotions. Sadness, like he felt at this moment, left him feeling vulnerable and that type of raw, open pain had always been seen as a weakness by his father. Anger was easier. Anger was a "man's emotion" and anger is what replaced his overpowering grief.

He walked to his friend's body and placed a hand on Jim's arm to stop his movement. He was close enough to Jim that he could feel the rats moving around in the sack, looking for another soft meal.

Rage bubbled inside Ricky's chest. He tugged at the knotted rope that held the sack over Jim's face. The bag began to sag as the ropes loosened. He pulled the bag downward off of Jim and tried not to look at his skull that was now mostly stripped of flesh. One rat tried to jump out of the opening but Ricky closed the bag before it could escape. *Not today you little prick.*

Ricky held the top of the sack closed with one hand and spun it with the other, as one might do with an opened bag of bread. He wrapped the rope around the twisted end and tied it tight. The rats, their bellies full of his friend's face, clawed at the sides, trying to break free. They weren't going anywhere.

He clasped the end of the sack with both hands and let it drop to his side, the bottom nearly touching the ground. Ricky let out a primal scream of anguish as he swung the sack in a looping motion, moving slightly behind him and into the air. When it was at the full height of its arched orbit, directly over his head, he violently pulled downward. The motion looked like a man swinging an axe into a felled tree.

Ricky swung the bag so emphatically that he bent forward at the waist, nearly falling over as the bag made contact with the unforgiving earth. He had to take a step to regain his balance. Crunching of small bones and pained squeals filled the air. Ricky stood and swung again and again, each motion more savage than the last. Tears ran down his blood covered face.

Ricky looked at the sack in his hands, chest heaving from the exertion. Sure, the rats were just doing what animals did when they ate Jim's face, and it was not their fault for being in that situation. But Ricky needed something to blame. He couldn't have the revenge he wanted—yet.

Ricky spun in a circle twice, the bag suspended in midair, outstretched at the end of his hand until he let go of the knotted end. The bag of dead and dying rats landed somewhere in the woods, out of his visual range in the darkness. Some other scavengers could have them.

He turned his attention to his friend. He was surprised that someone hadn't come to put Jim's body into the truck as they had the others. Ricky found the lone wheelbarrow and pushed it over to the tree. He placed it under Jim's hanging body and looked for a way to get him down. He worked at the knots on the rope around Jim's feet but they were pulled too tight.

He followed the rope to see where it was the other end was tied to. It was looped around a tree branch about 8 feet off the ground, but it was tied off on another tree somewhere in the woods. Ricky didn't know which side of the boundary the other tree was on, so he didn't dare to risk searching for it. He would have to cut the rope on this side.

He didn't have anything sharp with him other than his own teeth so he tried to fray the knots by dragging his open mouth over it. His front teeth split a thread or two, but not much else. He would need a new plan.

Ricky looked around the clearing and finally found something that might work. Some of the stones used to crush Stephen were piled up on the edge of the clearing. He pulled out one that looked like shale and placed it on the ground in front of him. He picked up a second, larger rock and held it above his head. He dropped it onto the first stone and was greeted by the sound of stone cracking, as well as a sharp pain from pieces of shattered rock stabbing into his shins.

Ricky dug around in the pile of broken pieces and found a shard that was dangerously sharp. He walked back to the tree and shimmied his way up the trunk and onto the thick branch that held Jim's suspended body. After striking the rope with the rock several times, and it started to cut. Unfortunately, the rock began to splinter as well, so he reverted to a sawing motion. A full minute later, the rope was severed and the loop unwound from the branch.

Jim's body landed on the side of the wheelbarrow, tipping it over. Ricky scrambled down and pulled his friend into the wheelbarrow with as much care as possible. Jim's savagely damaged face stared back at him. Ricky couldn't handle seeing Jim like that. The only option he had was to take off his brown tee shirt and cover Jim's face.

Ricky struggled to push his friend through the narrow path, the field, and finally the trail before arriving at the back of the pickup. He would not put Jim in the back of the truck. They could do that task themselves. As he saw Smalls walking his way, Ricky felt for the sharp piece of shale that he had brought with him.

Attacking the young, stronger man head on would be suicide. Ricky would have to wait for a more advantageous opportunity to present itself. When it did, Smalls would pay for what he had done. Instead, he said a silent final goodbye and thank you to Jim, and promised him that he would honor his dying request.

Chapter 28

For the third morning in a row, Mick stepped into the shower after less than four hours of sleep. Then energy surge that kicked in after he made the pivotal connection between the unsolved homicides had long since dissipated. The unfortunate drawback to adrenaline rushes is that once they are gone, you are even more exhausted than you were before the hormones flooded your body.

Mick stood under the falling water and pressed the top of his head against the cool tile just below the showerhead. His thoughts drifted through the events of the last few weeks and he wondered what he would be doing at this very moment if he hadn't climbed into the back of that town car.

Mick watched the last of his shampoo bubbles circle the drain before plunging into the darkness. He shut the water off and reached for a towel. He dressed in yet another Alex-approved outfit and headed down the cream colored carpeted stairs to the kitchen.

Mick didn't see any sign of Christian, but he did hear what sounded like something heavy being slammed around somewhere nearby. He looked out through the living room windows and saw a car in the driveway that he didn't recognize. Another loud thump landed somewhere, and a frightening thought entered his mind. Was someone attacking Christian?

The thumping seemed to be coming from the other end of the house, and Mick rushed past the kitchen and into the laundry room. The noise was in the garage!

Mick slowly opened the garage door and immediately saw a large man squaring off with Christian. He was just about to rush to Christian's aid when Christian held up a hand. The attacking man stopped crouching and stood straight up.

"Good morning Mick," Christian said, catching his breath. "We didn't wake you, did we?"

"No. What is going on? I thought someone was attacking you or something."

"I should have mentioned it before now, but I completely forgot," Christian started. "This is Roddy. He is in my Cross Fit group, and a couple Saturdays a month, I help him with his MMA training."

"Hey man, nice to meet you," Roddy said as he walked over to greet Mick. Mick was still standing on the bottom step but he was only slightly taller than Roddy in his bare feet. He had to be 6' 5" or 6' 6", and was slightly more muscular than Christian. While Christian had large, well-defined muscles that gave the appearance of usable dominating power, Roddy had the bulky musculature of a body builder. When he shook Mick's hand, it completely swallowed it up.

"You can join in if you want to," Christian extended an invitation to his new protégé.

"I think that I will just watch for a bit if that's ok. I don't think I am anywhere near Roddy's weight class," Mick laughed. "What are you helping with, anyway?"

"Grappling—it's Roddy's weak area. He has crazy knockout power, but his ground defense is weak. His last two losses have been to inferior fighters who were able to get in close, take him down, and get an arm free for a submission."

"Yeah, I keep losing to guys that I shouldn't. They don't want to stand with me, they just dive in on me and then get lucky," Roddy said, his anger evident. "If I can stop the takedown, or get better at protecting myself on the ground, the ref will stand us up and boom, they are going out cold."

"Ok, time to stop talking and get working," Christian said, putting in his mouth guard.

Christian stared across the thick mat that had been laid down on the garage floor at Roddy. The enormous man adjusted his size XXXL 4 ounce open fingered MMA gloves and stared back at Christian. The two had been working on Roddy's ground defense for weeks now, and the date for his next amateur fight was only two weeks away.

At 265 pounds, Roddy weighed in at the very top of the heavyweight division. Most of the men in his weight class were on the lower end of the scale and were generally faster than he was. They had been using that speed to their advantage, and unless Roddy learned to take that speed away, he was unlikely to win again.

All Roddy needed to do in order to stop the men from taking him down and using his size against him was to block their attacks and wear them down. If they got through, he would be as vulnerable as a turtle on its back.

The morning's lesson had been "stuffing the takedown", which was not a lot of fun for Christian. The technique was simple enough but effective if used properly. Roddy would stand in a low crouch and wait for his opponent to dive forward for his waist or legs. When they came within range, Roddy simply needed to lay flat. He would slide his legs back and outward, making them harder to grab, and at the same time he would push down on his opponent's back with his hands. This basic combination would end with Roddy lying flat across his opponents back.

As the men struggled to get out from Roddy's considerable weight, they would use a significant amount of energy, making them cautious about attempting another takedown and leaving them vulnerable to his powerful hands. Once his opponent started dropping his hands lower, Roddy would know that he was worn out, and that was Roddy's moment to strike.

Christian and Roddy had been sparring at half-speed and Roddy was noticeably improving. Time after time, Christian pretended to shoot in and grab at Roddy's legs, and each time he would be crushed to the ground under Roddy's massive bulk. The only way to know if Roddy would be able to use this technique in his next fight was to move on to full-speed sparring. If he could stuff Christian at actual pace, he would be ready.

"How about we go full on this one?" Christian suggested.

"Fine with me," Roddy responded, growing cockier from the morning's successes.

Roddy stood in the standard striker stance with his left foot in front of him and his right foot back, accompanied by his sledgehammer of a right hand. Christian adopted a mirroring stance but leaned forward more than his sparring partner. The purpose of the training was to work in ground control so why pretend that he wasn't going for the take down?

Roddy paced to his left and then to his right, like a prowling leopard. He looked for an opening to strike at Christian's upper body or head but Christian held his hands close to his face with his elbows in, protecting most of his vulnerable spots.

Strikers, the nickname given to fighters who prefer to punch and kick their opponents, are always looking for that one opening to show their skill and power. They also have a tendency to get overly frustrated when that opening takes too long to appear. Roddy is no different. After 15 seconds of not being able to throw a power punch, like a cross or hook, he settled for using his jab. Unfortunately for him, even that swift, straight punch only found open air as Christian moved his head out of the way.

Four missed jabs later, Roddy grew more agitated and tried a lower body kick. He stepped forward and swung his right foot toward Christian's chin. This was the desperation move that Christian was looking for. He stepped forward as soon as Roddy had moved his weight to his left foot and dove for Roddy's waist.

Christian caught Roddy's right leg with his left arm and the larger man wobbled momentarily before Christian's shoulder slammed into his hip. Down went the giant, landing squarely on his back. Christian landed with his body on top of Roddy who tried to wrap his legs around Christian to stop his progression. Christian was fine with being in Roddy's "guard".

Just as Christian had suspected, Roddy had gotten lax during the half-speed practice, and now that he was in a position that he wasn't comfortable with, he was freaking. Christian knew that when an opponent was as mixed up as Roddy was, there was no point in trying to find an opening. One would be provided. It didn't take long.

Roddy attempted to use his strength to push Christian away, but Christian was pressed tightly against his body. Christian's head was pressed against Roddy's chest, with the top of it under Roddy's chin. He let his legs drop to the ground, and Christian moved his legs to the outside of Roddy's without lifting his upper body off of the much larger man.

Feeling the pressure get lighter on his lower half, Roddy tried to roll to his right, away from Christian. Huge mistake. Christian allowed Roddy to move, and as soon as Roddy's back was exposed, Christian wrapped his legs around the man's waist. His feet met in front of Roddy's belly button, and Christian hooked his ankles together. Roddy struggled to sit up and Christian followed along, sticking close to Roddy's back. Christian saw the fatal opening and took it.

Christian slid his arm around the front of Roddy's massive neck and leaned back. Roddy immediately tapped, bringing an end to the sparring. Roddy and Christian stood and Roddy wanted to try again. The technique was different each time, but the results were all devastatingly similar.

In the next match, Christian again easily took Roddy to the ground, but this time he waited until Roddy left his left arm unprotected. Christian grabbed the wrist and moved his legs to either side of the arm and across Roddy's chest. The behemoth struggled and thrashed but Christian held tighter and arched his back, locking the arm in a painful arm bar. Roddy tapped.

Roddy wanted to try one last time and the results were exactly the same, except when Christian went for the arm bar, Roddy kept his arms bent and locked his hands together. As long as Christian couldn't straighten the tree-trunk-like arm out, he couldn't lock it. This was a great sign of improvement in Roddy's defense. Being proud of his student didn't stop Christian from finishing him off.

While Roddy focused on his arms, Christian moved his legs up Roddy's upper body. Eventually his legs were on both sides of Roddy's head. He bent his right knee so that his foot was near his left knee. He moved the foot under his knee and hooked his ankle into the space behind the back of his knee. Roddy's hands were still together, but with one arm inside of Christian's legs and the other on the outside, his grip would no longer matter. His left arm and head were between Christian's legs; Christian tightened his grip and pulled Roddy's face down by the back of his head. Roddy was trapped in a "triangle" and wasn't going anywhere. His breathing was once again cut off and he had no option other than to tap.

Mick hadn't moved from his seated position on the garage stairs. Once again, his new friend left him in awe. He watched the overmatched giant stand and hug Christian. They quietly spoke for several seconds before Roddy walked out through the door with a smile on his face. Christian sprayed a combination of bleach and water onto the mats and wiped them off. He folded them and stacked them in the corner.

"I am going to hit the shower but after that, I was thinking of going to grab some breakfast. You interested?" Christian asked Mick.

"Sure, I could eat. I think I'll go for a stroll around the yard until you are done," Mick responded.

Mick walked through the open garage door and started to walk down O'Connor's Glen toward the "busier" Main Street. It was a gorgeous morning, and he soon found himself lost in the sights and sounds of the country road.

Mick had been walking for about fifteen minutes when the sound of an engine overpowered the chirping of birds in the trees. He stepped to the side of the road and waited for the vehicle to pass. Only, it didn't drive past him, it stopped. The window rolled down and a deep voice said, "Hey Mick, how's it going?"

Mick squinted in the bright mid-morning sun and put his hand over his eyes to darken his view. He thought he recognized the face in the window. He had only met two men that large recently, and Roddy had just left. "Clint?"

"Hey, you remembered! What are you doing out here?" the deep voice asked.

"Just going for a walk. What brings you back out this way?" Mick asked Clint. He thought he saw a second person in the truck but he wasn't sure.

"My brother and I had to make an early run into Portland, and Andy asked us to drop off some stuff for Christian on our way back. Want a lift back to the house?"

"Sure, why not?" Mick replied and he climbed into the back of the truck's body. A large blue tarp covered most of the truck's bed, so he couldn't see anywhere to sit. There were a couple of old tires sitting and some rope sitting on top of the tarp, so he just sat down on one of them and held on to the side.

Christian was just walking out of the house when they pulled into the driveway. He looked puzzled as to why Mick was in the back of a truck until he recognized Clint.

"Good morning, Christian. Andy wanted us to swing by and drop off those pickled beets and jam you wanted," the big man said as he stepped out of the truck.

"Wow, I didn't expect to see them so quickly. Thank you. I appreciate it. Is this your brother?" Christian said, nodding to the slightly smaller man who climbed out of the passenger side.

"Yup, that is Marty. Marty this is Christian," Clint answered.

Marty carried two boxes over to Christian. Mason jars clattered together inside the wooden crates. He balanced them on his hip so that he could shake Christian's hand. "Good to meet you. Clint wouldn't shut up about how much he liked your place when he got back last night. I almost had to sleep outside."

Christian laughed and shook the man's hand. Marty pulled his hand away slightly as they shook, causing Christian to look down. He noticed that Marty's hand had gauze and tape covering the space between his thumb and forefinger. "Sorry, I didn't realize your hand was hurt. What did you do?"

"Oh, nothing really. I just pinched it on something last night. Damn thing won't stop bleeding," Marty replied.

"Make sure you keep it clean. I am sure that won't be easy around the farm. Andy's father used to put an old bread bag on his hands when he had a cut. Worked pretty well."

"Andy said that you had a place that we could maybe go fishing sometime?" Marty said, ignoring the medical advice.

"Oh sure, it is right over there if you want to take a look," Christian answered as he started walking toward the boat house. He had only taken a few steps when his phone rang. "Can you excuse me for a second? I have to take this."

Mick and the brothers walked to the edge of the river. They asked questions that Mick had no idea about, regarding what type of fish were in it and how deep it was. Thankfully, Christian interrupted the conversation.

"Mick, that was Brooks. He needs us to come in to his office. He says he has something big to discuss."

Chapter 29

Brooks was so wired from coffee and lack of sleep that he was pacing in the parking lot as Christian pulled to a stop next to Brook's office. The stores in the strip mall were just starting to open for the weekend rush, and most of the parking spaces were wide open.

Christian watched as Brooks walked in circles, oblivious to their arrival. "Looks like we are dealing with a caffeine zombie this morning. This should be interesting."

Christian and Mick walked over to Brooks, who genuinely seemed to be startled by their sudden appearance. "Jesus, you scared the crap out of me. I think you guys need to wear bells or something. You are going to give me a heart attack."

"So what is this good news that you needed us to rush over for?" Christian asked. He ignored the comment about being sneaky, but the ability to approach someone without them knowing had served him well over the years.

"Let's walk and talk," Brooks said, holding the door open. "We didn't have any luck on our stakeouts in the parks, but one of the techs knew about one of those online groups that you were talking about, and he put me in touch with the guy who runs it. He lives in Saco and is on his way here right now."

"Fantastic! Are you looking at him as a potential suspect, or just someone who might know who we are looking for?" Christian asked as they entered the office suite. Several young men in jeans and tee shirts were milling around, presumably the techs that Brooks had mentioned.

"Right now we are looking at both of those options as being possible. I am thinking that we can talk to him together and see where the conversation leads us," Brooks answered.

"That is fine with me. I will sit back while you take the lead and jump in where I can," Christian said.

"Ok, I don't want to spook him as soon as he walks in, so I am going to have you wait in Interrogation, and Mick, you can sit in my office or the Observation room. Either one is fine."

"I'd like to watch. I'll be in Observation," Mick responded.

It was Christian's turn to pace. He waited in the empty room for almost 30 minutes before the door opened. Brooks and another man entered. The fan club moderator fit the classic 1980's nerd movie clichés. Shorter than Brooks, no more than 130 pounds, and dressed in khaki pants and a red short-sleeved polo shirt with a small Spiderman logo on the lapel, he timidly took a couple of steps into the room and stopped. A food stain of some sort next to the left collar was bugging Christian as Brooks guided the young man to his seat.

"Chester, thank you for coming in on such short notice," Brooks started, "This is Dr. Rinaldi, and he will be joining us today. Do you prefer Chester or do you go by a nickname?"

"My friends call me Chet, but I am fine with whatever," Chet answered. "What kind of doctor are you?"

"I am a forensic psychologist," Christian answered, tweaking his title a little to help convey his role better. Knowing that the man was going to be very nervous in this setting, he decided to speak first. "Like Agent Brooks said, we really do appreciate you coming in here today. If you had to change any plans, we do apologize. We wouldn't have asked you to rush if it wasn't for the fact that we have some very time sensitive work that needs to be done, and we believe that you are uniquely qualified to help us."

"I did have to reschedule some prior commitments, but assisting the FBI is as good of a reason as any to break plans," Chet said. His ego had taken Christian's bait—hook, line, and sinker. With his natural suspicion fully suppressed, he would be more willing to open up. "How can I be of service?"

Brooks stepped in to answer. "I understand that you run the Maine chapter of a fan club for the TV show *Serials*. Is that correct?"

"Actually, I am the *President* of the entire New England *Chapter*," Chet said, emphasizing the differences. "I am also the Membership Committee

Chair, and oversee many of the Club's events throughout the region."

"Then you are definitely the man we are looking for," Christian said. "Agent Brooks has some pictures to show you, and we would love your thoughts."

Brooks opened a manila folder and spread five pictures from the last two crime scenes on the table in front of Chet. Chet stared at each one for several seconds before moving on to the next.

"This is exceptional work," the strange young man answered.

"How so?" Christian asked.

"Well, everything about them is astounding. All of the details are well thought through. Even the technical analysts' uniforms look real. The blood, the body, it all looks so…. so lifelike. Is this from an event? Because if it is, someone did it without my authorization. I need to know who it was, because they are in violation of our bylaws."

"These are real crime scene photos. There is nothing fake about them," Brooks said.

Chet's face became even more ashen than it was. He dropped the pictures back onto the table and pushed away, turning. "Wait, these people are really dead? Who did it?"

"That is what we need your help with," Christian said.

"It wasn't me, I swear," Chet interrupted.

"No one said it was, but we do have to look into all possibilities," Brooks said. "Can you tell me where you were Wednesday and Thursday evening?"

"Umm, yeah. I was with my girlfriend," Chet answered. The surprised look on Brooks' face irritated him slightly. "Yes, I have a girlfriend, and we were in Manchester for a viewing party. We left Wednesday morning and stayed until yesterday. We went to the party on Thursday night and just stayed an extra day."

"I assume you will provide me with contact information for her as well as anyone else who attended the party," Brooks said.

"Yes, no problem. Am I seriously a suspect? Do I need a lawyer or something?" Chet asked, frightened.

"No Chet, I don't think you are the person we are looking for, but I believe he is someone that you would know," Christian answered.

"No way, none of my friends would do this," Chet protested.

"I wasn't necessarily meaning that the man we are looking for is someone you are close to. I do believe that they are a fanatical follower of *Serials* and would likely be a member of its fan club," Christian explained.

"I don't know. I am not in contact with most of the members. A lot of them just like the swag we send out and don't get very involved with Club activities."

"That is fine, Chet. The person we are looking for wouldn't be one of those passive members. He may not attend your get-togethers, but he would be very involved in some sort of communication, like a message board, for example. If they did attend an event, they would try to interject themselves either in the planning or in discussions about it." Christian continued.

"No, I can't think of anyone who would do this. I am telling you that none of our members would kill someone," Chet said.

"Eleven," Brooks interjected.

"What eleven? What do you mean by eleven?," Chet asked.

"He has killed at least eleven people, possibly 16 or more," Brooks answered.

Christian tried to get Chet focused back on his profile, "He would be a very organized person. He would have to be at least 5 foot 10, possibly taller, and in good physical condition."

Chet shook his head. "No, doesn't sound familiar."

"If he did go to an event, he would be more focused on what people wore or what they did that was inaccurate," Christian further explained. "He would also be obsessed with how the killers got caught in each episode. He would be very vocal about how they could have done it better."

Chet, who had been staring at his hands and shaking his head no while Christian spoke, suddenly sat straight up in his chair. "Wait, I do know a guy like that. I don't know if he is that tall, because I have never met him but he is always going on the boards late at night and talking about how the show isn't realistic. He goes on and on about how the killers are morons, and that he wouldn't have gotten caught."

Christian and Brooks looked at each other. This could be their best lead yet. "Do you know his name or where he lives?"

"No, I know his chat name, but if you have a computer, I can get the real one."

"Adam Newell," Chet said after 10 minutes at a tech's computer.

Brooks wrote down the address displayed on the screen and handed it off to a pair of waiting Agents. He looked at Christian and Mick who were standing nearby. "Do you have time to stick around? This might get fun."

"There's no place I would rather be," Christian answered.

Chapter 30

"Adam, can you tell us where you were Wednesday through Friday morning?" Brooks asked the man shackled to the table in front of him.

Adam Newell sat silently across from Christian and Mick. He leaned forward and touched the tips of his fingers to his bleeding lip. He had a bruise forming under his left eye, as well as a myriad of other fresh scrapes and cuts.

When the Agents had asked him to come in for some questions, he began screaming about Big Brother and Government Overreach, and then attacked the two men. As is so often the case, he got the worst of the altercation.

"I ain't got nothin' to say to you. I'm a sovereign citizen, and I don't recognize the fascist U.S. government or any of its jackboot agencies. I'm going to sue the hell out of you for police brutality," Adam said, spouting off one antigovernment propaganda buzzword after another.

"Adam, my name is Christian, and I am not here as a member of any federal agency. I am just a private citizen like you. I don't want to talk about anything related to mainstream media or politics or anything else. I just need your thoughts on television. Actually one show in particular that I have been led to understand that you are an expert in," Christian said in hopes of calming the man down.

Adam turned toward Christian and seemed to be calming down. "I ain't got nothing to talk to you about either."

Christian stood, playing a game of cat and mouse with Adam. "That is fine. We can probably get more accurate information on the *Serials* Wiki page anyway. Let's go, Agent."

"You're not going to get anything good from there. It's just written by a bunch of kids who don't know nothin' about it. I have to fix most of what they put on there," Adam snapped at Christian.

"Well you can either answer my questions, or I can go on the web. It doesn't matter to me either way," Christian retorted.

"Fine, I will let you ask two questions," Adam said, smugly.

"Okay, this isn't really a question as much as I want your opinion," Christian said as he returned to his seat. "Agent Brooks and I were watching it last night, and I think that it is good show but poorly written. He thinks that it is just inaccurate from start to finish. What do you think?"

"I think it is a great show, not just good. It is one of the best shows in TV history, but it has some major flaws," Adam answered.

"What kinds of flaws?" Christian asked.

"Some of the acting is mediocre at best, and that makes the writing seem worse than it is. They have to make the government censorship Nazis happy, so the show is backwards."

"What do you mean by it is backwards?" Brooks asked.

"They make the cops look too smart and the killers are morons. You expect us to believe that for the first three quarters of the show, the cops don't know what is happening, and the killer is getting away with murder after murder but all of a sudden the cops figure it out and the killers start making stupid mistakes? That is unrealistic. If they were smart enough to get away with the first few, they would just keep on killing," Adam explained.

"So you think that it is a good show, but it just doesn't play out the way it would in the real world?" Christian asked.

"Yeah, they make these killers all out to be nut jobs who hid so well for so long, and then for no good reason, they just fuck up. It doesn't make sense."

"You wouldn't make those same mistakes, would you?" Brooks pushed.

"No, I am not an idiot. Wait, what is that supposed to mean?" Adam asked.

Brooks dug the same five pictures back out of the file and tossed them on the table. "You don't make mistakes, do you?"

"Whoa, I didn't do this. Are you crazy?" Adam argued. "I see what is going on here. You haven't got any idea who did this, and you need a fall guy. Screw you. I'm done talking. I want a lawyer."

After hearing the magic words, Brooks and Christian got up and left the room. Brooks made a call to the public defender's office and sat behind his desk fuming.

"What do we do now?" Mick asked.

"Scumbag knows that we have him so he lawyered up. I can't ask anything else until his free lawyer shows up and tells him not to speak. Well, I've got news for him. He may not believe in the Federal Government, but I do, and he assaulted a Federal Officer. He can sit in jail until he wants to talk," Brooks ranted.

"So, you think he's the guy? What about his partner?" Mick asked.

"We'll catch him, too." Brooks said, chewing on his fingernails. He paced when nervous and chewed when angry. Lots of unresolved issues there, Christian thought to himself.

"I don't think he did it," Christian said.

"Doc, you don't seem to think anyone did it lately. What is your reason this time?" Brooks asked in exasperation.

"We are assuming based on the types of the murders and boot prints left behind that we are looking for two men. Correct?"

"Yes," Brooks answered.

"The only way that killing pairs work is for one to be the dominant partner, and the other is submissive. The dominant is almost always the one who makes the plans. He has to be organized and in control. Adam Newell can't play either of those roles." Christian explained.

"He seemed pretty damn dominant to me," Brooks quipped.

"There is a difference between being domineering and being dominant. The dominant person that we are looking for is a fan of Serials, as is Adam. That is a match, but he is extremely volatile and emotional. He is not capable of the level of organization necessary."

"Fine, he is the submissive then. They can both be fans, can't they?" Brooks said.

"They both can be fans, certainly, but he is not a submissive. Again, he has too volatile of a temperament. He doesn't like authority. A submissive craves an authority figure. His emotions would have carried over into the killing. The murders, while they were gruesome, were well executed, and there was no overkill component," Christian answered.

"Right now, I think he is our guy, and since we are in my office and not yours, we are going to do what I want. He stays until I say so," Brooks stated.

Christian didn't respond. He understood why Brooks was upset, and at this point there was no reason to continue the conversation. It would only lead to more arguing. Thankfully he didn't have a choice when Brooks' cell rang.

"This is Brooks," he said, and then paused to listen. "I appreciate the call, but what makes you think that this is related to our case? We are expecting a fire, not what you have."

Christian and Mick waited patiently as Brooks finished.

"Ok, well, thank you for calling. Can you send me photos of the body ASAP? Thank you."

"Is it another of ours?" Mick asked when Brooks hung up.

"I don't know. They found a body on the East End Beach. Coincidentally, do you know who lives in the East End? I'll tell you. Adam Newell does," Brooks said.

"Well that is great. Isn't it?" Mick asked.

"No," Christian answered.

"Why not?" Mick asked, confused.

"It wasn't a fire, so if this was done by the same people, our theory just went out the window."

Chapter 31

"There it is, right there on the left leg," Christian said, pointing to the patch of hairless skin on the lower leg of the new body. The crime scene techs had emailed some of the early photos to Brooks so that they could confirm whether or not this crime scene belonged to him or not.

"It just doesn't make any sense," Mick said. "What are the odds that all 16 other murders have this same...what is the word I am looking for?"

"Signature," Christian answered.

"Yes, that is it. How could the rest have this same signature, match the order of the Serials episodes, and then after 2 or 3 years of the same thing, they suddenly change? It doesn't make sense."

"I agree. It doesn't make sense. We have to be missing something here," Brooks said.

"So what do we do now?" Christian asked.

"We can still hold him on the other charges, but I am not sure how this fits with the others. I still think it is him but we need some time to tie this one to the rest," Brooks answered.

A knock on his door interrupted the conversation. Agent Patton stood in the doorway. "Sorry to bother you, sir, but Newell's lawyer wants to talk to you."

"Okay we will be right there. Thank you, Patton," Brooks said before turning to the others. "He has only been in there for 10 minutes. This can't be good."

Christian followed Brooks into Interrogation and Mick headed in to the Observation room. As they entered, the young public defender was still whispering to Newell. Neither man could hear it clearly, but it sounded like, "Let me do all the talking."

"My name is Special Advisory Agent Brooks, and this is Dr. Rinaldi. I understand you wanted to speak with us," Brooks said to the young man. He liked to use his full title when speaking with fresh-faced defense attorneys. It helped to tilt the tables in his favor to remind them that while they may be new in their roles, his first day on the job was ancient history.

"Yes, Agent, that is correct. I have discussed the matter with my client, and he has something he would like to say, against my advice," the attorney said.

"Unless it is a confession, I am not interested in what your client has to say," Brooks responded, attempting again to set his rules.

"I wouldn't exactly use those words," the attorney started before Newell jumped in.

"I want to make a deal," Newell blurted out.

"Please, let me do the talking," his attorney interjected.

"Shut up junior. Let the big boys talk," Newell snapped.

"What sort of deal are we talking?" Brooks asked.

"I will admit to everything, but I want to do it on camera. I want you to call a press conference, and I want you to invite all the channels. I want them all here," Newell demanded.

Christian and Brooks sat in shock. Brooks was thrilled, but Christian was dubious of the surprise turn of events. Something didn't smell right.

"Mr. Newell, why are you confessing all of a sudden?" Christian asked.

"I've been waiting for you boys to figure it out, but it is taking too damn long. I have a message that I need to share with the world, and I am getting tired of waiting," Newell said smugly. "Hell, I'd be dead if I waited for you to catch me."

Christian was not convinced. If it really was Newell, then he would be able to explain the latest killing. "Mr. Newell, I need you to fill in the gaps for me here. Why did you kill all of these people?"

"I wanted to show that real killers aren't what this government wants you to believe. They control the media, everything we hear, see and read. They even controlled this show. I wanted to prove them—and everyone else—wrong. You G-Men don't have the skills to match wits with someone like me. I think I did a good job of proving it."

"Ok, let's say that I believe you," Christian said. "Then why did you make a mistake on the latest killing?"

"What do you mean? I didn't get anything wrong," Newell said defiantly.

Christian pulled out the printed copies of the newest crime scene. He placed them in front of Newell. Newell didn't look away, but his attorney looked as though he may throw up at any second. "This is what I mean. The next episode was a fire. This man appears to have been attacked by some sort of animal."

"See, once again, this shows how little you know," Newell laughed. "Any real fan of the show would know that I didn't make a mistake."

"How so?" Brooks asked.

"The season finale that was shown here and in Britain was an arson, but it isn't what the original finale was supposed to be."

"What was it supposed to be?" Brooks asked, tired of Newell's games.

"The original was a man who had his face chewed off by rats. It was epic, but the fascists in charge at the studios and here at the FCC refused to air it. They had to make a new finale. They used the lame-ass arson scene to replace this one," Newell said as he leaned back, grinning like he had just won a contest of wits.

"If the show never aired, how did you know about it?" Christian asked.

"It was an underground rumor until the DVD came out. They put it on the special features. So, do we have a deal or what?" Newell demanded.

"I will run it by the District Attorney," Brooks said as he stood to leave.

Once outside the Interrogation room, Brooks ordered the IT techs to look into Newell's explanation. Mick emerged from the Observation room and joined them.

"That was a strange turn of events," he said as he stood with Christian. "Does that happen often?"

"No, this is a first for me," Christian answered as they walked back to Brooks' office.

Brooks entered the room a few seconds later. "Techs confirmed that he was telling the truth about that show. Everything lines up. Looks like we have our guy."

"I still don't think it was him," Christian said.

"Doc, the guy confessed and explained what we didn't know. What else do you need?" Brooks asked, his exasperation shining through.

"His motive doesn't make sense. He is saying that he wanted his message to get out there. That is the type of crappy line that you see on those shows. No one actually talks that way. The real killers, who are driven by exposing an injustice or to make themselves known, as he is claiming to be, don't wait for years without getting recognition. Killers like the Zodiac have always tried to make contact with the police or the press. This is the first time that anyone involved in this series of killings has made themselves known."

"They have been dumping the bodies in parks. That is pretty damn public," Brooks responded.

"Yes, but that is completely different. The type of killer who wants his work seen by the world doesn't necessarily want the recognition for it. They want to see their handiwork on the news, and they want the police to be baffled. They live for the feelings of intellectual superiority and the terror that it fills the community with. If these guys had wanted us to know it was them, they would have shown us that a long time ago, when no one was putting these cases together as being linked. That didn't happen. He is only saying this now because we have him in custody. He wants the fame, but he isn't our guy."

"Doc, I believe him, and he is screaming from the rooftops that it is him. Unless you come up with some reason that I don't see, I am calling the DA." Brooks said.

Christian's phone beeped, interrupting the conversation. "I don't think I am going to change your mind, but I do have to leave. I am on call at St. Lucia's this weekend, and I have to run up to Lewiston to do an evaluation."

"Ok, well, I have plenty to do here, so I will check in with you later. Relax Doc; we've got our guy. Before long, we will have the full confession, and he will give up his partner."

"We'll see. Mick, I don't know how long this is going to take, but you are going to have to sit in the car at the hospital. You aren't cleared to do rounds with me yet. Sorry. St. Lucia's is 45 minutes away, so I don't have time to take you home first," Christian explained.

"I can have one of my guys take him to your place. No worries," Brooks said.

"That is fine with me if it is fine with Mick."

"Sounds good," Mick responded.

* * * * *

Thirty minutes later, Christian was almost to St Lucia's, and Brooks was neck deep in paperwork when Agent Patton and Mick reached the end of O'Connor's Glen. Mick's jovial mood disappeared when he saw the dusty pick up and two large men waiting in the driveway.

"I thought you and the doctor lived here alone?" Agent Patton asked.

"We do," Mick responded.

Chapter 32

"Do you want me to stay?" Agent Patton asked as he pulled to a stop behind the large pick up. The two men walked toward them.

"No, I should be fine," Mick answered.

"So you know these guys?" Patton asked.

"Not really, but I know them as well as I know anyone else up here." Mick said as he got out of the car.

Clint and Marty walked up to Mick as the car pulled away.

"Hey guys, what brings you by?" Mick asked his unexpected visitors.

"Andy gave us the afternoon off, so we thought we would get away and do some fishing before he came up with something else for us to do," Clint the giant answered.

"Yeah, we have been busy day and night over there this week. It isn't going to get any better for a while, so we have to take the time where we can get it. You want to go with us?" Marty asked.

"I don't have a license," Mick answered.

"Bro, you roll with the FBI. I am pretty sure you can get away with catching a trout or two on your first weekend here," Marty laughed.

Mick mulled the idea over. He hadn't relaxed much in the last couple of weeks, and as worked up as he was after solving his first case, he wasn't going to be able to take a nap, so why not? "What the hell, let's go. I don't have a rod though. I'll have to grab one from the boathouse."

The three men walked across the lawn to the boathouse, and as expected, Mick found several rods to choose from. Clint picked one out for him while Marty admired the rest of the structure's contents. They walked through the back door and took up positions on the dock on the back side of the building. Several minutes passed before anyone spoke. Mick was enjoying the simplicity of casting the line out, letting the slow current drag it downstream, and then reeling it back in.

"Where's Christian?" Marty asked, breaking the silence.

"He had to go see a patient in some town called Lewistown," Mick answered.

"Lewiston. It's *ton* not *town*," Marty corrected. "So what were you doing with the Feds without him?"

"Long boring story," Mick answered. "Okay, not really boring but long."

"Well, we have plenty of time," Marty said.

"I guess it can't hurt. It will be all over the news tonight anyway," Mick said, his excitement clouding his judgment.

"Atta boy. Tell us all about it," Marty laughed.

"Okay, so when I got up here Thursday, Christian and Brooks were working on a murder case. Some sick bastards had crucified some poor guy and dropped him off in a park," Mick started.

"Holy shit, that is friggin' nasty," Marty said, feigning disgust.

"That isn't the worst of it. Friday, another body was found, and this guy had basically been barbecued in the ground, dug up, and left in a park. The only thing we could find to tie them together was a bald spot on their legs," Mick continued.

"What was that from?" Marty asked.

"We still don't know. We are assuming it was some sort of restraint," Mick answered. "So anyway, we found a bunch of other old unsolved cases with the same thing. So we tried to figure out what they had in common after your brother and Andy left here the other night."

"Did you figure that out?" Clint asked, joining the conversation.

"Actually, I did. I noticed that the killings matched a TV show."

"A TV show? That's kinda lame, isn't it?" Marty said.

"I don't know. All I know is that we found a guy who knew a lot of people who were obsessed with the show, and he led us to this other guy and BAM, the guy confessed today," Mick said, smiling.

"That is awesome, you guys got a killer off the streets," Marty said.

"Yeah, I am pretty excited. Christian doesn't think we have the right guy, but who the hell would confess if they didn't do it, right?"

"Who knows, there are a lot of sickos out there," Marty said. "You never know who they could be."

*   *   *   *   *

Christian stepped through the sliding glass doors of St. Lucia's and walked to his car. He still couldn't shake the feeling that Adam Newell was confessing to crimes that he didn't commit. He needed to find the answer, but where?

Christian turned onto East Ave, heading back toward the Interstate, when a good starting point came into view. He pulled into the parking lot of Black Bear Music, a store that specializes in new and used music and movies. They were always priced under the big box stores, and the employees all knew their products.

Black Bear was one of the only stores left in this particular strip mall, and its popularity would keep it open as long as the owners wanted it to be. Christian walked through the door and past the vinyl records and new releases to the back wall where DVDs of TV shows were kept. He searched the wall for the "S" section and found seasons 3-7 but not the one he needed. He walked around the corner to the Blu-ray section and found the same thing.

"Hey Christian. Long time, no see," said Kat, one of the employees that Christian had dealt with many times over the years. "What are you looking for?"

"Hey Kat, I was just looking for Season One of *Serials*. You don't have it in another store, do you?" Christian asked.

"Lemme check," Kat responded with a smile. She searched her internal system to find a new or used copy in one of the six other stores throughout the state. "Sorry, I don't have it, but I can order it. It would take two or three days to get here, unless you want the British version."

"I want the one that has the unaired episode," Christian said.

"Oh, the rat bag episode. That is some nasty shit," Kat said with a laugh. "That is the British version."

"Can you get it?" Christian asked.

"Yeah, I've ordered a few, so I can get one. They aren't easy to find, but I can do it," Kat answered. "It could take a couple of weeks."

"Yeah, that is too long," Christian said. "Don't worry about it."

Christian started to walk out when an idea struck him. "Hey Kat, do you think you could do me a favor?"

"Sure what's up?"

"Is there any way you could tell me who has ordered it through you?"

"I can't print you a list or anything, but if I happened to be looking it up and you happened to be standing on that side of the counter, I can't help what you saw," Kat answered with a wink.

Kat slowly scanned through the short list when a name caught Christian's eye. "Can you highlight that last one? I need to see the address."

Christian's eyes widened and sweat broke out on his forehead when he read the address. He yelled a "thanks" as he ran out of the store and into the parking lot.

* * * * *

Mick's phone rang, interrupting his conversation. "Hey Christian, how are you doing? I am sorry. I can't hear you. Can you repeat that? I will run to the house and call you from the landline."

"What was that?" Marty asked.

"It was Christian. He was saying something about us having the wrong guy, but the reception out here sucks so I lost him. I am going to run up to the house and call him. I will be right back," Mick said.

"I need to use the bathroom so I will head up with you," Marty said.

They walked into the house and Mick placed his cell on the kitchen island and ran into Christian's office to return the call. As soon as the door closed behind him, his cell lit up with a text. Marty picked it up and read the screen as Mick returned.

"No answer, it went straight to his voicemail. He must be in a bad spot too," Mick said as he walked into the kitchen.

"He sent you a text while you were in there," Marty said as he handed Mick his phone.

Mick looked down at the four-word text, and fear rushed through his body.

Marty is the killer.

Chapter 33

"Brooks, can you hear me?" Christian yelled into the phone.

"Yeah, Doc, I can hear you fine. You don't need to yell," Brooks said, the irony lost on him.

Christian swerved around a slow moving car and narrowly avoided a head-on collision with an oncoming car. Horns blared as his large grey SUV crossed back into the right lane. "You have the wrong guy in custody."

"Doc, I have a lot to do. I don't have time for thought exercises," Brooks said.

"Just listen. I need your help. I need you to get in the car and go to my house. I will explain as you go," Christian said, the urgency apparent in his voice.

"Ok, I am grabbing my keys, what is wrong?" Brooks said, picking up on the panic in his friend's tone.

"I stopped by Black Bear to ask about getting the missing episode and they didn't have it, but I did get to see who else had ordered it," Christian said, breathlessly.

"Yeah? Who is it?" Brooks asked.

"Marty. He is Clint's brother, and one of Andy's farm hands. I think he and his brother are the pair that we are looking for. They drive a pickup that is the right size. They fit the description for the pair of men. They have a huge farm where they could do this without anyone knowing," Christian said.

"Ok, then why I am I rushing to your house?"

"I called Mick to let him know what I found, but the reception was bad. I lost him, but I thought I heard other voices. He called me from the house phone but I was leaving him a message so I didn't get it. I tried calling the land line and his cell, but he isn't answering," Christian explained.

"So what is the big deal? Maybe he didn't hear them," Brooks said.

"I think the voices were Clint and Marty. I sent him a text saying it was Marty. I am worried that something has happened. I am closer to the farm than I am to my house. I am going to talk to Andy and I need you to check on Mick," Christian said.

"Ok, I am on it. I am sure everything is fine," Brooks responded.

"I am at the farm now. Call me as soon as you find Mick," Christian said before hanging up.

Christian turned onto the long dirt road that led to the old Melanson Farm. It had been two decades since he had been on this stretch of dirt, and even seeing the tall trees that lined it made the world feel like it was closing in. His heart started racing and the trees felt like a tunnel that was getting tighter and tighter.

Finally, the landscape opened, and the farm came into view. The pastures were not as well-kept as he remembered. Grass rubbed on the horse's knees as they ran in the fields next to him. The early setting springtime sun backlit the house and barns with an almost demonic orange hue. In the distance, Andy stood and shielded his eyes as he looked in Christian's direction. He ran down to the wide gate to open it for his former foster brother. He was at Christian's door before it opened.

"Hey Christian, I didn't expect to see you out here. What a wonderful surprise," Andy said as he attempted to hug Christian.

"Andy, I need your help. Are Clint and Marty here?" Christian asked. His words rushed out before his breath caught up.

"Yeah, I think so. The truck is back. What is going on? You seem all spooked or something," Andy asked.

"What do you mean 'back'? Where have they been?"

"I thought you knew, they went over to your place a few hours ago to see about going fishing. They didn't ask you?" Andy asked.

"No, I haven't been home. I was with the FBI this morning and was seeing patients until an hour ago," Christian said.

"Well, I am really sorry. I told them to ask you first. I will yell at them as soon as I see them," Andy said, shaking his head.

"I have some serious questions for you, Andy. How well do you know these guys?" Christian asked, placing his hand on Andy's left shoulder.

"Not all that well. They work with the other helpers, and I don't really see them that much. They have their own bunk house, and once they are done work for the day, they are on their own to do whatever they want. Why?"

"Do you think they could get violent or hurt anyone?" Christian asked.

"Like I said, I don't know them all that well, but they have always been good with me. Marty has a little bit of a temper, but he is still young. He isn't much older than I am. What is this about?" Andy asked, his eyebrows wrinkling with concern. "Did they do something?"

"We think it is possible that they have been killing people in the style of a TV show, *Serials*. Are you familiar with it?" Christian asked.

"Can't say as though I am. We still don't get great reception out here, and I don't even have a TV," Andy said. "But you think that they are killing people? Who are they killing?"

"I am not sure on that part yet, but I am thinking that it might be some of your other workers. Have any gone missing?"

"I wouldn't know. They handle all the hiring and firing. I just give them the money to give to the others. I see them around, but I never really talk to the hands," Andy said. "We can go ask them if you want. I am sure they are just settling into their bunkhouse after dinner."

"Okay, just don't say or do anything that would spook Marty or Clint. I want to ask them when they aren't prepared for it," Christian said.

"Okay, hold on a second. I am going to pop into the house to see if I have something to protect us with. If they are as bad as you think, I don't want to take any chances," Andy said before disappearing into the farm house.

* * * * *

Brooks slammed on the brakes and the back end of his FBI-issued sedan slid out at an angle. He jumped out of the car and left the door open as he ran up the stairs and onto the porch. The front door was still open, so he drew his sidearm and cautiously entered.

The house appeared empty, but a couple of overturned dining room chairs showed signs of a struggle. Brooks took the carpeted stairs two at a time as he raced to the second floor. He didn't expect to find anyone, but he needed to know for sure.

Christian's expansive master suite was empty, as were the guest rooms. That only left Mick's room. The room was silent and the door was closed, so he turned the knob slowly, and quietly opened the door. He had never wanted to catch a man napping so badly in his life.

Mick's bed was made and the room was completely empty. Brooks walked into the last part of the room, Mick's den. It was also empty aside from his belongings. Most of the items in Mick's den said ARMY on them. *I thought he was a college student interning for Doc,* Brooks thought as he looked out of the second-floor windows.

Brooks opened the doors to Mick's balcony and surveyed the grounds. Everything looked normal—

everything except for the boathouse. The door was open. *Is that a hand on the ground?*

Brooks didn't waste time by going back through the house. He closed the balcony doors, stepped over the side, and did a running tuck-and-roll jump off the porch. When his feet touched the ground, he bent his knees and rolled forward to lessen the impact.

Brooks stood and walked slowly toward the mystery hand. As he came within 15 feet, he was able to see the whole body. The man's body was stretched out in front of the boathouse as though he had been struck from behind. Blood-matted hair on the back of the skull backed Brooks's theory up. He checked for a pulse and didn't find one.

Even though Brooks had just met the man a couple of days earlier, and they had only spoken a few times and shared a meal, he felt a deep sadness. He dug out his phone to call Christian. The static in the ring reminded him that the reception wasn't good. He walked away from the body and hoped that Christian could hear him.

* * * * *

Andy emerged from the house with a yellow and black striped metal stick. Christian gave him a quizzical look. He had been expecting a rifle or something more intimidating.

"Cattle prod. It's not lethal, but it will lock a guy up pretty damn fast," Andy said, holding the weapon above his shoulder.

"Ok, I am ready when you are. You lead the way," Christian said, waving his arm toward the back of the property.

Christian followed Andy past the edge of the house, and the tops of the bunkhouses had just come into view when his phone rang with that familiar tone.

"It's Agent Brooks. I need to take this," Christian said and both men stopped moving. "Brooks, tell me you have good news."

The reception was so bad on both ends that Christian made Brooks repeat himself several times, but even then all he could make out was, "Sorry....found a body....boathouse... It is..... trust Andy."

Chapter 34

"Who was that?" Andy asked Christian when his call ended abruptly via a lost signal.

"Agent Brooks. He said something about a dead body at my house. I hope it isn't Mick, but I don't know who else it could be," Christian said, shaking his head.

Even though Mick was a new addition to Christian's life, he was someone that Christian felt an instant connection to. After losing Franklin and Reston, and now Mick, Christian was going to tell Grayson that he was out. Their rule was that no innocent people were to be killed, but it seemed like a lot of them were dying because of Christian.

That call would have to wait. So would the anger, the pain, the sorrow, and the tears. He would cry for Mick tomorrow. Tonight he had two murderers to Cleanse. Fuck the rules, Clint and Marty weren't going to see another sunrise.

"Are you sure you want to do this?" Andy asked. "We can call the police and let them sort this out."

"I am going to find them and handle this on my own. You can either go with me or not. That is up to you," Christian answered.

"I'm in all the way. I just wanted to be sure, because if we walk down that hill, there's no turning back," Andy said ominously.

"Let's go."

Andy turned and walked down the narrow dirt path between the farm house and the same huge red barn that filled Christian's nightmares. Seeing it night after night hadn't prepared him for seeing it in the fading light of late spring. It looked larger than its 100 foot by 60 foot, three-story frame. The old paint was peeling away in long strips and wide patches, forming a pattern that could easily be mistaken for a scowling face.

Christian pushed the twenty year old memories out of his mind and looked straight ahead at Andy's muscular back. He must have been doing more than just sitting around the house all day and crunching numbers. Between the knotty muscles and deep tan, he had to have been out in the fields more than he had been letting on.

They crested the small hill, and the rest of the farm's dilapidated structures came into view. The twin bunkhouses sat at the far end, one on each side of the path they were standing on. A field, maybe 500 feet long, stood between Christian and the home of his friend's killer. The left side of the path was empty from where he was standing to the first bunkhouse. It was slightly uphill from the other. The bunkhouse on the right was on lower ground and had eight picnic tables spread out on its field.

"Which one is their bunkhouse?" Christian asked.

Before Andy could answer, Marty appeared at the far end of the left-side bunkhouse. Christian wanted nothing more than to tear down the hill and take his revenge, but the element of surprise would be lost as soon as he crested the hill. If his opponent was armed, he would have plenty of time to get a bead on a 6'3" 225 pound man barreling toward him. No, he would have to wait and see what Marty was doing before he could risk it. Besides, he still didn't know where Marty's giant of a brother was.

If Marty noticed them, he didn't let on. He walked around to the front of the building and onto the small porch on the side closest to Christian. Marty looked across the field at the other building before opening the door and turning on a light. Christian caught a glimpse of another figure inside, but it didn't look like Clint. Christian couldn't be sure who the other person was, or even if it was a person. The deepening darkness mixed with the distance made any guesses completely unreliable.

Andy stepped closer to Christian and whispered, "Try to be quiet when we go down the hill and back up the other side. Stay behind me just in case they look out that window, but I doubt they will. When we get up to the porch, I want you to stand around the corner while I knock."

"Fine with me," Christian said. "Do know if they are armed?"

"Not with guns. I don't allow guns anywhere besides the main house. They do keep their personal tools in there with them, so they could have any number of things within reach. Just be ready for anything," Andy answered.

Christian stepped off the path and onto the grass next to it. He didn't want any unnecessary noises as they approached. Andy didn't follow suit and each time his foot ground gravel against the hard sole of his boot, it sounded like a shotgun blast to Christian. Even the creatures of the night seemed to know the importance of a stealthy approach, as they had gone silent during the normally busy predusk hour.

One harrowing minute later, Christian disappeared around the corner of the bunkhouse while Andy made his way up the steps. Three thunderously creaking steps and a four-foot walk placed Andy at the front door. Christian's heart pounded in his chest so loudly that he barely noticed Andy's knocks.

"Who is it?" asked Marty's voice from the other side.

"It's Andy, you decent in there?" Andy answered.

"Yeah, come on in,"

Andy opened the door but he held his hand out telling Christian to stay where he was. Christian couldn't see anything other than light spilling out onto the single Adirondack chair that took up most of the tiny porch.

"I need to talk to you about something," Andy said as he stood in the open doorway, blocking Christian's view. "Where did you go this afternoon?"

"We went over to Christian's and did some fishin'. Why, is there a problem?" Marty asked. Christian thought he heard a grunting or groaning but it was too faint to understand.

"Did anything out of the ordinary happen while you were there?" Andy asked.

"Nope. We got there and there wasn't nobody home. We waited a couple minutes and were getting ready to head back when that Mick fella showed up," Marty said. Just hearing the bastard say Mick's name fanned Christian's anger. "We asked him if he wanted to go with us and we went down to the river and fished and talked for like an hour. Mick got a call from Christian that he couldn't make out and he went back to the house. He didn't come back, so we left."

"Good enough, see you in the morning," Andy said and began to close the door.

Good enough? Christian couldn't take it anymore. He wasn't going to sit here and let that be the end of this conversation. If Andy didn't have the balls to ask the right questions, he certainly did.

Christian jumped from where he stood and landed loudly on the top of the porch. He gave Andy a slight push to move him away from the door, squared his body to the building in front of him, and slammed his size 14 boot into the door just below the knob. It burst open so quickly that it crashed into the wall and bounced back toward him. He caught it before it closed again and stepped into the room.

Marty popped up from the ratty old recliner that he had been sitting in and looked at Christian in complete shock. Christian stepped toward him, but a loud grunt to his left caused him to look away. On a bunk bed on the opposite side of the room, cuffed to the frame with a rag stuffed in his mouth was Mick!

What the hell? Christian thought as he stared at his friend in disbelief. His mind raced. Surely, Andy would have seen Mick when he opened the door. Why didn't he say anything? Unless...

Christian turned to look at Andy, but it was too late. A searing pain filled his body as Andy pressed the cattle prod to the back of his neck. All of his muscles flexed and tightened. He tried to fight it, but he couldn't. No amount of conditioning or skill could prepare you for "riding the lightening" as Mr. Melanson loved to call it. Christian's muscles locked and he felt himself falling backwards. His world went black as his head struck the floor.

* * * * *

Ricky heard a loud thump coming from the other bunkhouse. He didn't look or even sit up from his bed. This had to be what it was like to be desensitized to such a horrible place. Either that, or he had just given up. He wasn't sure he liked one choice more than the other.

Suddenly, the whole room got dark. The wooden panel that ran the length of the building crashed against the windows. The heavy sheets of plywood were positioned just above the windows and were used by most farmers as a quick way to protect the glass during a nasty storm. That didn't make any sense. The night was perfectly clear. The next sound Ricky heard was clicking of padlocks on the ends of the panels.

The other men stood and rushed to the only door at the far end of the building. First one and then another turned the knob and pulled. The door opened about a half inch and stopped. The metal clasp that ran from the doorjamb to the door itself was latched, and another padlock hung from it. They were trapped!

A dozen panicked men ran around the room. Several strained as they pulled on the door to no avail. Others opened the windows and kicked at the plywood with similar results. As the wood flexed against their feet, a new smell filled the room. It took Ricky a second to place it, but not much longer. He had pumped gallon after gallon of the stuff into the tanks on the lobster boat every morning for years. The thick, acrid smell was most definitely diesel fuel. The rest of the men soon noticed the smell, and the chaos momentarily stopped. Questioning voices filled the air. What could they do? What was happening?

Ricky knew the answers to both questions, but he kept them to himself. He sat back down on his bed. He needed to think. They were locked in a wooden box with no way out, and it was about to be set on fire.

* * * * *

Christian opened his eyes and waited for them to adjust to the darkness. Every muscle in his body was a kind of sore that he had never felt before. He sat up and tried to stand, but a set of handcuffs on his left wrist ended his attempt.

A bright light flashed on and he could see the entirety of the room around him. Mick sat on a similar metal bed across the room from him, and he still had the rag in his mouth. His left eye was bruised and had swollen nearly shut. Andy and Marty stepped into the room and closed the door behind them.

"What the hell is going on here, Andy?" Christian asked, even his throat hurt as he spoke.

"Just having some fun," Andy answered. "You should know what it is like. Dad told me all about the games you two used to play. I still can't believe it. Sweet little too-good-for-the-rest-of-us Christian got off on stabbing other men. Did you know that, Mick? Did you know that your new mentor has been killing people since he was 9 fucking years old? Don't deny it. Dad told me everything, you sick fuck."

"If you want to call someone a 'sick fuck', you should start with the bastard you keep calling 'Dad'," Christian snarled. "He started all of this. He was the one who forced me to do it."

"Maybe so, but he loved you like his own flesh and blood. It broke his heart when you left," Andy snapped back. "None of us were ever good enough for him after you left. He still loved you the most, and now I know why."

"He didn't miss me. He missed slaughtering innocent people. He missed being able to watch them die. He didn't care about me; he just knew that Vinnie was going to kill him if he started again. How long did it take until he started making you do it? A week? A month?"

"He never killed again, and he never asked me to when I lived here. I didn't know anything until I came back to visit after Mom died. He said your old man was gone and he was ready to pick up where he left off. The only problem was that he couldn't do it himself." Andy said. He paced back and forth in front of Christian, cattle prod in hand.

"So he asked you to do it and you just jumped at the chance to make the old man happy, is that it?" Christian's anger built and built.

"No, I asked him if I could do it. You should have seen the look on his face every time I ended someone. He just smiled and laughed. Boy, did he laugh."

The maniacal sound of Melanson's laughter echoed in Christian's mind. He turned his face away, but the memory continued.

"I started looking forward to the days I was on leave and I could come up here. Dad would just pick out someone from the crew and I would tell them they were fired. They would always come begging for their job, and then I got to end them," Andy continued. "Then Dad got really bad and he didn't recognize me anymore. I stopped even trying until he was gone. The crazy thing was—I missed doing it. I just needed a new reason."

"That's where my brother and I came in," Marty laughed. "When Andy got drunk one night and told us about it, we told him some stories of our own."

"So it was your idea to copy *Serials*?" Christian asked.

"Not copy. *Perfect*. We perfected what they fucked up," Marty corrected.

"Fine, you are all a bunch of fucking psychopaths. I get it. The only thing I don't understand is why you killed your brother," Christian said.

Marty's face flashed with rage. "I didn't kill him. I went into your house to get Mick and when I came back he was laying there, dead."

If Marty didn't kill him, who did? Christian wondered.

"Time for talking is over. You boys get comfy. We will be back in a few to get you. You can be our guests of honor at a little season-ending bonfire, and then we can start Season 2 with you," Andy laughed before exiting the room. Christian heard a scraping as the Adirondack chair was wedged under the handle of the damaged door.

Christian couldn't afford to waste any time. As soon as he heard the last man step off the porch, he sprang into action. He couldn't break the cuffs or the bedpost, so he would need to do something he didn't want to. Desperate times call for desperate measures, right?

The cuff on his left wrist wasn't tight against his skin. When he slid it down to the base of his hand, it had about a third of an inch of looseness. He grasped his left thumb in his right hand and yanked. He pulled slowly and methodically until he heard a wet pop and felt a sharp pain rush up his arm. He pressed the freshly dislocated thumb into the middle of his palm and pushed the cuff upward. It dug into his soft flesh and compressed tightly around his injured thumb. He wiggled it back and forth and moved it little by little. He used his good thumb to push into the damaged one and as the muscle depressed, the cuff slid right off. A quick pull on his thumb and it was back in its socket. Good as new. Okay, not really, but close enough.

Christian rushed to Mick and pulled the rag out of his mouth, resisting the urge to hug him. "Are you okay?"

"I'll make it," Mick answered. "What are we going to do?"

"I am not sure yet, but I will come up with something," Christian responded. He saw a pile of supplies in the back of the darkened room and remembered that Andy had said that the brothers kept their tools in there. A quick visual search gave him a plan.

Christian didn't see a saw of any type to cut through Mick's cuffs, and even if he had, the noise would have alerted their captors. Instead, he settled for a roll of tape, an old manual drill, and a small jug that smelled like it contained gasoline. He returned to his bunk and placed the items on the bed.

"What are you doing with that?" Mick asked.

Christian pushed one side of the hanging cuff through the other so that it was completely open on one side. He would need to reattach it to his wrist later for his plan to work. He then walked over to the broken door and removed the light bulb from its socket to the left of the entrance. It was still warm, so he blew on it to cool it.

"We are going to set a surprise trap for our friends," Christian said. "They are going to need that light when they come in, but when they flip the switch, they are going to get more than they bargained for."

With the bulb now cool, Christian held the tip of the drill against the glass neck of the bulb, halfway between the metal cap and the widest end. He placed his hand on the wooden knob of the drill and slowly turned the metal handle. The metal bit scraped against the glass, and Christian waited patiently to hear the results. The bulb would either shatter in his hand, or the drill would make a small opening. He heard a tiny popping noise as the tip of the bit pushed its way through the glass. Christian slowly turned the handle in the opposite direction and removed the bit.

Christian held the bulb between his knees and grabbed the gas can. Gently he poured a small amount of the flammable liquid into the tiny hole. As soon as there was enough gas to fill the bottom quarter inch, Christian pressed a finger over the hole. Tape was then wrapped around the opening to form a tight seal.

"As soon as they hit the switch, the filament is going to spark in the bulb and ignite the fumes. The gas will expand rapidly and the bulb will explode in a ball of flames. I just hope they are close enough to it," Christian explained.

Christian didn't dare to put the bulb back without testing the socket. Old wiring wasn't reliable, and if there was even a small amount of current passing through the socket, even though it was off, the bulb would blow as soon as the connection was made. His only option was to lick his finger and stick it in the exposed socket. He rubbed his wet finger around the entire interior or the light and felt nothing. He screwed the bulb back in just as he heard voices coming his way. He rushed back to his bunk and closed the cuff around his wrist. He only closed it until he heard a second click. It would slide right off when the time came.

"Lie down and cover your face with the pillow. Turn away from the door and curl up to protect as much of your body as you can," Christian whispered to Mick as the chair was removed from the outside of the door. The counted down in his head. *Three.....two......*

Chapter 35

The door handle turned, and metal hinges creaked as the old wooden door was pushed open. Christian had followed the same instructions that he had just given to Mick, but he kept the back side of the pillow off the mattress an inch or so. He wasn't facing the door, but he wanted to see if any other light source was used. No light, but why hadn't they flipped the switch?

An unknown hand scraped against the wall in the dark, searching for a familiar switch. The index finger on Marty's right hand found the small nub and pushed it upward. A bright flash of light filled the room followed by screams of pain. Marty fell to the floor and stopped moving. Shards of glass covered his horribly burned face.

Christian rolled over and pulled his hand through the cuff just in time to see Andy run into the darkness of the open field. He had been a step or two behind Marty and while he didn't feel the full blast, he had to be injured. Christian ran to Marty's prone body and searched his pockets until he found what he needed: the handcuff key.

Christian ran back to Mick and removed the cuff from his wrist. Mick rubbed the red lines circling his lower arm. His cuff was closed much tighter than Christian's had been. Together, they ran toward the door and stepped over the barely breathing body of Mick's kidnapper.

Christian jumped off the porch and searched the darkened field for any sign of Andy. Aided only by the moonlight, he saw his brother's silhouette half way up the hill. He held a short stick in his left hand, but Christian couldn't see what it was. Mick joined him at the bottom of the stairs, still flexing his hand and wrist.

"Why are we standing here?" Mick asked. "Shouldn't we go after him?"

"Not yet. We have no idea what he is holding or if he has something planned. Scared people run. People who feel in control let you come to them, and he hasn't moved since I got out here. Something doesn't feel right," Christian responded.

"So are we just going to wait here until he makes a move?" Mick asked.

"No," Christian answered. He took a single step forward and when Andy didn't move, he decided to feel the situation out. "Andy, this has gone far enough. One of your men is dead and another is circling the drain. If you don't call for help, he isn't going to make it."

"It is too late for Marty," Andy yelled back. "It is too late for all of us."

"It doesn't have to be," Christian called up the hill. He took another step forward as he spoke. "You are not yourself. I can get you help."

"That is the problem. You can't see that I don't need help. I am happy. Dad was happy until you took that away from him," Andy screamed. "I promised you a bonfire, and even though Marty and Clint won't be here to see it, I owe it to them to finish this."

Marty pulled at the top of the stick that he held in his hand and yellow and red flames shot from the top. A road flare? What was the point of a flare, Christian wondered.

"There are thirteen men locked in the building next to you. You can either save them or follow me. That is your choice," Andy yelled. He took two quick steps forward and threw the flare toward the building. It landed a yard away, but that was close enough. A blue flame spread around the sides of bunkhouse as the men inside screamed and begged for help. Andy turned and ran up the hill toward the giant barn.

"I'll go after him. You get those men out of there," Mick said to Christian. He started sprinting toward the fleeing Andy before Christian could respond.

Christian ran to the burning building and leapt over the growing wall of flames. He stood on the top step and pulled on the padlock but it didn't move. He didn't have the space to generate enough momentum to kick it in. He needed something to increase his leverage on the bracket. He jumped off the steps and back onto the ground.

"I need something to pry the door open. I will be right back," he yelled to the men inside the building. He rushed to the other bunkhouse and stepped over the still motionless Marty, and dug through the pile of tools until he found a thick screwdriver. It wasn't as strong as a crowbar, but it would have to do the job.

Christian ran back to the burning building and prepared to jump onto the steps a second time, but paused when he saw that they were now on fire. He looked back up the hill and saw Mick entering the barn very slowly. A second shadow emerged, this one holding a round pointed shovel. Before Christian could open his mouth to yell, the shadow swung the shovel and Mick crumpled to the ground. Christian started to run toward the barn but the screams of the trapped men stopped him in his tracks. The barn doors closed.

"I need you to stand back away from the door. Do you understand?" Christian yelled to the men.

"Yes!" several voices screamed in unison.

Christian only had one option left and he prayed that it would work. He tucked the screwdriver into his back pocket and took a deep breath to clear his mind. He sprinted at full speed toward the building, and just before he reached the edge of the flames, he dove forward, turning his massive body into a human battering ram. He pressed his head to his chest and slammed shoulder first into the door, just to the right of the lock. The door shattered from the impact and he crashed to the floor. His leg was burning. His pants must have brushed the flames.

Most of the men rushed out the door and jumped for safety but one stayed behind and tossed a blanket over Christian, putting out the flames. Christian stood and shook the man's hand. They both left the burning building, and once on the ground he turned to the men.

"Thank you for saving us," said the man who had stayed behind. He limped toward Christian and patted the last of the flames off of his shirt.

"My friend is in that barn with Andy. Does anyone know how I can get in without going through that door?" Christian asked.

"There is one way," a second man said. "If you crawl under the left side, you will find an old root cellar about halfway in. One of the walls has collapsed, so you could squeeze in through there."

"Root cellar" were two words that Christian didn't want to hear. When no other suggestions were tossed out, he started running up the hill leaving the group of men where they stood.

* * * * *

Ricky watched as the large young man who had just saved his life ran toward the barn at the top of the hill. He thought about following him until he heard a familiar voice.

"Help me," Smalls groaned as he stumbled down the steps of his bunkhouse. He landed hard on his stomach and struggled to stand. Burnt skin filled with broken glass hung loosely from his face. He staggered toward the group of men, his arm extended; fingers spread open in a silent request for assistance. No one moved.

Ricky was standing so close to the burning building that he could feel the flames licking at his back. Marty fell forward toward him and Ricky let him. Ricky could smell the burnt hair and flesh as he held the injured man.

"Thank you, Dickey," Marty said as he lifted his head to look Ricky in the eyes.

Ricky turned Marty's body so that their positions were reversed. "My name is Ricky you pathetic piece of shit."

"I know that. I was kidding," Marty said, faintly.

Ricky reached into his pocket and pulled out the sharp piece of stone that he had used to cut Jim's body down. He thrust the razor sharp rock upward and into Marty's chest. Marty stepped back, pawing at the exposed weapon. He stood wobbling at the edge of the flames. Ricky rushed forward and pushed Marty with both hands.

"That was for Jim, you fucking asshole," Ricky screamed as tears streamed down his ash-covered cheeks.

Marty slammed into the burning building and fell to the ground. A blood curdling scream filled the air as his clothes caught on fire. He burst forward out of the flames, and fell to the ground. The rest of the men stood in a circle as he crawled forward. No one offered to help, and he stopped moving. Thirteen men silently watched his final moments, just as they had watched so many others die by his hands.

Chapter 36

Christian paced along the left side of the barn, looking for any opening to get under the enormous structure. At nearly the halfway point, he got his wish. Four boards had rotted away from the base, leaving a gap that was about three feet wide and two feet high. Diving into the burning building had been no issue, but plunging into the darkness was terrifying.

Christian's heart began pounding harder and harder until the blood pulsed in his ears. The sound was eerily similar to standing at the base of a tall waterfall. Cold sweat broke out across his forehead, and waves of nausea washed over him. The fear had paralyzed his muscles.

A loud thud echoed from inside the barn and shook the cobwebs from Christian's anxiety-filled mind. Mick needed him and he had no other choice. He had to move. He crouched until his knees grazed the grass and stretched his arms forward into the black abyss under the barn. He took a final deep breath and stuck his head into the emptiness.

Silken nets of dusty spider webs spread across his face and hair. He swatted at them, but knew that he couldn't get them all. The entirety of his path was bound to be covered with them, so wiping them away was an exercise in futility.

His shoulders scraped the splintered wood as he leaned further into his own personal hell. His belt caught on the lip of a board and he had to balance on one hand while reaching back with the other to free it. His legs lifted off the ground and he pulled the rest of his body in, landing shoulder-first in the loose dirt.

Christian turned his head slowly in one direction and then the next in hopes of finding anything that could guide him. Thankfully, a dim light seeped into the space through the cracks in the floorboards. It seemed to be coming from the center of the room, and just below it Christian could see the vague outline of his childhood prison—the root cellar.

Christian inched along the crumbing dirt, his stomach rubbing against the occasional oddity: a rock, a termite mound, and even a mouse's skeleton or two. The floor of the barn was three or four feet above him, but he still had to crawl like a soldier trying to stay under barbed wire because of the low-hanging supports. He tried to avoid thinking about the 40 foot tall building above him or even look behind him to see the moonlight fading in the distance. He focused on one thing: getting to the light. Twenty feet became fifteen, which quickly became ten, and then five feet. Five feet further and he would reach the cellar.

The farmhand had been correct. One wall had broken apart, and Christian was able to pull himself over the broken cement and into the remaining structure. Once inside, he could almost smell the onion skins, but he knew that was only his imagination. It is all in the past, he told himself as he sat with his back pressed against the rough cement.

He pulled himself into a low crouch and lifted his body as high as possible without opening the door above him. Time had not been kind to the door and he could easily see through the widened cracks. The lock was no longer there, and it would be very easy to open it this time. He looked around the enormous barn and soon found Mick and Andy. Mick was hanging motionless upside down from a pulley hook. His hands were bound and dangling below him. The gentle rise and fall of Mick's chest filled Christian with a sense of relief.

Andy was looking at the barn doors, away from where Christian was hiding. He must have been expecting Christian to come charging in like a bull to save his friend. His underestimation gave Christian a big advantage—the element of surprise.

Christian placed both palms on the underside of the wooden door and gave it a gentle push. The door lifted effortlessly from the ground, allowing Christian to stand. The only trouble with this was that the door didn't swing open. It was in such bad shape that the whole thing lifted—all four sides. Christian tried to set it off to the side, but a large chunk bowed from the end and fell, clattering to the ground.

Andy turned to face Christian upon hearing the crash. He seemed startled to see Christian standing waist deep in the floor behind him. Christian expected Andy to rush toward him, but instead he stepped closer to Mick.

"I have to give you credit, Brother. I didn't expect to see you there. What a pleasant surprise!" Andy said, holding Mr. Melanson's favorite skinning knife in his right hand.

"Andy, step away from Mick. No one else needs to get hurt here," Christian said as he pulled himself out of the pit. He held his hands up to show that he was not intending to be aggressive.

"You still don't get it, do you?" Andy laughed. "Of course no one *needs* to get hurt, but what fun would that be?"

"You are on the losing side here, Andy," Christian reasoned. "The police are on their way by now. Your workers have been freed. Clint is dead and Marty is headed that way. You don't have to follow them into the ground. Just put the knife down."

"They were fun, but they were also weak," Andy said dismissively. "I see now that I needed a stronger partner. That should be you, Brother. Join me and we will have more fun than you could ever imagine. Dad would be so proud to have us working together. His memory could live through us."

"He was a sick man, Andy. He killed for his own amusement. None of those men deserved to die. We can end this right now," Christian pleaded.

"That sounds an awful lot like you are turning down my offer, Brother," Andy said, waving the knife back and forth.

"I'm sorry, Andy, but I don't agree with what you are doing. I am going to have to take you in," Christian replied.

"Is that your final answer?" Andy asked.

"It is. I think you are not seeing things clearly. You need help, Andy. Let me help you," Christian responded.

"Wrong answer," Andy said. He turned to face Mick's hanging body and in one swift motion he plunged the knife into Mick's abdomen, just below his ribs.

Mick's eyes popped open and he screamed. Andy seemed unprepared for the reaction and his lapse in concentration allowed Christian to get closer. Unfortunately, he didn't get close enough.

Andy turned and slashed at Christian with his arm moving in an arc from right to left and then back again. Christian had to jump backward to avoid the razor sharp blade and nearly fell into the open root cellar.

Andy regained his balance and circled to his left, trying to get closer to Christian. Christian looked past Andy to his bleeding friend. The blood oozed out of Mick's wound at a slower pace and Christian knew he would need to end this quickly in order to save Mick's life.

Andy took two quick steps forward and thrust the knife at Christian's stomach. This time, instead of backing up, Christian reached out to meet the knife. His hand just missed the blade on its way to Andy's wrist. He clasped the wrist and twisted, locking out Andy's arm just as he had practiced hundreds, if not thousands, of times.

Christian took another step closer to Andy and slammed his forearm down across Andy's hyperextended elbow. The knife fell silently into the hay as a loud crack and Andy's screams filled the air, his elbow and forearm shattered. Andy fell to his knees clutching his broken arm.

"I am going to fucking kill you! Do you hear me? You are a dead man!" Andy screamed.

Christian picked up the skinning knife and walked toward his kneeling adversary. He stood in front of his former foster brother and thought about using the blade one last time. The knife that started his killing career was back in his hands, and it felt...normal.

Mick groaned and Christian turned to look at him. He started to step toward Mick but at the last second he spun in a half circle, his leg lifting into the air as his right foot collided with the side of Andy's head. The spinning roundhouse kick sent Andy flying backwards into the open root cellar.

Christian ran to Mick and cradled his shoulders with one arm while cutting the rope. He tossed the knife to the side to catch his falling companion. He cradled Mick and pressed against the bleeding wound with his palm. Now that the opening was below Mick's heart, the blood gushed out.

"Stay with me Mick," Christian pleaded.

Sirens in the distance grew louder as they moved down the dirt road. Mick's eyes fluttered open and then closed. The next time they opened, they quickly flashed with surprise. He started to open his mouth to speak, but before he had a chance, Christian felt something large slam into him.

When they rolled to a stop, Andy was on top of Christian and swinging wildly with his only good arm. His broken right arm hung at his side, swaying with each punch. Christian tried to punch back but couldn't get any power behind it. Andy continued to connect with one powerful blow after another.

Christian felt a strange poking sensation in his right back pocket and remembered the screwdriver was still on him. He reached under his body and pulled the plastic handled weapon from his pants. The next time Andy pulled his arm back to punch, Christian moved his hand upward, burying the steel spike into his chest until the plastic handle pressed against his flesh.

Andy fell backward off Christian who climbed on top of his fallen foster brother. Rage took over, and Christian slammed fist after fist into Andy's face. His nose was bent at a sharp angle to the left and blood pumped from it and into Andy's mouth. He screamed for Christian to stop, but it was no use. Christian had lost control.

Ten punches landed and then fifteen. Christian saw Mick moving out of the corner of his eye and snapped back into reality. He rolled off of Andy and returned to his friend's side.

"I hear them Mick. They should be here any second," Christian said.

Christian heard a pounding on the outside of the locked barn doors. "We are in here," he screamed.

"I am going to go let them in. I will be right back," Christian reassured Mick.

Christian staggered toward the locked doors. He was five feet away when he heard a scrapping noise behind him. He turned just in time to see Andy kneeling over Mick, the screwdriver that Christian had stabbed him with was in his hands. He held the weapon over his head and prepared to plunge it into Mick's helpless chest.

Christian ran as fast as he could and dove onto Andy just before the weapon found its mark. Christian landed on Andy's back and wrapped his arm around Andy's throat. This time he wasn't letting go. He reached up and grabbed the side of Andy's head, and with one violent twist, he snapped his neck. Andy fell to the ground, the life gone from his eyes.

Christian raced to the barn doors and lifted the plank from the lock. Paramedics rushed by him and checked on Andy and Mick.

"This one is dead," one paramedic shouted to the other.

"This one is still breathing, but barely," the second man shouted.

The first man ran to his side to help save Mick. Christian collapsed from exhaustion. The paramedics frantically worked to stop Mick's bleeding. The blood had slowed to a trickle. The last words that Christian heard before passing out were, "Get the paddles. We are losing him."

Chapter 37

Christian sat in the waiting room for Maine Medical Center. Mick had been in surgery for hours and would likely be in recovery for many more if he made it.

The deer skinning knife had sliced through his diaphragm and liver. Initially, the surgeons had been unable to stop the bleeding until they found a small cut in his spleen. They were working on that at that very moment.

A young woman in her early thirties sat silently next to Christian. She had been bouncing her knees up and down for the last twenty minutes. She had rushed into the room crying saying "I don't know what is happening. They just told me that I couldn't see him!" over and over.

A doctor in dark green scrubs walked into the room and she stood to meet him. Christian couldn't hear what the doctor said, but he certainly heard her reaction.

"What do you mean he had a heart attack? He came in here for knee surgery and was going home today. Why would he have a heart attack?" she screamed.

The doctor led her away from the waiting room with his arm on her shoulder. She pushed his attempt at comfort away and then pushed him with both hands. She began pounding on the doctor's chest with closed fists before collapsing to the floor. Nurses rushed to help her to a wheelchair.

* * * * *

Mick slowly opened his eyes and stared at the florescent light above him. *Where am I?* He wondered to himself. He tried to sit up, but pain in his chest and abdomen stopped his progress.

"Look who is finally awake," Christian said cheerfully.

"Where am I?" Mick asked, his voice hoarse from lack of use.

"You are in your very own semiprivate hospital room," Christian said, trying to keep the mood light.

"What happened?" Mick asked.

"Andy stabbed you after he had you tied upside down. You had to have a couple of surgeries to fix the damage. He nicked a couple of organs. It was touch and go for a little while, but you are going to be fine," Christian answered, his tone more serious now.

"Have I been out long?"

"Three days," Christian answered. "You have been on some pretty heavy doses of morphine so you could rest. Your lungs collapsed, so you have a couple of tubes in your back. I wouldn't try to get too frisky for a while."

"How long am I going to be in here?" Mick asked.

"The doctor said it would be at least a few more days, and then you would be off your feet for a week or two," Christian said. "Less than a week on the job, and now I have to play nurse. I even picked up an outfit."

"No sponge baths," Mick joked. His own laughter hurt his chest, so he stopped.

"Brooks, Alex, and Asher all stopped by. They were pretty concerned about you," Christian said. "They want to throw you a party when you get home."

"That was nice of them. What happened to Andy? Did he get arrested?" Mick asked.

"He didn't make it," Christian said without elaborating.

"What about Marty?"

"Nope."

"So none of them survived? I guess that means it is over for good?" Mick asked.

"Looks that way."

"Did you ever find out what was causing the bald spots on the victims' legs?"

"Andy had some homemade bombs strapped on them. C4 sewn into ankle weights with a GPS transmitter in them—some really weird stuff. We managed to save 13 of them in total," Christian answered.

"I am glad some good came out of it, then," Mick said.

"I have a question for you. What happened to Clint? Brooks found him dead by the boat house," Christian asked.

"All I remember is that when Marty was dragging me to the truck he yelled something to Clint about watching out behind him. He kept saying over and over that someone snuck up behind Clint and bashed his head in. I didn't see anything though."

"Very strange. Sounds like someone did us a favor. That big bastard would have made things a whole lot tougher that night," Christian said, shaking his head.

Mick looked around the room at the flowers and gift shop stuffed animals. Christian brought them to him one by one and told him who each was from. The thoughts behind the gifts filled Mick with a happiness that he hadn't felt in many years. Maybe he had found a new family after all.

Christian brought the last gift bag over and handed it to him. He said that he had no idea who had sent it, but there was a card in the bag. Mick pulled out a small blue bear wearing an "It's a boy!" tee shirt and felt around for the card. The envelope had the smell of burnt plastic as he opened it.

Mick turned the envelope over and pulled out the card. As he opened it, a partially burnt plastic rectangle fell onto his woven hospital blanket. He picked it up and turned it over. A cold wave of fear rushed down his spine.

"What's wrong?" Christian asked when he saw Mick's face go white.

Mick handed Christian the card. Christian opened it and read the block printed message. There were only two words: *I'm watching.*

Mick handed Christian the burnt piece of plastic. He turned it over in his hands as Mick spoke.

"I put that in the fire pit myself," was all that Mick could say. "I put it in myself."

Christian looked down at a face he had only seen twice before, once when he was at Christian's house, and a then again a day later when the two police officers came to his office with the same picture that he held now. In his hands was the partially melted Pennsylvania Driver's License belonging to Dean Costa.

The words from the card echoed in Christian's head.

I'm watching.

<u>About the Author</u>

Derek lives in Maine with his wife, Janene; 5 year old son, Connor; 3 year old daughter, Mackenzie; and 1 year old daughter, Paige.

When he is not writing, Derek enjoys spending time with his family, sports, and traveling.

How to find Derek Dorr:

Facebook:

https://www.facebook.com/pages/Author-Derek-Dorr/761191490571729?ref=br_tf

Website with blog, updates, and signed copies:

www.AuthorDerekDorr.com

Twitter: @DerekDorrAuthor

Goodreads:

https://www.goodreads.com/author/show/8221016.Derek_Dorr

www.ingramcontent.com/pod-product-compliance
Lightning Source LLC
Chambersburg PA
CBHW032130190626
46814CB00005BA/1638